RENAISSANCE
Primordium – Book 2

William E. Mason

RENAISSANCE

DOUBLE DRAGON

A DOUBLE DRAGON PAPERBACK

ISBN 978-1-78695-487-9

Double Dragon
is an imprint of
Fiction4All

This Edition Published 2020
Fiction4All
www.fiction4all.com

Cover art by Deron Douglas
www.derondouglas.ca

Dedication

to Zoe

Acknowledgements

I would like to thank members of my critique groups, who, over the years, have devoted countless hours reviewing my work.

Robert Spiller
Beth Groundwater
Annette Kohlmeister
Jimmie Butler
Barbara Nickless
Maria Faulconer

John Stith
Sasha Miller
Dave Wheeler
Edward Bryant
Christopher Barili

Prologue

Approach to Earth

The Shepherd slid along convoluting stellar fields following the path of least resistance. His unpretentious front and gray, seamless sides contrasted little against the immutable void. Nothing abraded his smooth outer surface but the slightest pucker, a tight sphincter dialed closed sealing entry to his womb.

Inside, standing perpendicular to the line of travel, Truman Justis slept, unaware of where he was or how long he had been there. On a long curling arc, the Shepherd homed to the distant star his passenger called the Sun.

"It is time," the Shepherd said, giving Truman a gentle nudge. "We are almost there."

Truman awoke. "The players! Those vermin!" He struck randomly at unseen tormentors.

"You are shaking. Be calm." The Shepherd relaxed tissue to absorb Truman's tight-fisted struggle.

The future had been a hideous place. "What about Cathcar? The guardian?" Truman felt again the heavy body blows from the Neanderthal, saw his massive build, the reddish hue of his hairy body, his dead eyes.

"Cathcar is in the future." The Shepherd's voice was devoid of emotion. "The guardian is here in the present."

Truman inhaled. "Where are we? I can't see a thing."

A vision opened inside his mind. The backside of the Moon loomed large with a smaller Earth floating emerald-blue and swirling white in the distance. The Moon slipped past. The Earth rushed toward him.

As he stared at the vision, his mind locked up. "When?" Breathless, it was all he could manage to say.

"Two thousand five. A very precise return given the vagaries of time-past re-entries."

Truman blew out a stale breath. *Home*. A giddy rush of excitement washed over him. It had seemed an impossibility hours, or was it years ago? He no longer knew. His space-time travel could have spanned centuries.

The Horn of Africa broke through the center of surrounding equatorial clouds. Truman let his mind's eye follow the Great Rift Valley from Eritrea, down, southwest, in a line connecting to Lake Turkana. The speed of their approach brought the landscape into stark relief. The dry desert south of the lake showed pink and beige with the Loriyu Plateau standing above it like a broken aircraft carrier. Orange, afternoon sunlight pierced the dense atmosphere and cast a long shadow off the plateau's eastern flank.

The scene rushed toward Truman and stopped. A flat table of red rock stretched out on all sides and ended at an edge, then nothing except desert below, the distant horizon and pale blue sky.

"I had forgotten how dry it was. We've landed on top of something. Where are we?"

"Two degrees, fifty minutes, thirty seconds north latitude, thirty-seven--"

"Please..."

"We are atop the plateau, facing west. The fossil fields of Kanapoi are on the desert below."

"The last time I was here, I thought I was a dead man."

"That is understandable."

The fossil fields of Kanapoi. Mankind had begun here and here mankind would end. Maybe not in this time, but perhaps in another. Truman tried to shift position, but couldn't. The cloying walls of the womb pressed close like stiff pillows. "Okay, we're here. Now what?" He was anxious to get out and back to his life. He was also tired of being used.

"You must meet some people."

"Will that end it?"

"I thought we had...a deal. I showed you how to reverse the degradation of the human genome and you agreed to meet these people."

"Are they players?"

"Yes, some of them."

A tingle of apprehension shot through his body. "Jesus Christ, is mankind ever rid of them?"

"The players will be neutralized long enough for mankind to fulfill its destiny."

"That doesn't sound reassuring.

"Without mankind's survival, I cannot exist."

"But you exist."

"Yes. Mankind survives...long enough."

"But for what purpose?"

"It is very simple. Humans must build A4-Ni."

"Who the hell is A4-Ni?"

11

"She is my creator. The people I want you to meet are already here. You must go."

Truman resigned himself to what he must do. A deal was a deal. The orifice that led from the Shepherd's womb to the outside world dialed open. Sunlight flooded the chamber. The walls tightened around Truman and thrust him from below. He rose, an infant in a birth canal.

Outside, he sat on the Shepherd's rounded exterior and slicked a residue of clear mucus from his arms and legs. The Shepherd had clothed him and given him boots. His head was bare, his beard gone as well as the deep body bruises and lacerations inflicted by Cathcar. The mucus evaporated ahead of his efforts to remove it.

Beside him, the butt of a rifle eased through a tight opening in the Shepherd's skin-like exterior. The rifle slid straight up, a thorn emerging from a festering wound and fell on its side next to him. He picked up the rifle with both hands, hefting it. "What's this for?"

"When the time comes, you will know. The people you must meet are below the plateau's western edge."

The womb's sphincter-like opening sucked closed.

"Wait!" Truman shouted. "Will Azizah be there?"

"Yes," the Shepherd said dryly. "Proceed with caution."

"What the hell--"

"Goodbye, Truman Justis."

An instant of panic numbed his mind. "Will...will I meet myself?" Did he hear a chuckle? No, the Shepherd was only a machine.

"You will not meet yourself," the Shepherd said. "That is impossible."

"But--"

"Go now. I will wait for you here."

Truman hesitated. *Give me more*.

"You need not worry, Justis," the Shepherd said. "You will succeed."

Truman wasn't afraid of failure. He had a gun. His whole life had been one of meeting challenges, and he had always succeeded.

A gunshot cracked through the still air. The sound originated from beyond the plateau's western edge. A moment later, a second shot followed.

Truman slid off the side of the Shepherd and jogged toward the edge of the plateau. He squinted into the glare of the desert sun. Beads of sweat forced from his brow. With his heart thumping, he leaned forward and raised the rifle close to his chest in a ready position. His strong legs pounded the earth beneath his feet, raising puffs of dust. He hadn't felt this good since basic training.

Chapter One

"God damn flies."

Deputy Director for Military Support Jim Brubaker slapped a flyswatter at a pirouetting black speck. That a fly could penetrate his room, let alone the facility of which it was a part, never ceased to amaze him. National Reconnaissance Office Headquarters, Chantilly, Virginia was one of the most secure office headquarters in the nation.

Having knocked over a book, scattered papers and spilt a glass of water, he gave up on the fly, tilted his considerable bulk into his chair and swiveled back to his desk.

His computer beeped, then launched into a piezoelectric rendition of *Hail to the Chief*.

With a pudgy finger, he punched function key F2, swore under his breath at his mistake and stabbed F1--the secure video feed.

The screen darkened. A time display came on at the bottom edge of the screen and started flipping...Thursday, March 31, 2005: 0712hrs 35sec...36sec...37sec.

"Brubaker." Brubaker fidgeted.

The screen cleared and the image of a uniformed officer came into view. "General William Morehouse, here, NORAD. We tracked a bogie heading to contact somewhere in Kenya. Thought you guys might want to know."

14

"I'll be damned." Brubaker leaned forward, feeling the static electricity off the screen prickle the hairs in his nose. "You got details?"

"Yes, sir. Not much. But what we have, you can punch up on COMM.net. It came in real fast."

"Thanks, Bill, I'll take it from here."

Brubaker cut the reception and pressed the button on his intercom to the operations center. "This is Brubaker. You got anything from NORAD on this Kenya thing?"

"Yes, sir," squawked the intercom. "We're looking at it right now."

"I'm coming over."

He reached across his desk and fingered a Wintermans, a Dutch cigar, short, stubby, an after dinner smoke but he liked them anytime. Down the hall, he stepped into the NRO Military Support operations center.

It wasn't as big as its name suggested, maybe ten meters by thirty. In the dim light, clone-like officers hunched over monitors, manning lines of computer consoles. On the far wall, across from the door, multiple projections of the incoming craft's trajectory splayed across three large screens, all showing a different magnification.

Brubaker studied the center screen while unwrapping clear plastic from his cigar. "Where's it headed?"

"It's down, sir. Detection to contact, one-point-nine-five seconds."

"Two hundred-fifty kilometers in two seconds? Where'd it hit?"

15

The duty officer consulted his computer console. "Kanapoi, Kenya. Ah...sir, it didn't hit. It landed."

That's fast even for a UFO. That it hadn't drilled a hole in the desert was even more remarkable. Brubaker twirled the cigar deep into his mouth, wetting the dry tobacco, wishing he could light it. He pointed the cigar at the board. "Kanapoi. We closed that project twelve years ago. Give me a satellite image of the area."

Brubaker paced behind the duty officer as the man punched in the coordinates. An image of the desert seen from two hundred kilometers up replaced the hatch work of lines on the wall screen.

"What the hell am I looking at?"

"That's Lake Turkana, sir. The Kanapoi site is south of it." The officer used his thumb to rotate a ball on a joystick.

Video games. That's where these guys get their skills.

The camera view zoomed to fill the screen with the southern lakeshore and the northern part of the Loriyu Plateau.

"There're the ruins of the Loriyu research station."

"What's that?" Brubaker pointed.

"Sir?"

Brubaker snatched a laser pointer from his pocket, thumbed the switch and, with a thin red beam, pointed to a dark spot south of the ruins on top of the plateau.

The officer shifted the view to the spot and zoomed in. The spot grew in size until it filled the

16

center third of the screen, then stopped. "We're at the limit of optical resolution, sir."

Brubaker peered at the image. A gray, rounded shape threw off a shadow to one side. "Doesn't show us any more detail than before. How big is it?"

The officer punched a button, and a calibration grid layered the image. "I make it to be twenty meters across. Almost circular."

A speck separated from the object and moved to the northwest.

"Did you see that?"

"Sir?"

"That thingy-dot that separated from the bogie and is moving off to the left?"

"Yeah, I see it now."

"Can't we make it bigger?"

"I can go to digital mag but the resolution will be degraded."

"Please, Lieutenant, proceed." Brubaker chewed the end of his cigar.

The dot on the screen expanded, breaking into definitive pixels.

"Looks like a man running," Brubaker said.

"Yes sir. I think he's carrying something, like a rifle at port arms."

Brubaker sucked on the cigar, tasted something he didn't like and stared at the cigar's moist end. "So," he said taking a handkerchief out of his pocket and spitting into it, "we've maybe got a man separating from a presumed alien craft and carrying a rifle."

"Yes sir."

"Shit." Brubaker paced in thought. "We're going to have to coordinate with the JCS and the ASD on this."

"Yes, sir."

"We got any assets in the area?"

The duty officer's fingers tapped his keyboard. He studied the screen for a moment. "The Eisenhower is cruising the north end of the Persian Gulf. We could get a couple of F/A-20s to Kanapoi in--" He did a quick calculation. "--two hours and fifty minutes if the Saudis give us permission to fly over."

"Fucking rag heads. Not likely. Anyway, I'm thinking more in terms of people. We got anyone on the ground who's up to speed on the Kanapoi Incident?"

The officer typed some more. He stopped at one screen, then flicked to another. "Here's a live one."

"What's his name?"

"Truman Justis."

"Where's he at now?"

"Zen retreat, Kyoto, Japan."

"Japan? I'm talking closer."

"No one with his background, sir. It says he's a geneticist."

"I need a commando, not some fucking sushi-eating academic."

The duty officer typed. "His portfolio says he's seen combat. Gulf War."

"That wasn't no war. What'd he do?"

"CIA counter-intelligence. Biological weapons. Nerve gas."

"What's his profile?"

18

"Black American by naturalization, thirty-five, single." The officer placed his finger on the screen and moved down as he read. "Sir, this is *the* Truman Justis, the guy who missed the sarin ID. Two soldiers dead. But he gets a Purple Heart. Shot in the leg, friendly fire. He claimed it was retribution but it was never proved."

"Is that all we got to send against this thing?"

"Yes, sir."

"What else you got on this bozo?"

"Joined the NRO after the war. Been passed over twice. Top marks in his field."

"All right. What's his clearance?"

"SCI-IV."

"After that screw-up?"

"Sir?"

"Gimme a cross-link on genetics."

More keyboard work. "Hits on alien genetics. Kanapoi Incident." He paused. "Let's see—" He slid his finger down the screen. "--another cross-link to Kamau Jubali." The duty officer looked up.

Brubaker shoved the cigar in his mouth and tongued it to one side. "Who's Kamau Jubali?"

"Truman's father. Jubali worked for the paleoanthropologist John Lohner twenty years ago when the Kanapoi Incident came down."

Brubaker leaned over the seated man's shoulder and read the screen. "Jubali was killed by a lion. Same time Lohner died when his camp was fired. Wife, Judith Jubali—English, Caucasian, and son immigrated to the States. She took the name Justis. Anything else?"

19

The duty officer shifted the cursor and clicked on another link. "Truman stays in touch with an Amboseli Moye, Kenyan police constable who radioed in the Kanapoi Incident."

"Looks like Justis is our man. How fast can we get him to Kanapoi?"

"Assuming he answers his cell--" The duty officer changed screens. "--there's a flight out of Narita in three hours, two stops to Nairobi. Let's see...seventeen hours total flight time." Screens changed again. "Embassy's got a helicopter. Two hours to Kanapoi. Say twenty-four hours at the outside."

"That'll work. Get him on the phone. And contact CENTCOM. While we're waiting for Mr. Justis, I want a flyby."

"Yes, sir."

Brubaker bit off the soggy end of his cigar and spit toward a wastebasket. "Might as well put some muscle in ahead of our man."

***

Truman Justis sat on a bamboo mat at the center of the Ryutaku-ji *zendo* hall, Kyoto, Japan. His legs folded beneath him. On his robed thighs, his hands rested palms up, cupped in a *mudra*, his dark skin a contrast to the beige silk of his kimono. The smell of rosewood veneered walls mixed with decades of burnt incense conjured images of molding earth, of things growing in darkness, creeping spirits flowing in dim light. He tilted his shaved head forward, trying to concentrate on his *koan*, repeating each syllable rapidly but clearly, his breathing controlled.

The door of the *zendo*, four centimeter thick planks strapped and bolted by wrought iron bands, ground open.

Number one monk *Kurusai* entered.

Afternoon sunlight fanned orange behind his stocky frame and cast his shadow long. The door swung closed and shut with a dull *thunk*.

Candles flickered on the altar-shrine, tossing *Kurusai's* shadow across the room. He swaggered to one end of the altar, lifted the *kyosaku* from its rack, then raised the bamboo paddle over his head and brought it down in a practiced swing. It cut the air with a whoosh.

He duck-walked the perimeter of the room and took up a position behind Truman. "Who are you?" *Kurusai's* voice issued in a level tone, just above a whisper.

Though the temperature in the *zendo* was cool, a trickle of sweat ran off Truman's scalp, slid down his cheek and fell from his chin. He raised his voice, uttering his *koan* louder, faster.

"Answer!" *Kurusai* shouted.

The word fell like a physical blow on the back of Truman's neck. To demonstrate his answer, he drew a hand before his closed eyes in a sweeping gesture, his fingers trailing.

"Good," the monk said. "Now, who am I?"

From behind, the gravel crunched beneath *Kurusai's* wooden sandals. Truman demonstrated another answer.

The *kyosaku* whistled fast beside his ear and hit hard across his back.

"No!" *Kurusai* spit the word out. "Who am I?"

Pain radiated down Truman's spine. He imagined one of his ancestors sagging, hands tied to the whipping pole, the slave trader's lash laying onto flayed skin. The *kyosaku* smacked one shoulder, then the other.

"Answer!"

Truman suppressed his rage and demonstrated his response.

"No!" *Kurusai* flailed the *kyosaku* at Truman's back.

His shoulders slumped. A fiery sting streaked from each side of his body, intersected mid-chest and dropped to the pit of his stomach.

"Sit straight!" the monk screamed. "Who am I?"

Truman flinched and uttered a cry of anguish, thrown up like vomit from his gut.

"Ex-cell-ent," *Kurusai* whispered. He stepped around to where Truman could see him. "But this is a better answer." He demonstrated the correct response.

"Thank you." Truman rose, wiping wet hands on his robe, and bowed at the waist, then limped from the *zendo*. His war-wounded right leg had stiffened with the prolonged sitting.

Outside, he skirted a small courtyard. A bell chimed. Its sound drifted in the still air like a coiling ribbon that was reluctant to leave. The bell signaled the start of his interview with the *roshi*. Truman was late.

He entered the *roshi's* chamber and prostrated himself on the floor.

The *roshi* sat calmly. His baton in one hand lay across his lap.

"My *koan* is *Who am I?*" Truman tried to focus his eyes on the mat centimeters from his face but saw only a yellow-brown blur.

"Do you have any questions?"

"Yes," Truman said. "When the *godo Kurusai* strikes me with the *kyosaku* I feel he enjoys hitting me. The blows do not push me to greater effort and concentration. They have the opposite effect. I become discouraged."

"You may sit." Though the *roshi's* deep voice rumbled like gravel in his throat, he projected an air of infinite patience. "You must not think it is this *godo* or another who is hitting you, or try to analyze your reaction. You should raise your palms in gratitude. But there are many like yourself who find being hit with the *kyosaku* a distraction to their meditation. The monitors can be told not to hit you unless you request it."

"Thank you." Truman shifted his position, easing the pain that had returned to his leg.

"Do you have another question?"

"Yes." Truman tried to meet the *roshi's* gaze but wavered. Instead, Truman stared at his hands on his lap. "Once I am distracted by the *kyosaku*, my meditation is flooded by unpleasant feelings about myself and thoughts about my work. You have said to achieve *kensho*, I must empty my mind of all thought. I cannot do this. My ego enters first and refuses to leave."

"You are a geneticist and a black American. Powerful sources of distraction. Your ego uses these to place obstacles along your path to enlightenment. The higher these obstacles are, the harder it will be to achieve *kensho*."

23

"Why would my ego do that?"

"Your ego makes you feel you are the emperor of the universe but in truth, you exist halfway between a speck of dust and the Buddha. As long as you remain at the midpoint of existence you will try to enhance yourself through the control of others and the accumulation of material possessions. When your spirit awakens with *kensho*, you will be able to overcome the obstacles your ego has placed before you. You will turn from these worldly pursuits and embrace the whole universe as yourself. It is then you will find the tranquility you seek."

"Thank you, *roshi*. My work tells me humans are devolving. In my meditation I see as men become less, their ability to see the path to *kensho* becomes more obscured, until they can see no path at all."

"Your problem is your thinking. It puts you on one side of a wall and that, which is not you, on the other. When you stop thinking of your two selves as separate, the wall will crumble, and you will experience *kensho*."

"A wall," Truman said. "I have spent my life standing on the outside looking in."

"The obstacles to your enlightenment are great."

The interview ended. Truman rose and bowed at the waist.

Outside the *roshi's* chamber, Truman stood on the polished wooden deck above the courtyard. Sand-raked water patterns swirled in silence, a bird chirped from a dwarf fig tree, and a cloud scudded across the afternoon sun.

With a shuddering intake of breath, he absorbed the tranquil scene. The *roshi's* words echoed in his mind. Mankind's genome was crumbling, as though there were indeed two selves, one devouring the other. If the degradation continued, mankind would devolve to archaic humans in two thousand years, to Homo erectus in tens of thousands, then to Australopithecus.

Does it matter? Despite knowing the problem existed, Truman didn't care what happened to mankind. He shivered at the thought of how far he had drifted to the edge of cynicism. He knew he was being selfish. Muttering a *koan* over and over in a vain hope to discover who he was seemed futile. He knew less now than he did before. Would he ever know more?

The cell phone clipped to his belt vibrated. A small LCD blinked red, the secure line.

Chapter Two

A warm breeze pushed a dust devil across the dirt road that ran between Kanapoi's sun-bleached clapboard buildings. Broken windows stared at the emptiness of the town. A sign creaked back and forth on a single hinge, the other long ago rusted through in the humid air off the lake. In front of an empty store, a hitching post for camels lay cracked and bent. Down the middle of the street, an overturning bucket caught in the windswept sand and twirled crazily, before banging on its way.

Constable Moye leaned against his Land Rover, waiting for his appointment to show. His khaki uniform of shirt and shorts was starched and proper. The tight curls of his hair showed touches of gray at the temples. His dark wraparound sunglasses matched the black of his skin and hid the expression of his eyes from the world.

He had parked where he could view the main approach from the south. In the distance, a vehicle sped across the landscape, raising a rooster's tail of dust behind.

Cutting through the shimmer of heat mirage, a late model Toyota Land Cruiser loomed large and pulled to a stop ten meters from where he stood. A cloud of sand, carried by its own momentum, blew past, forcing him to shut his eyes and throw an arm across his face.

Damn, doesn't the son of a bitch know what he's doing?

But the driver wasn't the man Moye expected.

A woman opened the door and stepped out, showing a long, tanned leg ending in a sandal, toes painted blood red. She stepped away from the SUV and slammed the door.

She was tall with dark brown, almost black hair shoved under an Aussie hat pulled low to designer sunglasses. Bronzed complexion, perhaps an Arab mulatto. About thirty. Between full lips, a bit of chewing gum peeked out as she worked it around her mouth. A dust-stained white bandana wrapped her neck. From broad, square shoulders a pink tank top hung over tight, small breasts. No bra, no watch, no jewelry, no makeup.

All in all a good lay, Moye thought but she had a gun slung low in a holster on a belt around her hips. *What the hell is she doing out here?*

"Are you Moye?" She removed her glasses and let them drop on a cord to her chest. Blue-green eyes stared at him from under the shadow cast across her face by her hat. They had a haunting look, bright dots of intense color in a perfectly proportioned face.

He gazed at her muscled thighs stretching athletically below the single cuff roll on each leg of her shorts. *Yes, indeed. She would be nice in bed.* "I'm Moye," he said instead. "I expected a man."

"I've come in his place."

She spoke without emotion. Her gaze drifted from left to right, focused behind him, as though she were checking the place out. Her attention returned to lock him in a stare.

"My name is Azizah." She stepped forward, extended her hand and offered a winning smile backed by two rows of perfect, white teeth.

27

Moye grasped her hand and found her grip strong, almost too strong.

"Do you have the guardian?" She sounded impatient.

Her confidence made him uneasy. "You don't waste any time do you?"

"Time? How can one waste time?"

Moye snorted and shook his head. "You got me there, deary." He pulled a handkerchief from his pocket and wiped his forehead. "Yeah, I've got the guardian. You got the money?"

"Of course."

"Show me."

Azizah sauntered to the Land Cruiser and returned with a hard-shell aluminum attaché case. She banged it onto the hood of his vehicle and shoved the two slide latches open. She lifted the top and stepped back. "Two million dollars."

Arranged in neat rows and filling out the area of the case were stacks of bills drawn snug in paper wrappers marked *Ten Thousand*. Azizah closed the cover and shoved the case across to him.

"You're trusting," he said. "How do you know I won't shoot you and take the money?"

"Believe me, I know." She smiled. "And you won't."

Moye swallowed hard. *Tough bitch.* "Yeah, I guess not. Still, it's a lot of money to pay for a bauble."

Azizah stared past his shoulder. "Let me worry about that. May I have it?" She extended her hand, curling her fingers toward her palm.

Moye squinted at the manicured nails flashing red in the sunlight. "It's not here. I don't like having it around. Gives me the willies."

"That's too bad." She rolled the gum over her tongue, formed a small bubble and bit through it with a pop. "Where is it?"

"Not far. I'll take you." This woman was getting on his nerves. He put the case on the ground and reached into the front seat of his Land Rover to withdraw a holstered gun on a belt. He threw the buckle end around his hips, laced the tongue of the belt into it and pulled tight. "Ready."

"Do you always travel armed?"

"I do nowadays. Used to be you could reason with people, even bad ones. Not anymore. You want to take my car or yours?"

"Let's do it in mine." She ran her tongue over her upper lip.

Moye shrugged. Having had his manhood shaken by her attitude, he didn't appreciate the sexual innuendo in her offer. Tossing her in bed was now the farthest thing from his mind. "What about the case?"

"Bring it with you. It was safe in my vehicle a minute ago."

Moye grabbed the case and climbed in on the passenger side of the Land Cruiser. He placed the case under his knees against the seat.

She started the motor. "Where to?"

"Go back the way you came, ten kilometers, then turn left off the road toward the plateau."

She put the vehicle in gear and made a tight turn to head south. After ten kilometers, she slowed. A beaten, earth track led toward the plateau. She engaged the four-wheel drive and turned off the main road.

"Does this lead to the camp of John Lohner?"

"Yeah." Moye leaned forward. "But there's nothing left of it. Government trucked in here right after the fire. Joint US, Kenya job. Dug up everything and hauled it all away, burnt tents, fossils, equipment, everything. There's nothing left."

She raised the power windows and switched on the air-conditioner. She drove expertly over the uneven track, one hand on the wheel, the other resting in her lap. "How did you come into possession of the guardian?"

Moye glanced at her and grabbed a handhold over the door to steady himself. "John Lohner gave it to me before he died."

"If I recall, he died in your arms. That must have been traumatic."

Moye didn't mind talking about the incident. Talking always washed away some of the fear and confusion that had stayed with him over the years.

"I met Lohner on a couple of occasions before he was killed in the fire. The first time, he tried to get me to take custody of a girl, Mia, who had showed up one day at his camp out of nowhere. That didn't work out and she stayed with him.

"The next time, I was called out to his camp where he reported some guy named the Shepherd had forced Mia into a spaceship and taken off. Nuts if you ask me. That was the day before Lohner died. Next day, Lohner called me on the radio and said he was being threatened by his laborers. By the time I got there, the camp was a total loss, burnt to

30

the ground. Witnesses said they had seen Lohner staggering into the desert carrying a woman. I took out after them.

"When I found him he was alone and burned real bad. There was this big round object sitting there, like the spaceship he had described to me that had taken off the night before. Next thing I knew up it went. The government investigators grilled me good. Was it the same spaceship or a different one? Hell, I didn't know and told them so."

"Whatever happened to the woman Lohner was carrying?"

"Beats me. We never found a body. Maybe she took off in that spaceship like Mia did in hers. It was all crazy as far as I was concerned."

"Lohner didn't elaborate in his diary?" Azizah asked.

Moye was surprised. "So, you know about the diary. No, Lohner didn't elaborate. The last entry was before he reported this Mia had left, then later I suppose we can assume dead men aren't writing their memoirs while they're in the midst of dying."

"You sound bitter."

"Yeah, I guess. After I discovered the diary, I turned it in. No thanks from anyone. Damn bureaucrats."

"Governments can be intimidating. Tell me, did you read any other parts of the diary?"

"I took a glance at it. Most of it was nonsense, at least to me. But I told the investigators what I'd seen, and they couldn't get past the UFO they'd tracked and it being when I reported it to them."

"I know."

31

"Do you?" Moye regarded her suspiciously. "Bet you don't know what Lohner told me before he died?"

"That's a bet I'd lose." She played him with a smile. "There's nothing in the records about your conversation with the paleoanthropologist."

"That's because I never told no one. He said *Afareni* built the spaceship I saw taking off."

Azizah raised an eyebrow. "*Afareni*. She'd be the Earth-mother of myth."

"Yeah. I figure Lohner was far gone."

"But you're sure he said *Afareni* built the Shepherd?"

"No, she built the spaceship."

"We are experiencing a semantic confusion. The Shepherd is the spaceship."

Now it was Moye's turn to be surprised. "I thought the Shepherd was the leader of whatever group Mia was a part of."

Azizah smiled and shook her head.

Moye peered at her. "Something I should know about?"

"No. It's interesting how the truth can be seen by so many people and interpreted in so many different ways."

"I'm no philosopher, miss. Anyway, I figured if Lohner wanted to think *Afareni* made the craft then that's what he should think. I wasn't going to tell a dying person what to think."

"You were very kind."

Is she putting me on? "You don't think she built this Shepherd?"

"Perhaps she did. Perhaps she wasn't *Afareni*. Did Lohner ever say anything about A4-Ni?"

Moye squinted at her. "Yeah...I get it. I'd almost forgotten. He wrote A4-Ni in his diary and noted how it sounded like *Afareni*. Course I didn't pay it much mind. He also said this A4-Ni was a voice he heard."

"It's obvious the poor man was under a lot of stress."

Moye shook his head. "Pure loony-ville. But what do I know? I'm a small town cop, Miss Azizah. It all happened a long time ago. All I'm interested in now is getting you the guardian, and I'll be on my way with the cash, thank you."

Moye took out his handkerchief and wiped his forehead. Not a day passed he didn't think about the incident. He had filed his report, and it got a lot of attention. Soon, it seemed like the whole world descended on Kanapoi. Scientists, military, international press. The town grew from a sleepy camel herders' stopover to a boomtown. Then after eight years, the scientists and the military pulled the plug and left. The town died.

"So," Azizah said, "you had the guardian all along?"

Moye chuckled. "That's the only funny part of this whole damn affair. I drove the scientists nuts. I made up stuff about good spirits and the bad spirits and how they lived in all human beings and controlled our lives."

"Did they believe you?"

"Don't know but they wrote it all down. Anyway, I never told them where I kept the guardian. I wasn't afraid of them neither. I'd sit there and give them a big smile. They knew I had

33

the thing. But what were they going to do, torture me?"

They neared the plateau. Raked by its convoluted escarpment, it loomed out of the surrounding desert. At its top toward the north end, overlooking Lake Turkana, stood the outline of an abandoned two-story structure.

Azizah pointed. "What's that building up there?"

"That's what's left of the research center. Government didn't fool around. They built the center, stayed eight years and left. Waste of money, if you ask me."

"I understand they drilled a tunnel through the plateau."

"You've done your homework. Since the research center sat on top of the plateau, they tunneled through so they could drive from the Lohner base camp on the west side to where the alien craft took off on the east side. The center is connected by a passageway down through solid rock to the middle of the tunnel."

"Do you know why they abandoned the center?"

"They were tracking something with a big telescope they had. Guess they lost sight of whatever they were looking at."

Azizah stopped the Toyota at a jumble of rocks across the road. A sign to one side warned about trespassing on government property.

"We'll have to hike the rest of the way," Moye said.

"Where are we going?"

"The tunnel." Moye got out of the SUV and led her up a track that climbed to the tunnel entrance.

Iron gates hung ajar across an opening ten meters wide. He stepped through, and Azizah followed. He waited a moment for his eyes to adjust to the dim interior. The tunnel floor rose with a slight camber as it penetrated the plateau, hiding the exit at the opposite end.

"Where's the guardian?" Azizah surveyed the tunnel nervously.

"Don't get so jumpy. It's over here." Moye strode deeper into the tunnel.

At the midway point, Azizah pointed to a door-sized opening four meters off the floor in the north wall. "What's that up there?"

"That's the end of the passageway I told you about. Leads back to a flight of steps that climb to the research center. Used to be a rung ladder going up from here but it rusted away long ago. Over there--" He pointed to a gaping recess in the north wall at ground level, below and to the right of the passageway. "--that's where an elevator used to come down. They'd drive trucks in here, unload them and take stuff by elevator to the upper floors. Once the place was abandoned, everything got striped away. Doesn't say much for the folks around here."

He stepped over to a large rock and pushed back some wood debris to expose a neat concrete box half a meter on a side with a hinged iron cover. "It's in here," Moye said, breathing hard.

"You went to a lot of work."

"I never liked the thing. The scientists were always pestering me about it, so I figured to put it somewhere safe, away from me."

"So you constructed this vault?"

"Yeah. Seemed a good way to preserve the guardian. Seemed like it belonged hereabouts, anyhow."

He took a key from his pocket and unlocked the iron lid, then raised it. The hinges protested with a rusty squeal. Sticking his hand inside, he felt around until his fingers closed on a metal sphere that lay on the bottom of the vault. He brought out the sphere, not quite as large as a golf ball, and held it between thumb and forefinger.

"It's smaller than I expected," Azizah said, taking the sphere from him and hefting it. "Heavy, too."

"I figure it got burned in the fire and never worked. That's why it got left behind."

"You are very perceptive." With a pleased smile, she started toward the entrance.

"Wait up." Moye turned back to the vault, replaced the lid, locked it and put the key in his pocket. As he stood, a shadow fell across the tunnel floor.

A powerfully built man stood silhouetted in the entrance. He was shirtless with cut-off shorts. Light from behind reflected white off the black skin of his muscled shoulders. He stood, legs spread in a balanced stance with thighs as thick as a man's waist. In one massive hand, he held an AK-47 as though it were a pistol.

Action figure, Moye thought. "Now what?" He glanced at Azizah off to his right. She stood stark still. He reached for his gun.

The man rotated the rifle at his hip and fired at short burst, one-handed.

A bullet thumped as it tore through Moye's khaki shirt, drilled into his stomach and exited out his back. He gasped in pain. His gun clattered to the ground. He clutched his midriff and crumpled to the floor, staring in disbelief at the blood seeping through his fingers.

Before Azizah could get her gun out, the man leveled his at her chest. "Give me the guardian."

"Who the hell are you?"

"Call me Jomo but that don't matter." He pulled the trigger.

A bullet caught her in the left shoulder, splitting her halter strap. She cried out, spun and fell. Blood oozed from her wound, coursed across her half-exposed breast and spread out on the rocky floor.

Jomo stepped over to Moye and kicked his gun out of reach. "Sorry about that." Jomo waved his rifle at Moye's wound. "We all gotta die sometime."

Moye tried to talk but the pain took his breath away. Instead, he gazed at Jomo's red hair, dark and slicked across his black forehead like some Nairobi pimp. *Who did his mother sleep with?*

Jomo stepped over to Azizah and nudged her hand with the toe of his boot, all the while keeping the rifle trained on her. The guardian rolled out of her curled fingers. He stooped, picked it up and placed it in his pocket.

He exited the tunnel and returned a moment later, carrying a canvas satchel. After dropping it on the floor, he took out two clear plastic boxes, a handful of dynamite sticks and fuses. He worked quickly, screwing the fuses into the ends of the dynamite. When the explosives were assembled, he parceled them into the plastic boxes to which timers were glued.

He trotted over to the entrance with one box and attached it to the rusted jamb of the gate with multiple wraps of duct tape. He returned, picked up the other box and jogged out of Moye's sight to the entrance at the opposite end of the tunnel.

The light dimmed, and Moye was startled to see a second man silhouetted at the entrance to the tunnel. He hefted a 450 Marlin big game rifle. *What's he hunting? Rhino?* He resembled a Kenyan but his head was shaved. He seemed familiar. "Truman? Is that you?"

The man squinted into the dim interior and rushed to Moye's side. "You don't look too good, Constable," he whispered.

"Thank God, it's you." Moye spoke in a pained whisper. "What are you doing here?"

"Later. Who did this to you?"

"I don't know. He called himself Jomo." Moye winced. "Ugly fuck. He's at the other end of the tunnel. Get the girl out of here."

"She's here?" Truman scanned the floor of the tunnel and located the girl. "Azizah? Oh, God." He hurried to her side and touched her neck for a pulse.

Azizah moaned.

38

Jomo reappeared. "What the--" He raised his AK-47 and began stitching fire from Truman's left to right.

Truman dropped to one knee as the rounds sizzled overhead. He brought his rifle to his shoulder, took careful aim and fired.

The shot hit Jomo in the chest--a bullet going through a thick melon, blowing out a chunk of his spine. He fell flat on his back, twisted onto his stomach and began dragging himself with his arms deeper into the tunnel.

Truman stalked after him.

"You are not part of this," Jomo said before another shot from Truman silenced him.

He came back into Moye's view, grabbed Azizah under her armpits and dragged her out of the tunnel. He returned to Moye.

"God, I hurt," Moye said.

Truman hesitated, then hurried to the vault. He tried the lid. "Where's the key?"

"I've got it." Moye winced.

"Where?"

"Pocket."

Truman fumbled inside Moye's pocket and grasped the key. He stepped to the vault, knelt beside it and inserted the key into the lock. It snapped open. He threw back the lid and peered inside. "Who's got the guardian?"

"How do you know about...the guardian?"

"Come on, Constable. We don't have a lot of time."

Moye shook his head. "God-damned guardian. I should have given it away."

With a sense of rising urgency, Truman shook Moye. "Where's the guardian?"

"Shit, Truman. That really hurts." Moye's eyes shifted. "He has it."

Truman disappeared from view in the direction of the dead Jomo, and returned a moment later with the guardian clutched in his hand.

A shot rang out. The bullet whined overhead and splattered rock from the top of the tunnel.

Truman spun around. "No!"

Azizah rolled onto her stomach, both elbows propped on the sand with her gun clenched in her hands.

"Go to hell." She steadied the gun and pulled the trigger.

Truman grabbed his chest in agonized surprise. He toppled face down into the dirt. The guardian pitched from his grasp and rolled toward the vault.

"I will carry this day if it kills me," Azizah wheezed as she staggered to her feet. She gazed at Truman's still form for a moment as if waiting for something to happen, and when nothing did, she shrugged.

"Help me." The pain in Moye's gut was like a giant vice, squeezing the life out of him.

She ignored him and limped into the tunnel toward the fallen Truman and the guardian.

"Get me out of here," Moye cried. "The tunnel is going to blow any second."

Azizah glanced ahead to the guardian lying twenty meters from her in the dirt near the vault, then staggered for the box of dynamite at the entrance.

"He was trying to help us!" Moye screamed.

40

"He was interfering in my business. He deserved to die." She knelt beside the plastic box and tried to dismantle the explosive. "No time."

She hesitated at the entrance. "Get in there and throw me the guardian."

"Fuck you." Moye coughed up a mass of blood.

Looking desperate, Azizah started into the tunnel.

A scraping sound emanated from the tunnel's deep shadows. Jomo lurched into the light. Besides the wound in his chest, half his forehead was gone, leaving what was left of his brain cratered in his skull surrounded by a pool of coagulating blood. His AK-47 flashed rapid fire in random arcs.

Moye thought he'd seen a ghost. "He was dead!"

Azizah stood her ground, raised her pistol and squeezed off three shots in rapid succession.

Jomo jerked as the bullets punched holes in a neat triangle on his bare chest.

"Players are hard to kill." Azizah took a step toward Jomo, then stopped.

Jomo's remains shriveled from his feet toward his head as if he was a balloon with the air leaking out. A moment later he was gone. His boots, lacking feet to support them, fell sideways and rocked below his crumpled shorts.

"What the hell happened to him?"

"Recycled. Happens all the time when there are too many players in one place. I thought that jobbie over there--" She indicated Truman's corpse. "--was a player but he's still here. I don't usually kill humans but it happens."

"What are you talking about? Where'd Jomo go?"

"How should I know? I'm just doing my job. Now throw me the guardian."

"Go fuck yourself."

Azizah stared at the guardian resting beside the vault deep in the tunnel, then at the winking red LCD on the explosive charge taped to the tunnel entrance.

Smart girl. You might get trapped in here if the charges go off.

She disappeared in the direction of the Land Cruiser. The door opened and closed. The engine gunned to life. Tires spun, crunching gravel. The sound of the vehicle receded.

Moye crawled. He got as far as the entrance when the charge at the tunnel's eastern end blew. A blast of dust-laden air billowed over him. *Odd. The eastern entrance blew before the western one.* But he figured he didn't have long to wait.

Chapter Three

Truman stood at curbside outside the arrivals area of Nairobi International Airport.

Where the hell's my ride? It didn't make sense a heavy hitter like Brubaker would jerk him halfway around the world only to leave him hanging.

Truman glanced at his watch. Twenty minutes late already. He waved over a taxi, threw his bag in the back seat and climbed in next to the driver. "New Stanley Hotel."

Twenty-five minutes later he was standing at the hotel's front desk signing a hotel card and getting the key to a room.

He glanced at his cell phone. No messages. No incoming calls.

"Do you want help with your bag?" The clerk behind the desk graced him with a smile while smoothing her hair back along the sides of her head.

Is she the one going to help? "Nah. I've only got the one case."

She looked disappointed. "I hope you have a nice stay."

"Thanks." Truman lifted his case and headed for the elevator.

An *Out of Order* sign hung across the doors.

Great. Fortunately, his room was on the second floor. He found the fire stairs and huffed his way up to the floor, stepping first with his good leg, then lifting the gimpy second one behind him. He located his room and pushed in.

Nothing to do but wait. Brubaker hadn't been specific about why they wanted him in Nairobi *ASAP* except to say they wanted him to look up Amboseli Moye, his father's friend. But that seemed a cover, and anyway Brubaker didn't have to tell him why he wanted him here. Brubaker was the boss.

The sounds of traffic from Kenyatta Avenue below his room drifted through the open window on hot, humid air.

A fan twirled above him. A queen-size bed with tall, carved wooden posters crowded half the room. Two sets of French doors led to identical small balconies overlooking the avenue below. A painted white wicker chair sat angled to one of the doors next to a small writing table with a day-old clutch of red hibiscus hanging limp in a frosted glass vase. Very colonial.

He leaned both hands against the dresser and flexed his leg. Sitting hours on a plane was never achieved without pain. He glanced at himself in the mirror above the dresser. Except for his lighter skin, he'd pass for a Kenyan. Hell, he was half Kenyan by a father he'd never known--only a vague memory of a large man, a kind man who was never around much.

Truman peeled off his shirt. In the bathroom he leaned over an old-fashioned washbasin with a cold-water faucet handle consisting of four spokes with a scripted "C" on a white porcelain cap. His attention to detail never left him. He cupped his hands to catch the warm water and splashed it onto his face, then rubbed his hands over his scalp.

Scratchy stubble reminded him he'd have to shave his head again soon.

Back in the bedroom, he dropped his carry-on onto the bed and took out his laptop computer. While waiting for his computer to boot-up, he sat in the wicker chair and gazed out the doors at the bustling city.

Kenyatta Avenue disappeared west, clogged with honking afternoon traffic and lined with blue, flowering jacaranda trees, purple bougainvillea, hibiscus and oleander. Mini-skyscrapers of anonymous design formed an irregular backdrop, dwarfing an odd collection of colonial era buildings and shops below. Puffy clouds hung motionless in a pale blue sky.

Once the operating system steadied, he opened his organizer and clicked on the "M" tab in the address book. "Constable Amboseli Moye, GPO Loiyangalani, Kenya." He hadn't seen the constable in five years. How had the NRO guys picked up on his relationship, and what did that have to do with all this dial nine-one-one bullshit? He could see Moye anytime. Why now?

And why doesn't someone call? He was about to go online with his cellular phone to check with the home office, when the LCD blinked red. *Finally.*

"Hello." He hoped it would be Brubaker.

"Truman Justis?"

"Speaking."

"This is Jim Brubaker."

"Yes, sir."

"Where the hell...ah, excuse me, may I please have your ID?"

"Yours first." Truman tired of the cloak and dagger. Did Brubaker think he had been waylaid since his departure from Narita? Paper rattled in the background at the other end.

"...the dead man walks."

"He thinks silent thoughts." Truman stilled the quaver in his voice. Given the high level exchange, the call must be important.

"God damn it, Truman. Where the hell are you?"

"I'm at the New Stanley."

"You should be on a chopper heading for Kanapoi."

"You could have told me. I waited at the airport, and no one showed."

"Something got screwed-up. Embassy was supposed to send someone to meet you. Obviously, that didn't happen. We're looking into it."

"What's in Kanapoi?" Truman didn't know whether to be surprised or intrigued. Things were happening, and he was somehow at the center.

"We registered a UFO homing to the site."

"You told me I was to meet Amboseli Moye."

"Forget Moye. He was our cover. Look, trust me. You've got the background for this."

"What do you want me to do?"

"Sit tight. We're in contact with the Embassy. They seem confused. They sent their military attaché, a guy named Hopkins. When this gets ironed out, he'll fly you up to Kanapoi. He's been briefed and can bring you up to speed. I want you to check out the UFO site. We're organizing backup."

"Yes, sir."

"I want a report in three hours."

"Three hours, sir?"

46

"Just do it." Brubaker hung up.

Truman was left holding the cell phone and frowning at it. He had never gotten used to the chicken-little mentality that always escalated around an affair when the sky began to fall. These career types were great for stepping into the breach and cranking up the volume. He found them hard to take.

Though UFOs were spotted all the time, he supposed Brubaker had considered this one serious. The report on the Kanapoi Incident was rife with sightings of alien craft. Should he call the Embassy and ask for the attaché? But if this was coming down as fast as he thought it was, they'd fix the screw-up, and there'd be a knock at his door in no time.

He had opened his suitcase and pulled out a change of clothes when there was a knock on the door. He opened it.

A solidly built man, who could have been a linebacker in the National Football League, stood before him.

"Truman? I'm Brad Hopkins, US Embassy." He stuck out a beefy hand.

"That was quick." Truman grasped the hand. The man's freckled complexion was flushed pink, like he'd run up the stairs. His disheveled red hair lay limp in a sweaty mat on top of his head. "I expected you to pick me up at the airport."

"Fucking screw-up. You know how these things are." Hopkins drew his hand across his brow and wiped his open palm on his pants. He fixed Truman in a stare, then winked. "The dead man walks."

Hopkin's cavalier attitude startled Truman but he answered. "He thinks silent thoughts."

Hopkins smiled. "Had to get that out of the way."

"Of course." How had the embassy's military attaché gotten his ID? "I was getting a few things together. We can be on our way in a minute."

"All right but step on it. You know how these guys get once their ass is in the wringer. You got to drop everything and piss bullets."

Truman pulled on a shirt and stuffed a change of clothes into a small nylon bag. He added his laptop to the jumbled contents, then paused to take a quick look around, trying to think if he had forgotten anything. "Okay, I'm ready."

Hopkins held the door for him. "We'll take the stairs. My car is out back. I didn't want to attract any attention parking in front, diplomatic plates and all."

***

They double-timed down what were supposed to be fire stairs but the concrete walls smelled of dank urine, the pipe railings rusted through in places.

Hopkins kicked open the door to the lobby. The reception desk was around a corner wall out of sight. They turned a sharp right and headed down a narrow hallway with a wooden wainscot and peeling wallpaper top and bottom. The hallway led to a fire exit at the back of the hotel.

This Exit To Be Used In An Emergency. Alarm Will Sound.

After pushing through the door, the alarm didn't go off but not much worked in Kenya as Truman would have expected, anyway.

They got into the car, a black, late model Cadillac with US Embassy seals emblazoned on the doors. Hopkins eased it to the end of the alley and paused at the busy avenue crossing in front of him. When traffic refused to give way, he cut in, honking his horn, practically daring other drivers to run into him, then made a turn south toward the airport.

"Cock-sucking nationals," he said.

Truman decided he didn't like Hopkins. The man's speech had a vulgarity that set Truman on edge. *Try conversation.* "The left hand drive doesn't seem to bother you."

"You get used to it." Hopkins shifted his football shoulders into the tan, leather seat. "Problem comes when you go back to the States."

"I bet. Where you from?"

"Here and there. I move around a lot. You?" He hit the horn, slammed on the brakes, spun the steering wheel hard right, then accelerated past a donkey that had entered the roadway. Hopkin's expression didn't change.

Truman pulled his seat belt tighter. "New York City, West 116th Street."

"That'd be south Harlem."

"You know New York. I grew up in the shadow of Columbia University. Joined the Air Force, let them put me through school, all the way to a PhD in biochemistry with a break somewhere in between for the Gulf War. Now I'm paying them--"

"Wait a minute." Hopkins glanced at Truman. "I know you. You're the agent sarin guy."

Truman stared at his hands resting on his lap. "That I am." Would he ever be free of agent sarin?

"Don't look so glum." Hopkins returned his concentration to the road. "From what I read, it wasn't your fault."

"Doesn't help much. Two soldiers died." The missed sarin ID had changed his life. In one horrible moment he had fallen from a know-it-all, get-out-of-my-way, brilliant Afro-American to a failed ghetto product succumbing to the years of abuse heaped from above by an aloof, white society. Then the friendly fire. A white boy took a shot at him. Shattered his kneecap. Nothing he could do. Nothing he could prove. Payback. Though the youthful fires still seethed deep within, he now made sure the smoldering energy no longer reached the surface.

Hopkins glanced at him. "That how come you got shot?"

"I... yeah, I guess that's why I got shot." How could anyone be so insensitive?

Hopkins drove with a quick abandon and passed under a pair of giant plaster elephant tusks arched over the roadway, the entrance to the airport. He turned off the main approach and circled round on a service road that led to a fence that surrounded the runway.

A red-and-white striped bar, counterbalanced by a block of concrete, rested across the road, controlling access to the runway beyond. A tilting guard's shack with sun-bleached, peeling paint stood to one side. In it, a Kenyan soldier lounged against one wall, half asleep. He shifted to loose attention when they stopped and held an automatic rifle in front of him, finger straight off the trigger guard, muzzle pointed down.

Hopkins flashed his diplomatic passport. "We're going to take a spin in the company chopper. This here's my passenger."

The soldier eyed Truman and nodded. Clearly, the soldier hadn't understood a word of what Hopkins said. The soldier stepped to a sliding chain link gate beyond the barrier and slid it open.

Hopkins chuckled. "Tight security."

The soldier returned to the barrier and leaned his weight onto the concrete. The bar rose clear of the roadway.

Hopkins eased the car through the tight opening and headed for the Embassy helicopter.

He parked next to the aircraft. "Ever been on one of these?"

"During training. I never liked the idea the only thing keeping me up were four blades."

"You don't have to worry about this baby. Those are twin Allison 250-C40 turbines. No way they're going to let you down." He patted the polished, dark-blue shell of the cab above a white US Embassy seal showing an eagle holding in its beak a ribbon with the words *e pluribus unum* written across it.

"Stow your gear in the passenger compartment back of the front seat. I'm going to do a quick pre-flight, then we'll get going."

Truman dumped his gear and climbed into the co-pilot's seat. He pulled the harness over his shoulders, buckled it across his lap and waited.

Hopkins finished his inspection, then climbed in and handed Truman a helmet with a mike on a boom protruding from one side. "Wear this. We won't be able to talk otherwise unless we shout."

Hopkins busied himself with the controls. He called the tower to let them know his destination. In a moment, the engine coughed to life and the rotors began a slow turn.

"You okay?" Hopkins' voice crackled from earphones inside Truman's helmet.

Truman nodded. He glanced back over his shoulder at the passenger compartment. "Pretty plush."

"Top of the corporate line. Seats six."

"How long's this going to take?"

"We'll be there in a couple of hours, give or take five minutes. It's five hundred kilometers as a vulture glides."

Once the rotors reached speed, Hopkins taxied a short distance away from the car, and they were airborne. He banked the copter in a steep, tight turn and headed north over the sprawling city.

"Look at that shit." Hopkins indicated the sprawl of shantytown that surrounded the larger buildings of the capital. "Fuckers multiply like rabbits." He glanced at Truman. "No offense."

Truman had gotten used to intentional insults. Careless figures of speech had long since ceased to bother him. He put a mental shell around the obscenity, boxed it up and tossed it to one side. Though his anger stirred, the lid he kept over it remained in place. "How long you been here?"

"Almost four years." Hopkins stared at him with a hint of a smile. "You're okay, Truman."

He didn't care what Hopkins thought. Racism lurked in all guises. Hell, Kenyans put him in a

52

class with white Americans even though he was half Kenyan. So much for brotherhood.

He stared out the window. The city thinned and gave way to yellow plains interspersed with stands of forest. Most of the land appeared to be farmed. Mount Kenya towered off to the east, its snowcapped peak rising above surrounding clouds.

Hopkins settled the helicopter on course and leaned back. "All right, Truman, not much to do for the next hour or so. Here's the scoop." He turned his head to see if Truman had heard him.

Truman nodded.

"At zero-five-hundred hours Mountain Standard Time, which would be yesterday, USSPACE in Colorado detected a UFO entering the atmosphere. They tracked it to the vicinity of Kanapoi. Satellite imagery shows the sucker on the ground. It's just sitting there. We don't know why it's there or what it's going to do." He smiled. "You and I are going to try to find out."

"I suppose," Truman said, "the assumption is it's the same or similar craft that left Kanapoi twenty years ago."

"That's the assumption." Hopkins laughed. "Not many alien UFOs come and go from a place as remote as Kanapoi."

"Why us?"

"They're sending me because I can pilot a helicopter, and I know my way around Kenya. They're sending you because you work for them."

"That doesn't sound like a crack team to put up against an alien presence."

"Don't worry. The heavy muscle has already left the Eisenhower but they'll arrive thirty minutes after we do. More backup is behind that, all the good stuff C-130's carry."

"What are we supposed to do?"

"Play dumb. We're the only bodies available. First in, first out."

"This sounds a bit ad-lib."

"It is." Hopkins tapped his finger on the altimeter. "Being a geneticist, you might look at it from a scientific point of view. Great opportunity to meet our rivals face-to-face."

"That's not what I was led to believe we were going to do when they fingered me to come out here."

"What'd you have in mind?"

"They told me to meet the constable who filed the report on the Kanapoi Incident."

"Moye?"

Truman hesitated.

"Come on, Justis." Hopkins gave him a pained look. "I'm not the enemy."

"He's still in the area and a friend of the family."

"What do you think he'll tell you that wasn't in the NRO files?"

"It's been twenty years. I thought Brubaker wanted me to follow up on the Incident. Maybe Moye would be willing to say more than he did at the time. Reports indicate he wasn't too cooperative."

"How does that line up with your work?"

"I'm studying the human genome. A couple of months ago, I isolated a section of DNA code that had changed in the short time we've had the code spelled out.

"Is that bad?"

"It's taken four million years for the human genome to evolve after humans split from the great apes. At the rate this section is degrading, we could be back swinging through the trees in a couple of thousand years."

"No kidding?"

"No kidding."

"What's that got to do with Kanapoi?"

"I did a search of NRO files, keying on genetics and got hits relating to the Kanapoi Incident. There were references to alien genetics."

"So what."

"There are other identified cases of rapid human genome degradation. They all began after the Kanapoi Incident. I wondered if there was a connection. I wrote it up and got linked to Moye, then this shit happened."

"I don't know how Moye could help. He's a stubborn son of a bitch. Always going on about spirits and some guardian he took from the alien craft."

"So you know about the guardian. Not many people do."

Hopkins waved a hand in the air. "That's the best part about being in this business. You come to a place like this, you get to learn all sorts of things no one else knows anything about." Hopkins adjusted his harness and pushed his hand across the bottom of his nose, a nervous gesture. "When you contact Moye, you going to ask him about the guardian?"

"Yeah, I'll ask him, if I ever get to see him. The documents are ambiguous. Although they indicate that Moye has the guardian, there's a second opinion the shaman Watombo got it before he died and hid it."

"I've heard that one." Hopkins shook his head. "Don't believe it. I'm guessing Moye has it."

"You seem very interested in the guardian."

Hopkins grinned. "Shit. Give me a break. There's not much else going on out here. TV's worth crap. If I didn't follow stuff like this, I'd go insane."

"That would be interesting," Truman said.

Hopkins frowned, probably not the response from Truman he expected. "That paleoanthropologist...what's his name?"

"Lohner?"

"Yeah. His diary wasn't clear about the guardian. A lot of what he wrote was unintelligible. Some of the pages got burned in the fire that killed him."

Truman leaned back in his seat and stifled a jet lag induced yawn. He rubbed his eyes. "Yeah, I knew that. It's a wonder anything survived."

"Anyway, Lohner wrote the guardian could see into the future of anyone using it, if it was calibrated on that person's past."

"And the investigators believed him?"

"I didn't say they did," Hopkins said. "Of course him being paranoid didn't help."

"I didn't know he was."

"Had a history of depression in his family. A bit touched. He thought an alien controlled his life and was after his DNA."

Truman smiled to himself. "And I thought I had problems."

Hopkins snorted a laugh.

56

At least he has a sense of humor. Truman gazed out the window at the landscape rushing by beneath them, seeing a peacefulness in the vast expanse he didn't feel in his heart. Here and there a herd of wildebeest or water buffalo grazed. An isolated elephant stood out, a gray shape casting a darker shadow onto the bleak landscape. How did any of the animals manage to survive with so little to eat and no water in sight?

The steady throbbing of the helicopter and his lack of sleep on the trip out made him drowsy. His eyes fluttered, and he dozed. He thought Hopkins took a revolver from a holster strapped under his armpit inside his shirt, checked the clip and returned the gun out of sight.

Hopkins glanced at him but didn't seem bothered Truman might have been watching.

***

Hopkins gave Truman a nudge. "Rise and shine, Tru, baby."

Truman sat up and frowned. He could never get over people wanting to shorten his name. At least Hopkins hadn't called him brother.

The sun brushed the horizon, casting everything on the plain below in sharp relief.

"Not much to look at," Truman said.

"That's the Loriyu plateau sticking up over there." Hopkins pointed. "Kanapoi's off to the west."

Truman stared down at the plateau as they passed over it. "There!" A round, dark object rested on the plateau midway between its east and west edges and a half kilometer south of the abandoned research station. "Is that the UFO?"

"Don't know but we're going to find out."

Hopkins banked the helicopter into a sharp turn for another pass. "There's a car."

A sport utility vehicle raced north along the western side of the plateau. Passing beneath the helicopter, the car hit a soft mound of sand, careened sideways and rolled twice before coming to rest right-side up in a cloud of dust.

"Shit! Did you see that?" Hopkins aborted his flyby, brought the helicopter to a hover and descended toward the wrecked vehicle. "The little green men are going to have to wait. We'll make this quick."

He brought the helicopter down, bouncing it on its shock-absorbing, wheeled runners.

Truman leapt out and sprinted to the SUV before Hopkins throttled down the rotors. The SUV leaned at an angle with the passenger-side wheels sunk in the sand. The driver, a woman, was still strapped into her seatbelt. He stepped onto the running board and grabbed the edge of the open window. After pulling himself up, he gazed inside.

Money littered the interior.

The woman moaned and lifted her head, fixing him with penetrating blue-green eyes.

Hopkins ran up and stood beneath him, hands on hips. "What's the situation?" he shouted over the noise of the idling helicopter.

"One occupant. Female," Truman shouted back. "She's been shot."

"Ten-four. I'll get the first-aid kit." Hopkins ran back to the helicopter.

The twin turbine engines cut out and began a descending whine from their idling pitch. The landing lights snapped on, casting two hollow beams through the deepening twilight.

Truman pushed the door up and propped it open. "I think she's pinned," he said over his shoulder.

Hopkins jogged from the helicopter, a first-aid kit was in one hand and his semi-automatic in the other.

"What the hell's that for?" Truman indicated the gun.

Hopkins shoved the gun into his belt and shrugged. "Never know when it'll come in handy. Looks like we're going to need something to lever her out. There's a pry bar strapped to the back of my seat in the helicopter."

Truman stared at him.

"Let's go, Truman." Hopkins dropped the kit onto the ground and opened it. "I'll get the first aid started."

Truman hesitated. *Why should I go for the pry bar?*

"Jesus, look at all the money." Hopkins glanced around, then returned his attention to the woman. He reached in and pressed his hand over the wound on her shoulder. "She's bleeding badly. Get going."

Truman jumped down and returned to the helicopter. He had freed the tool when a shot rang out.

"What the hell?" He ran back to the SUV.

Hopkins lay on his back on the ground. A neat hole, coagulating with blood, marked his right temple. The other side of his face disappeared in a bloody mess.

The girl in the SUV leveled a gun at Truman's mid-section. "You can drop the pry bar."

Truman dropped the bar, shaking his head, trying to make sense of what had happened. "Hopkins?" He knelt beside the body and stared at the wound. Hopkins was dead.

Truman stepped away from the corpse.

The girl waved the gun toward Hopkins. "Look."

The corpse shriveled from its feet up, then disappeared. Hopkins' clothes and shoes cluttered the ground.

Truman gasped. "What the..."

"Don't feign surprise," the girl said. "He tried to kill me. You know damn well he would have killed you, too."

"Me? He worked for the embassy."

"Really?" She peered close. "At first I thought he was an assassin named Jomo, red hair and all but you say you've come from Nairobi."

"What's that got to do with anything?"

"He couldn't have recycled. I only killed him a half an hour ago."

Truman blinked, dazed. "But..."

"Who are you?" the girl demanded. "You look familiar."

She's insane. Buy time. "I'm Truman Justis."

She waved the gun at the US seal on the side of the helicopter. "What're you doing out here?"

No way to close the distance to the gun. She looks distracted but that could only be a ruse. "We're on official business."

"With him?" She indicated the scattered clothing.

Truman stared, dismayed. "I only met him a couple of hours ago."

"Sure you did." The girl grabbed the car door and eased herself out.

Guess she wasn't pinned after all.

Swaying, she stood before him. "Put the kit on the hood where I can reach it."

The pry bar. Truman did as told, then inched toward the pry bar on the ground.

"Come on, Truman. I'm not stupid. Over there." She indicated the desert away from the pry bar.

Truman sidestepped into the lights of the helicopter.

"All right, that's far enough."

He stopped and realized he was too far away to lunge for her gun, yet not far enough he could run anywhere before she would have a good shot at him. "What happened to his body?"

"Player kills player. Player recycles."

"What're you talking about?"

"You're either human or a dumb player, and I hate dumb players. I suppose there are plenty more where you come from."

He took a step toward her. "Where I--"

"Ah-ah." She waved the gun in his direction.

Sensing the determination in her voice, he froze.

"Stay there for a second." She put the gun on the hood of the SUV and rummaged through the first-aid kit. She pulled out bandages and dressed her wound. After fumbling in the bottom of the kit, she found a vial of morphine, cracked it open and sucked out its contents.

61

"That's better." She made a face and picked up the gun. "All right. This is what we're going to do. I'm going to get in the backseat of my vehicle, and you're going to drive where I tell you."

"And if I don't."

"You don't look stupid. You'll cooperate, thinking I'll make a mistake, or maybe this morphine will make me groggy, then you'll try to overpower me." She smiled, lighting up her blue-green eyes. "But I'm not going to make a mistake, the morphine is doing what it's supposed to do, and you'll stay alive as long as I think you should."

He lowered himself into the driver's seat, and she climbed in the back.

"See if you can get this thing started."

Truman turned the key and depressed the accelerator. The engine turned over with an agonizing groan but caught.

"Good boy. Now get us out of the dirt. The differential lock is that button on the left."

Truman bent over and located the switch. He put the Land Cruiser in reverse and eased it off the soft shoulder back to level ground. "Now what?"

"Go north."

After turning the SUV around, he drove over a rough track. The windshield was cracked but still in place, one of the headlights still functioned. To see where he was going, he peered below the windshield cracks into the gloom ahead. After driving for five minutes, he arrived at the end of the plateau and stopped.

"Turn right," the girl said. "We're going around the plateau to the other side."

The Land Cruiser bounced on the uneven desert over mounds of sand-clogged grass. Thorny acacia bushes scratched its sides, producing an irritating sound like distant screams.

Truman glanced in the rearview mirror. The girl was sitting upright despite her wound and staring at him. She seemed determined. Who the hell were players? Obviously, there was some connection with the UFO. He forced himself to be calm. They all seemed human, though they were alien enough when they died. She had thought Jomo was Hopkins but he couldn't be in two places at the same time. So that meant at least three players or whatever and one UFO. It didn't seem they had come from the UFO. What was the connection?

Be patient, he told himself over his thumping heart. She will tire and let her guard down. Then again, maybe aliens don't tire.

The dark waters of Lake Turkana slide by on his left, reflecting a dull palette of ochre from what was left of the sunset. Truman rounded the north end of the plateau and headed south on the other side. After another five minute drive, a weed-infested track cut across the desert in front of him.

"Stop here," the girl said.

"Where are we?"

"We're on the eastern side of the plateau. That track goes through the tunnel. Connects the Kanapoi side to this side." She shifted the gun. "You first."

Truman got out of the SUV and preceded her on the track to the tunnel entrance. A pile of rocks barred his way. "It smells like dynamite."

"Good guess." She surveyed the pile of rubble. "We'll never get in this way." She looked around, frustrated, then up at the escarpment. "Okay, back to the vehicle."

She ushered him with her gun. "You stand there," she said, indicating Truman should stand in front of the SUV's only headlight. She went to the back, dropped the rear window and pulled out a coil of old rope and a flashlight.

"We're going to do a little climbing." She threw the rope to Truman, then switched on the flashlight and indicated the escarpment. A number of faint animal trails led to the top. She picked out the least steep among them. They climbed, Truman in the lead.

"You going to be all right?" she asked.

Startled, Truman stopped and turned around. "What do you mean?"

"You're limping."

"I'm surprised you care. You shot and killed my pilot, and you say you shot and killed someone else before that."

"I still need you."

"I'll be all right." He tried to find an opening but she stayed far enough away. He continued climbing.

Whenever she called a halt to rest, she remained ten paces from where he stopped in front of her. At the top, she directed him to the ruins of the research station.

It loomed in the pale light, a two-story concrete and steel bunker with its windows broken out. Drifted sand piled against the walls and flowed out the open door.

Truman scanned around. He could see nothing on top of the plateau to the south. The dark object he had seen from the air would blend with the night sky, if indeed the object was still there. Off to the west, below the edge of the plateau, glowed the lights from the helicopter.

"Inside," the woman ordered.

He ducked his head and entered a vestibule the size of a small bedroom that must have acted like an outer airlock to the air-conditioned station. Azizah goaded him through a facing door opening into the ground floor of the station. On the far wall to his left was where an elevator must have come out. He peered into the gloom for some kind of weapon but the place had been stripped clean.

The woman ushered him across the large empty room to another door opening on the far side. She flashed her light onto a landing for a flight of steps that dropped off to the left into an inky blackness. "Down there. Go slow. It comes to a hallway."

"Does this lead to the tunnel?"

"Bingo." She smiled.

Truman thought that she was very beautiful. Her tough demeanor didn't seem to fit.

"Call me Azizah." She motioned with the flashlight for him to begin descending.

Truman cleared the steps and entered a down-sloping hallway. Though Azizah shone the flashlight back and forth from behind him, he stepped cautiously, right hand sliding along a roughhewn rock wall. The wall of the passage on his left opened into a void.

"The abandoned elevator shaft," Azizah said. "Used to be a wall here but it rotted away. We're going to the end of the hallway. There's an opening there that gives access to the tunnel."

After feeling his way for a minute, he groped empty space and assumed he had come to the hallway's end.

She shone the flashlight on the remnants of iron plugs that once anchored a gate to the stone wall. "Tie the rope to one of those anchors, then throw the end over the side."

Truman tied the rope, tossed the loose end into the darkness and heard it hit bottom.

"Down you go," she said.

"The rope doesn't look like it's going to hold my weight."

"It'll hold."

Truman turned around, eased over the edge and began rappelling down into darkness.

He reached the floor of the tunnel and estimated he had climbed down four meters. He stood back.

She held the flashlight on him. "There's something I want you to get for me. It's over that way." She indicated the direction with a thrust of her beam before putting it back on Truman. "Take it slow. I'll guide you."

Truman glanced to his right. A recess in the tunnel wall led to the abandoned elevator shaft. If he could get in there, she wouldn't have a clear shot at him.

"Don't even think about it," Azizah said.

God, I hope she was guessing and not reading my mind. "What am I looking for?"

"The guardian."

"It's here?"

She didn't answer his question. "See that concrete vault?" She flashed the light briefly on a concrete vault on the other side of the tunnel.

"I see it."

"The guardian is off to the left about a meter." She played her flashlight across his body indicating the direction.

Truman shielded his eyes and peered at the ground. "Can you get that light out of my eyes?"

She angled the light so it partly fell on him and partly in the direction she intended him to go. "Get moving."

Truman started walking, and she shifted the light ahead of him. After twenty paces, the light stopped and fell on a small sphere. Truman knelt. "Is this it?" He held the sphere up to the light.

"That's it. Bring it here."

Truman walked toward the rope, then realized if he gave her the guardian, it would end his usefulness and get him killed. He made a quick movement one way. The light followed and overshot him. He danced back the other way and ran for the elevator recess. The light swung back to pinpoint him. A shot rang out. He staggered and fell. A burning sensation erupted from his left thigh.

"That was stupid," she called. "Why not be reasonable and toss me the guardian?"

"I can't move." Truman clutched his leg. Warm blood eked out of a flesh wound. The bullet had hit muscle and gone straight through.

The light went out. Silence. Then scraping sounds. A moan of agony and the light switched on again. Azizah had reached the floor of the tunnel and was moving toward him. She stopped two meters from where he lay.

"The guardian, please."

"Come get it."

"You *are* going to be stupid." She seemed to consider the situation. "With that limp, it's very unlikely you're a player but one never knows. I don't want to kill you unless I have to."

"I wish I knew what you were talking about."

"This isn't your game." She waited.

Resigned, Truman tossed the sphere the short distance to her feet.

She knelt, wincing with pain and picked it up. "Thanks. Have a nice eternity."

Truman cringed, thinking she would shoot him but she didn't. Instead, she strode back to the rope and turned off the flashlight.

He realized if he didn't do something soon, he would die in the dark tunnel. In agony, he frog-crawled across the rough floor to the end of the rope. She hadn't gotten very far, it being a lot easier for her to descend with her wound than to go up. He still had the strength of his arms, whereas she had to fight the wound in her shoulder.

He grabbed the rope and climbed hand-over-hand as fast as he could. He reached her foot and latched onto it.

She kicked. "Let go, you idiot."

He clawed his way up her leg and grabbed her belt.

She struggled.

If she tries to use her gun she'll lose her grip.

He worked his way up her body, circling his good leg around her legs, and grabbed her halter with one hand while reaching the other to her hair.

She screamed.

The rope broke.

His foot dragged on the wall, tipping them around in mid-air. They hit the floor hard. The last thing he felt before blacking out was his elbow pressing into her neck below her chin and the crunch of her larynx collapsing.

Chapter Four

Terror. Oppressive darkness. Truman lay on his back. Rain splattered his face as if poured from giant buckets, big spherical drops, liquid missiles, pounding the ground, splattering dirt and leaves.

Where am I?

He shielded his eyes with his hand and squinted upward. *Still dark.* His mouth gaped, filling with water. He gagged and rolled onto his side, spitting. He gagged again, then more sucking until he managed a slow steady breathing.

He dragged himself to his knees and wiped muck from his arms with jittery hands. His clothes hung in shredded wet strips, his boots torn, the soles missing.

Azizah shot me. I fell.

He gripped his thigh. No pain. He pawed where the wound should have been. Nothing but smooth skin. He reached up and felt his scalp. His fingers tangled in tight curls of hair that led through thick sideburns to a full beard.

He felt again.

Hair? He couldn't have been unconscious that long. Or could he?

How'd I get out of the tunnel?

Lightning flashed, followed by a ripping thunderclap. The ground shook and darkness returned. A false image burned his retinas, showing a small clearing surrounded by dense growth. Desperately, he struggled to adjust his eyes to the gloom.

Dim shapes. Massive tangles of brush and grass whipped in the wind. Shielding his eyes, he gawked at a towering canopy of trees and palms backlit by stroboscopic flashes of lightning. Snaking vines laced back and forth snaring the swaying trees in a tight chaotic knit.

The bush emitted a frantic rustle, then a pinched-off squeal followed by a wet chomping. He imagined sharp teeth crushing the bone-stiffened flesh of a small animal.

Truman crawled across the clearing away from the sounds. With each agitated movement, his knees and hands sank into thick loamy earth smelling of rotted vegetation. It oozed between his fingers and gummed his legs. At the clearing's edge, he stood, glanced back to see if he was being followed, then lunged into the underbrush.

Staggering forward, he forced tired legs to propel him into a wobbly run. Branches clawed his hair, tore across his chest and scraped his thighs. He flailed his arms ahead of him, pushing branches from his face, willing them out of the way.

He slammed into a wall of dirt and rough stone, and dropped to his knees. Reaching shakily, he ran his hands over a slippery surface. Through rain clogged eyes, he made out crumbling rock rising to form a steep escarpment. It disappeared above him into the wet darkness.

A purposeful thrashing behind him cut through the steady rush of the rain. Whatever it was, it was big, the brush no barrier, just an annoying impediment.

Truman staggered to his left, following a narrow space between the bottom of the wall and the wind-whipped jungle.

After twenty slogged paces, his scrabbling hands met empty space. He'd come to an opening, a cave of some sort. A quick assessment. The entrance seemed a meter and a half wide by two meters tall. It loomed ominously dark but inviting.

The inside should be dry.

From deep within the cave, a faint, clicking drifted to him over the roar of the rain. Not a natural sound. He tilted his head back against the dirt of the escarpment. His stomach curled in knots of fear.

What to do? What the hell's in there?

A flash of lightning followed by a shattering thunderclap. A tree exploded and caught fire, hissing and smoking in the downpour.

That settles it. I need shelter.

He peered around the edge of the entrance into an inky gloom. The flash of a spark caught his eye, then another flash. A faint glow of flame grew and danced the shadow of a hunched figure onto the wall at the back of the cave.

Though he couldn't see the figure clearly, it was obviously that of a man, one of massive proportions.

The man sauntered toward the entrance, his attention concentrated on blowing onto smoldering kindling in his cupped hands.

As the scent of burning wood drifted out of the cave, Truman inhaled, gaining small comfort from the familiar smell.

The man raised his head.

Truman held his breath and flattened against the escarpment wall. In that moment, he had seen the man's face. Something about it put him off. Not because the face was ugly. But the face fell slightly to one side of a spectrum of faces that Truman would classify as modern humans. The man's head was larger in proportion to his body, his eyes wider spaced, his nose broader and flatter, lips fuller.

The firelight grew inside the cave and spilled out the entrance, illuminating a small clearing in front. Truman risked another look.

The caveman transferred the flickering tinder from his cupped hands to an earthen container. The thick stench of burning fat replaced the wood smell. In the brighter light from the lamp, the man's features became clearer. He was stocky, perhaps a head shorter than Truman, and naked except for some sort of loincloth. Fair-skinned, almost pale. He had a developed musculature, massive chest, coiling biceps and strong thighs. A chaotic mass of stringy, blond hair cascaded off his head in loose curls.

Blue Lagoon's Christopher Atkins on steroids.

A crash behind Truman made him turn. From the wall of underbrush, a caricature of a lion, cross bred with a bear, thrust its head clear and snarled at him. The beast leapt into the clearing, hunched low. From its open lower jaw, two jagged canines curved upward, glistening in the dim light. Glassy, cat eyes flashed reflected light.

A whimper of desperation caught in Truman's throat. He lunged into the cave, tripped and sprawled onto the dirt floor two meters from the caveman.

His head snapped up. He fixed Truman in a piercing stare with shocking blue eyes.

The lion-bear huffed and leapt onto Truman.

Air exploded from his lungs.

With an angry snarl, the beast retreated, then sank sharp teeth into Truman's leg.

Truman howled in pain and panic.

Growling--a dog chewing a bone and warning all to stay away--the creature dragged him from the cave into the splattering rain.

A scream rose in Truman's throat, where it died as the beast let loose of his leg and stomped up Truman's back, hot breath pounding the nape of his neck.

With a grunt, the breath stopped. The animal loosed a plaintive howl that cut short in a high-pitched yelp. It pushed off hard and sprang from Truman. The beast slewed sideways in the mud and crashed through the brush.

Truman stared.

Blue Eyes stepped forward.

"Help me," Truman cried through bruised lips.

The powerful figure stepped nimbly and retrieved a sharpened lance from the thick growth.

Though Truman strained to see what Blue Eyes was doing, he couldn't rise. His legs no longer responded to the commands his brain issued. He got as far as coming to his knees, then toppled forward onto the soggy ground, expecting the point of the lance in his back.

Instead, Blue Eyes straddled him, grabbed him by his hair and pulled his head back.

With his mouth agape, Truman stared into the man's eyes, deep liquid blue pools, irises finely etched. He squinted, and Truman felt reassured. The eyes were human, inquisitive, intelligent.

Blue Eyes grunted, circled an arm around Truman's mid-section and draped him across his hip. With a powerful, measured stride, he stepped into the cave, put the flat of his hand over the lamp, ignoring its heat, and smothered the flame.

The dark night returned with a suffocating presence. Still carrying Truman, Blue Eyes spun around, exited the cave and loped along the path between the escarpment and the jungle.

Truman groaned at the rhythmic jostling to his body. His back seemed on fire from clawed scratches. His leg throbbed where he had been bitten.

Blue Eyes shifted Truman higher in an underarm grip and climbed the escarpment. Minutes later he emerged onto the flat summit.

Thick brush covered the summit. Beyond, rain-laden clouds swirled across the dark sky, showing no stars or moon. *Could this be the Loriyu Plateau?* But broad-leafed tropical plants had replaced barren acacias, and soggy ground, the sand and gravel. Below, tall trees carpeted what had been dry desert.

As Blue Eyes carried him into the bush, branches of undergrowth battered Truman's face and ripped off what was left of his shirt. He twisted his head, trying unsuccessfully to dodge their thrashing.

On the far side of the summit, Blue Eyes descended with bone-jolting strides on another trail, which ran level midway between the top of the escarpment and the jungle floor below. The trail ended at a large rock that appeared to have sheared from the mass of the plateau and slewed across the path, leaving a slit opening to something beyond.

Another man appeared through the slit. He and Blue Eyes exchanged quick words, unintelligible to Truman. Then the second man disappeared behind the rock.

Truman was released and dropped to the ground.

Blue Eyes stepped into the opening, then reached back to sink his fingers into Truman's hair and dragged him through.

Truman's head cracked hard on the side of the rock. His stomach heaved. He retched. In a daze, Truman found himself again riding Blue Eyes' hip. The rain stopped, and Truman realized they had come out of the rain into a sheltered space. He sensed others were watching him but it was too dark to see anything. A shiver coursed through his body. He convulsed with a sneeze.

Blue Eyes climbed what seemed to be terraced levels and eased him onto flat, dry ground. A moment later someone laid a rough animal skin on top of him. Then he was alone. He felt chilled. He drew his hand under his nose and pulled the skin about him. It was poorly tanned, still stiff with a strong, animal odor. Truman tried to see where he was but it was too dark. He felt feverish. That and his fatigue saved him too much thought. The dinning roar of the rain, at a distance, cascading like a gray veil from some overhanging ledge, never ceased.

He lay back on the hard surface, shuddered and closed his eyes.

Where the hell am I?

***

Truman awoke before opening his eyes. In that brief instant, he hoped he had been dreaming. He shivered. His aching head felt ready to burst. In dim light, he examined his calf. Angry red teeth marks marched across the muscle, swollen to twice its normal size.

A gourd half-filled with what appeared to be water sat within arm's reach. He picked it up, tasted the contents, then, satisfied it was only water, drank. With his head upturned, he saw he was in a large cave. The escarpment must have collapsed at this location. The natural shelter formed was at least twenty meters high by a hundred wide and ran back into the plateau another thirty or so.

The roof of the cave arced overhead, framing gray sky beyond. For as far as he could see, thick water-laden clouds scudded over a dense carpet of dark, green jungle.

I wasn't dreaming.

Judging from the light, it was either mid-morning or mid-afternoon but the rain was falling as hard as the night before. Runoff coursed over the edge of the plateau above and fell in a fluttering sheet to pound eroded rocks below.

Men and women of similar stature to Blue Eyes busied themselves with unknown tasks on different levels of the layered terraces. Crude ladders, two poles with rungs lashed between them, linked the levels. Each terrace fronted narrow entrances into blocky rooms constructed of crude stonework and mud plaster.

77

He counted at least a couple of dozen persons, divided between male and female. The women wore loose-fitting skin wraps that hung from one shoulder by a halter that slewed across their breasts and dropped to their thighs. He saw no children, although to his astonishment, all the women appeared to be pregnant. *Why were they pregnant*? But he was too weak to wonder further.

***

A nudge.

He must have slept. He opened his eyes and shielded them. Someone held an animal-fat lamp close. A woman's face eclipsed the light. Piercing blue-green eyes stared at him.

The lamp-holder stood, and the light bobbed away.

Truman had been transferred into one of the rooms. It had a low-ceiling and felt cramped. A flat slab of stone served as a table on one side. On the other, a stack of gourds littered the floor. Behind him, a hanging animal skin covered the entry to a second room, perhaps a sleeping room.

The lamp holder approached another, whom Truman thought must be Blue Eyes. She spoke to him in an incomprehensible language, either because it was, or Truman was too delirious to understand. Blue Eyes grunted and replied with a similar stream of gibberish, though in a deeper voice.

Truman tried to stand but felt lightheaded with a stab of pain lancing his forehead. He shrieked in agony as he stumbled on his wounded leg. He fell back exhausted and crawled to the skin, then curled into a fetal position.

The blue-green eyes reappeared. They swam before his delirious gaze. He tried to focus but could not.

"What are you doing here?" Blue-green Eyes asked.

She speaks English! "I don't know," Truman answered, eager, confused. A strong hand raised his head. An earthen container touched his lips, and a warm herbal liquid entered his mouth. He swallowed. When he tried to go back to sleep, blue-green eyes shook him and made him finish the drink.

He lay back exhausted.

***

A loud noise made him start, and he realized he must have dozed off again. It was still light but he had no way to tell how long he had been there. He crawled to the room's entrance.

Only women occupied the cave. They seemed agitated, running up and down the terraces, screaming and pointing toward the entrance slit.

A man of ominous proportions strode up the path toward them.

The screaming increased like a chattering wave, infecting all of the women at once. They ran in all directions.

The brute ignored them and stomped his way toward Truman's enclosure.

Unlike Blue Eyes and the other males of the cave, this beast was thickset with arms as big around as his massive thighs. Reddish hair hung in ragged disarray from his head. A fine bristle of body hair peppered his skin, which was as black as pitch. He stomped, wheezing, shifting side-to-side, brushing massive thighs together in his effort to walk. He breached the terrace in front of Truman and peered at him.

Truman gasped. If Blue Eyes had been at the edge of human physiognomy, this brute was well below it. His forehead sloped back, accentuating small eyes, pinched close above his broad nose, giving him the look of a simpleton, though a terrifying one. Below the flat splay of his nostrils, his mouth turned down in a grimace.

Feeling trapped with nowhere to go, Truman scrunched to the back of the small room.

The brute thrust a hand into the opening, grabbed Truman's leg and dragged him onto the terrace. He shifted his grip to Truman's neck and forced him to his knees.

"Dead man," the horror croaked in passable English.

The women converged on the man. They howled and showered him with ineffectual blows.

With his free arm he batted one woman head over heels and punched another in the face. Otherwise, he took no notice of their onslaught and continued to stare at Truman. Then, possibly deciding this was not the time or place to end Truman's life, the beast shoved Truman hard to the ground and plodded away.

Truman clutched his throat. A female stepped forward and patted him on the shoulders and back as though he were a pet.

"Who was that?" Truman strained to ask no one in particular.

The women didn't answer him but he picked up the repeated word *Cathcar* in their exchanged gibberish.

Truman raised a water gourd with shaky hands and drank. The swelling in his leg was down. His fever seemed to have broken, leaving him feeling better but limp with exhaustion. He crawled back into the enclosure and covered himself with the skin.

Make it all go away.

But it didn't. He dreamed he was in the embassy helicopter making a joyous return from Kanapoi to Nairobi, to the New Stanley Hotel. In his dream he smiled and turned to Hopkins but instead of Hopkins, a grotesque hunched form manned the controls. The beast, Cathcar.

***

When Truman next awoke, the sun lay low on the horizon opposite the cave. A shaft of light spilled into his small room and across his legs. He examined his feet sticking out in front of him. His boots were gone. He still had his pants, though they were so torn they'd pass as shorts. He remembered his shirt had been ripped from his body sometime during the hike from the cave over the plateau.

He pulled up a tattered pant leg and examined his calf. Though still sore to the touch, there didn't seem to be any infection. He tried to remember the last time he had had a tetanus shot. But what time reference would he use?

He pulled the pant leg all the way up to his thigh. Twenty centimeters above his knee was a neat circular scar a couple of centimeters in diameter. He twisted around and strained to see the back of his thigh. A larger scar there indicated the bullet had exited. He was wondering how his wound could have healed so quickly, when he realized someone was watching him.

Blue Eyes squatted in the corner of the room.

Truman pushed his pant leg back over the scar and pointed a finger to his open mouth. "I'm hungry. Food."

Blue Eyes pointed to a gourd beside Truman.

He picked it up and smelled the gray, mashed substance inside, some kind of fruit. Using his two fingers, he scooped a portion into his mouth. The mash was edible, even tasty. He finished it all, washing it down with water from another gourd.

Blue Eyes continued to stare.

"Who are you?" Truman laid the empty gourds to one side and wiped his mouth with the back of his hand. The food made him feel stronger.

No answer or movement from Blue Eyes.

Truman reached out a hand. "Thanks for saving my life." He said the words deliberately and a bit loud, wondering if Blue eyes understood anything.

The cave man stretched out one long arm and engulfed Truman's small hand in his. The squeeze was measured, almost gentle. He didn't release Truman's hand when Truman decided to pull it back.

Okay, you go right ahead and hold on. "Where am I?"

Still no response. Truman leaned back as far as he could and brushed at the leaves and dirt clinging to his body.

Blue Eyes shifted closer.

82

Surprised, Truman stopped while Blue Eyes removed the remaining leaves and twigs.

Truman patted his hand against his chest. "My name is Tru...man."

"Tru...man," Blue Eyes repeated.

The rudimentary exchange pleased Truman. *Here goes.* He patted his free hand on the Blue Eyes' chest. The skin under his palm twitched at his touch.

"Ju...ven...al," Blue Eyes said.

Whoever he is, he's not stupid.

Juvenal stood and pulled Truman to a standing position. Though Truman was a head taller than the cave man, Juvenal could be half again his weight.

Holding Truman's hand, Juvenal guided him out of the enclosure, past piles of wood, animal skins, fire pits, earthen pots and past stacks of fire-sharpened sticks.

As Truman stumbled to keep up, he realized his feet hurt. He stopped and shook his hand free of Juvenal's. "I need shoes." Truman indicated his feet.

Juvenal's blue eyes narrowed. He jerked on Truman's arm, then said something unintelligible. He was not going to wait.

Juvenal started off again. On the way to the slit in the rock, he picked up a fire-hardened lance, hefted it as though checking its balance and gave Truman another pull on his arm.

They squeezed through the entrance, crossed the level part of the path and climbed back to the flat summit. The sun had continued to sink lower, indicating to Truman the cave faced west.

Juvenal headed north through the brush.

Truman followed, placing each foot carefully on the ground, trying to avoid sharp rocks and exposed roots. After a while they entered a clearing. Truman stumbled into the open area and gazed in awe.

On the far side, walls of moss-covered concrete and steel loomed two stories high. Vacant openings stared where once windows offered protected views of the outside. Here and there a tree thrust its trunk through the structure to spread branches above. Aerial roots hung from the overhead canopy and snaked into openings and across the interior.

His mind made an adjustment, and he realized he was looking at the ruins of the research station, more deteriorated than when he had last seen it but still recognizable.

Raw fear crept into his heart. He turned to Juvenal, who had remained at the edge of the clearing. "What is this place?"

Juvenal responded with something incomprehensible, then frowned and waved his arm in a motion indicating he didn't want to stop.

Truman ignored the gesture. He stepped to the ruin and climbed a concrete abutment that gave him access to the roof of what he remembered to be the vestibule. From there, he grabbed a vine and pulled himself hand-over-hand, to the roof of the second floor where he had an unobstructed view of the surrounding region.

To the north, a swollen Lake Turkana engulfed the end of the plateau. To the east, through the jungle, a large river flowed into the lake.

Farther south a snow-capped mountain rose above surrounding clouds. Mount Kenya. He peered west. No sign of Kanapoi. Probably long rotted away and overgrown by the jungle that spread out before him. Dark, puffy clouds ranged all around. If it hadn't rained yet, it soon would.

He knew with a cold certainty he was still in Kenya, standing on the Loriyu Plateau. *But when*? How long for the desert to be replaced by jungle, the lake swelled to it new shoreline, the research station overgrown? A thousand years? Had the climate changed that quickly?

Dismayed, he sat on the abutment and eased himself down. Streaks of red dappled the old concrete where his feet touched. He was bleeding.

"Shoes," Truman said angrily, letting his disorientation boil into frustration at not having his boots. He halted his descent to twist one of his feet up so he could examine its sole.

"Shooz." Juvenal leaned forward, hands on knees and peered at Truman's feet.

Truman held a vague hope Juvenal might carry him but the hulk turned around and crossed the clearing. After locating a path through the brush, he followed it to the edge of the plateau where another path continued on to the bottom of the escarpment. Without waiting, he plunged down the steep trail with abandon.

Truman followed, limping and holding onto bushes at the edge of the path to slow his descent. He passed into deepening shadow.

It started to rain.

Juvenal waited for him at the bottom. They were back to the cave where he had first seen Juvenal.

Stepping into the cave, Truman had the impression he was descending into the underworld. The cave roof sloped downward, forcing him to crouch lower and lower as he followed Juvenal into its depths.

Juvenal stopped, got down on all fours and scrabbled his hands across the darkened floor until he located fire-making materials. A moment later he had a flame flickering from the animal fat lamp.

The back of the cave held a small opening, which led to a chamber beyond.

Pushing the lamp ahead of him, Juvenal crawled through the opening. He paused on the other side and peered back at Truman, motioning for him to follow.

Truman emerged into a chamber five meters square and stood. With his hand extended, he touched the roof. The near walls of the chamber were contoured and covered with paintings. Men with spears chased images of bison. Herds of horses thundered across flat plains.

Juvenal grabbed Truman by the arm and led him to the back of the chamber. An altar-like rock, which had sheared from the wall, lay flat on the floor. On the rock, small, earthen containers sat in a neat row. Each contained a different color of pigmented dirt. A large gourd, filled with water, lay to one side.

Juvenal pulled Truman up to the wall and raised the lamp.

At first Truman saw nothing. Then closer examination showed the wall was covered with more painted figures--horned four-footed animals that could have been deer with large racks, and larger massive animals resembling elephants, white tusks curving outward.

Juvenal pointed to one side of the wall, an area where he had been working, judging from the location of the paints.

Truman stepped close. A crowd of figures, men and women, milled around a curved, dark object, not unlike the UFO he had seen from the helicopter. "What's happening here?"

Speaking what was gibberish to Truman, Juvenal tapped his chest and pointed to the figures,.

Truman nodded, hearing one word repeated more often than others. "Maraia?" Truman waved his finger back and forth across the assembled figures.

Juvenal's mouth widened to a big smile. "Maraia."

Truman glanced along the wall and noticed another group of figures painted at the opposite end. He leaned forward to examine them more closely. A female figure stood facing outward, raised arms touching the rays from an image of the sun.

To her right, facing her, the figure of a massive, dark man clutched the throat of another man.

Truman tapped the female figure. "Who's this?"

"Ah...zih...zah," Juvenal said, pronouncing each syllable.

Azizah. The name hammered Truman's consciousness, causing a momentary disorientation, a dizziness. *The woman who shot me. Depicted here? Here when?*

Truman strained to regain his composure. "And this?" He pointed to the ominous-looking dark man.

"Cath... car."

Truman shuddered, remembering the brute who had choked him and the name the Maraia women had called him. Could there be a relationship between Azizah and the evil-looking Cathcar?

Above the three figures was painted a male figure, very human in form. The image of the sun shone over his shoulder. He wore what appeared to be a hooded cape.

"And who's this?"

"Sed... roth."

The name meant nothing to Truman. He was about to look away when he noticed Sedroth held a small sphere in his outstretched hand. Truman studied the image of the woman again. Where he had thought she was reaching for the sun, it now seemed like she was reaching for the sphere Sedroth offered. Was that sphere the guardian? Painted here in a cave? A wave of nausea swept over him. The cave seemed to spin around him. Truman was back at his first *sesshin* with the *godo* demanding to know who he was. The only thing missing was the crack of the *kyosaku*. Truman's legs buckled.

Juvenal grabbed his arm and steadied him.

The fat in the lamp sputtered.

Juvenal led Truman back through the small opening into the main cave, placed the lamp on a sheltered flat rock and headed for the exit.

Outside, the jungle was quiet and dark. The rain had stopped. They retraced their steps to the top of the plateau where Truman rested. Scattered clouds revealed patches of stars and familiar constellations.

Despite being so close to the equator, he located the North Star at the end of the Little Dipper and very low to the horizon, then he found what he thought should be the Big Dipper. But the ladle tipped out, and the handle was much shorter, more bent. Could the stars have changed their relative positions? Only thousands of years would have produced such a shift. The ruins still existed. That put an upper limit, though a large one, on how far into the future he was. Concrete took something like fifty thousand years to degrade completely.

He smiled in the dark and shook his head. Sometimes events got so crazy all he could do was stand back and marvel at them. If he'd been an astronomer he could have determined his time more precisely. As it was, he could only guess, maybe six, seven thousand A.D., given the relatively good condition of the concrete in the research station. Not that it mattered. He definitely seemed to be in the future. Worse yet, he didn't have the vaguest idea of how he was going to get back.

Chapter Five

Something big crumpled the jungle beneath elephant-sized feet. Teeth flashed. Thump, plod, it rushed closer, a subway train crashing along a track, Brooklyn to West 85th, the express line. Its hot breath puffed in a ha-aha-aha cadence. Then it leapt.

Bulldozer pressure across Truman's back, a sluicing avalanche, gargantuan paws pinning him to the ground, zing, zing, a quick slicing of razor-sharp teeth, stripping flesh.

Truman slammed awake, perspiration streaming from his chest. He shook his head, trying to clear it, then rubbed fists against his eyes. *God, what an awful nightmare.*

The walls of the blocky room that had become home pressed close offering little comfort. In the back room, Juvenal slept, the sound of his breathing deep and regular. By the look of the light outside the narrow entrance, it must be early morning.

Truman eased himself through the keyhole opening and onto the terrace. Overhead, water slewed off the edge of the cave's towering overhang, caught in the wind and feathered twenty meters to the rocks below, producing a constant background splatter. Beyond this liquid veil, stretched the top of the jungle, a lumpy, green carpet softened by yellow accents in the dawn's streaming light.

He stepped toward the edge of the terrace thinking he would relieve himself where he had seen others do the same.

Pain shot up his legs, forcing him to his knees. *Damn, my feet.* They weren't going to take him anywhere unless he found a way to protect them.

He crawled to the terrace edge, knelt and relieved himself into the dark shadows below.

Maybe sandals. Leather.

The women worked tanned skins with sharp stones, scraping the hides, shaping them. Most of the material seemed destined for the rudimentary clothes they wore, the rest they cut into strips they used for tying things like rocks to sticks, or sticks to sticks, or hanging things like meat or gourds from sticks.

Find a knife.

He eased himself to a tentative standing position. The terrace on which he stood was smooth but small rocks lay scattered on its surface. Frustrated at the amount of concentration it took to avoid the pebbles, he limped to a vacated area strewn with skins and a cutting tool. It turned out to be a piece of black obsidian, chipped along one side in a series of practiced concave curves to produce a serrated edge of razor sharpness.

He grabbed the cutter and retreated to his enclosure. There, he picked up the stiff hide that had been his blanket for the past two days. Placing his foot on it, he scribed an outline, then sat and drew the stone blade around the pattern until a sole for his foot emerged.

Juvenal awoke and drew back the skin curtain between the two rooms. He glanced at Truman, then exited the enclosure without a word.

Truman changed feet and continued tracing. He produced another sole, then used the end of the stone to work a hole into the tough leather. After cutting holes in four places on each sole he laced a thin strip of leather through them and managed to tie the soles to his feet.

Bending over, he exited the enclosure and tested the feel of his new sandals. Though his feet still hurt, he was confident he would be able to walk while they healed.

Juvenal returned with his hands full. He laid two gourds with mashed fruit and a third with water on the terrace. He squatted nearby, took a handful of the mash and indicated Truman should do likewise.

Juvenal chewed the mash and pointed to Truman's sandals. "Shooz."

"Yes, shoes. They protect my feet."

After a rapid fire string of gibberish, Juvenal stuck out his foot, showing Truman the bottom.

Truman rubbed the tough skin with his thumb. "I know, you don't need shoes. Your feet are tough."

"Tuff." Juvenal grinned. He said something else Truman couldn't understand, then pointed toward the jungle and hefted his ever present spear in a manner indicating they might be going somewhere.

"Are we going hunting?"

"Hun...ting."

Juvenal was a fast learner or a good mimic.

After breakfast, they retraced their steps through the entrance slit and continued on the level path. Instead of heading to the top of the escarpment, Juvenal descended to the jungle below on the western side of the plateau.

What appeared as impenetrable growth seen from the cave was riddled with paths. Some probably had been formed by large animals pushing their way through. Others appeared cut. From what he had seen of the Maraia, they possessed the rudimentary tools, not to mention the brawn to slash through the dense tangle.

Juvenal had gone a short way when he held up his hand.

Truman stopped.

In a low crouch, Juvenal eased forward, raised his lance and shoved it into the bush.

With a squeal, a dark-haired pig staggered out of the bush, lance in its side. After removing his lance, Juvenal grabbed the pig by the hind legs and swung the still squealing animal in a circle to smash its head on a nearby rock. The pig went limp.

"Hun...ting," Juvenal said over his shoulder to Truman's horror.

He understood animals had to be killed in order to eat them. He just hadn't seen it done before, at least not this way.

A branch cracked up ahead, distracting Juvenal. He came alert, his lance held low with both hands at the ready, then he lowered it.

"Azizah." He raised his hand in a greeting.

"Juvenal." A woman's voice cut through the jungle.

93

She stepped into view. Truman recognized her, although her dress differed from the last time he'd seen her. Like the Maraia women, Azizah's wrap hung from a shoulder, across her chest, then dropped to her thighs. The shock of someone familiar in this strange place flashed through his mind. Desperate for contact with anyone from his past, he stumbled toward her.

She took one crazed look at him and ran.

"Wait, god damn it!" Panic drove him forward. When she refused to stop, he dove and clutched her ankles.

She fell, twisting, and came down on her back.

His breath heaving, he straddled her with his knees and pinned her arms above her head.

She lunged, freed an arm and brought it hard across his face knocking him to one side.

"You're stronger than you look," he muttered, ducking a second blow.

When she started to scramble away again, he lunged after her.

She kicked, catching him in the groin, all the while not uttering a sound.

Pain radiated from between Truman's thighs. It tucked under his diaphragm. His patience evaporated. He heaved himself on top of her, ignored her double fisted blows, and brought the four knuckles of his closed fist flat on her nose, one quick hard punch.

Startled, she stopped struggling. Blood gushed from her nostrils.

Truman leaned back, having regained his position astride her. "You didn't have to make it so difficult." Had he broken her nose?

94

Her blue-green eyes glared at him from a blood-smeared face.

She was beautiful despite her injury. The covering she wore had come loose, and she pulled it up and over her taut breasts with a lean and well-muscled arm. She gasped for breath, her chest heaving.

Thank God, she looks human.

"I see you are better." Sarcasm laced her voice.

"So it *was* you."

"Get off me."

Sensing she wouldn't try to run, he stood and offered her a hand up, which she ignored.

She pushed off a knee to her feet and leaned her head back, pinching her nose until the bleeding stopped. "You didn't have to hit me."

"Aside from me tackling you, you're the one who initiated the hitting."

She glared at him.

"What are you doing here?" he demanded.

After reattaching her wrap, she grabbed a large leaf and scrubbed blood from her hands. "I was going to ask you the same thing."

"You shot me," Truman said. "We struggled and fell into the tunnel. I felt your neck crush beneath my weight. You should be dead."

She leveled her head and stared at him. "You have a good memory."

"Then it's true."

"Of course it's true."

"Who fixed your throat?"

Her hand went to her neck and rubbed. "I'm a player, remember?"

"But I'm healed, too. I've got a scar where you shot me." Truman pawed at the puckered skin on his left thigh. "Does that make me a player?"

"Are you?"

"Come on, lady. I don't even know what a player is."

"If you are not a player, then who are you?" She stood with her hands on her hips, smiling. She seemed to be enjoying the exchange.

"You know damn well who I am. I'm Truman Justis, a geneticist. I work for the National Reconnaissance Office. I was sent to investigate the appearance of an unidentified flying object that landed in the desert. Kanapoi, Kenya, 2005."

"A U...F...O?" She stared at him as though he were stupid.

"Yeah, UFO. It landed in Kanapoi. Probably looking for the guardian." Hell, if she was going to be so evasive, he figured he'd go fishing for answers.

But she didn't react to his mention of the guardian. Calmly, she reexamined the gunshot on his thigh. "It looks like an old wound."

It did look like an old wound. But how old? Truman thought of Jomo and Hopkins, dead but not dead. Could Azizah have died and been resurrected here? He was unsure of himself. "You *are* the Azizah I met before, aren't you?"

"How nice of you to remember my name."

A small confirmation.

"After the fall, I woke up here, in the rain. Juvenal brought me to his cave."

"Juvenal is a nice man."

He grabbed her by the shoulders. "Cut the crap. You've got to tell me what I'm doing here."

She knocked his arms away. "I don't have to tell you anything. Why would you think I have something to do with your presence?"

"You're here but you don't seem at all bothered. I'm here and going out of my mind trying to figure out how and why. It seems to me you know something about what is going on."

"After what you did to me, I owe you nothing."

"Jesus Christ." He stared at her. "You shot me!"

She fidgeted under his steady gaze. "I'm sorry I shot you."

Truman laughed. "That's it?"

"What do you want?" Color flared into her cheeks. The first sign of emotion he had seen.

"I want to go home!" His voice came out hoarse such was his desperation.

"You've come to the wrong person. I don't have a first-class ticket to get you back to 2005."

Truman squeezed his head between the palms of his hands. He repeated what he knew, as if repeating it would yield more information. "I was in Kenya, in the tunnel with you. We fell. I blacked out. When I woke up, I was here."

She smiled, he thought sympathetically. "You're still in Kenya."

"Yeah, I know. Lots of things are familiar. But it's a different time."

"You've been observant."

"I saw the stars last night. The Dipper is skewed, not a lot but enough to notice." To keep from losing it, he dropped to one knee and poked out the six stars of the Big Dipper. "Alkaid on the handle and Dubhe on the cup have shifted." He indicated the new locations of the two stars.

"You are very perceptive. From these positions--" She pointed to the displaced stars. "--we are five thousand years into the future, 7005 A.D. to be precise. You wouldn't have been able to tell with only a short viewing but the axis of the Earth has precessed and no longer points to Polaris. It is closer to Alderamin in the constellation Cepheus." She regarded him with a steady, neutral gaze.

Truman blinked, feeling mesmerized by the deep color of her eyes as his brain struggled to adjust to the assault of the information she had given him.

He shook his head. "It can't be."

Azizah shrugged. "But it is."

"This...this weather must be the result of some greenhouse effect."

"That would make it understandable but greenhouse gas emissions dropped once humans began to degrade."

"So I was right."

"About the greenhouse effect? I thought I was clear that did not cause the weather to change."

"No, damn it. The degradation. I discovered humans were degrading. In 2005. And they did."

"You were very clever."

"So what do the Ma...Maraia call this place?"

"You know their name?"

"Juvenal showed me his paintings."

"He's very proud of his paintings." She surveyed the enclosing jungle. "Juvenal says they

98

have no name for this place as yet. They haven't been here very long."

Juvenal interrupted with a fast string of syllables.

"What's he saying?"

Azizah graced Truman with a half-smile, a twinkle in her eye. "He says he's tired of standing here. He wants to take the pig back to the cave, then show me his paintings. Do you want to come or are you going to stand here shoving your finger in the dirt?"

Truman refused to take the bait. He waved her away. "I've seen his paintings. How is it you understand him?"

"I just do."

"God damn, you're frustrating. Did you have to learn it or not?"

"When I arrived here, I was equipped with a number of languages and dialects, including his."

"When you arrived?" Truman's patience, if he ever had any to begin with, was depleted. "Do you think you could spare me the information as to how long you've been here?"

"I arrived four days ago. You arrived two days ago. Juvenal has indicated he and his people arrived six days ago."

"Six days! All of them? They act like they've lived here for centuries."

"Six days. All forty of them."

"Where'd they come from?"

A loud thunderclap announced the start of the day's rain. The sky opened up, and a torrent cascaded down on them.

Azizah flinched at the lightning and thunder.

"Where'd they come from!" Truman shouted over the roar of the torrent.

"Juvenal's paintings can wait!" She shielded her eyes and said something to Juvenal, then turned back to Truman. "Juvenal says I may stay and share his pig with him and his people."

They started moving off toward the cave. "Where would you go otherwise?" Truman leaned into her, frustrated by the interruption.

"Nowhere." She stopped and turned to him. "I'm a stranger here, too, Truman Justis. I have no one. Sort of like you."

***

At the cave, the women took the pig from Juvenal butchered it and began roasting it over an open fire.

Truman sat on a distant terrace that overlooked the activity. He didn't feel like participating, not that he would have known how to do so, anyway. Azizah's remark about being a stranger weighed on his mind. If she were a stranger, why did the Maraia treat her as one of their own? Though she differed from them physically, she mingled with them as an equal, one treated with respect.

She glanced up to where he sat. A moment later she broke away from the other women and climbed to his terrace. She sat beside him, legs dangling over the edge.

She seemed more feminine in the flickering light from the distant fire. It gleamed off her bronze shoulders and exposed breasts. Her dark hair fell, straight and unruly, still damp from the rain.

A lock fell across her face, and she pushed it back. "You look disturbed."

100

"Is that surprising? Everyone in this place seems to have only just arrived. Yet every one I've met so far doesn't have the slightest anxiety about being here. I'm the only one doing the wondering." Truman waved an arm out to encompass the cave and the jungle beyond. "Is this all a dream? What I experience seems real. There are thoughts that correlate with what is happening to me, so the connections seem real. There aren't any of those repetitive sequences that might tip me off it's all a dream. So most of the time, so far, I've been thinking that I must be going mad. Does that explain why I look disturbed?"

She folded her hands in her lap and stared down at them. "I know it's difficult for you." Her voice was low, almost sympathetic.

Truman sighed painfully. "That's the thing. I know, you know. Yet you won't give me any answers."

She frowned, a denial. "I think I've been forthright."

"Really? How did we all get here?"

"We? I know how I got here. I'm a player. If you don't know how you got here, then I'm afraid I can't help you?"

"Okay, let's start with how you got here."

She brushed at the flat rock on which she sat. "I see no reason to tell you. I know very little about you aside from a name and a profession and a short tragic encounter in Kanapoi."

Truman hunched forward, exasperated. "But there isn't any more."

She shook her head.

"What's that mean?"

She smiled and shook her head again. "There must be more."

"Well, sure there's more. But is it relevant?" Truman held up a hand and started ticking off points on his fingers. "Let's see. I'm thirty-five years old. I was born in Kenya. My father died when I was very young. I immigrated to the States. Does this track? I've also worked on the human genome project."

"So there *is* more?"

"Yeah lots but what parts?"

"I'd like to hear about the genome project."

She could certainly spot his area of greatest interest. Maybe talking about it would help to clear his mind and provide some rationality to the situation. "After the main sequencing was finished, I was assigned a section of the code to examine. I discovered my section was degrading. If left unattended, isolated chromosomes begin to disintegrate almost as if some external unifying force had been removed."

"That sounds ominous. I've never known a genome to degrade as you describe."

"It's not ominous. It's true. Others corroborated my findings. I was pursuing a solution, when I got the call to investigate the UFO at Kanapoi."

"Did it ever occur to you there was a coincidence between your scientific pursuits and Kanapoi?"

"Sure. I did an internet search and got a zillion hits, too many to track down. But Kanapoi was mentioned often."

"You didn't come across *Gilomir*?"

Truman did a double take. *Gilomir*. The Lohner diary. "You mean Humanus?"

102

"If you wish. They're one and the same. Different languages."

"Lohner had some pretty extreme ideas about why humans are human."

"Don't you wonder why?"

"Of course I wonder. Anyone who delves into the make-up of the human genome has to marvel at its complexity and wonder how it could evolve the way it has."

"Maybe it didn't evolve."

"Now you're getting into slippery territory."

"Slippery?"

"It's an expression. It was a strong scientific insight to have come to the conclusion humans evolved from lesser beings. But there are those, and I have to lump Lohner in with them despite him being a paleoanthropologist, who would have us believe humans were created after being injected with a quantum jolt of DNA. Lohner thought the Earth-mother, *Afareni*, from an African myth did the injecting. As a scientist, I can't take that seriously."

"Wouldn't that be easier to understand?"

"But how do you prove it?"

Azizah smiled. "Some things don't need proving, they just are."

"A lot of things just are. But scientists still try to figure out why." *Why is she taking the conversation in this direction*? So much for layering the situation with rationality.

Juvenal called from the fire, indicating the pig was cooked.

Azizah prodded Truman with a finger. "Don't look so gloomy. Come on, you must be hungry."

Truman sucked in a deep breath. "I suppose I should eat to keep up my strength."

"Look, Truman. I know you think we both carry a lot of baggage about each other but that is not the case."

"It seems like it to me. You shot me. I killed you in the fall. To me that's not carry-on."

She shrugged, presumably not appreciating his attempt at humor. "Are you hungry or not?"

He gazed at her bewildered. Here he was desperate, pouring out his heart and soul, and all she could think about was eating?

They rose and joined the others. Though Truman ate, he experienced no joy in doing so. His predicament overwhelmed all other thoughts and made him miserable. After a while he stood, grabbed a skin from his sleeping area and sought out a darkened terrace at the back of the cave.

He spread out the skin and sat, legs crossed in the lotus position, back of his hands on his knees, palms up. He let his breathing slow and dropped his mind through his body to a lower center of gravity. The sounds of the feasting, the cascade of the rain off the plateau receded. Tranquility embraced him. He remained there, suspended, letting time spread out around him and pass him by. Slowly, some relief began to dissolve his tension.

A light footfall intruded, signaling someone's presence. It was time to come back, anyway. He took a deep breath, then another, and opened his eyes.

Azizah stood before him. "I am bothering you, perhaps for the second time tonight?"

"No, I was finished."

She sat down opposite him, leaned forward and idly picked up a couple of pebbles. "What were you doing?"

"I was meditating."

She reached over and brushed a bug from his shoulder. "I know nothing of this...meditating. What is it like?"

"I find it relaxes me when I do it right."

"How do you feel after you have meditated?"

"Before meditating, I feel stress, like all the wrong connections have been made. After meditating, only the memory of those stresses remains. Although, they are always there, like the bitter peel of a fruit. I have gotten through the peel to the fruit within, the good part, to the right connections."

"That sounds like a very beautiful experience."

"It can be. But it's a small step in the direction of a much greater understanding."

"Understanding of what?"

Was she toying with him or did she really want to know about the beauty he experienced? "If I had achieved it, I would try to tell you. But so far, it remains beyond my grasp. In many ways it is a very lonely quest. Have you never had a similar experience, a moment of supreme introspection?"

"No. I can't say I have." She waved her arm to indicate Juvenal and his people. "I am different from you and these others. Juvenal and his people are kind but they have only just begun the path of life, the path to understanding. From what you say of your meditation, I sense you are farther along. I on the other hand, have traveled farther than you will ever know or can imagine." She sighed. A tear

105

formed at the corner of her eye and coursed down her cheek.

Truman leaned forward, cupped her face in his hand, and used his thumb to brush away the tear. "Why so sad?"

She lowered her eyes, distracted, studying the pebbles she still held. "My quest is lonely, too."

Odd how her moods change. Perhaps being here was as difficult for her as it was for him. "When I was in the cave with Juvenal yesterday, he showed me a painting of you opposite this guy, Cathcar."

"So, you know about Cathcar."

"He practically strangled me while I was sick. He's a scary character."

"He is...scary. You remember Hopkins."

"How could I forget."

"Cathcar is a player. Cathcar was Hopkins, ruthless."

"He...recycled?"

"Yes."

Truman felt a white flash of fear. "What is this, some kind of secret organization?"

"You could call it that."

Truman stared at her and blinked. "But from where? Who do you represent? Who is backing you?"

She seemed pained. She turned to gaze at the darkened jungle outside the cave and threw the pebbles over the edge of the terrace. They clattered lower down and were still. "Do not ask these questions, now."

The rain had stopped and the clouds parted, letting moonlight flood the top of the jungle below, turning it into a gray seascape. Her eyes reflected the light, twin jewels, sparkling, yet sad, concerned.

Truman refused to be put off so easily. "What's wrong with now?"

"Some of the answers I do not know. Some that I could give you would only confuse you."

"I can't be more confused than I already am. Juvenal painted another figure on the cave wall. A man, very human. Sedroth. Do you know who he is?"

"Yes." She seemed uneasy. "He is…a mystic. Juvenal says Sedroth taught him how to paint."

Truman remembered the sphere Sedroth had been holding. "The Sedroth Juvenal painted seemed to be holding the guardian."

"That must be a new painting I haven't seen, yet."

Truman's frustration renewed. She hadn't reacted to his mention of the guardian earlier in the day and didn't now, either. "But if this Sedroth is holding the guardian, then it must be here. Juvenal shows you reaching for it."

"Is that so surprising? You know I seek the guardian."

"You didn't seem very interested in the guardian when I mentioned it this afternoon."

She laid her hand on his arm. "What was I to do? We were in the middle of the jungle, you had just punched me in the nose, and you drop a hint you know something about the guardian?"

"So how come Juvenal knows you seek the guardian?"

She looked out over the rest of the cave. "It's getting late. The others have all gone to sleep."

"Tell you what, I'll help you get the guardian if you help me to get back to where I belong."

"That's a clever offer but you overestimate me. I have no way to get you back to where you belong. I don't even know how you got here."

"Then maybe this Sed--"

She reached out and placed a finger on his lips. "So many questions."

Truman pulled down her hand. "But you can't blame me for asking questions. I feel...I feel so insecure. I go over past memories only to find a certain resistance, or emptiness. It's like portions have been wiped clean. Like the Gulf War. I know I participated in it, but if you asked me details about what I did, I wouldn't be able to tell you. Once I get past that, I remember all the way back to growing up in Harlem."

"You see, there is reason for me to be circumspect for now about you and your existence here. You can't even remember yourself." She leaned against him. Her breast brushed his arm. "May I lie here with you tonight?"

Before he could answer, she pressed him down onto the skin and cuddled beside him. One hand rested on his chest. Her head lay next to his.

"Sometimes it gets chilly at night," she said before closing her eyes and falling asleep.

***

When Truman awoke the next morning, his first thought was of being happy. He realized it was Azizah who made him feel that way. Though she resembled the aggressive Azizah of Kanapoi, he sensed somehow she was a different person.

He felt for her at his side but she was already up. He searched and found her mingling with Juvenal and the others.

Truman stretched, then went barefoot, thinking to toughen his feet, to join them. Bad idea. He winced as the rough ground bit into the soles of his feet.

Azizah turned at his approach and seemed to notice his discomfort but said nothing about it. "You slept soundly."

"It's the first night I didn't have a nightmare about this place. I think having you with me made the difference."

Azizah favored him with her blue-green eyes.

A man would kill, he thought, to have her look at him like that and often.

"The men are about to hunt for food," Azizah said. "Do you want to join them?"

Truman surveyed the confident, muscular men walking about, picking up spears and stone adzes. "No, I don't think so. I'd only be in the way."

"Then come with me to the painting cave. Juvenal will join us there later."

"He's not hunting with the others?"

Juvenal knelt off to one side, packing a skin with some of the pork from the night before, fruit and a gourd of water.

Azizah shook her head. "He takes food to Sedroth."

"Ah, Sedroth. Where, may I ask, does he live?"

"It's no secret. He lives in the ruins at the top of the plateau. He's very reclusive."

"He must be," Truman said, surprised. "We were there yesterday. I didn't see anyone. Juvenal didn't even mention him, or call out to him."

"Sedroth wishes to remain apart."

"I suppose he showed up here a month ago as well."

Azizah laughed. "No, Juvenal says Sedroth was already here when he and the others arrived. Sedroth has never said when he arrived here, or whether he's been here all the time."

"But from the looks of the painting, he's human, like you and me."

She shrugged. "Like I said, I've never met him."

"I think now would be a great time for you to meet him. I'm dying to meet him, too."

Juvenal approached. He and Azizah engaged in a quick conversation.

She translated for Truman. "Juvenal says you cannot see Sedroth. Sedroth does not want to be seen."

"Screw that. As far as I know, Juvenal is not the one stuck in a millennium he doesn't belong to. I'm going to find Sedroth."

Juvenal said something rapidly, angrily, then followed the other men out the entrance slit.

"He's leaving now," Azizah translated. "You'll not find Sedroth. Juvenal will warn him."

"We'll see about that." Truman padded back to the sleeping area for his sandals. He sat and laced them on. *I'll have to hurry if I'm to catch up with Juvenal.*

Though his feet were still tender, the skin was healing well at the places where it had been abraded. He had finished lacing the second sandal, when a commotion below distracted him.

Cathcar stepped into the cave. He hefted a thick branch half the length of his body, its limbs broken off.

The Maraia women cowered away from the brute, who stomped to the center of the cave.

Azizah stood her ground. She and Cathcar spoke to each other with Azizah gesturing.

Cathcar shouted something.

Azizah flinched.

He stepped back, and in a lightning motion brought the club up from his side across the side of her head.

The blow tossed her to one side, where she crumpled, blood seeping from a gash above her hairline.

Truman jumped to his feet, stunned by the ferocity of the attack.

Cathcar raised his club across his body to deliver a *coup de grace*.

Truman screamed.

Cathcar stared at Truman. He lost interest in Azizah and stalked forward in a half-crouch, hefting the club, hatred glowing in his eyes.

With painful strides Truman limped to the edge of the terrace, closing the distance, and launched himself at the startled brute. He landed awkwardly, with Cathcar's massive head pressed into his stomach, his arms gripping desperately Cathcar's shoulders.

Cathcar grabbed him by the back of the neck and threw him to the ground as if he were a kitten.

Before Truman could recover his footing, the club flashed and thudded against his temple. Darkness descended accompanied by a shower of zooming sparks behind his eyes.

Chapter Six

The windows of the subway flashed, the wheels of the cars clacked on the rails, thirty meters per rail, clack, thirty meters, clack.

Truman opened his eyes. Gray terraces swam in an out of vision. Far, then close, clack. Far, then close. His head and shoulders bounced. Terrace to terrace. *Let me off. Stop the train.*

The bumps stopped and transitioned into a smooth lope. He was draped over Cathcar's shoulder, a sack hung backward over a raging bull.

The beast padded to the entrance slit, turned his shoulders and scraped through without a care for his human baggage.

Truman groaned as his head hit first one side of the entrance then the other--a bell rung twice.

Outside, Cathcar traversed the level path, came to where it forked to the jungle below or the plateau above. He chose the path to the plateau and ascended the escarpment like a mountain goat, his thick legs planting solidly, his thighs bulging, springing forward despite the weight he carried. He cleared the top with a leap, crashed through the brush to the other side, then descended in long jolting strides. Each lunge was accompanied by an expel of breath, a bassoon of wind through blocky teeth.

He covered the last two meters to the bottom of the escarpment in a single plunge, then headed east, away from the cliff face and into the jungle.

All Truman could see was back from where he had come. He hoped Juvenal and the others would be in close pursuit. But they were nowhere to be seen.

Truman's head swelled from the blow, its downward position and the constant jogging up and down. The pressure sought out his eyes, which bulged in their sockets. He tried to scream. All that came from his throat was a dry, reedy sound followed by a wet retching. The remains of his breakfast coursed from his mouth and splashed off Cathcar's hips, hit his Herculean thighs and slipped to the ground.

The close jungle receded, and they entered a clearing. Cathcar dumped Truman face down in matted grass next to a tree trunk. He went out of sight for a moment, then returned clutching a handful of leather straps. He dragged Truman by the hair to a standing position. Cathcar's flat hand slammed hard against Truman's chest, pressing him against the tree. Cathcar spun the leather straps like a web, pulling tight, lashing him to the tree.

"Help..." Truman called but the jungle remained silent and dark, his voice more a mewing than a shout. He shook his head in disbelief and spit to rid his mouth of gorge aftertaste.

Cathcar stepped back.

The man-beast was flushed from his run. His body glistened with perspiration. He sucked his breath through an open mouth. A dark rancid smell of death and unseen horror washed over Truman to mix with the stench of his own vomit.

Without warning, Cathcar drove a fist at Truman's chest.

A sharp pain cut through to his heart. He thought it might stop beating.

Cathcar slammed his other fist into Truman's stomach.

His breath exited his lungs with an explosive whoosh. He struggled to breathe and dry-heaved at the same time. His vision clouded. His eyelids no longer seemed large enough to fit over his eyeballs.

"Who you?" Cathcar croaked.

Truman tried but he couldn't speak.

Cathcar brought the back of his hand across Truman's cheek, snapping his head hard to the left. Then another blow snapped it hard to the right.

"Who you?" Cathcar repeated. "How Hopkins dead?"

"Who? I don't--"

Cathcar stamped on Truman's foot. The pain shot up his leg, knifing his groin.

"Where guardian?"

Think. Azizah had the guardian when we climbed the rope. Maybe she dropped it. Could it still be there? Had Sedroth found it? Say anything to stop the beating. "The tunnel," he said with all his effort. He wavered at the edge of consciousness.

"Tunnel?" Cathcar raised his hand.

"Beneath...ruins." Truman ran his dry tongue over swollen lips, tasting blood.

"Tunnel blocked. Where in tunnel?"

Truman knew he must answer quickly, or Cathcar would kill him. "I'm not sure. On the floor. In the middle. Maybe in a...box, a concrete box."

"You player." Cathcar gripped both of Truman's cheeks in a tight pinch and shook his head back and forth.

115

"No, no, no," Truman wheezed, his head wobbling, his speech in cadence. Truman's legs gave way. He sagged in the leather restraints, letting them cut more deeply into his skin. He sobbed. "I don't know...I don't know."

Cathcar left him. The man beast approached a dark rounded shape, twenty meters in diameter, sitting on one side of the clearing. He climbed up on top of the shape and disappeared into it, as though it had opened and swallowed him whole.

***

God help me. I don't even believe in God. Maybe I should? How can this be happening?

Truman wasn't there of his own choice. He had nothing to do with these people. *Give me Zen.* But Zen didn't help. Only pain. And tears from swollen eyes. His tongue fished around his mouth. A loose tooth. *I know nothing.* His shoulders shook as incontrollable sobs wracked his chest.

"Truman."

The voice was a hard whisper, coming from the edge of the clearing. It penetrated his pain, a cold sharp pick. "Azizah?"

"Shhh..." She stepped from the bush, glanced from side to side and hurried to him. "I'm sorry."

Her apology barely registered. "Get me out of here," he blubbered. Tears of relief streamed down his cheeks. He lunged at the restraints.

"Be still. You'll only succeed in hurting yourself." The blood from her head wound had dried to a dark cake that covered the side of her face. She struggled with the knots but they held.

A movement near the object caught his attention. "He's coming back."

116

She whirled, arms raised. Too late.

With a grunt, Cathcar chopped his thick forearm across the back of her neck.

Her head whip-lashed. Her mouth opened in surprise. She dropped like a stone.

He stepped over her, then sat down hard on her chest. One hand thrust forward to grip her throat.

Her eyes fluttered open. Air hissed through her open mouth but she made no effort to resist him.

"I kill you, soon." Cathcar's mouth opened in what could have been a crooked smile, except his lips remained turned down. He stood, still gripping her, and pushed her to the tree, holding her tight. Ignoring Truman's shouts of protest, Cathcar pulled on one of the lashes until it broke, then looped it around Azizah and reattached it.

After satisfying himself they were tight, he disappeared from view. When he returned, he carried a prying stick and an assortment of gourds and stone scrapers. He checked the tethers once more and stepped into the bush in the direction of the sealed tunnel entrance.

"Are you all right?" Azizah swallowed hard, trying to clear her throat. The tethers dug deep into her skin.

Truman didn't answer. He was lost in a painful inventory of the damage done to his body. *Vision failing. Teeth loose. Cracked chest? Lacerated stomach?*

"Truman!" She brought her lips to his ear. "Truman, don't die."

"I'm getting tired of this. Look at me." One eye swelled shut. Blood streamed from his nose. An ugly purplish bruise spread across his chest. He blinked his good eye trying to focus on the dark round object Cathcar had entered and exited. "What's that thing over there?"

She swallowed hard and turned to see past him. "The Shepherd."

Truman shook his head and immediately wished he hadn't. "What's a Shepherd."

"It's the alien craft that was at Kanapoi. The UFO. The one you and Hopkins were sent to investigate."

Truman stared at her with pained surprise mixed with bitterness. "So you do know a lot about Kanapoi."

"Please, Truman."

"What's it doing here?"

"I don't know."

"How come Cathcar can come and go from the Shepherd?"

"I don't know."

Dark shades threatened to draw across Truman's consciousness. "Is that how he and you got here?"

"No."

Truman stared at her, surprised. "An answer." He started to laugh, then coughed and spit blood. "Why tell me now?"

"It doesn't matter. You seem to be dying."

"Don't count on it." He began to feel a bit lightheaded. Probably loss of blood from somewhere or internal bleeding.

"I'm sorry. I didn't mean it that way." She squirmed, trying to loosen their bonds but could not. *We'll never get free.* "Cathcar spoke to me in English."

She stopped her struggling. "He probably remembers something of Kanapoi, from his presence there as Hopkins."

"Yeah, Hopkins. He thinks I had something to do with Hopkins dying."

"Maybe you did?"

"God damn it!" Truman winced. "No maybe. You killed Hopkins."

"It wasn't me. I mean it was but not the me, here."

Truman thought furiously. *What was it players did?* "You recycled."

"Yeah. Players recycle." She stared at him, concerned. "I'm sorry you're involved in all this. Possibly, you shouldn't be. Since you are here, and shouldn't be, he suspects you're a player."

"Player...player," Truman wheezed, then licked his bruised lips. "Always players. I don't know anything about players! Tell him I'm not a player!"

"I could but he wouldn't believe me."

Truman's jaw slacked open in wonderment. "I protest," he said feebly.

"What else did Cathcar want?"

Truman leaned his head back and closed his eye. "The guardian."

Azizah glanced around. "Is that why Cathcar left us?"

"I told him the guardian was in the tunnel."

"I don't think so."

Truman struggled to regain his posture. Was she being factious? "But you had it when you fell. What happened after I blacked out?"

"I don't know."

119

"Stop this I don't know!" Truman gagged and coughed up more blood. He spit and took a moment to settle his breathing. "What happened after I blacked out?" He could see her at the edge of his vision.

She stared ahead. Determined, angry. "I did have it. Then…my presence there was…terminated."

"So you came here?"

"Yes."

He glared at her, then comprehension dawned. "Sedroth has it."

"Please, not now."

"Why would Juvenal paint Sedroth with the guardian?"

"You'll have to ask him. Maybe he was painting what might be."

A noise from the edge of the clearing distracted him.

Juvenal stepped from the bush and hurried over to them. He took a sharpened stone from his belt and cut the leather thongs.

Truman collapsed to his knees. "I don't think I can walk."

Azizah spoke to Juvenal, who gathered Truman in his arms and lifted him.

"Thanks," Truman said, feeling for the first time in many minutes like he might survive this ordeal. "I'm tired of being thrown around like a sack of potatoes."

It started to rain. *Relief.* Truman leaned his head back and opened his mouth, letting the warm water fill it to flooding and wash it out. The rain pounded his battered body in a throbbing massage.

"Get me out of here," Truman said in a hoarse whisper.

A minute later, they came to the escarpment.

"Where are we going?" Truman asked.

"The tunnel. It's got to be over that way." Azizah indicated north along the escarpment.

Truman's fear returned. "I don't want to go to the tunnel. Cathcar's there."

"I want to see what he's up to." She motioned Juvenal to follow as she headed north.

They came to the edge of the jungle growth that overlooked the collapsed entrance to the tunnel. A short distance beyond, the waters of the lake lapped against the shore.

"Jesus, is that Lake Turkana?" Truman whispered. "It used to end three or four kilometers farther north."

"Quiet." Azizah pointed to the hunched figure of Cathcar by the sealed entrance.

He pried rocks loose, picked them up and threw them to one side. He rolled large rocks out of the way. Alternately, he grabbed one of the scrappers and, holding it in both hands, used it as a hoe to claw dirt and silt away from the entrance.

"It's going to take him a long time to get through all that," Azizah said. "Luckily he doesn't know there's another entrance into the tunnel through the research center ruins."

Disabled as he was a plan began to take form in the back of his mind. "Ask Juvenal if he painted Sedroth with the guardian because he knew Sedroth has it."

Azizah gave Truman a stubborn look, then had some quick words with Juvenal. "Juvenal says he's not sure if Sedroth has the guardian. Sedroth has only spoken of it."

"That's great. What if we snuck in there and got the guardian before Cathcar does? We'd be holding all the cards."

Azizah looked stricken. "We're not even sure it is still there."

Azizah's reaction confused Truman. *I thought she lived and breathed for the guardian*. If she didn't want it, he did. "It's worth a try. The passageway is probably still open. We could be in and out with the guardian before Cathcar breaks through."

"I'm not going in there," Azizah said.

"Why not."

"I'm not going near Sedroth."

Truman stared myopically in amazement. "I'm surprised a mystic would frighten you."

"I have my reasons."

The rain increased.

Cathcar straightened and squinted up at the escarpment. Silt and water washed off the top and down, filling his excavation faster than he could remove it. He threw his scraper into the muck in disgust and headed back to his clearing.

"We better get out of here before he discovers we're missing," Azizah whispered.

They hurried back to one of the paths that led up the escarpment. Once on top and feeling safe, they slowed.

"The tunnel comes out on the other side," Truman said as he continued to take an inventory of his battered body. Though he was sore and bruised, he decided Cathcar's blunt blows hadn't broken any bones.

Azizah stopped. "So?"

"From what I saw from the top of the ruin, the west entrance is underwater."

"That's possible. It's lower than the eastern entrance."

"If the lake has inundated the lower half of the western entrance," Truman said, "then it's possible the entrance is clear somewhere, although submerged."

Azizah started walking again, moving ahead of Juvenal and Truman.

"Hold up," Truman called.

"I don't like where you're going with your reasoning," she called back over her shoulder. "You're going to propose we swim down there to find out."

***

The rain stopped sometime during the night, leaving water to trickle over the edge of the cave and dissipate into a fine mist before reaching the bottom. The morning sun shone clear.

Truman nudged Azizah awake. "We have to get going. With good weather, Cathcar will waste no time trying to dig through the eastern entrance."

"I'm not doing this," Azizah said.

"I don't understand. You were willing to kill for the guardian in Kanapoi."

"You have no idea of the power Sedroth holds."

Truman shook his head. "That's why we are going in the western entrance. We don't have to disturb Sedroth." Truman sat up and groaned. "God, I ache all over."

"I thought you'd be more interested in seeing the Shepherd. Something tells me he knows how you got here or is directly responsible."

"The Shepherd can wait. I don't want to risk running into Cathcar again," Truman said. "If the guardian can do what I've read it can do, foresee the future, then we have to get to it before Cathcar does, or at the least make sure it's no longer there." He stared at her. "I thought that would be obvious. I don't understand your reluctance."

"I've tried to tell you and you won't accept any of my reasons."

"All right, be stubborn. I'll go myself." He stood and started to stretch, then doubled over in agony. "God, that hurts. I hope I haven't cracked a rib or something."

"You're not going anywhere." Azizah reached her hands to his chest. "Let me see."

Truman turned so Azizah could examine his side.

She pushed and prodded gently with Truman flinching. "I don't see any swelling. I think your ribs are only bruised."

"How do you feel? I don't see you hurting."

"I heal rather quickly. It's a player thing."

Truman twisted a bit, testing his range of motion. "I can hold together long enough to get in and out of the tunnel. Maybe I'll even get to meet this Sedroth." He picked up one of the animal-fat lamps and fire-making materials and wrapped them in multiple layers of animal skin. "This should stay dry if I'm not underwater too long."

Azizah looked away. "There's Juvenal. You better get some breakfast before you go."

While Truman stuffed some of the fruity gray mash into his mouth and washed it down with water, Azizah engaged Juvenal in an animated conversation.

She came over to him. "Juvenal agrees with me you shouldn't go to the tunnel."

"I'm not surprised. You and he seem to always be on the same page. I'm going anyway."

Azizah put her hands on her hips. "He also said if you insisted on going, I should go with you to see that nothing happens to you."

Truman smiled. "Hey. Tell him thanks. That's a first." Truman picked up the bundle with the lamp in it and struck out for the lake.

Azizah hurried to catch up. "As far as I know, Sedroth stays in the ruins."

"I still think it would be easier to say *hi* to Sedroth and use the passageway to get to the tunnel."

"I am only trying to protect you...and me."

They hiked along the base of the escarpment to the lake. The tunnel entrance was nowhere in sight, the waters being deeper than Truman had expected.

Truman started into the water.

Azizah grabbed his shoulder. "You are being foolishly stubborn. Wait here. I'll do the swimming around to see if there's a way in."

Truman gave an inner sigh of relief. There was no way he was going to be able to swim underwater in his condition. He had hoped she felt somewhat responsible for his safety and he was right. "I knew you'd come around."

She gave him what amounted to half a glare, then waded into the water. When it came to her waist, she dove forward and disappeared.

Truman tried to see where she went but the water was cloudy from silt stirred up by the rain. After five minutes she surfaced, took a deep breath and went under again. She surfaced again and again, as she worked her way along the submerged base of the escarpment.

Finally, she came up and waved to him. "I found it."

Truman waded into the water, holding the bundle above his head. When he could go no farther without losing touch with the bottom, he stopped and waited for her to come to him.

"You're in luck. There's what feels like a way in."

Truman began to have some doubts about his strategy. But it was too late now to back out without looking like a fool. He'd have to join her. Besides he didn't want Azizah to think he was afraid.

She took the bundle from him. "I'll go first. After I get through I'll come back and guide you." She disappeared under the water.

Truman waited in neck high water for ten minutes until she resurfaced.

"It's clear."

"Ten minutes?" Truman asked, worried she would expect him to remain submerged for that length of time.

"No, not even a minute. I found a way through to an inner chamber and lit the lamp. I don't think there is much material beyond blocking access to the tunnel proper." She grabbed his hand. "Ready?"

Truman took a deep breath, and they went under. There was no way he was going to open his eyes in the silty water, better to let her pull him along. He had no idea how she could see.

She swam strongly.

He bounced off some rocks but kept moving forward. When he thought he could hold his breath no longer, she pulled him up. He surfaced into a small chamber.

The lamp burned to one side, its light reflecting off uneven stone walls.

Truman sniffed the air. "Smells like a tomb." The walls surrounding him probably hadn't seen any daylight in thousands of years.

"Don't be so morbid." Azizah heaved herself out of the water and picked up the lamp to shine the light on a wall of dirt and rock facing them. "It doesn't look very stable."

Truman stepped up to the wall. "It's been here this long. It'll hold for the next half hour. Help me dig some of these rocks out of the way."

Azizah set down the lamp and they bent to the task.

After a few minutes a small avalanche of debris fell away to expose an opening into the tunnel beyond.

"See, I was right," Truman said feeling vindicated. He picked up the lamp and shoved it ahead of him as he squirmed through the opening and stood on a loose pile of rocks.

Azizah followed.

The rocks shifted beneath his feet. "Maybe this isn't as safe as I thought."

"We can leave, now?"

"I'll give it fifteen minutes, then go."

The rocks led down to a shallow pool at water level. They splashed through the water and climbed the cambered floor into the main tunnel space. A trickle of water washed from the far end of the tunnel, along an eroded groove in the floor and emptied into the shallow pool at their end.

"That must be rain water leaking through somewhere at the eastern end," Truman said.

Azizah paid the trickle scant attention. "Let's get on with it."

Truman retraced his steps and stood where he thought she had shot him. "After you shot me, you took the guardian and tried to climb the rope. I crawled after you, the rope broke and you fell…over there." He gave the lamp to Azizah and walked to the tunnel wall beneath the opening leading to the research ruins.

"There's the vault." Truman said, surprised. The vault was pushed up against the wall below the opening. "How'd it get over here?"

"I don't know."

Truman thought for a moment she sounded evasive but dismissed it. "We fell somewhere around here." He pointed to a spill of rock and dirt that must have eroded off the walls over the years and partly covered the vault. "If the guardian is buried in this mess, we'll never find it." But he dropped to his knees and began dragging his fingers through the loose dirt hoping to snag the guardian.

A hollow knocking sound of rocks rolling together into the water distracted him.

"I hope that's not what I think it is." Without waiting, Azizah hurried back toward the tunnel entrance. The light she carried bobbed in the dark. Her silhouette climbed the pile of rocks at the entrance. "The rocks have shifted," she called. "The entrance is blocked."

A crash reverberated from the opposite end of the tunnel. A shaft of light shot into the gloom followed by the increased sound of rushing water.

"Cathcar," Azizah whispered.

"Our only chance is through the research ruins," Truman said.

Azizah hesitated.

"We have no choice," Truman urged.

"Okay. You first. I'll lift you to the opening."

Truman took the lamp and climbed onto Azizah's back. She braced herself against the tunnel wall. When he stepped onto her shoulders, she slipped her hands under his feet and pressed him straight up to the opening. He set the lamp down and climbed into the passageway. Once secure, he reached down and grasped her outstretched hand. After she crested the lip of the tunnel, he blew out the lamp.

Cathcar widened the opening and wormed his way through. He stood for a moment, the light from the opening throwing his shadow long onto the tunnel floor. His head swung, scanning the area. He glanced at the opening where they hid but did not see them. Then he spotted the vault below them. He plodded over to it and tried unsuccessfully to open the lid.

Not to be deterred he cleared away the debris and circled both arms around the vault. Then with a grunt he lifted it. He duck-walked back to the open entrance, set the vault on the ground and pushed it through. A moment later, he crawled after it.

"He thinks the guardian is in the vault," Azizah said.

"There'll be hell to pay if it isn't."

"Let's get out of here." Azizah re-lit the lamp and started to ease herself over the edge to the tunnel floor below.

Truman grabbed her shoulder. "You can't go that way. He might be right outside."

She pursed her lips. "I don't want to run into Sedroth," she said.

Truman couldn't reconcile her inexplicable desire to avoid Sedroth. "Maybe Sedroth isn't home," he said, hoping to encourage her.

She stared over his shoulder at the dark passage leading up to the ruins.

Truman grabbed her hand and felt his way up the inclined passageway. He came to the flight of stairs that led to the first floor and waited for Azizah to catch up to him. "Come on. Stop dragging your feet. I can't see without the lamp."

"Here you take it."

He held the lamp out in front of him and climbed the stairs two at a time. At the top landing, he pushed through a thick layer of branches that covered the door opening where it exited into the ruins.

"These look freshly cut. Sedroth?" Truman gazed around the interior of the ruins. Someone lived there. A makeshift bed stood against one wall. A rudimentary table and rock to sit on was near one of the window openings.

"Let's get out of here," Azizah whispered.

"Why can't we wait a bit and see if he comes home?"

"No." She grabbed Truman's hand and dragged him across the space toward the vestibule on the far side.

Halfway there, he stopped dead in his tracks and yanked his hand free. "What the hell's that?" He strode to the bed and picked up a toothbrush.

"How should I know?" Azizah said.

Truman held the toothbrush up to the light. "Ultra-brush Medium," he read. "Sedroth's from my time."

"We've got to get out of here."

"Bullshit. He knows what's going on, and I think you know he knows. Where is he?"

Azizah's shoulders slumped in despair. She raised her hands in resignation. "Look, if you think he's coming back, then wait for him. I'm out of here." She stomped across the floor and after looking back once over her shoulder, disappeared into the vestibule.

Chapter Seven

Truman stood, a bit confused. *What's with not seeing Sedroth*? Obviously, being a player didn't preclude Azizah from exhibiting some very typical human female traits.

He glanced around the room. No place to hide here. Farther along the wall through which the passageway exited, was an overhead opening that must have anchored a stairway to the second floor. He jumped up and caught the edge, then pulled his head level with the floor. It too was clear. Some small rooms off to one side, maybe closets. He thought to climb up and investigate but his body was already telling him he'd undone whatever recovery he had been feeling. He lowered himself back down, replaced the toothbrush on the bed and stepped out of the ruin after Azizah.

Outside, he squinted in the bright sunlight.

She stood a couple of meters away, arms crossed, tapping her foot.

He felt a bit more of a connection. Her behavior gave him something human to relate to. "I guess he's not home. I'm sorry I was so brusque in there." Take the high road.

"I wouldn't have acted any differently if the roles had been reversed."

She can be reasonable. Back to neutral ground. "You've never met Sedroth?" Would she lie to him?

"He's very reclusive. Only Juvenal sees him to bring him food."

"You didn't answer my question."

132

She stared him in the eye. "No, I have never met the man."

Truman realized even if she were lying there was no way he could tell. "Do you think we can we see Cathcar from the edge over there?"

She seemed relieved at the change of subject. "Maybe. Let's find out but keep low."

They crept to the edge of the plateau.

A hollow thud cut the still air.

They flattened to the ground on their stomachs.

Cathcar staggered below them, muscling the vault on the trail heading south. The lid banged free on its top.

"Where the hell is he going?" Truman asked.

"He's probably looking for you. Obviously he didn't find the guardian."

"I'm cooked if he finds me. I'm cooked if he doesn't find me." Truman sat up and brushed dirt from his stomach.

"Cathcar may seem dull witted but he's not. He's a realist. He won't kill you until he has the guardian."

Whose side is she on? "Am I supposed to gain strength from that? I'm destined for annihilation once this son of a bitch gets what he wants? The hell with the guardian. I want to get out of here."

"Of course you do." She patted his shoulder. "But I know of no way out."

The stark reality of his situation came over him in a wave of self-pity. He struggled for composure. "What about the Shepherd?"

"Something doesn't seem quite right," Azizah said, "if Cathcar can come and go from the Shepherd with impunity. If I were you that's the last

133

place I'd want to go. It'd be like going into the lion's den and waiting for the lion to return."

"I don't think he controls the Shepherd."

She stared at him with an exaggerated stare. "Suddenly you know so much?"

"Stop that." He felt angered by her condescension. "There's only one way to find out." Truman got to his feet and headed for the trail leading to the jungle below. He stopped at the edge of the plateau. "You coming?"

"I'm not going to the Shepherd."

Truman gazed at her, a supercilious smile on his face. What was her problem? "Why not? First Sedroth, now the Shepherd. What gives?"

"I...I don't want to."

"That's the best excuse I've heard in a long time." Truman thought she had given up on being evasive. He decided to try accommodation. "Do you have another option?"

"I don't, aside from not doing it. I don't think I'll like doing it."

A subtle shift but she fell in step beside him, all the while looking south to see if Cathcar had decided to turn around.

At the base of the escarpment, Truman led the way through the brush until they came to Cathcar's clearing. The Shepherd sat at its center. A small lean-to, a pile of rough-cut branches piled against a bracing branch, sat off to the left.

Truman indicated the dilapidated shelter. "Cathcar doesn't bother much with amenities."

"No, he wouldn't. I don't even know if he bothers to sleep. From what I've seen of him, he's an automaton, committed to obtaining the guardian."

"Aren't you?"

"Truman...." She gave him a pained look.

"Come on. We're wasting time." He grabbed her hand and pulled.

She came up short. "You go."

"You know I have no choice." He released her hand and circled the Shepherd, then stepped close. He pushed its outer surface. "Feel this," he called over his shoulder.

Reluctantly, she pressed her hand against the surface. "It's like skin," she said with distaste and pulled her hand away.

"I thought the Shepherd was some sort of spaceship."

"It is but it's organic. It's also artificially intelligent and self-replicating."

"How come you know so much about it?"

"It comes with the territory."

Truman shook his head in frustration, put one foot on the Shepherd and tried to climb, only to slip back. "Give me a hand up."

Azizah cupped her hands together into a foothold. He stepped into it, pushed hard and clambered across the smooth surface toward the center. At each step, his feet depressed the taut skin.

At the top center of the Shepherd, he stopped and peered at a tight pucker. "Look at this."

Azizah strained her neck. "I can't see."

He returned and lay down on the surface, hoping there would be enough friction to prevent him sliding off. He offered Azizah his foot. She grabbed hold and pulled herself up.

Truman helped her stand. "What do you make of it?"

She inched forward to peer at the sphincter. "It looks like an entrance of some sort."

"Cathcar climbed up here and disappeared. This...this Shepherd swallowed him whole." Truman knelt and ran his hand over wrinkles radiating out from the center of the tight constriction.

The pucker started to open with a sucking sound, like the final gurgle of water spiraling down a drain.

Truman jumped back, tripped against Azizah, and they both fell. He kicked himself farther away as the pucker continued to open.

It stopped.

Azizah headed for the perimeter.

"Hang on," Truman said. "Take a look at this."

Azizah looked at him incredulously, then to where he pointed at the opening.

He beckoned her closer and leaned forward to get a view of the inside. He stared into a pink, fleshy throat, ribbed, not unlike that of a fish.

Tentatively, she stepped closer to get a better look.

The opening convulsed once and overtook them, dropping them into the interior.

***

Truman struggled but could not gain purchase on the slick walls. He slid to the bottom, a distance twice his height, hit a soft membrane and bounced. Cloying walls rippled--a smooth muscle twitching, a clearing of the throat that closed around him, pressing Azizah against him in an intimate embrace. The opening above him dialed shut. He felt a moment of claustrophobic panic in the dark, then the lights came on.

We're dead. "How are we going to get out of here?"

"That's an odd question," Azizah said. "You're the one who wanted to come here in the first place."

"Thanks." Truman suppressed a sense of fear by trying to concentrate on the details of their predicament. He pulled his head back as far as he could from the wall of flesh and focused on its composition. Though it looked like freshly butchered meat, it was not sticky or wet. Rather the surface was smooth to the touch. Small veins, presumably carrying nutrients, formed a dense web. "How is it we can breathe?"

Azizah expelled her held breath. "I don't know. I guess we can. I think we're in some kind of womb."

She wriggled along the length of his body.

The feeling was pleasant despite his wounds. "No use struggling," he said.

She leaned her head forward. Her face was millimeters from his.

He brushed his lips against hers.

She pulled back, startled. "Why did you do--"

"The woman is of purer stock than the Neanderthal Cathcar." The Shepherd spoke in a deep, resonating male voice. "Homo sapiens. An interesting choice."

Truman breathed a sigh of relief, giving thanks to this mass of pink tissue for distracting Azizah from her question.

She craned her neck to see where the voice had come from. "You're very astute. How is it a

137

Neanderthal like Cathcar has such a way with something so technologically advanced as you?"

If she hoped to involve the Shepherd in a conversation, her effort failed.

Truman felt instead a firm prodding at his body, then the slightest needle prick in his side. He imagined a medical doctor holding up a patient's chart, examining its stats, then prescribing an injection.

"What's happening?" His voice held an edge of fear.

"You are hurt," the Shepherd said. "I have repaired the damage."

"Amazing," Truman whispered to Azizah. "I no longer feel the effect of Cathcar's beating."

"Why does the Shepherd take such an interest in you?"

"I don't know. I'm happy that he does. I want to confirm that he's the same craft I was sent to investigate at Kanapoi?"

"You didn't believe me when I told you he was?" Azizah's voice was laced with tension.

"Just collecting data, and cross checking. It's a research thing." Truman didn't know where he was supposed to look if he was to address the Shepherd and chose to stare straight ahead. "Are you the UFO I was--"

"Yes."

"I guess he was listening." Truman felt contrite, but at least they were getting somewhere with questions and answers. "Are you the craft that was tracked leaving Kanapoi in 1985?"

A long pause.

"There were two craft that left Kanapoi in 1985. Please refine your question."

"Were you one of those craft?"

"I was."

"Which one?"

"The second one."

"Then what was the first one? Could it have been you?"

"I do not know."

"You don't know what? I asked two questions."

"I do not know the answer to either of your questions except to say it might have been me, somewhere up my world line that I have not traversed yet."

If the Shepherd was in Kanapoi in 1985 and 2005 and now he is here, then the Shepherd traveled with impunity through space and time. I might find out why I am here and have my ride home. Cut to the chase.

"Why did you bring me here, anyway?"

"I did not bring you here."

Truman almost screamed such was his shock and disappointment. He had been so close. If the Shepherd didn't bring him here then who did. *Back up. Take it slow.* "Can you return me to 2005?" He crossed his fingers.

"Yes."

"Really?" Truman's gloom transformed into sudden elation.

"Really."

"Now?"

"No!" Azizah shouted, struggling against the confining tissue. Her hands disappeared to her

139

elbows in the fleshy wall. "Look at this! I'm being absorbed."

"I am restraining you," the Shepherd said. "You were hurting me."

Azizah struggled for calm. "Truman, I expected more from you. You can't leave Juvenal and his people to the mercy of Cathcar."

"Oh yes, I can. Shepherd, can we leave now?

"No."

Truman shook his head. It seemed whenever he was given reason to hope, some sort of setback popped up. "Why not?"

"It is not yet time."

Who's keeping track? "What the hell are you waiting for?"

If the Shepherd was offended by Truman's language there was no such indication. "Events."

Truman fought down his frustration. This step by painful step process was as bad as pulling teeth out one at a time. "Events, events," he muttered. "What events? I don't belong here. You come and go at will. What the hell are you, anyway?

"I am a universal constructor."

Truman knew he'd read about universal constructors somewhere before. Maybe the Lohner diary. He couldn't remember what they were. "What's a universal constructor, anyway?"

"A universal constructor is an artificially intelligent, self-replicating machine," the Shepherd intoned, "designed to spread life throughout the universe from a genome. I make people."

"I told you," Azizah said, impatiently. "Who made you, Shepherd?"

140

A prolonged silence. *Is the Shepherd ignoring Azizah or doesn't he want to answer?*

She looked at Truman and shrugged. "Who made--"

"Please," the Shepherd said in a tired voice. "I was reviewing the impact of answering your question. From my calculations, no temporal paradoxes will arise if you know. A4-Ni made me."

"Temporal paradoxes." Azizah snorted a laugh. "I have anecdotal knowledge A4-Ni built you. Moye already told me in Kanapoi."

"I know," the Shepherd said. "I was referring to what that knowledge might do to your present companion."

Truman searched his memory, trying to recall what he had learned about A4-Ni from the remains of the Lohner diary. "Lohner wrote A4-Ni and *Afareni*, a mythical mother figure, were one and the same."

"Lohner was only correct in realizing that they sounded the same," the Shepherd said. "Although Afareni was at times the name applied to A4-Ni, the former was in fact entirely from myth, whereas the latter indeed had a physical presence."

"But his assertions were dismissed as the ranting of crazed man. He also thought A4-Ni was still around and talking to him."

"He wasn't as crazed as you think," Azizah said. "Isn't that right, Shepherd?"

"You are quite correct."

One step at a time, Truman thought. "Lohner also wrote that this A4-Ni stole a--"

"What I don't understand is where A4-Ni came from," Azizah said, ignoring Truman.

"Future humans built her," the Shepherd said.

"Then they must have had help." Azizah's voice rose in agitation. "With hominids degrading, even enhanced by *Gilomir's* DNA, they would not be intelligent enough to build A4-Ni by themselves."

"The guardian helped future humans to build A4-Ni," the Shepherd said. "The guardian also helped A4-Ni build me."

"How is it you even know about future humans?" Azizah asked.

"I have already stated the guardian assisted A4-Ni in my construction. The guardian also gave me a view of the future to an extent it deemed necessary for me to complete my mission."

"And what is your mission?"

A long pause. "I am surprised you have the audacity to ask such a question."

She's beginning to piss him off. "Come on Azizah," Truman said, annoyed she had taken over the conversation. "You're a player. He's not going to give away the store. What did you expect?"

"Sometimes I get surprised."

When she started to speak, he'd had enough and put his hand over her mouth. But there was something else bothering him. The Shepherd had piqued his interest before Azizah interrupted. "You make people?"

"Indeed," the Shepherd answered.

"Like humans?"

"I can make humans."

"Then you might know the answer to something I discovered. While working on a section of human genome, I found that--"

142

"--Humans are devolving," the Shepherd finished.

Azizah ripped Truman's hand from her mouth. "You're beginning to sound silly. He knows all about you and what you do."

Truman didn't care what Azizah thought. *If the Shepherd knows about human de-evolution, does he have a solution? And if he does, will he tell me?* "Can you help me solve this problem?"

"I can. And I will at the appropriate time."

Another roadblock. "The events."

"Yes." The walls of the Shepherd's womb constricted. "It is time for you to exit."

"I don't want to exit!" Truman shouted.

"It's the events, Truman," Azizah said sarcastically.

"But I don't want to go anywhere. I feel safe. I don't mind waiting here for these events, whatever. Then I'll get to go home."

"You don't understand," Azizah said. "You are a part of these events."

They rose inside the womb to be deposited onto the Shepherd's slippery exterior.

"Why the hell didn't you stick up for me in there?" Truman demanded. You seem to know I will go back. But it's not the right time for it to happen. Is that it?"

"That's it." Azizah grabbed his hand. "Come on. We better get out of here while we still can."

Truman hesitated, then followed her pull as they slipped off the side of the Shepherd. He turned back and gazed at the silent, rounded form. *Don't leave without me*, he thought morosely.

***

A flash of lightning sizzled, splitting a nearby tree, followed by a stuttering, rolling thunderclap. Rain pelted from the cloud-blackened sky. Heavy drops splattered and stung. The wind whipped bushes and trees in a heart-stopping frenzy.

Truman ducked reflexively. "Jesus, I hate this lightning shit!" He dragged on her hand. "We'd better find shelter. Juvenal's painting cave is the closest!"

He pulled her through the bush, nearly ran into the escarpment again, then followed it south until he reached the cave entrance. Water cascaded over the rim of the plateau in a waterfall they squeezed behind to get into the cave.

Truman stood back from the opening, dripping wet and gazed at the muddy torrent. "God, why does it have to rain so much? I feel like I'm ready to rot away."

"The rains started hundreds of years ago and will continue into the near future."

"You'd make a great meteorologist."

"I would? Why?"

Truman shook his head, wondering at her lack of humor. Were all players so driven? "Never mind." Truman slicked the rainwater from his body.

Azizah gathered her hair together and wrung it out, then shook her head, letting dark curls fall around her face.

She stepped to the back of the cave and located Juvenal's fire-making materials. A moment later a flame flickered on the earthenware lamp. "I'd light a bigger fire but there's no draft in here. The cave would fill with smoke."

Truman started pacing back and forth. His shadow rippled over the uneven walls in the dim light. The tension that had been building ever since being in the Shepherd threatened to overwhelm him..

"Sit, Truman. You won't figure anything out walking, and you're driving me crazy."

He stopped in front of her. "I need answers. I thought I was getting somewhere with the Shepherd but you wouldn't support me."

"I'm sorry you feel that way. But unlike you, I thought we were getting nowhere. The Shepherd seemed focused on certain things happening before he was prepared to even talk about returning you to 2005. Besides, it wasn't me who called time. The Shepherd did."

Truman stopped pacing. She was right. It wasn't her fault. The Shepherd was adhering to a time table that had nothing to do with what he might say or do at the moment. He struggled to maintain some sort of rationality. If he let go for an instant he feared he would be plunged into insanity. Review the facts. Maybe by saying them over and over again he'd burn them into his consciousness and have them there as a last grab, a desperate resort to reach for when all else failed. "Somehow I ended up here. You don't know how. Cathcar doesn't know. And the Shepherd says he didn't bring me here. Who does that leave? Juvenal? I think not. Maybe this Sedroth but he'd have to use magic."

"Please, Truman, calm down." Azizah took his hand. "I'll try to answer your questions but I only see one part of the whole story." She led him to a smooth spot on the floor near a side wall.

They sat, and he leaned back. "God, this is all so complicated." He rubbed his eyes with the heels of his hands. "I don't know where to start."

Azizah brushed her thumb over the puckered scar on his leg. "Aren't you curious why this wound is healed?"

"I assume I had it longer than I remember--" Truman blinked. "--I see what you're getting at. You're suggesting the Shepherd healed it."

"He did a good job repairing the damage you suffered from Cathcar's beating."

"He also said he didn't bring me here. So if the Shepherd did heal me, I don't know when he might have done it. I don't remember any of it."

"He does make people."

The now familiar feeling of disorientation swept over Truman followed by the persistent question, *who am I*? He sensed where Azizah was taking the conversation, and he didn't like it. "That's absurd."

She smiled. "You said yourself you can't remember certain parts of your past."

"I don't think that qualifies me as a clone."

"Perhaps not but you must admit the Shepherd knows a lot about genetics."

"That would be an understatement. His only concern seems to be genetics."

"He knew right away Cathcar was a Neanderthal, and I was a Homo sapiens."

"Yeah." Truman squinted at her. "What did he mean when he said you had made an interesting choice?"

"There are other hominid forms here. Not close by but they exist. Cathcar prefers the Neanderthal physiognomy and I prefer something more advanced."

"You talk as though you both decided who you wanted to be."

"Is that so strange? You yourself said you didn't know who you are. Once you decide, then you you'll be no different than Cathcar and me."

"If I've led you to believe I don't know who I am, then I meant it in a philosophical sense. You guys chose a physical form. How did you do that?"

She picked up the lamp and placed it between them. The light shone from below her face and cast sinister shadows.

"Since you're being philosophical," she said, "I'm going to tell you about players."

"Finally." Truman raised his hands above his head in a sign of false jubilation.

She ignored his sarcasm. "First some background. Consider two opposing forces. Call them good and evil, or Yin and Yang. Whatever you call them doesn't matter. I know them as *Gilomir* and *Zug*. Though they are identified by their extremes, they cannot exist one without the other."

"Dynamic dualisms."

"Precisely. *Gilomir* and *Zug* existed in a kind of harmonic balance. One couldn't go too far one way without the other being able to pull back."

"Existed?"

"Somehow the balance shifted…in *Zug's* favor.

"So who's evil and who's good?" Truman thought to ask a light question but Azizah took it very seriously.

She gazed into the flickering flame. "It would be a mistake to place such labels on either of them.

147

They each have their goals, which are mutually exclusive."

"Right," Truman said. "Gods fighting other gods but joined at the hip. I think all that went out thousands of years ago. Next you are going to tell me there's a heaven and a hell."

"I might. It would be easier in a way. The truth is far more complex."

"I was joking."

"I know you were. Players have a sense of humor, too, Truman, even if you don't think so. Let me give you a sense of perspective. Civilizations, for want of a better term, can be categorized by the amount of energy they can control. Humans are, or potentially were, on a path to harness the capacity of this entire planet, 10^{16} watts of energy. Let's call that a Level I civilization. A Level II civilization might be one that harnesses the capacity of an entire solar system. A Level III, a whole galaxy. A Level IV, clusters of galaxies, and so forth, maybe up to a civilization that could span your known universe. *Gilomir* and *Zug* are at the latter level. A level so far advanced from yours, you have no way to comprehend who or what they are."

"Sounds like voodoo metaphysics to me."

"You and I both know from the Lohner Diary that A4-Ni stole the *Gilomir* genome. In fact, Lohner believed *Gilomir* DNA was inserted by A4-Ni into an ancient hominid and is responsible for the evolution of conscious beings. Homo sapiens."

"If you hadn't interrupted me, I was going to ask the Shepherd if Lohner was right."

"Lohner *was* right."

Truman stared at her, shocked. "I guess I'll just have to take your word for it. How'd *Gilomir* get here to be stolen, then inserted?"

"I don't know."

"For a player you don't seem to know much more than I do."

"I never claimed players knew everything."

Truman struggled to his feet and began pacing again. There was sure a lot of ignorance going around. At least he didn't have the lion's share of it. "Do you even know where you came from? Why you are here?"

"Yes, of course, I do know that."

"Really?" Truman was surprised. Maybe she knew something after all. "Tell me."

"Players are the time present, physical manifestations of...strings...for lack of a better word, of programmable strings that have been sown throughout your universe by *Zug*.

"You lost me. *Zug's* here, too?"

"Not that I know of. Instead of entering your universe in pursuit of *Gilomir*, *Zug* sent in strings.

"And as to why you are here?"

"Primarily, strings are meant to harass *Gilomir* on *Zug's* behalf. Strings are also looking for the guardian, which you know from Lohner's diary, can view the past and the future as a continuum. Possession of the guardian would enhance the power of a string. Without the guardian, a string can only sample reality, a laborious process of inserting a manifestation, like me, into a time present. I check around for *Gilomir* or the guardian, and if I don't find either or think they are somewhere else, I withdraw and reinsert elsewhere."

"But what of Cathcar, or Hopkins or whomever?"

"Strings exist within time zones of varying length, thousands of years, tens of thousands of years. The time zones are scattered throughout your space-time, past and future. Strings can enter time present as players anywhere within their respective time zones. Time zones can overlap, so it's possible to have two or more players from different strings in the same time present.

"My string has a zone that spans 7005 years, beginning a few hundred years before your 2005 and ending somewhere in the year 9000. Cathcar's string and mine overlap. I don't know what the time limits are for his string."

"If you are all from *Zug*, why the competition, the deadly competition."

"All strings used to be controlled by *Zug*. Then something happened and that coordinating control was interrupted. Now it's every string for itself."

"I don't understand. If strings are so powerful, why do you waste time taking human form instead of creating some sort of superman? You've got nothing but sticks and stones to work with here, or cars and guns back in Kanapoi."

"A string can't manifest itself in something that doesn't exist in the time present. Maybe in the distant future there are supermen. Then a string entering that time present would probably utilize that form. But you're right. As a player I have little to work with. I'm like an ant with the knowledge of how to build an automobile."

150

Truman stared in wonder. "You're telling me we're assaulted by beings that come and go from reprogrammable nothings?"

"You asked, Truman."

"So that explains that stuff you laid on me after you killed Hopkins, player kills player, player recycles."

Azizah nodded. "You remember well."

"I was rather traumatized. I think it got seared in permanently."

"Players don't actually die. They are merely withdrawn by their string. It will decide whether or not it is in its interest to persevere or recycle into the same or a different time present. I thought Hopkins was Jomo recycled but he wasn't. It's very unusual to have three players in the same time present. But Hopkins did recycle to Cathcar. My string had me follow him here...when I recycled

"You recycled? What did happen to you in Kanapoi? The last thing I remember was falling on you when the rope broke. I blacked out, then I woke up here."

"I died."

"How can you know?"

"I was there, so I know. Now I'm here."

"So you retain your memory of the past even though you've recycled?"

"My memory is cumulative. It's not always perfectly cumulative. I find there are gaps, sometimes."

Truman smiled. "Sort of like me."

"Sort of."

"What about the future? Do you know the future?"

151

"Nope. Just the past."

He reached for her chin and raised her head with his finger to stare into her eyes. "If everything else going on wasn't so weird, I'd say you've been smoking a controlled substance. Lots of people go around thinking they're omnipotent."

"But I am." She reached and clasped his hand.

"Yeah. So am I." He spoke with a bravado he didn't feel. Her answers were testing the limits of his ability to understand. *Was it all true, or was she spinning a story?*

Azizah set the lamp to one side and snuggled against him. "I see you need convincing." She slipped her hand under his arm, and nuzzled his neck.

Her soft breasts pressed against his chest. Then she disappeared and reappeared, nuzzling from his left side. Before he could react, she disappeared again and returned to his right side.

"What the hell?" He stood and tried to grab her. "Stop that."

She stopped and faced him. "I don't often show off. Do you still think I've been smoking a controlled substance?"

"Why didn't you do that to get away from Cathcar?"

"First, I didn't want him to know I was a player. Second, it would have been of no use. He could have pursued me anywhere if it had served his purpose."

He saw her in a new light. She really was practically omnipotent. The big picture just got a whole lot bigger. Where the hell did he fit into it? "I'm sorry I was flippant. You'll have to excuse me if I don't understand everything you've told me. It's almost more than anyone can accept."

"Take your time. It's a lot to assimilate."

"What about the two Shepherds that left Kanapoi. Are there two purveyors of the *Gilomir* genome.

"That's a good question. I don't know the answer."

"I'm surprised."

She smiled. "Players do have their limitations."

"I'd like to know what my place is in this mess."

"I'd like to help you but I can't."

"You can't, or you won't?"

"Truman, please. This is as difficult for me as it is for you. In time, certain truths will out, and you will understand."

"I get it. Be patient."

"Yes, please."

Truman fussed. None of this was making a lot of sense to him. Even worse, he had the feeling it should be making sense.

Her arms drifted around his waist. "Why did you kiss me when we were in the Shepherd?"

"I...I..." He stopped trying to speak and gripped her shoulders. "I was being impulsive. I'm afraid. I'm alone. I'm glad you're here. If I didn't know better, I'd think I'm falling in love with you." The sudden admission surprised him.

"No, you don't love me." Her head rested against his chest. "You need me."

He laughed and rubbed his hands up and down her back. "There's that, too. I'm okay with it."

She shivered. "It's a pity we can't build a fire."

He pulled her close, then brushed aside a stringy lock of hair that had fallen across her forehead. "Feel warmer?"

"Yes." She gazed at him. The evanescent color of her eyes sparkled despite the weak light. Her forehead creased with the slightest frown. "Truman, do you really love me?"

"I admit I'm a bit confused. I feel love but I don't know who loves, or who is receiving that love."

She pulled on his beard, bringing his mouth to hers. Her kiss was warm, passionate.

"You seem to enjoy kissing," he said.

"Just because I'm the instrument of a god doesn't mean I'm immune to the pleasures of the flesh."

"Does that mean you can make love to mere mortals?"

"Yes. I will show you."

154

Chapter Eight

Morning sun cast a shaft of light deep into the cave, bringing the colors of Juvenal's paintings to life. Bright red and deep ocher resonated with yellow and orange.

Azizah still slept.

Truman tried to move but she pressed against him.

"Azizah," he whispered. He gave her a gentle nudge. "It's time we headed back."

She murmured. Without opening her eyes she stretched, then looked at him. Smiling, she brought her arms around his neck and pulled him into a close embrace. "I slept so soundly. I think you wore me out."

"I thought you would never tire." Truman kissed her. His hands drifted down the smooth skin of her arms. He inhaled her musky scent mixed with the damp air of the cave.

She dipped a shoulder and leaned away from him, all the while observing his ministrations. "You were very gentle. Look. The light is beautiful. See how the paintings glow."

"I've been watching them. The first rays hit the painted sun above Sedroth, then descended to the guardian, you, and Cathcar."

"Cathcar. I wish I could forget him." She stood, reached for her skin wrap, and reattached it over her shoulder and about her waist. "I'm starved. Hopefully, we can find some fruit on the way back."

Truman led her out of the painting cave. He paused at the entrance in the misty light. The morning air hung with the smell of rain and vegetation. He put his arm around her square shoulders and gave her a hug. For a moment he forgot where he was and why he couldn't find a way to get back to Kanapoi.

A distant cry broke the tranquility.

"That sounded like a scream," Azizah said. "Close by. The ruins."

"You think Cathcar is there?"

"Let's find out." Azizah started up the path alongside the escarpment..

Truman lagged behind.

She stopped when she realized he wasn't following her. "Are you coming or not."

"I can't"

"You can't?" She seemed shocked. "What about the Maraia."

"I don't owe them anything. If Cathcar is there, I don't want any part of him after what he did to me. You go. I'll wait for you here." Truman turned back toward the cave entrance.

"Truman, wait." Azizah grabbed his shoulder. "I can reason with Cathcar. Please, we have to try."

Truman hesitated.

The screams grew louder, more frequent.

He knew he was being a coward and that it didn't become him. So what if Cathcar was going to beat him to a pulp? *Yeah, so what? I'm dead here, anyhow. No way back. Why not make the most of what is left?*

"All right but I've got a bad feeling about this." He grabbed Azizah's hand and ran.

156

As he stumbled into the clearing in front of the ruins, a chorus of agitated cries washed over him. Pandemonium.

Swinging his club, Cathcar stood surrounded by Maraia men.

The men ducked back and forth, looking for an opening, stabbing with their sharp lances, keeping him at bay.

The Maraia women milled around behind the men, screaming and offering encouragement.

Lid open, the vault lay on its side at Cathcar's feet.

The crowd fell silent and turned to stare at Truman.

Despite his earlier devil may care convincing of himself, his stomach churned with fear at the sight of Cathcar. His knees felt weak. "I'm out of here." Truman ran.

Cathcar's head jerked in the direction of Truman. He charged, a steam engine on rails, swift for his bulk, knocking Maraia out of his way.

Truman stumbled and lost ground.

Cathcar was on him. He grabbed Truman by the shoulder, whirled him around and hit him across the face with the back of his massive hand.

Truman's feet left the ground. The force of the blow sent him sprawling backward.

"You lie!" Cathcar bellowed.

"Leave him alone!" Azizah cried, racing at Cathcar.

She got as far as his outstretched hand, which smacked her hard in the forehead. Her eyes rolled up in their sockets, and she crumpled to the ground.

"You next," Cathcar said, staring down at her.

157

Truman struggled to his feet, touching his lips with his hand. It came away bloodied. "You dumb fuck! I didn't lie. The last time I saw the guardian, it was in the tunnel. If it wasn't lying around on the ground then I supposed it might be in that stone box!"

Juvenal and the Maraia men closed in a circle around the three of them. When Juvenal stepped forward to help Truman, Cathcar gave him a baleful stare from his close-set eyes.

Juvenal froze in his tracks.

Cathcar turned back to Truman. "Players all alike." He leaned sideways and gave Truman what amounted to a clean Karate kick in the side.

Bent over, Truman gritted his teeth, gasping for breath. He clutched his chest, sure the rib Cathcar had managed to bruise before had now given way. *This is getting old.* "I'm no player."

Cathcar grabbed Truman's hair and raised him with one arm to a standing position.

"No. Look. Please." Truman pleaded. Each intake of air convulsed his chest in pain.

Like a heavyweight boxer working a training bag, Cathcar buried his fist in Truman's mid-section. Cathcar retracted his arm like the piston on an ancient combustion engine, then plunged it forward, driving his fist home, each thudding blow swinging Truman--still gripped by his hair.

Azizah rose to her hands and knees, shaking her head, trying to clear it. She fixed Cathcar with a stare. "He is not a player. You and I are the only players here."

Cathcar grunted, something akin to astonishment or was it satisfaction? He released

Truman, who slumped to the ground, holding his stomach and choking for air.

"You seem surprised," Azizah said.

"Surprised." Cathcar's rasping baritone made the statement ominous. "No Homo sapiens here but him and you. Why you choose form?"

"It becomes me." Azizah smiled nervously.

"Save female wiles. If not player, what this miserable turd?"

"I thought you might know," Azizah said. "He says he's from the past. He doesn't know how he got here, though I suspect the Shepherd had something to do with it."

"Shepherd? Excremental lump of organic protoplasm. I enter. It ignore. I leave. It ignore."

Truman regained his breathing with difficulty and listened dreamily to the exchange. "Azah...zah," he moaned through thickened lips. His vision clouded from his eye puffing shut again.

Azizah knelt beside him. "Poor Truman." Tears welled in her eyes and streaked her cheeks. "Someone, somewhere is making you suffer very much."

"I don't understand," Truman mumbled. "How can you talk to him like that? As though you were old pals."

"We are players." She stroked his forehead. "Though our game is played out on a human landscape, remember our goals have nothing to do with the interests of humans."

"Then why the tears?" Truman winced at a sudden stab of pain in his chest. "Are you just a good actor?"

159

"My goals may be obscure to you but the characters I become feel in a human way."

"Cathcar doesn't have a sympathetic bone in his body." As soon as he said it, Truman regretted his statement and braced for another pummeling..

Cathcar stepped on Truman's foot instead, pinning him to the spot, then spat on the ground. "I eat you for dinner."

Truman struggled in vain, trying to dislodge the massive foot.

"You would do well to move cautiously," Azizah said to the hulking beast, "at least until you know with whom you are dealing."

"Dealing?" Cathcar cocked his head idiotically.

"I find it interesting the Shepherd is here," Azizah said, obviously trying to turn Cathcar's attention elsewhere. "Since he's not here for you or me, then he must be here on behalf of someone else."

Cathcar grunted. His lips curled all the way up into a crooked smile. "*Zug* gone. You know. I know. Where other manifestations?"

Azizah stared at the beast. "I told you there are no other players here."

With lidded eyes, Cathcar regarded Juvenal.

"Surely you don't suspect him." Azizah rattled off a quick phrase to Juvenal, who stepped back behind a protective wall of Maraia men.

"Everyone suspect. What of Kanapoi? Hopkins dead."

"You expect me to keep track of your reincarnations?"

Truman jerked his foot free and glared at Azizah. Everything Cathcar said confirmed what

Azizah had already told him. They talked as though he didn't exist, their own goals paramount. He flicked his tongue around his mouth, leaned forward, and spit blood. "She's lying. She killed Hopkins."

"Ehhh?" Cathcar turned on Azizah.

She backed away quickly. "My presence in Kanapoi was also terminated. The guardian was in my grasp."

"This excrement--" Cathcar pointed a finger at Truman, "--say guardian in tunnel. He duck-walked over to the vault, his massive thighs brushing against each other. He picked it up by the edge with one big hand. "Empty. You know?" Cathcar cast the vault in front of Truman.

"I didn't know for sure." Truman raised his arms to protect himself. "I really didn't. She had it last. She shot me and left me for dead. I blacked out and woke up here."

"Talk nonsense." Cathcar dismissed Truman with a downward wave of his hand. "Guardian move. Worm go to Kanapoi. Find."

"Find?" Truman's interest piqued, and for a moment he forgot his misery. "I'll find it for you."

"Your loyalties are very thin," Azizah said.

"Loyalties?" Truman blinked, feeling frustrated as he felt his way in this surreal situation. But these players didn't seem to have a clue either about what was going on. His only hope lay with the Shepherd. Were these the events? Would the Shepherd agree to ferry him back to Kanapoi?

"What about last night?" Azizah glared at him.

Truman longed for her embrace, remembering the passion of their lovemaking. But it seemed

161

every time he gave in to her, she took the advantage. "You said yourself you have no interest in mankind, except a passing compassion because you have to take our form. Why shouldn't I feel the same way about you?"

"I thought you were human."

Cathcar watched the exchange with a bemused look on his face. He bellowed a hollow, choppy laugh. "Use female charms to advantage. Think rutting in cave bring guardian?"

Azizah turned him a cold eye. "Why shouldn't I? You chose brawn and dim wit to play this part. Who's to say it won't be won with guile?"

Truman was dumbstruck. She couldn't care less about him. "This is all about the guardian and always has been!"

"Shut mouth," Cathcar said. "Waste time. I decide. You go back. Put guardian in vault."

Azizah's mouth gaped open in surprise. "Are you assuming if Truman places the guardian in the vault in the past, then it will appear here, in the vault in the future?"

"Quantum physics. Many worlds. Do math." Cathcar turned a dull stare to Truman. "Where worm after black out? Where worm before here? Change past. Change future."

"You assume it will turn out favorably for you."

A satisfied smile spread across Cathcar's face but no joy shone in his eyes. "Truce now," he said squinting. "Find guardian. Then play more."

He grabbed Truman and heaved him to his feet.

162

Truman let out a cry. The weight of his bent legs pulled on his chest. He shut his eyes and waited for the beating to resume. It didn't come.

"Worm to Shepherd," Cathcar said.

***

Truman struggled, feeling that the skin on his back and bottom would soon be worn away as Cathcar dragged him over the rough ground.

Azizah and Juvenal trailed behind. The rest of the Maraia men brought up the rear in a ragged array. Not a single one of them was a match for Cathcar, and without some strong coordinating effort from Juvenal they were helpless. Still, they had followed, despite Juvenal's admonition to not become involved. Truman couldn't resent Juvenal for telling them to stay behind. He was after all their leader and had to think of their ultimate survival.

Cathcar raked Truman through the bush, crossed his clearing and dumped Truman at the base of the Shepherd.

Azizah put a staying hand on Juvenal and approached Cathcar alone.

Truman, on hands and knees, considered, then abandoned, a dim thought to crawl away.

Cathcar leapt onto the Shepherd and stomped across the top, looking awkward as each heavy step depressed the Shepherd's rebounding surface, putting the beast off balance. Presumably, he wanted to verify the puckered entrance remained where he had last seen it. A moment later he slid off the Shepherd's side and landed on the ground with a thump.

"Entrance no move," Cathcar grunted. He grabbed Truman by the arm, leaned back for leverage, and gave him a great heave, depositing him onto the Shepherd's side, halfway up.

Truman felt himself sliding off.

Cathcar bounded up onto the other side, came into sight above him, and caught his foot, then dragged him across the Shepherd's skin-like surface.

From the perspective of four centimeters, the surface material was rougher than Truman had remembered. It also was not gray but a deeper dark green, like looking into the depths of an algae-filled pool of water.

Cathcar deposited Truman at the pucker.

With a leg up from Juvenal, Azizah came over the side and scrambled up to stand beside Cathcar.

Juvenal ranged back and forth below the Shepherd, craning his neck to get a look at what was going on above. The rest of the Maraia spread out, two or three deep on one side of the clearing.

"How enter," Cathcar growled, looking at the closed opening.

"I don't know," Azizah said. "He let you in before."

"Always open. I go. I come."

"He let us in. We just stood here and it opened."

Cathcar stamped his foot on the pucker and set the whole Shepherd bouncing up and down like a water-filled balloon.

"Open!" he bellowed. When the Shepherd refused to respond, Cathcar dropped to both knees and tried forcing his fingers into the center of the pucker. "No open. Like clay!"

"Perhaps it will respond to Truman." Azizah gave him a quick glance.

But he could only stare past them both at the tangle of jungle beyond, wondering when his ordeal was going to end.

Cathcar shoved Truman's face close to the pucker. "Ask open."

Truman coughed. A drool of blood escaped from his lips, splashed on the radiating wrinkles, then oozed toward the center.

Cathcar kicked him, reminding him why his face was so close.

"Open," Truman said weakly. "Please open."

The entire surface of the Shepherd twitched, then the pucker relaxed and dialed open.

At that moment, the sky, always spotted with dark clouds, released a torrent of rain. It pounded the back of Truman's head reviving him, washing through his hair and dripping onto the Shepherd to drain into the open pucker.

Cathcar stared myopically at the widening orifice and stepped back when it got too close to where he was standing. He bumped into Azizah, tripped, and the two of them rolled off the Shepherd to the ground.

Juvenal waved an arm at the Maraia men.

They rushed Cathcar.

As soon as he hit the ground, he bounded up, into a crouched stance.

A lead Maraia fell into his clutches and was hoisted bodily and flung at the rest.

Their erstwhile assault ended before it had a chance to develop.

Fists clenched, Cathcar whipped around and glared at Juvenal. His rage rose to his face. His mouth curled into a snarl. The whites of his small

165

eyes discolored red and swelled, seeming to test the confines of their sockets. He grabbed Juvenal by the hair and pulled him close, bending back his head to expose the white flesh of his neck below his chin.

Juvenal strained. His jugular pulsed on the side of his throat.

"Let him go!" Azizah screamed, regaining her feet. She lunged at Cathcar.

Cathcar ignored her ineffectual blows and reached to Juvenal's thong belt. He grabbed the sharpened piece of chert tethered there. "Maybe Truman go now!" With one quick movement, he brought the knife's razor edge up under Juvenal's chin.

"Don't!" Truman cried. He slapped the hide of the Shepherd in frustration. "I can't move. I'm too weak."

"You go to Kanapoi. You put guardian in vault. I wait. No guardian? No Maraia. I kill all."

Cathcar started the blade across Juvenal's throat, all the while peering cross-eyed at the crimson trickle the blade set free. His lips pulled back exposing a blocky toothed grin.

Juvenal struggled but was no match for Cathcar's strength.

Cathcar shrugged Azizah off his shoulders to the ground.

She hit hard but bounded to her feet. "Wait! If you're looking for the guardian, Sedroth has it."

"Lie!" Cathcar's nose twitched, his lips fluttered. He seemed insane. His eyes rolled in their sockets, giving him the look of an enraged simpleton. Then with a sudden movement, he drew

166

the blade across Juvenal's neck from ear to ear, slicing deep.

Juvenal choked, a wet, gargling sound caught in his throat. He sagged and tipped forward onto his face, both hands at his throat.

Azizah stared at the hemorrhaging Juvenal. "Why?" she cried in anguish.

Truman gaped, horrified at what he had witnessed.

"This Maraia first!" Cathcar bellowed. "No guardian, then others." Cathcar grinned. "Bye-bye, Worm."

***

Dazed by Cathcar's brutality, Truman hardly felt the tug at his shoulders. He slid toward the pucker now dialed open to its full extent. His head went first. He tipped, hips rising into the air. Once his shoulders filled the pucker, it closed snuggly around him. The rest of him was gulped in, a rodent ingested by some unseemly serpent.

Though he knew he had entered upside down, he had no sense of up or down once the opening closed at his feet.

The lights came on.

"He slit Juvenal's throat!" Juvenal's fear-filled eyes remained fixed in Truman's mind.

"Do you wish to return to Kanapoi?" the Shepherd asked.

"What about Juvenal?" Truman was overcome with guilt.

"Do you wish to return to 2005?"

Truman cringed. *What to do? None of this is real, or is it?* But all he could see was blood spurting from Juvenal's neck. That was real. And

167

making love to Azizah but she betrayed him in the end. "Get me out of here." *I'll never understand what happened, anyway.*

"You have become damaged again. I will repair you."

"Forget it." Truman despaired. "I feel like I want to die but can't. It's hard to live with these memories."

"Of course you can." The Shepherd busied himself for a moment. "Feel better?"

"Yes, damn it." Truman did feel better, though he would have slumped with fatigue if he could have. "Now what?"

"I will return you to Kanapoi, 2005."

"No, wait." Confusion overwhelmed Truman. "Can't we help Juvenal?"

"Yes. Do you want to return?"

"Yes...I mean, no. What's happening?"

"Please narrow your question to something more specific."

"Where are we?"

"We are now three-hundred thousand kilometers from Earth and accelerating."

"Shit. Do you know that Cathcar wants me to locate the guardian?"

"Yes. Do you wish to do that?"

"The guardian is irrelevant, now." Truman groaned. "I want my life back."

"You can have that, too."

Why was the Shepherd so accommodating? He wasn't taking him back to 2005 because Cathcar thought it was the best way for them to obtain the guardian. "I get it. You want the guardian, too?"

"I already have it."

"You do?" Truman paused, confused. "Then why tolerate all this bloodshed? You could have told them you had the guardian. They would have stopped pestering the Maraia about it. Juvenal wouldn't have to die. Why am I involved, anyway?"

"I do not have it...now."

Truman sensed some faint whirs and clicks. Some background computing by the Shepherd? "You're confusing me. Either you have it or you don't. What gives?"

"The guardian comes into my possession farther along on my world line. I do not have it in my possession, now, at this point in my world line."

"World line? I thought that was a hypothetical graph of someone's journey in space-time."

"It is but it is not hypothetical."

"You know the future?"

"Sometimes the past is the future. In that case, you could say I know some of the future."

"You've lost me. But I'm easily lost after what I've been through. Tell me, does Juvenal survive?"

"He is still alive. Not by much. He can be saved."

"Who's going to save him?" Truman didn't see Azizah being able to, not with Cathcar standing over her.

"Sedroth."

I should have known. "Who is this Sedroth?"

The Shepherd remained silent and seemed to busy himself with other matters.

"I wasn't able to meet Sedroth while I was--"

"I heard you." The Shepherd shifted his position around Truman. "I could remove your hair and beard, if you so desire."

God, that would be great. He'd forgotten how clean and refreshing a smooth scalp and chin could be. The Shepherd wasn't going to tell him any more than he wanted to, anyway.

"Yeah, go ahead. It itches."

After the briefest of dislocations, Truman's head pressed flesh-to-flesh against the wall of the womb.

"Feel better?"

"I assume the hair's gone."

"It is."

This is crazy. "Where are we now?"

A vision opened in Truman's mind, or so it seemed. Everything around him disappeared as he gazed into a holistic view of space, though one oddly skewed. Stars at the focus of his vision appeared as points of light, whereas those on the periphery were blurred streaks.

"What am I seeing?"

"It is a temporal view of our travel. I must attain the black hole in the Cygnus formation, round it on a precise orbit and hope to re-emerge at our predestined time and place."

"If you thought you were explaining something to me, you lost me."

"I use spinning black holes as accelerators."

"Sounds like a sports car."

"Perhaps. Probably a bit more involved. In a Newman-Unti-Tamborino universe--"

"A what?"

"A NUT universe, a special solution to Einstein's General Theory of Relativity in 1963. Come Truman, you cannot be so ignorant to have not known about these things in 2005?

"I'm beginning to believe I was. Azizah thought I was stupid as well."

"She is a very astute Homo sapiens, even for a female."

"Female or not, your universe seems as nutty as its name."

"I am not here to educate you given the limits of your cosmology. Using a Kerr solution to Einstein's General Theory of Relativity, a spinning black hole warps space and time in such a way a precision orbit around it will accomplish leaps in time and space. Am I making myself clear?"

"It sounds like a very iffy maneuver."

"It is. Wherever a black hole is located, space-time coils around it a fixed number of coils depending on the size of the black hole. I skim around these coils, which are located at the event horizon, until I arrive at a desired time in the past or future. Sort of like climbing or descending a spiral staircase."

"When I exit the coil I remain spatially near where I started but removed in time."

"So, how long is this going to take?"

"Subjectively, five months."

"Five months!" Truman couldn't imagine standing suspended in a fleshy womb for that long without going insane. Maybe he already was insane.

"Do not worry. I will sedate you. You will not experience any passage of time."

"Are you going to sedate me now?"

"If you wish."

"No." Truman felt uneasy, as if he were about to go under for an operation and wasn't in any hurry to begin. "Can we talk a bit more?"

"Of course."

Truman tried moving his arms but found he couldn't raise them above his shoulders. He gave up trying. "I want to know more about this A4-Ni."

"Anything in particular?"

"Was she really built by humans?"

"Three thousand years from now humans build a universal constructor. They christen her A4-Ni, a play on the historical name *Afareni*."

"What do they hope to achieve?"

"The preservation of the human race. By then humans are reduced to a non-sustaining population. They seek to disperse their genome elsewhere, elsewhen, hoping it will flourish. They build A4-Ni and send her into space to use the black hole in the Cygnus binary to achieve a space-time jump to a time and place where no players exist."

"She couldn't have gotten very far if she's mentioned in Lohner's diary as being everywhere present in 1985."

"A4-Ni's space-time jump was flawed. It landed her in the same place but five million years in the past. The human genome she was supposed to use to disburse humans to the stars was destroyed, and her memory banks so scrambled she could not remember her origin, nor her mission.

"She lingered near the Cygnus black hole, and being organic, like myself, evolved into a life form quite alien to her original design."

"Why did she evolve?"

"She had a capacity for self-replication. That capacity was not adversely affected by the turn around the black hole."

"So, how long did she evolve?"

172

"A million years. Then a Shepherd, the second Shepherd you referred to that was seen in 1985 at Kanapoi--"

"The one you weren't sure if it was you or not."

"Correct. That Shepherd emerged coincidentally from around the same black hole. He was carrying the guardian and the genome *Gilomir*, transporting them from nothingness to reach a place of being."

"Nothingness to...what the hell does that mean?"

"The answer would confuse you."

"God damn it, Shepherd or whatever the hell you are, quit the *I don't really want to tell you* stuff. From my point of view, I've got a few months or years, I don't know which, to listen to whatever crap you can come up with."

"None of this is as you say...*crap*."

I don't have to know what nothingness and being are. "Go on. And I'm sorry I yelled at you."

"Thank you. A4-Ni damaged this Shepherd and stole the genome for her own use. With her muddled memory, she thought her destiny was to bring a genome to Earth. At that point any genome would do, and of course, this was the exact opposite of what she had been programmed to do. Nevertheless, she attained Earth, planted *Gilomir* into a primitive species of primates, your hominid ancestors, and retired to the role of caretaker. She oversaw the evolution of the primates, always ensuring some of them carried a pure copy of *Gilomir*."

Truman could not contain his excitement. "So mankind's humanity is a mistake?"

"You could call it that. Without the *Gilomir* genome, men would still be apes."

If true, the implications were profound. Man wasn't some cherished construction of a creating god, or the result of millions of years of progressive evolution. Man was a fortuitous accident resulting from a cosmic theft.

"The creationists are going to love this."

"Be that as it may, the Shepherd in question pursued A4-Ni but being damaged, he did not track her down for millions of your years. Not until 1985."

"The Kanapoi Incident." Big chunks of information rubbed up against each other like icebergs. They fit perfectly.

The Shepherd sighed. "Yes. A rather messy affair. But to make a long story short, the Shepherd obtained a copy of *Gilomir* DNA from the one human who then carried it in a pure form, the paleoanthropologist John Lohner."

"So Lohner wasn't crazy when he wrote aliens were after his DNA?"

"He did not see and could not have seen the big picture of what was happening around him."

"So where's A4-Ni now?"

"She attacked the Shepherd and compounded his damage, mortally wounding him. After leaving the guardian behind, the Shepherd fled."

"You said he was mortally wounded. What happened to him?"

"That is an interesting question. The guardian has chosen not to inform me as to his fate. Indeed, I have wondered that if this Shepherd were me somewhere up my world line, then knowing my fate

174

might compromise my ability to execute my mission...in a philosophical way of course."

"So one Shepherd left, and the guardian had A4-Ni build you."

"A4-Ni used the guardian to view her past and future. The guardian showed A4-Ni her true origin, a construct of future humans but misled her to believe she was originally a Shepherd. By attacking the departed Shepherd and possibly precipitating his eventual death, the guardian convinced A4-Ni she had compromised the very effort she had been constructed to achieve."

"Whoa. Whoa. You're saying the guardian manipulated everything?"

"Yes. Everyone overlooks all the guardian can do. The fact remains its sole concern is seeing to the safety of *Gilomir*. Had that been known, perhaps the visions the guardian produced would not have been taken at face value."

"What did A4-Ni do?"

"Overcome with guilt, she was swayed to believe her destiny now lay in building, under instruction from the guardian, a Shepherd...me. The guardian told A4-Ni she must charge me with *Gilomir's* genome, which she now believed to be the genome of future humans, and send it on its way to populate the universe. Of course this was all nonsense.

"Nevertheless, A4-Ni believed the guardian and bent to the task of building me with all her remaining energy. I was supplied with a fresh copy of *Gilomir's* genome, albeit one corrupted with hominid DNA. Then I went on my way."

"What happened to A4-Ni?"

175

"With her energy depleted, she died, leaving the existing copies of *Gilomir* in Homo sapiens to degrade. Without her care, humans devolved."

Truman's excitement spilled over. "That's why devolved hominids existed back there."

"If you are referring to the time you have left, then, yes, to some extent that is an accurate statement."

"But what of the guardian? Why was it left behind?"

"For a purpose I am only now beginning to understand."

"It misled you, too?"

"I cannot be misled. I am here to follow. The guardian instructed me to return to Earth, year 7005 A.D., pick you up and return you to 2005, which I am now doing. You are important to the future of mankind. Unless you are returned to 2005, humans three thousand years from now will not be able to construct A4-Ni. If she is not constructed, I cannot exist."

"But you exist," Truman said, wondering at the complexity of the situation. "How could humans fail to construct her, and she you?"

"Yes, I do exist. Humans do not fail. You will not fail."

Truman wasn't sure he understood but he was beginning to see the role he might play in this complex scenario. "You said you could tell me how to solve the problem of the degrading human genome. Is now the right time?" Truman hoped for the best.

"Yes. This is how to save mankind." The Shepherd was quiet for a moment. "Now you know."

"Amazing." Truman reviewed a new stream of knowledge that appeared in his mind. "It's not simple but I understand."

"Good. Are you ready to be sedated for the trip?"

"No, no, not yet. One more question. With all this time travel stuff, will I meet myself?"

"No, that is impossible."

"But I am some sort of catalyst?"

"Yes, a...catalyst. You will precipitate a chain of events that will ensure mankind survives in the future...the near future."

Truman rubbed his eyes, feeling exhausted. So much information coming in, so much of it barely understood. He yawned. "I think I've had enough. I'm ready to go under."

A needle pricked his thigh.

"It will be a moment before the narcotic takes effect," the Shepherd said.

"Will I dream...?" He struggled to focus his thoughts. A dream drifted like a wisp across his mind. Why the *sesshin*? It had been years--years?-- since he was into all that Zen crap.

"Shepherd. I'm having the clearest memory of my first *sesshin*."

"You are not asleep?"

"Does it look like I'm asleep?"

"I tried to find a soothing memory for you to think about." The Shepherd's voice resonated from all sides. A faint hum of working systems formed a background.

"But the *sesshin*? It wasn't very successful."

"Talking about it will help you to assimilate the memory, perhaps make you sleepy."

The intravenous fluids keeping Truman alive ebbed and flowed through his body. He felt a heavy grogginess weigh him down. "The first monk always beat me. These Zen types...can be obtusely motivated. He tried to push me to enlightenment. But the beatings distracted me. I failed. I always failed."

"Always?"

"I came close. Now, I live with my nullity." Truman felt like he was on a cloud, high above his body. "Do you know what it's like not knowing who you are?"

"I do not. I have always known who I am."

"I meant in an enlightened way. Your purpose in the universe."

"I know that, too," the Shepherd said.

Was his perception of the Shepherd being distorted by the narcotic, or was the Shepherd only going through some preordained motions, waiting until reality caught up with them? "You remind me of Yakitani-roshi."

"I do?"

"Just a feeling, maybe your voice. That's what I don't get about the memory...of the *sesshin*. I seemed different. Obsequious, groveling. I don't think I'd ever let a Jap monk hit me, even if it was to attain *kensho*."

"I find your use of the Japanese pejorative interesting, especially from someone of your race."

"Give me a break." Truman experienced a long period during which he couldn't think. Then his

178

mind lurched forward. "Blacks can't have prejudices?"

"I will give you...a break. To clarify your confusion about memory, sometimes the memories we have of ourselves are different than the way we were. If I erred on the side of accuracy with the projected memory, then I apologize."

Truman thought about that. It was the last thought he had for a while.

Chapter Nine

The sound of two gunshots rang in Truman's ears.

Clutching the heavy rifle the Shepherd had given him, he threaded his way between scattered rocks and clumps of dry, yellow grass. His boots crunched gravelly sand underneath. A wind off distant Lake Turkana, swirled dust into his face. Low-angled sunlight caught bent reeds and cast flickering shadows onto the plateau's rust colored floor. Hot air beat up from beneath him, easily fifty degrees Celsius, enough to make a Finnish sauna seem air-conditioned.

He squinted and pushed on.

The Shepherd knew full well Truman felt an obligation to comply with Cathcar's demand to put the guardian in the vault. Truman sensed doing so wouldn't make a difference. But if it held out the slightest hope Cathcar wouldn't slaughter the Maraia, the least he could do was try.

Disconcertingly, the Shepherd didn't seem to care one way or the other. His only request had been for Truman to meet some people in exchange for having learned the remedy for the degradation of man's genome. But why the rifle?

"Why do I need a rifle?" Truman asked.

The Shepherd shoved it into his hands. "You'll know when the time comes."

Great.

At the plateau's edge, Truman flopped onto his stomach, then inched his way forward to peer over.

Down and to his right, the western entrance to the tunnel gaped open. The Shepherd must have deposited him minutes before it was dynamited. Were the shots he had heard fired at Moye and Azizah? Her Land Cruiser stood undamaged on the road below. No sign of the helicopter. Still too early for that. Could he trust the Shepherd's confidence that he would not meet himself?

He pushed the thought out of his mind. Presumably, the Shepherd knew what was going on, and wasn't going to let some temporal anomaly get in the way of what he told Truman to do, even if none of it made much sense.

As he eased over the edge, a large man, carrying a rifle, exited the tunnel and headed for a canvas satchel that rested fifteen meters from the opening. He picked up the bag and returned to the entrance.

Truman experienced a moment of déjà vu. Though he struggled with the memory, he could not penetrate a foggy barrier that separated what was happening from what he thought he knew. Had the Shepherd messed with his mind?

A moment later, the man hurried to the edge of the tunnel entrance and taped what Truman assumed was an explosive charge to the rusted, iron gate. After checking the charge was secure, the man thumbed a switch, which set an LED blinking. He stood and returned inside.

Guessing the man would cross to the opposite entrance to mine it, Truman scrambled down the escarpment. When he got to the bottom, he ran to the entrance and peered into the tunnel.

A man slouched against the wall of the tunnel, holding his gut with both hands in a failed attempt to stop the hemorrhaging of blood from his mid-section.

Is that constable Moye?

"Truman?" The man's face contorted with pain.

It is Moye. Truman stepped to Moye's side. "You don't look too good, Constable." He kept his voice low, glancing all the while into the dark eastern depth of the tunnel.

Moye took two quick breaths, his face slick with sweat, his eyes wide with fear. "Thank God it's you. What are you doing here?"

"Later. Who did this to you?"

"I don't know. Called himself Jomo. Ugly fuck. He's at the other end of the tunnel. Get the girl out of here."

"She's here?" Truman scanned the floor of the tunnel and located Azizah. She lay off to Moye's right nearer the entrance. A pool of blood stained the rocky floor around her.

"Azizah? Oh, God." Though she seemed dead, she couldn't be. He'd meet her later when he came up from Nairobi with Hopkins. He rushed to her side and felt for her pulse. It beat weakly.

She moaned.

The sound of footsteps echoed off the rocky floor from the east. Truman stared, a sudden fear seared his mind. Now he knew why he had the rifle.

A hulking man appeared from the shadows.

"What the--" He raised what appeared to be an AK-47 and fired a continuous burst moving from Truman's left to right.

Bullets whined overhead.

182

Sweat stung Truman's his eyes, blurring his vision. He brought the heavy hunting rifle up to his shoulder and fired.

The 450 caliber, belted magnum cartridge thwacked into Jomo's chest and blew through like it was piercing a thick melon.

The force of the blow lifted Jomo off his feet and slammed him onto what was left of his back.

Twitching in agony, Jomo rolled over and crawled deeper into the tunnel, dragging his legs after him.

Truman followed.

Jomo's hands clawed at the floor, seeking a grip to pull himself forward.

Then, with what seemed a supreme effort, Jomo turned his head around and stared. "You are not part of this," he said through clenched teeth.

The man should be dead. Shocked, Truman trained his rifle at Jomo's head.

Jomo lunged for something near his thigh.

Truman fired.

The top of the man's head snapped back and splattered the area with shards of brain and cranium.

Truman stepped forward and, with distaste, pushed up Jomo's shorts. A gun rested in a holster strapped to his thigh. The iron smell of blood thickened the air.

Truman retraced his steps to Azizah, who appeared to have fainted. Grabbing her under the arms, he dragged her out of the tunnel and part way down the road. Then he ran back to Moye.

He sat ashen-faced, his breath sucking into his lungs as if passing through dry reeds, then rattling out with a long hiss through his teeth. "God I hurt."

183

The constable appeared done for. Better to focus on getting the guardian into the vault. At least that way the Maraia stood a chance. He stepped to the vault and tried the lid. "Where's the key?"

"I've got it." Moye winced.

"Where?"

"Pocket."

Truman fumbled inside Moye's pocket for the key. He stepped to the vault and inserted the key into the lock. It snapped open. He threw back the lid and peered inside. Empty as he supposed it would be. Obsessive as he was, he relocked the lid. *Why would I do that?* A moment of insane introspection. Then he remembered the vault had been locked when he and Azizah had penetrated the tunnel. But had his locking of the lid been his last act? He was supposed to reverse the future. "Who's got the guardian?" he demanded of Moye.

"How do you know about...the guardian?"

"Come on, Constable. We don't have a lot of time."

Moye shook his head. "God-damned guardian. I should have given it away."

"Where is it?"

Moye's eyes went to Jomo. "He's got it."

The last thing Truman wanted was to revisit the dead Jomo. Understandably, the constable was feeling his pain but was probably telling the truth. Azizah didn't have it, or she wouldn't still be here.

Nothing to do for the little guy. The wound was mortal and Truman didn't have any first aid at hand. Nothing to do but return to Jomo. *I should have frisked him before.*

184

Truman stepped to Jomo's corpse, trying to ignore the gore above Jomo's neck. Truman rifled the dead man's pockets. In his left front pants pocket, he closed his fingers around the guardian. He returned to where Moye lay bleeding to death.

A shot rang out. The bullet whined overhead and splattered rock from the roof of the tunnel.

Azizah lay on her stomach in full sunlight outside the tunnel entrance, holding her gun unsteadily, both her elbows splayed out on the ground for support.

"No!" Truman shouted.

"Go to hell." She pulled the trigger.

A searing pain tore through his chest. A dense blackness closed in around him. The guardian slipped from his grasp. He staggered toward Azizah.

She gazed at him passively.

He grabbed the iron gate as his knees buckled under him. He twisted and fell. His last thought was that Azizah must have known who he was when she shot him.

***

On top of the plateau, the Shepherd monitored the gunshot from Azizah's revolver. Then a minute later, the explosives blew the tunnel entrances shut, first the eastern entrance, then the western, burying Truman and Moye.

Azizah started the Land Cruiser's engine. She backed up, braked, turned sharply, and sped toward the north end of the plateau.

To the south, the Shepherd picked up the steady throb of the approaching embassy helicopter.

Still hundreds of miles away over the southern Ogaden Desert in Ethiopia, two F/A-20s from the carrier Eisenhower closed rapidly.

The Land Cruiser sped along the base of the escarpment, hit a stone in the track, careened, and rolled onto its side.

The helicopter changed course, circled and landed.

Truman jumped from the helicopter and ran to the crashed SUV.

Some shouting and a gunshot cracked onto the Shepherd's sensitive receivers. That would be the end of Hopkins. Another player dead. Would humans ever be free of the players? They seemed to multiply as fast as they were killed off. The possibility of obtaining the guardian had shifted them into a frenzied search.

Azizah accosted Truman and forced him to do her bidding.

The Shepherd powered up, rose half a meter and shifted his position away from the ruin in anticipation of Azizah's next move. It would not do to have her or Truman see him when they climbed the escarpment to enter the research center ruins.

With Azizah giving directions, Truman righted the Land Cruiser and drove around the north end of the plateau, then headed south to park at the sealed eastern entrance to the tunnel.

Truman and Azizah stepped out of the Land Cruiser. Rope in hand, she forced him up the escarpment to the ruins.

The Shepherd adjusted internal systems in anticipation of what was to come. Truman would need first aid. That had been foretold by the guardian.

The next gunshot was the one that put a bullet through Truman's thigh. He would have to overcome pain to crawl back to the rope and climb to engage Azizah before she could leave him to die.

The Shepherd flinched as his sensors recorded the subtle parting of hemp fibers when the rope broke and the two of them tumbled to the hard floor of the tunnel.

The only consolation he could offer himself was it would not be long, now.

***

Truman awoke. It was dark. He opened his eyes, and it was still dark. Holding his hand in front of his face, he saw nothing. He touched his head and felt the sticky remains of a wound on top of a swollen contusion.

Then he remembered. *Azizah. The fall. I crushed her larynx. I must have hit my head.*

He tried to stand. His left leg buckled under him. He screamed in pain.

Azizah shot me.

He felt around for her but couldn't locate her. Had she survived and left him to die, or had she disappeared like Hopkins? Then again, she could be lying out of his reach in the dark, and he would never know it.

Still passing his hands over the ground about him, he felt the cool surface of a small metal sphere. The guardian. He snatched it up. Azizah must have perished and disappeared. She wouldn't leave the guardian behind. Not after going to so much trouble to obtain it.

He shoved the guardian into his pocket and assessed his situation. He was wounded, on the floor of an abandoned, sealed tunnel, and the only way out was from a doorway four meters above his head.

He lay back and stared unseeing at the darkness above. *The rope broke. At least half of it must be left.* That cut his escape distance to two meters. Still more than he could reach or jump in his condition. He couldn't even see the rope.

What to do?

If he could move the concrete vault, he could try to stand on it to reach the rope.

He fanned out his arms and located the broken half of the rope lying on the floor of the tunnel. He anchored it with a rock to a spot he hoped was beneath the entrance to the passageway where the rest of the rope was tied. Then he crawled with the other end, laying it on the floor, straight out from the wall.

After reassuring himself he could find his way back, he began a slow crawl across the tunnel to the opposite wall. The wound in his thigh shot flashes of pain into his mid-section. He reached to his thigh. Sticky wetness covered his fingers. Though the bullet hadn't hit bone, he was bleeding freely. Not much time. If this kept up, he'd pass out and bleed to death.

He felt the opposite wall in front of him and remembered the vault was closer to the eastern entrance than the passageway opening. After turning left, he crawled until he came to the large rock that hid the vault.

He sat back against the rock, his breath heaving, his thigh throbbing. The darkness provided an odd disorientation. He didn't know at times if his eyes were open or closed, whether the images going through his mind were only there or actual images in the cave.

Besides pain induced flashes of virtual light, he imagined he saw Hopkins, red-haired and red-faced. He probably hadn't been with the embassy. There wasn't enough time between the phone call and when Hopkins appeared for him to be connected with the embassy. Then there was the hotel fire alarm. Hopkins must have dismantled it, as he dismantled whoever had been sent to meet Truman.

Who were these people? They died and slithered away. What was all the money for? Could Moye have been prepared to sell the guardian? It didn't matter now. They were all dead, and he soon would be if he didn't get back to saving himself.

He rolled onto his knees and dragged himself around the rock. The vault was where he had remembered it to be. It was too heavy, at half a meter of concrete on a side, to carry, even if he'd been able to stand. But he could roll it end-over-end. He pulled it away from the wall, then put his back to the wall and took a bearing, hoping he could roll the vault straight across the ten meters to the opposite wall.

He pushed with his good leg, feeling like the mythical Sisyphus. The vault rolled on its side and stopped. Truman shoved it again, loosing a shout of agony, as pain shot like a white light up his leg. Every fourth turn the lid thumped hollowly, sending an echo reverberating the length of the tunnel and back. He had stopped counting the number of rotations when he came to the other side.

After pushing the vault a couple of turns, he stopped to feel for the rope he had laid out on the floor. Not finding it, he pushed again. Finally, the soft fibers brushed his hand. He stopped and rested.

When he thought he had the strength to continue, he jockeyed the vault so its longest dimension lined up vertically, then he began a tortured crawl to get on top of it. Bracing himself against the wall, he put his good foot on the vault and pushed himself up. His screams of pain echoed from the ends of the tunnel, a lonely sound that died without response before it was renewed. He clawed himself to a standing position.

His face wet with tears, he leaned his head against the wall. Its cool surface revived him. He reached one arm above his head and waved it back and forth against the wall. Panic. Nothing but air. Then the fibers of the old rope brushed his hand.

Elated, he grabbed the rope with both hands, and hoping it would not break again, pulled himself up. Hand-over-hand, centimeter-by-centimeter, he rose above the floor. His strength was at an end when a cool draft of air drifted over his face.

He felt for the wall but it had disappeared. The passageway. A few more centimeters up the rope, and he grasped the iron anchors of the rusted gate. He grabbed hold and pulled himself onto the passageway floor.

After lying exhausted for what seemed an eternity, he crawled up the sloping floor toward an easing gloom. *One flight of stairs to climb and I'm out.*

He flopped hard against the lowest step, then dragged his good leg with both hands and shoved his foot onto the tread. With a scream, he lunged upward, clawing desperately. Four steps at a time. He didn't have time to do it any other way.

Finally, he spilled out onto the ground floor of the research ruins, sobbing with relief. His exertions had left his mouth dry, his lips cracked.

He dragged himself over to the vestibule, crossed it and leaned outside. A dark sky arched overhead, studded with stars. The moon had yet to rise. Relief washed over him. *I made it. Water.*

He wasn't even sure if there was water in the SUV. With a sinking feeling, he realized he didn't have the SUV's keys. Though it might be unlocked, getting to it would be a problem. Still, he must try or die.

A glow of lights diffused from below the western side of the plateau. The helicopter. He could go there, then what? He couldn't fly the thing but it had a radio.

His body ached. He started crawling again, angling toward the helicopter. He'd still have to get down the escarpment. He supposed he could breach an edge and tumble the rest of the way. His gunshot leg dragged behind him. His delirium increased, causing him to stop for long periods of time with no desire to continue. Unable to stay upright on his hands and knees, he toppled sideways onto the sand, too weak to go any farther.

A slow scraping sounded behind him. Then a groan and more scraping.

Truman's head filled with a searing realization. *God damn it. She's still alive.* Desperation sent him into a frenzy. His good leg pumped. His hands reached out to claw the sand. But he barely budged.

Her hand latched onto his foot.

He kicked.

Help me. Help me. Only thoughts, getting no farther than his parched throat. *What the hell is she? Zombie. Undead.*

Her clutch was too firm to kick off. Her other hand fell like an iron rake on the back of his thigh.

I'm going to die. He stared blankly, gathering moments to contemplate his death.

A looming darkness slid between him and the canopy of stars.

Azizah's grip loosened.

Truman blinked. For an irrational moment, he wondered if he were back in the tunnel and had only imagined his escape. But he could see the defining edge of what appeared to be a circular object.

He reached a hand skyward, sensing salvation lay above him, anywhere but where he lay. Though he tried to speak, the words died in his throat.

The bottom center of the object dialed open, growing to manhole-size. He peered up at an illuminated interior that resembled an open wound. Then an unseen force raised him up. His head went into the opening first. He slid upward. Close, cloying walls pressed in against him, rippling, drawing him in.

Azizah's hands slipped away.

Does she know what's happening? Her touch is gentle. A send-off? A good-bye?

One panic replaced another. He tried to scream but his throat was too dry.

The orifice closed. An ethereal light filled the distance between his eyes and his brain.

A male voice resonated.

"Welcome, Truman Justis."

***

I've been swallowed whole.

Panic transmuted to terror.

Wet, cloying walls pressed in on Truman from every side. Light bathed his sight wherever he turned his head. He struggled but the walls gave way where he punched and kicked, absorbing the force of his blows.

"Be still," the voice said. "You only exhaust yourself."

Truman's mind went into overdrive. He tried to focus on something, anything but all he saw was the uniform light. Fear washed through his body in shuddering waves.

Damn Brubaker for dumping him into this mess unprepared. Who was Hopkins? Who was Azizah? Did Brubaker know these people? He hadn't been explicit about anything. Hopkins must have made up everything as he went along. At least he was dead, as was Azizah. Or was she? What a ruthless piece of work she turned out to be. Did they have a connection with the UFO?

The light vanished and was replaced by a panoramic view of the terrain outside.

"What the hell? There's the plat--"

The scene shifted. The plateau loomed large in the center of the vision before him. The research center. The scene shifted again.

He didn't have to move his head to see up or down, left or right. He merely turned his mind's eye

193

in the desired direction, and the scene shifted. He was suspended at the focus of some giant IMAX theater with a spherical view and full surround sound. The familiar context of the plateau, the research ruins, the dark sky overhead, and the soughing of a breeze off the lake through the dry grass calmed him. Azizah lay prone on the plateau, somewhere, somehow beneath him.

All reports suggested the alien craft had been benign in nature, showing no hostile intent. Still, none of the reports mentioned being swallowed whole.

Anger seeped in, dissolving his panic. "Are you the alien craft of the Kanapoi Incident?"

"Yes. You have nothing to fear."

"I've been hijacked, shot and left for dead, and you say I have nothing to fear?" Truman tried to maintain his newfound courage but his voice wavered.

"You are safe now."

A rejuvenating massage rippled over his body. Slight pricking sensations on his skin indicated something like needles were being inserted into him. In his mind he protested but his aches and pains dissolved.

He soon felt relaxed and strong. Though he still couldn't move, when he flexed his legs and twisted his head he felt no pain.

"I want out."

"One moment, please. I have to attend to a small problem."

Two jet fighters streaked in from the northeast and passed over the Shepherd with a thundering roar.

194

The fighters began a sharp climbing turn for another pass.

"This is Alpha-Tango leader," the lead pilot chattered. "Bogie remains on the ground. No response to initial flyover. Passenger vehicle parked at eastern entrance to tunnel. Embassy craft is down two klicks north of the western entrance. No signs of life. We're turning for another pass."

"I must leave," the voice said.

"Let me out first!" Truman's panic threatened to overwhelm him.

The image of the turning jets altered, reduced to specks against a fast-receding desert sky, which in turn was replaced with the turquoise blue sphere of the Earth diminishing in size.

"Negative that," one of the pilots said from a barely visible Earth. "It's gone."

The Earth diminished to marble-size, then disappeared altogether. The sun appeared off to one side. It, too, shrank from a discernable disk to a star that merged with a vast field of other stars.

Vertigo swept over Truman. He was in an elevator in free fall, waiting to hit. His heart thumped inside his chest.

"Remain calm," the voice cautioned. "You are hyperventilating."

Truman gulped. "Where are you taking me?"

"To the future."

"The future!" *How did I ever get into this mess*? He felt tugging around his body. He fought to get free. "What are you doing to me?"

"I have removed your clothing. It is damaged and not worth repairing. I shall provide you with a substitute when the time comes."

"When what time comes?"

"Be patient."

Why doesn't this thing ever answer a question? Truman tried blinking, wondering if he could restore his sight so he could see the inside of the object without all the stars in the way. "I don't want to see stars anymore."

The vision vanished to be replaced by the uniform light.

A positive response, Truman thought, a good sign. "I don't like that either."

"What do you prefer? Something from your past, your future?"

"Stop hiding. Please tell me who or what you are." His fear toiled at his resolve to see this through. He was in one of his recurring nightmares where he kept getting farther from his destination no matter what he tried. "Show yourself!"

"You are becoming agitated again. There is nothing more to show. You have seen me, you are in me, and we are traveling to the future. I am the Shepherd."

Truman's mind fumbled with the information. He was obviously in the UFO. So the UFO was calling himself the Shepherd. "Do you know those people? Hopkins. Jomo. Azizah. She should have been dead but she wasn't. Jomo should have been dead. Hopkins, he stayed dead. Are they all...players?"

"Unfortunately."

Truman reeled at the confirmation, given with nonchalance, but having a major impact, causing confusion. "I don't understand."

"There is no reason you should understand. Players are manifestations of *Zug*. Zug and *Gilomir* are extreme expressions of the same entity, a Yin and Yang, or good and evil. You do know of *Gilomir*?

"The Lohner diary was full of references to *Gilomir*, some sort of genome he claimed was responsible for mankind's humanity."

"Correct."

"If I am getting this right, *Gilomir* is here and *Zug* doesn't like it, so he sends players out to mess with him."

"In a rough sense you have grasped what has happened."

Truman felt he'd been rebuffed but he wasn't going to make a big deal about it. If in time the Shepherd would let him know that was fine. In the meantime, the Shepherd seemed open enough that he might expound on other matters. "I get the feeling players are hard to kill."

"Not really. But, although they take human form, they do have certain...capacities as regards dying that humans do not have. For example, if a player kills a player. The player shrivels, disappears and is recycled."

Wow, this Shepherd cut right to the quick. Not like he was withholding anything. Ask away. "Like Hopkins?"

"Like Hopkins. If a player is killed by a non-player, then the player need not actually die. It takes him a while to recycle and continue with his mission. Like Jomo."

"Jomo?"

"Right. You do not know about Jomo. Excuse me. Another possibility is if a player is killed accidentally."

"Azizah. The fall. I didn't mean to kill her."

"Exactly. When a player dies by accident the player can decide to recycle or not."

"That's why Azizah came after me."

"Yes. She was not…dead. Unfortunately, I had to neutralize her."

"Unfortunately? She would have killed me. What do you mean you neutralized her?"

"When I neutralize a player, I do so by injecting them with *Gilomir* DNA. I say unfortunately because, although the injection eventually converts the player to our side, it also alerts other players to what has happened and invites them to converge on the spot."

"I get it, you don't want to call attention to yourself from this *Zug* guy."

"Something like that."

Another pricking sensation, this time low on his thigh. Truman couldn't remember what question he had asked and wondered if he had been injected with a sedative.

"By the way, thank you for obtaining the guardian," the Shepherd said.

The guardian? It held some significance but he couldn't remember what it was. "Is that what this is all about?"

"Why, no. This is all about you."

"Me?" Truman smiled dreamily, amused. How could he be what *it* was all about? The twitching bodies of the two soldiers who had gotten a whiff of the sarin nerve gas rose in his mind. How could he be important after a mistake like that?

The Shepherd must have sensed his confusion. "Ah, yes. You have no way of knowing. I keep forgetting where you are on your world line."

"I don't--" Another needle pricked his skin. He no longer cared about his situation. His life became a pleasant dream.

Truman's inner vision shifted to a stroll he had taken along an isolated beach in the Bahamas. Coconut-laden palms tipped out from the forest and hung over a stretch of white sand. Afternoon sun dazzled off placid, transparent water.

"Is that better?" the Shepherd asked.

Truman nodded. The real walk had lasted for an hour. He had come to the end of the beach where it met a resort development, and he had decided to return to his hotel. He met some local toughs on the way back and an ugly encounter marred the former serenity of his walk. Was the vision going to replay that incident, too? But it didn't. He saw a slight jump as though a filmstrip had slipped in the projector. He was back at the beginning of the walk again.

"Enough," Truman said. "I'll be okay." He drew a deep breath and tried to relax.

"Good. Then I can proceed with your orientation."

"What orientation? I want to go home."

"Please be patient. You cannot go home yet. The guardian instructed me to pick you up and take you to the future. I am sure it has foreseen all the details."

"What does all this have to do with me?"

199

"A lot."

"Who told you that?"

"Ah, such inquisitiveness. I like that. It must issue from the residue of *Gilomir* still in your genomic structure."

"*Gilomir*?" A connection, between one fact and another shorted somewhere in Truman's brain. So alien genetics *were* involved during the Kanapoi Incident. "Who is *Gilomir*?"

"I will show you."

Show me? How? Truman's his whole consciousness imploded to a singularity and dropped to the pit of his stomach. From there it radiated out into an all-encompassing embrace of the universe. It was as though his body lost corporality and expanded to infinity. Then his disorientation returned. The vision vanished as quickly as it had appeared.

"What the hell was that?" Truman still tingled from the experience.

"*Kensho, satori,* enlightenment, *Nirvana,* all manifestations of *Gilomir.* Is that not what you have been trying to attain all your life?"

"How did you induce it?"

"For a brief moment, I put you in touch with your humanity, your *Gilomir.*"

"But you speak of *Gilomir* almost as if he were something separate."

"He is, or was."

"The Kanapoi Incident?"

"The so-called Kanapoi Incident set *Gilomir* free. Since then, you and other men have lost the path to your humanity, which gave you the capacity to achieve oneness. Call it what you will. The

200

greater the degree to which humans were able to connect with their inner selves, the more they were able to achieve the enlightenment you have so ardently sought. Humans with purer strains of *Gilomir* have an easier time, when they bother to try. But, alas, so few ever do."

"That's all that holds me back? Not being able to get to some alien genome I carry?"

"Yes, that is all."

"I want to experience it again."

The Shepherd obliged.

Truman reveled in near ecstasy.

"Enough," the Shepherd said. "You do not want to overdo it."

"But I do." What had come over him? The feeling had been so powerful, so transporting. "I want to be able to go there over and over again."

"And you could, if you are willing to forego your hominid roots."

Truman thought for a while. "I can't really be separated from my hominid roots, can I? It's not a fair question."

"Perhaps not. In any case, you do not have to answer it, now."

"But I--"

"There will be time to know all things."

Chapter Ten

The sympathetic man who stood before Truman wasn't real. That was obvious.

"You came to America when you were ten years old," the man said. "Do you remember your life in Kenya?"

Truman floated, disembodied. He knew he had been drugged and why but he didn't care. If he was indeed in a state of suspended animation, did these thoughts now take months to evolve?

"I lived in Nairobi with my mom. She was British. My dad worked for Lohner...the paleoanthropologist, John Lohner. I never saw Dad much. He'd come home after a dig and stay a while. Then he'd go away. I liked him but he wasn't home much."

"Your father died tragically."

"He died. No one told me how until much later. My mom grieved. A lot of stuff happened right after his death. Lots of officials talking to Mom. Most of them American. Soon after that we took a plane to America. New York. I don't know why we went to New York. If I had been older, maybe I could have figured it out."

"Did you like New York?"

"It wasn't Nairobi. But I guess I liked it. You could be as big as you wanted to be in New York."

"And you became big?"

"I grew, and I struggled. Harlem was a tough place. But Mom pushed me, and I suppose I stayed on track long enough to survive."

"You went to Columbia University and were brilliant in your field."

"Yeah, Columbia..."

The man who wasn't real faded away. In his place, Truman felt a strengthening sense of his surroundings. He was in the Shepherd. But how long had it been?

"We are almost there," the Shepherd said.

"Already?" The memory of Truman's dream lingered. *Why that dream*? Then it evaporated in the fleeting moments of wakefulness to be replaced with a vague anxiety of arrival. An image in his mind's eye showed a flat, forested landscape rushing toward him. An overgrown plateau came into view next to a large lake fed on one side by a river. Inactive volcanic mountains reached skyward, their tops capped with snow.

"Is this Kenya?"

"Kenya of the future. The weather has changed in five thousand years. It now rains a lot."

"That must be the Kerio Gorge." Truman returned his view to the river. "It's running full."

"Lake Turkana is also full. Its shores now encircle the northern base of the Loriyu plateau."

"I see the research ruins." Truman was barely able to contain his excitement at seeing something familiar. "How can any of it still be standing?"

"They built it well. Some of the concrete has dissolved or been overgrown but the stainless steel beams holding it all together remain and should be around another five thousand years."

The view rushed toward him, then stopped.

***

203

The Shepherd landed in a clearing. A hedge of red and yellow hibiscus formed one edge of the clearing, concealing what Truman supposed was the Kerio River beyond. A tangle of jacaranda and tall palms laced with purple bougainvillea and leafy vines formed a wall on the other side. Shiny blue and orange parrots sailed between the trees. Smaller, darker birds flitted between branches and soared above the jungle canopy against a backdrop of puffy gray clouds with dark undersides. The sky, where it showed through, was pastel blue.

Truman tried to look at his wrist but his arms were still pinned. The Shepherd had probably removed his watch, anyway.

A disconcerting pressure pushed at his feet, followed by a swift rise. The Shepherd's sphincter opened to the outdoors. Truman emerged from the fleshy chamber headfirst, a reorientation that wasn't lost on him, and slid off the Shepherd's exterior to the grassy clearing.

He collected himself and stood, feeling very much alone. The air hung with humidity almost thick enough to drink. Though the sun had not reached its zenith, the temperature was suffocating. He stood in knee-high, green grass, laden with droplets of water from a recent rain. The Shepherd had placed lace-up boots on Truman's feet and dressed him in a pair of khaki bush shorts.

"What's going on?" Truman pulled at the legs of his shorts. He had a sinking feeling the Shepherd intended to leave him there.

"It is quite warm." The Shepherd's voice resonated through the humid air. "Since it rains all the time, clothing is of little use. However, I thought you might feel uncomfortable without something."

"That's not what I meant. I'm not staying here!"

He tried to climb back up on the Shepherd but his boots kept slipping. Frustrated, he pounded his fist on the rubbery surface.

"Please stand back," the Shepherd said.

An orifice opened on the side of the Shepherd. A hollow pseudopod two meters in diameter, its end ringed by oscillating cilia, snaked out of the opening and slithered toward the edge of the jungle.

Truman jumped back to avoid being knocked over.

The pseudopod stopped at the dense wall of vegetation. An escalating whine broke across the damp silence of the clearing. A leaf shuddered on a tree, broke free and sailed into the gaping maw. Other leaves left their branches, then vines quivered before coming loose from their moorings to whip after the leaves. All the while the cilia waved the vegetation into the vacuum cleaner-like hose.

A large branch cracked loose. The tree to which it had been attached leaned, then came free, its trunk, roots and clumps of dirt digested in seconds.

Truman stepped back, hands over his ears, fearing he might be sucked in. The tearing noise from the intake became deafening.

Something bulged on top of the Shepherd.

The head of a man appeared, followed by his pale shoulders and the rest of his body. He rose straight up until his feet were even with the Shepherd's surface, tipped sideways as though frozen stiff, bounced, and rolled to the ground.

The man lay enveloped in a thin layer of mucus, which evaporated, leaving him pink-skinned and blinking. He rocked his head back and forth as though loosening his neck. His arms came free from his sides, and he rolled onto his knees. Though Truman stood right next to him, the man paid him no attention but stared at the Shepherd.

A female emerged, similarly sheathed in mucus, fair-skinned and obviously pregnant. She came to rest next to the man and went through a similar unwinding. The fall from the Shepherd didn't appear to have hurt either one of them.

The man helped the woman to her feet, and the two of them stumbled a few meters away, hand-in-hand, then stood together as though waiting.

To Truman they seemed like Adam and Eve, except Adam was shorter than average for a modern male, thickset and muscular. Blond hair hung wet over his ears and formed curly bangs on his forehead, which sloped back at an angle that was more reminiscent of an earlier hominid. Otherwise, he could have stepped out of a bodybuilding magazine. The woman, her condition aside, was no less endowed.

More sucking in of the forest was followed by more people plopping out onto the ground. Organic material went in the side like celery into a food processor and people came out the top. A crowd soon formed. Truman counted forty individuals evenly divided between male and female. Though the first arrivals helped the others to get oriented, they all seemed in awe of their surroundings. Some of them stared at Truman as though waiting for him to assist them in some way or at least tell them what to do.

The high-pitched whine of the pseudopod wound down. The tube and cilia deflated and were retracted into the body of the Shepherd.

"Are they real?" Truman indicated the newcomers.

"They are real," the Shepherd said.

"Why did you make them?"

"They are the solution to our problem."

Truman frowned. "Our problem?"

"Have you forgotten humanity's degraded genome?"

"Of course not."

"Your scientific assessment of the future of the human race was correct. All that remains on the planet of mankind's twenty-first century genome is a race of proto-humans, dispersed and still in decline."

"So, these--" Truman swept his arm to include the pale group of individuals. "--these people are the..."

"Maraia. They will call themselves Maraia."

"So these Maraia represent a rejuvenation, the future of the human race?"

"Yes. Look at them as a booster shot of DNA into the human gene pool. Humans of the future must retain their intelligence. If they do not, then I cannot exist."

Dumbfounded, Truman stared at the Shepherd. "What do humans of the future have to do with your existence?"

"With the aid of the guardian, they will create my creator."

"You're beginning to sound like Doctor Seuss. Are you telling me you are of human origin?"

"I am indirectly of human origin. Unfortunately, I do not have the time now to educate you on the history of my origin."

"What's the rush?"

"I must leave."

"Whoa, whoa." *I've got to stall him.* "In my opinion, forty individuals are hardly enough to secure the integrity of a gene pool. Are the genes of these Maraia so perfect they won't degrade?"

"I have been able to rectify the problem that you so ingeniously uncovered. Hominid DNA entwined with Gilomir DNA no longer seeks to restore an earlier status quo. These Maraia, though somewhat degraded from pure Homo sapiens, for reasons purely of my own confounding, will evolve rapidly into the future. They will not be impeded as you were by the conflict of opposing DNA. What else could I have produced if indeed they were to progress to where they will fulfill their destiny?"

"Your creation. Great. So how do I fit in?"

"I want you to help the Maraia."

Truman laughed. The Maraia would need all the help they could get, judging from their disorientation, but he was only one man. "How?"

"You are a product of the Twentieth Century. It should not be hard."

"So that's why I'm here?"

"It is one reason."

"There're others?"

"Most certainly. Your world line is not complete. You are somewhere along its line and will confront...shall I say...forks in the road. As you

208

then make your decisions, you will begin to understand."

Truman regarded the Maraia with disdain. Something about them bothered him. "Did you have to make them all white?"

"I did not consider the choice important," the Shepherd said. "There is very little sunshine for a thousand years. Plenty of time given their accelerated evolution to evolve darker pigmentation should they need it."

A flash of lightning and a thunderclap caused Truman to jump. "They can't stay here."

"True. They will need to get organized and find shelter."

To Truman the Maraia men all appeared the same, as did the women. No, it wasn't *seen one whitey seen them all*. The Maraia were beautiful humans by any definition, white or black. The women--

"Why are all the women pregnant? Doesn't that add to the complications of trying to figure out how they're going to survive?"

"See, you are already beginning to worry about them. And yes, there will be a certain attrition. They will need your help."

An awkward silence followed.

The Shepherd seemed to shift as though he were anxious. "I must leave now. I have done everything that needs doing."

"Leave?" Truman shouted. "You can't leave me here."

"Do you really want to go back?"

Truman was stunned. "Why the hell would I want to stay?"

"Given time, you might think of a reason. In any case, you do not have to decide now. When next you see me, you can tell me your decision."

"When's that going to be?"

"Two days, plus or minus."

"Don't you already know what I'm going to say?"

"Yes but you could always change your mind."

"That's nonsense. Why do you have to go now?"

"I cannot be here at the same time my past shows up in the future. You have time to think about your decision. Initially, the Maraia will not be able to survive on their own. They need you. Think of yourself as a messiah."

Truman snorted. "You've got the wrong guy for the job."

"You underestimate yourself." The Shepherd began to vibrate.

Truman blanched. *He's serious.* "I'm not going to last very long like this!" His voice rose in desperation as he spread his empty hands. "You've got to give me some tools, food, anything. What about them?" he indicated the Maraia.

He wondered if the Shepherd had heard him, when on the side of the craft, a slight swelling appeared. The surface split, and out popped a black oblong case.

"You should find everything you need to sustain you in that," the Shepherd said.

Truman regarded the case. It was a meter and a half long and about the same around, though flattened. The surface was ribbed and handles protruded, two to a side. He knelt beside the case, located the latches and snapped them open. Inside, he found neatly packed, various articles of clothing, an extra pair of boots, a first aid kit, assorted toiletries, and packets of food.

"This doesn't look like it's going to sustain me for very long."

"It does not have to," the Shepherd said. "The food is for emergencies. You must supplement your diet from local sources."

Truman pushed the clothes and food packets aside. "I don't see a weapon of any sort." He did find a waterproof wristwatch. A Casio. He hoped it had a new battery. He glanced at the time, eleven-fifteen in the morning, April 1. It had been April 1 when he left Kanapoi. The year showed '05. Very clever these watch makers. Replace the first two numerals with an apostrophe and the watch was good for hundreds of years. But what year was it?

"Thanks for the watch. I assume the time and date are correct. What year is it?"

"7005 A.D."

That hit Truman like a bucket of cold water. "You don't mess around, do you?"

"Mess…around?"

Something was telling Truman the Shepherd wasn't all there. At least part of his programming hadn't covered the normal clichés. But what could he expect? "What about a weapon?"

"Here, take this," the Shepherd said. The guardian plopped out of another smaller opening in his exterior.

Truman parted blades of grass to pick it up. "This is a weapon?"

211

"It is all you will need. When next you see me, let me know you have it."

"I don't understand. You already know I have it."

"I do now. Please do as I ask."

Truman hefted the small sphere, then placed it in one of the button-down pockets of his shorts. The Maraia closed ranks and stood as a forlorn group eyeing him and the Shepherd. "Do these Maraia have a leader?"

"Yes, he will identify himself after I leave."

"Does he speak English?"

"He does not have to."

"Then how am I to communicate with him?"

"You have the capacity to speak and understand their language."

"Couldn't you have let them speak English?"

"I suppose I could have but I did not." The Shepherd paused. "Goodbye, Truman Justis."

Exasperated, Truman raised his hands in the air. "How will I know when you return?"

"Ask the guardian." The Shepherd rose above the ground, drifted over Truman's head, then disappeared straight up. A sonic boom reverberated across the forest, and a rush of air clapped together in its wake. Darkened clouds released their rain.

The Maraia stood stock-still and gazed skyward, mouths open to the splattering drops. Given the heavy downpour they could drown doing that. They seemed as dumb as the day they were born, then Truman realized they probably could be.

"Okay, which one of you is the leader!" he shouted. Propelled by thoughts in English, foreign words issued from his mouth. *How had the Shepherd achieved that*?

A male separated himself from the others and approached. "I am the leader."

"Do you have a name?"

"I am called Juvenal." He stood a head shorter than Truman but otherwise looked very similar to the other males. His face was pale, his eyes a deep blue. He stared at Truman, expectantly.

"It's raining." Truman raised his arms from his sides and let the torrent wash off them. "Shouldn't you get your people to some shelter?" Truman wondered if he was projecting his own civilized concern for finding shelter in a downpour. None of the Maraia seemed to be bothered by the rain.

"Who are you?" Juvenal asked. "You are not like one of us, yet you also come from our creator."

They're not as dumb as I thought. "You're right about that. I'm not one of you. I come from a different time and place and have no business being here."

"Nevertheless, you are here, like us. It must be good you are here. What is your name?"

"Truman. Truman Justis."

Juvenal smiled as though embarrassed. "Your name has no meaning. I will call you Sedroth, son of the god who created us."

"My name is Truman. I'm no son of a god, and that thing that created you is no god. It's a machine designed to produce people."

"That is what a god does. So it must be a god."

Frustrated, Truman wiped both hands over his scalp and flicked the rainwater away. "Never mind. Are you going to get out of the rain?"

213

Juvenal tilted his head up at the torrent, squinting. The large drops splashed on his face. "We will do as you say." He stuck out his tongue and drank the moisture.

Perplexed, Truman wondered if the ruins of the research center could provide shelter. Perhaps they could make their way into the tunnel from above if it had not collapsed. "I know a place that is safe and dry. Follow me."

Juvenal cupped his hands to his mouth and shouted to the others.

Truman crossed the clearing and located a break in the hedge. Beyond, the languid water of the Kerio River glided past.

Juvenal caught up to him.

"We'll have to--" No word came to Truman from memory. "--*swim*." Truman used the English word. "Though we'll be carried downstream a ways, it's running slowly enough we can make it to the other side."

"How do we get across?"

"We'll swim," Truman repeated.

"No one knows this...*swim*. If we enter the water we will all die."

A woman, as pregnant as the rest, came up beside Juvenal and whispered something into his ear.

Juvenal stroked her shoulder and motioned for her to rejoin the others. "She is my mate. Her name is Lela. She is with child as are all the other women. Even if the men could swim, the women would never be able to make it across. He addressed his people, something Truman could not make out, and they all headed back across the clearing toward the jungle on the far side.

"Damn," Truman muttered. He decided he'd swim the river anyway and check out the ruins. No sense in everyone crossing if the ruins were in such a dilapidated state they would offer no shelter. "I will go alone. Keep your people together. I'll come back as soon as I can and let you know what I've found out."

Juvenal nodded and turned to rejoin the group.

Poor bastards, Truman thought, how are they ever going to make it?

***

The last of the Maraia disappeared into the thick jungle.

Standing in the warm downpour, Truman felt very much alone and exposed. He imagined predatory animals lurking behind every bush, waiting for a chance to seize him. He returned to where the supply pod lay in the grass, grabbed it by one of its handles, and returned to the river.

At the hedge, he eased himself through and almost lost his footing. The riverbank tucked under the overhanging vegetation, leaving a fall of a meter to the water. Large raindrops splashed the surface of the water raising an agitated mist. Shielding his eyes, he was able see the opposite bank. It was forty meters across the river, which flowed with a strong but sluggish current. If the gorge hadn't filled with silt over the years, the river must be twenty meters deep.

Truman had no doubt he could swim across. He removed his boots and shorts and stuffed them into the pod. After making sure the pod was sealed, he grabbed two of its handles, swung it out into the river, and jumped after it. The pod sank but bobbed to the surface. He pushed it ahead of him and kicked.

Though the current carried him downstream, he made headway toward the opposite bank. When he arrived, he found it was not as steep as the side he had left. He grabbed a low branch with one hand and pulled himself and the pod ashore.

The rain stopped. The sun came out, lighting up the landscape with a million sparkles. He retrieved his boots and shorts and sat for a while looking down at the coursing water as it flowed, hemmed in by the low banks, on its way to the distant lake. So different from the northern Kenyan desert he had left behind.

After catching his breath, he pushed through another brush hedge. It opened onto flat ground. The jungle on this side of the gorge was less dense than what he had left behind.

The plateau rose in front of him. Tangled brush covered its reddish side but there appeared to be a number of ways up its convoluted escarpment. He selected a path less steep than the others and headed for it.

His boots slipped in the wet soil--every two steps forward followed by one back. He would secure a foothold, sling the pod ahead of him, hoping it would catch in something, then pull himself up.

He reached the top, thirty meters above the surrounding area. The clearing where he had left the Maraia lay farther upstream. Snowcapped Mount

Kenya formed a backdrop in the far distance to the south.

His gaze drifted along with the river as it flowed below him to the north. It emptied into Lake Turkana, now swollen beyond its former shores so it engulfed part of the northern end of the plateau. Low trees and shrubs on top of the plateau made it impossible to see the research ruins from where he stood. Had the lake waters swelled so far they engulfed the east and west entrances to the tunnel?

To his relief he hadn't seen any large animals. They must exist but probably didn't venture out into the open during the day. He should have told Juvenal to get up into the trees at night if he didn't return before then. *Do I have to think of everything?* Hopefully, Juvenal was smart enough to have thought of that himself.

After walking a short way, dragging his pod, a glint of light off an exposed stainless steel girder helped him locate the station. Without that clue, he could have passed it by--such was the density of vegetation surrounding it.

It's smaller than I remember. Just as well the others didn't come.

The sun disappeared behind a cloud and it started to rain again.

This is worse than Seattle. He ranged along a wall of tangled vines looking for a way into the ruin. Having seen the place in the dark five thousand years ago, he had only a vague recollection of where the entrance was.

A shadow loomed behind the snaking green vines. The entrance. He squeezed through to the inside of what had been the vestibule, then stepped into the main room on the ground level. It had a low ceiling, which he could almost touch if he stood on his tiptoes and raised his hand. Slotted openings, where long ago glazing had formed windows, stood open to the outside. Roots that had heaved up the concrete and broken through snaked across the floor. Stepping carefully, he crossed the room, looking for the passageway to the tunnel below.

Though the light dimmed, he could still see. As he approached the passageway, he noticed to his left and overhead, a square opening in the ceiling. A brighter light shone from what he supposed was access to a second floor level. Rain coursed through the ceiling opening, so he assumed the roof was only partially intact.

The landing to the stairs leading down to the passageway wasn't as root damaged as the rest of the station. The floor outside also was relatively smooth. Truman dragged the pod up against one wall near the opening and sat down. From there he thought he could do a quick duck into the passageway if he awoke to danger, or run to the second floor opening and try to climb up. He'd investigate the second level later, maybe when he had some help to get up there.

Though the temperature was high, the evaporating water on his skin made him shiver. What a miserable situation. How would he get food? He didn't know the first thing about surviving in the wild, much less in a jungle five thousand years in the future. Hunkering down, he opened the pod and withdrew some hooded raingear. It fit snugly over his head and shoulders. That would stop the shivering but he was still hungry.

The hell with emergencies.

He snatched one of the food packets, tore it open, and removed a cookie-like piece. He bit into it and found a tasty combination of oatmeal-like grain and meat flavoring.

This is more like it. I don't know shit about living off the land.

After finishing his cookie, he felt better. The rain stopped pounding outside. Through the dripping runoff from the roof, twinkling shafts of sunlight dappled the convoluted floor of the bunker. He stood and entered the dark passageway. It seemed like yesterday Azizah had forced him down into it at gunpoint. He called into the darkness, only to hear his voice fade with no hint of an echo. Though it gave him the willies, he inched his way down the flight of stairs, recalling with each step the last time he was there and his subsequent agonizing ascent. His hand played along the wall to his right, the other hand held out in front of him.

He came to the end of the wall. The iron anchor to which the rope had been tied was gone. He picked up a stone and tossed it into the darkness. It hit the tunnel floor a second later with a dry clatter. The sound reverberated from the ends of the tunnel. Still closed, he thought but otherwise clear, no lake water inside.

He returned to the main room, pulled his hooded rain gear tight around him and tried to relax. He concentrated on his breathing, forcing all thought from his mind.

It didn't work.

How easily the Shepherd had made it work. How ironic all of mankind had it within them to

219

experience such a transporting enlightenment. Truman tried to recreate the experience but failed to find the path that had led to the ecstasy. Frustrated, he reached into his pocket and withdrew the guardian.

Hold it and ask, the Shepherd had said.

Truman closed his hand around the sphere. What now? Would it work for him?

Something resembling a screen opened inside his mind with a menu of options down one side. Though he tried, he was unable to decipher what they meant. Maybe he had to think his question? Like thinking where he wanted to look when he was inside the Shepherd.

What am I doing here, anyway?

"*You are integral to the survival of the Maraia. They must survive if they are to build A4-Ni.*"

The voice inside his head startled Truman but gave him some reassurance. Getting information from the guardian wouldn't be difficult at all. *But according to the Shepherd they won't do that for another three thousand years. I'm not going to live that long.*

"*What you teach them will carry beyond your death.*"

Why me?

"*There is an eighty percent probability you are the correct person. You are a geneticist. You also seek knowing....the spiritual kind. The two will serve you well as you teach the Maraia.*"

Truman didn't like what he was hearing. Eighty percent meant he could be stuck here. What did the other twenty percent hold? *How long do I have to wait for the Shepherd?*

"The Shepherd is in transit having exited orbit around the Cygnus X-1 black hole. His estimated time of arrival is two days from now at eight-twenty in the evening."

Truman closed his eyes and returned his attention to the menu of options, focusing on one. The display changed and offered a number of other options, each one showing varying degrees of strength from weak to strong. He picked one at random. The guardian took up a narrative while showing him a scenario.

***

I see Truman is concerned despite his previous feelings about not wanting to get involved.

"You can't stay here," he says to Juvenal. "You can't defend yourselves."

"But there is no place to go," Juvenal says. "We cannot cross the river--" A woman in the group gives out an anguished cry. "--and another starts her labor."

***

Truman marveled at the object in his hand. It was projecting in his mind something that hadn't happened to him yet. A possible future scenario? Did the strengths of the display options have anything to do with the probability of the scenario coming true? The one he had examined had been relatively strong.

Interesting. He directed his thought to one of the dimmer displays.

His head filled with strange images and feelings of fear and anxiety. They tumbled in, swirled around then settled, each tucking away in what

221

seemed the right place, integrating with his existing knowledge.

***

I see a fog, a veil lift as Truman's sight clears. He stumbles toward a cave.

A horrific beast pursues.

Truman falls, then struggles to rise.

The beast grabs and pulls him back through the mud. Sharp teeth and claws tear at his body.

***

Truman tried to pull out of the vision but couldn't. In desperation, he threw the guardian against the opposite wall.

The vision ceased.

Covered in sweat, his heart thudding, an overwhelming sense of foreboding lingered in his mind. So, not all the visions were pleasant. What else could the guardian do? But he had had enough for the moment.

The light had dimmed outside. His watch told him it was past six. Normally, he wouldn't be tired but after what he'd been through, sleep beckoned. He found a level area of the floor, spread his hooded rain gear out onto it, and lay down. Sleep came slowly. He'd have to do something about building a bed in the morning.

Chapter Eleven

A deer-like animal poked at the growth of vines outside the ruins. Morning light shone on the animal's dappled coat and reflected from leaves still wet from the rain. The deer sniffed at a leaf, bit, and pulled, then stood chewing before selecting another leaf.

Truman stretched and yawned.

The deer froze. It peered into the gloom of the ruins, then stepped away from the entrance and bolted toward the south, out of sight.

Truman's body ached from sleeping on the hard floor. His mouth was dry, and he was hungry. He rummaged in the supply pod. His hand hit a small container, which he picked up and opened. Inside, he found a piece of steel and a chunk of flint. Fire-making materials. He closed the container and placed it in his pocket.

He dug in again and grabbed a food packet. Until he found another source of food he would be dependent on the contents of the pod.

Truman ambled to the edge of the room, munching on a cookie, when he remembered he had cast the guardian against the far wall the night before. After locating the small sphere and seeing that it appeared undamaged, he stuffed it in another of his pockets. He headed for the exit, unable to dispel the feeling the ruin could give way at any moment and crush him.

Outside, the hot and humid air pressed around him. The low morning sun gave the flat red rock of the plateau a deep ruddy hue, contrasting with the riotous green bush scattered over it. Here and there indentations in the rock held water from the night's rain. Truman knelt by the nearest one and ducked his head to take a long drink. The water, already warm, was at least pure, not having been there for more than an hour since sunrise.

He splashed the rest of the water over his smooth scalp and face. There should have been a stubble. He supposed the Shepherd had depilated him. Truman rubbed his finger over his teeth, toothbrush fashion. There had been a toothbrush in the pod but he was not inclined to return for it. Instead, he walked to the eastern edge of the plateau.

Shielding his eyes, he tried to locate the clearing where the Shepherd had created Juvenal and the Maraia. He followed the line of the river south until it came to a clearing, hopefully the one he sought. If the Maraia were up and about, they were out of sight in the thick jungle.

From his location on the plateau he could look down on the expanded waters of Lake Turkana. Its shore came all the way inland, almost as far as the blocked eastern entrance of the tunnel below him. The Kerio River emptied into the lake a kilometer away, splaying out into an alluvial plain and pushing its cloudy spill into the main body of the lake.

He tried to remember the level of the western entrance relative to the eastern. From a dim memory, the western was lower.

He hiked across to the western edge of the plateau, following one of many animal paths that snaked through the brush. Looking down, he confirmed what he had thought. The lake extended inland on that side, submerging the western entrance to the tunnel.

He hiked south along the edge, searching for an easy way to descend to the lake shore below. A short distance later he picked up another animal trail that eased over the edge and descended across the contour of the steep escarpment.

The path leveled out halfway down the escarpment. Truman continued around a bend, where the trail seemed to end at a large rock that had sheared away from the main mass of the cliff. The path snaked behind the rock and disappeared through a small opening between the rock and the face of the escarpment.

Truman got down on his hands and knees and crawled forward. The opening was tight but passable. The passage continued for two meters. At the far end, Truman stared in awe.

A huge section of the escarpment had fallen away, leaving behind a deep recess into the plateau. He reckoned the length to be a hundred meters across. The roof of the cave soared high over his head to form a natural shelter.

He climbed to the rear of the cave, some thirty meters in. With his back to the wall, he surveyed the site. The bottom lip of the cave was five meters above the tops of the trees. The lumpy green carpet stretched out for as far as he could see to the west. To the north, he could just make out the shore of the encroaching lake.

What a perfect spot to shelter the Maraia. The cave was dry. It had access to water and food in the jungle. And it was defensible, since the floor of the cave came to an edge and dropped precipitously. The only entry was through the opening behind the rock.

Truman cupped his hands to his mouth and shouted. The sound ricocheted off the cave roof and spread out across the jungle, giving vent to his excitement. He retraced his steps to the slit in the rock, climbed back over the top of the plateau and descended the other side.

He came out farther south along the wall near another cave. It was much smaller than the one he had left and penetrated the cliff through a door-sized opening.

Truman peered into its dark interior but decided not to investigate, not knowing what might lurk inside. He began beating his way through thick growth to the river. He climbed over vines and fallen trees hidden by brush. Every once in a while he came to a small clearing and made quick progress through long grass before reaching the now familiar thick vegetation along the edge of the river. His shorts were soaking wet from the moisture of the jungle. Here and there, angry scratches snaked across his chest.

At the hedge, he pushed through and stood on the shore to take his bearings. He had emerged across from the clearing where the Shepherd had landed. Still no sign of Juvenal and the others. Truman marched upstream, gauging where he should enter so his forward motion, vectored with the current, would land him near the clearing on the other side. He dove in and set out for the opposite shore. Aided by the current, his strong strokes and clumsy kicks with his boots on brought him to the other side, downstream from his intended destination.

He hauled himself out and sloshed back to the clearing.

"Juvenal!" Truman peered at the surrounding wall of silent vegetation. Panic flashed through his mind. If the Maraia didn't show, then he was alone. He realized how much he wanted to see them again.

Juvenal stepped into the clearing and waved.

Relieved, Truman jogged over to him. "I'm glad to see you." He extended his hand, surprised at his own enthusiasm.

"I am glad you are here, too." Juvenal grasped Truman's hand in both of his and squeezed. "We are all on the other side of those trees." He pointed. "There has been some difficulty."

***

As Juvenal led him through a copse of trees, chaotic shouts from the other Maraia mingled in the still air with the grunts of animals.

The Maraia were huddled along one edge of a smaller clearing with their backs up against a stand of trees. In front of them three hyenas snapped at each other and pawed at something on the ground.

With raised sticks, the Maraia men closed ranks in front of the women. One woman lay bloodied on the ground. A Maraia man, scratched and bleeding from a head wound, attended to her.

A baby's cry split the morning air.

The hyenas glanced in the direction of the sound, then returned to their bickering.

"One of the women has given birth," Juvenal said. "The hyenas came and are fighting over the afterbirth."

"You can't stay here," Truman said. "The hyenas may not stop with the afterbirth."

"I have armed the men with clubs and told them to gather the women and move to that grove of trees over there. They can defend themselves there if the hyenas decide to attack. But there is no other place to go. We cannot cross the river--" A woman in the group gave out an anguished cry. "--and another starts her labor."

"I have found a large cave on the other side of the plateau. Once we get across the river you will have a place of refuge."

"But how can we cross? It was impossible before and will be even more difficult with infants."

Truman thought for a moment. "We'll build--" A Maraia word did not appear in his mind. "--a *bridge*."

Juvenal stared at him with puzzlement.

Truman knelt and grabbed a stick. He drew a groove in the damp soil, then he laid the stick across the groove. "This is the river," he said. "This is a bridge." He traced his finger across the stick. "If we can find a downed tree long enough in the forest we can float it across the river."

Juvenal's face lit with comprehension. "We will begin at once." He ran to the Maraia shouting orders. Three men broke away from the group and returned with him.

"We must hurry," he said to Truman. "The rains will come again, and I fear the hyenas will develop a taste for our flesh."

Led by Juvenal they pushed into the thick forest. Felled trees lay on the ground rotting. Healthy trees towered overhead, rising forty and fifty meters to the canopy above. Their trunks were long and slender, their root systems shallow. Together they held each other upright but here and there the wind had pushed the trees, toppling them at crazy angles to be held in place by vines and lanyards.

Truman located a candidate. The tree had been uprooted and appeared to be long enough, yet not so big around it would be too heavy for the combined strength of the men to carry.

He and one of the Maraia men began pulling away the vines.

"I will get the others," Juvenal said.

Truman nodded.

Juvenal had only been gone a short time when he reappeared, his face contorted with fear. "Sedroth! We are being attacked!"

"By the hyenas?"

"A man-beast!"

What now? The Shepherd had given no indication other hominids existed or posed a threat.

He hurried behind Juvenal, who ran back to the clearing.

The high-pitched screams of the women, and the tenor grunts and cries from the men interspersed with resounding thumps of wood smacking onto bone.

Truman stepped from the jungle.

Pandemonium met his eye. At the center of the clearing, a squat caricature of a man stood surrounded by Maraia. The beast was human in shape but out of proportion. Reddish hair covered a massive body with skin as black as coal. His torso was as thick as the trunk of a tree. In each hand he swung a wooden club. The beast raged at the circled Maraia, laying low first one man then another.

Truman shouted above the din, hoping to distract the brute.

The man-beast whirled on Truman, squinting with beady, bloodshot eyes that sat close together over his flat nose, giving him a demented look. Without warning, he brushed aside those standing in his way and bolted for Truman at a dead run.

Truman lurched toward the larger clearing, tripped and fell, then scrambled up and ran for his life. He cleared the dividing brush and started across the grassy field. He could hear the ah-ha panting of the man-beast gaining on him.

Truman's boots clumped through the wet grass. He came to the hedge, plunged through it, and dove into the river. He rolled onto his back and kicked out into the slow current.

The man-beast hurtled after him but skidded and grabbed at the hedge to stop his fall into the river. He regained his footing, then glared at Truman, who stroked out into the current.

Truman let the river carry him downstream. The man-beast stalked him from the shore, testing the water but refusing to jump in.

"Hey!" Truman shouted. He splashed water toward the beast who became even more agitated. Truman kicked and cajoled, then struck out for the opposite shore.

With a roar, the beast leapt into the river. Though he sank, he came up sputtering, flailing at the water in a parody of Truman's swimming. But the man-beast's efforts to stay afloat were ineffectual, and the current pulled him under, taking him bobbing downstream.

Truman gained the opposite shore and climbed out. He peered downstream but couldn't tell if the beast had drowned, crossed over, or regained the same side.

He hiked back up his side of the river until he was opposite the clearing. Juvenal and a couple of the Maraia men ranged the far side looking for him.

"I'm here," Truman called.

They waved enthusiastically.

Truman plunged into the river and swam to the other side. *We need the bridge. All this swimming is wearing thin.*

***

"What of the beast?" Juvenal asked when Truman came ashore.

"I hope he has drowned but I can't be sure. Where did he come from?"

"They say--" Juvenal indicated the two men with him. "--he appeared out of nowhere. Before anyone could react he grabbed one of the men and shouted, 'Guardian. Guardian.' No one knew what he wanted, and everyone was afraid. He threw down the first man who approached him, took his stick, and broke it in two. Then he attacked the others. 'Players!' he screamed." Juvenal shuddered.

The image of linebacker Hopkins came to mind. According to Azizah, Hopkins had been a player. He also had red hair and a massive build but that's where the comparison ended. "Is everyone all right?"

"No. We have lost two men. Their skulls were crushed." Juvenal brushed aside tears. "The beast kept coming. If you hadn't distracted him we would all be dead."

"We must build the bridge and get everyone to the cave. At least there, we stand a chance against this monster."

Tears falling freely now, Juvenal gazed at Truman. "We are not animals. We will attend to our dead first."

"But--"

"There is time. And if there wasn't, then we would make time."

Juvenal led the way back to the small clearing. When they arrived the others were grouped around two prone figures. Their women knelt beside them, rocking back and forth in grief. For the moment the commotion had scared away the hyenas but Truman feared they would return, perhaps with other scavengers.

Truman stepped up to the bloodied bodies and felt for a pulse in each. "There is no life in them. How do you propose to tend to them?"

"We will commit them to the waters of the river. Their spirits will tame the river and help us to cross." Juvenal motioned to the bodies, and four Maraia men stepped forward to lift them.

The Maraia carried the bodies to the edge of the river.

Truman wondered about the sophistication of the ritual Juvenal had proposed. The Shepherd must have taught them something. Then why not everything? Of course, whatever they did know was one less thing Truman would have to teach them.

232

"Will you say some words, Sedroth, to send them on their way?"

Truman gazed at the mangled remains. "Did they have names?"

"This one--" Juvenal indicated the near corpse. "--was assigned the name Eloh. The other, Saleh."

Truman glanced at the Maraia, who stood in a tight group, staring at him, waiting for him to say something. Truman cleared his throat, feeling out of his element, nervous.

"Eloh and Saleh. We give your bodies back to the earth from which they came. Though you lived but a short time, your souls are still carried by your brethren and your unborn children. We bid you goodbye. May you rest in peace." Truman took a step back to indicate he was finished.

The four Maraia men rolled the bodies to the edge and allowed them to drop into the river. They made little splash, sank, then bobbed to the surface farther downstream before disappearing in the brown swirl.

Juvenal came up to Truman. "Those were good words, Sedroth."

Though I have only known these Maraia a short time, I feel drawn to them and their struggle. His first reaction had been to leave them on their own. Why should he want to stay? He thought about what the Shepherd had said. "Given time, you might think of a reason..."

He put an arm around Juvenal. "We must now concentrate on building the bridge."

A sob caught in Juvenal's throat. "You are right." He ordered the remaining men to follow him into the forest.

At the selected tree, they removed the last of the restraining vines and pushed, letting the tree fall. Its leafy canopy snapped away, leaving a long straight trunk of forty meters. With the men lined up equally on either side, they lifted in unison and dragged the tree out of the jungle toward the river.

At the river they rolled the tree parallel to the bank where it narrowed somewhat to thirty meters.

"All right," Truman said to three of the men. "I want you to hold this end of the trunk. The others will push the top end into the river. We'll let the current swivel the end to the other side. Once there, we can lift the log above the surface of the water and secure it. I'll go with the end in the river. Juvenal, I want you to pick someone to come with me. He doesn't have to swim but he'll have to hold on tight to the log."

"I will go," Juvenal said. "The others can hold the log here."

Truman thought Juvenal should stay but wasn't about to waste time arguing. He showed Juvenal where he could hold onto the log, then instructed the others to ease the log out into the current. It picked up the log and angled it out into the river. Truman held on and swam along with the end. The mass of the water brought the log around with increasing speed. It slammed into the far bank and began slipping downstream. Water piled behind it.

"Hurry," Truman called to Juvenal. "We have to ease it up before the river takes it away.

Truman scrambled out of the water and with Juvenal's help heaved at the log. They managed to roll it up onto one of its broken branches, which was enough to lift it above the river. They stabilized the log by rolling large rocks up against it. The log hung suspended above the river, high enough to let the water slide beneath it, at least until the rain started again.

The men on the far side had seen Truman and Juvenal push rocks up to stabilize the log and did the same thing on their side.

Truman led the way back across the new bridge, finding its surface wide enough that balancing on it wasn't difficult. He noticed Juvenal was far more agile and could probably have crossed without losing his balance on a log half the size.

"I'll get the others." Juvenal ran back across the clearing.

A moment later he reappeared at the head of the Maraia. They were a bruised and haggard-looking group. Two of the women carried infants.

Truman worried about the infants but the group barely hesitated as the first of them started across.

Half of them were across, including the women with the infants, when a cry went up from one of the men at mid-bridge. He stopped and pointed upstream.

All eyes turned.

To Truman's horror the man-beast had secured a short log of his own. He was sitting astride it, waving his clubs in the air and bearing down on their bridge like a battering ram.

The rest of the Maraia scampered across the bridge and took up defensive positions at its western end.

The man-beast slammed into the bridge. His log rotated sideways.

The bridge shook its moorings. With a loud crack it broke in the middle and angled into the current. The river took both sides downstream with the beast still sitting astride his log.

At least the Maraia were all across. "We'll have to deal with the man-beast later," Truman said. "Let's get to the cave."

If the man-beast were a player, Truman presumed he and the Maraia were in trouble. From what he had witnessed of Hopkins and Azizah, players would stop at nothing to get the guardian. The beast didn't know Truman had the guardian. At least he didn't think the beast knew.

Had the Shepherd known players were in the future? To his dismay, he realized the Shepherd probably did know and was leaving it to Truman to sort out.

Chapter Twelve

The sun hung on the western horizon, skipping orange light across the top of the jungle canopy and setting the red escarpment of the plateau aglow. One by one, the Maraia came to the narrow entrance and squeezed through to emerge into the vast shelter of the cave.

Juvenal surveyed the overhanging roof. "This will be a good home."

"After everyone is inside, we need to decide how to defend this place," Truman said.

Juvenal raised a brow. "How can we do that? We have sticks and stones. We are no match for the beast's strength."

"We could build a--" Again the word did not appear. "--a *net*. We can collect vines from the jungle below and weave them together into a net, which we can suspend above the entrance slit. When the beast tries to come through, we will drop it on him. With him entangled, we should be able to subdue him."

Juvenal still didn't look like he understood. "What am I to do?"

"Have some men collect vines from the forest. They should take only long and strong ones. Ones that are still green. When they return, I will show you how to build a net."

Juvenal sent three men out to the jungle to gather the vines while the rest of the Maraia spread out on the terraced surface of the cave, staking out respective territories.

"I'm going back to walk on this side of the bank to see if the man-beast got out anywhere," Truman said to Juvenal. "If he got out on the other side, hopefully he's stuck there."

"I will go, too." Juvenal seemed determined.

Truman figured he could use the company if he met up with the brute.

They returned to the eastern foot of the plateau's escarpment. After pushing their way back to the river where the bridge had been secured, they began a careful examination of the soft bank looking for footprints. They saw none.

"He must have been swept far downstream," Juvenal said.

"I'm amazed he survived the first time he was in the water." Truman knelt. "Look here," he whispered.

Juvenal came up beside him.

A large human footprint pressed into the riverbank mud, followed by more prints that led into the bush toward the northern end of the plateau. Truman put his finger to his lips, and the two of them followed the trail into the bush. Thick growth merged overhead, blocking out the sky and any remaining light.

They penetrated the jungle to halfway between the river and the plateau. A rustling sound came from up ahead.

Truman motioned Juvenal behind him, and they proceeded single file until they came to the edge of a clearing. Crouching down, Truman peered into the clearing.

The man-beast stomped back and forth on the far side. He had erected the beginnings of a lean-to shelter. Poles stood at four corners with cross braces lashed to them with vines. He was in the process of attaching layers of palm leaves to the sides and roof. Scattered around the base of the lean-to lay an assortment of crude tools--scrapers, a stone adz, and a sharpened stick for a spear.

Juvenal's brow creased with concentration as he gazed at the tools.

The sky darkened and heavy raindrops began to splatter the leaves around them. Lightning flashed followed by deafening thunder.

Truman signaled they should retreat. After backing away from the clearing, the rain increased to such an intensity with multiple flashes of lightning that Truman feared for their lives.

They came to the escarpment. Truman felt his way along its slippery expanse searching for a trail leading to the top. Instead he came to the smaller cave he had discovered before.

The entrance was a couple of meters high and one and a half wide. The roof of the cave went in level four meters before curving down at the end.

A flash of lightning and Truman verified it was empty. "We'll wait out the storm in here."

He ducked inside and stepped away from the opening.

Juvenal followed him in.

Truman rummaged in his pocket for his steel and flint. He located some dry moss and sparked a fire, then transferred it to the moss and added small twigs. From near the entrance he dragged exposed dry roots from the ground and added them to his fire.

"That is magic." Juvenal reached out his hand to the flickering flame.

"Don't burn yourself." Why hadn't the Shepherd told them how to make fire? But there were a lot of things the Shepherd had failed to tell them.

Is that where I come in?

As the light grew the walls of the cave illuminated. They were flat and finely textured.

They made Truman think of caves discovered in his own time, carrying images from a distant past. Here he was in the future. A blank wall in front of him. What images might he convey given the chance.

As the rain continued its constant roar outside, Truman scooped up a handful of ochre mud near the entrance and returned to the wall. He thought a moment, then smeared some of the mud in a circular shape. The Shepherd. He took his fingers and began penciling in stick figures representing the Maraia.

Juvenal watched him with interest. "What are you doing?"

"Killing time."

Juvenal frowned.

"I'm painting," Truman said. "This here's the Shepherd. These represent your people."

Juvenal smiled. He went to the entrance and scooped up his own handful of mud. To Truman's right, Juvenal began dabbing in a larger figure. He glanced from the figure to Truman and back again.

"Not bad," Truman said, when he realized the figure was supposed to be him. The clay Juvenal had scooped up was darker than Truman's. "Here, use some of this, like this." Truman added some highlights to the figure. This was becoming fun.

An hour later they had found two more colors of clay and covered half of wall with a crude mural.

The rain stopped. The sun came out and shown through drips at the entrance, flickering rainbow patterns into the cave.

"I like painting," Juvenal said.

"You are a fast learner. We better get going before the others miss us.

They left the cave and made their way north until they came to the trail they had used to descend. A few minutes later they were on top of the plateau. They crossed and descended to the entrance rock.

Back at the cave, Truman set about showing the men how to weave the vines together to form a tight net. When the net had grown to a size Truman judged sufficient, he set the net on poles above the slotted entrance to the cave. The crudeness of the trap would require it be manned at all times. It was impossible with a lack of tools to fashion any sort of trigger mechanism. But Truman didn't think they would have to wait very long before the man-beast tracked them down and tried to attack.

In the deepening gloom before moonrise, two men positioned themselves on a ledge on either side and above the entrance, holding the net and waiting. Truman arranged for them to be replaced every couple of hours. Determined to stay awake, Truman decided it would be a long night.

Sometime after the fourth shift, a stone clattered off the trail outside the entrance and rolled down the escarpment. In the dim light from a moon just risen, a shadowy figure loomed. It knelt, then filled the slit entrance. A moment later it came out into the cave and stood.

The net dropped over the man-beast. The Maraia men pounced on him and pinned him down. He struggled, then, probably seeing he was outnumbered and overpowered offered no further resistance but glared up at Truman.

"Take those extra vines and tie his legs first. Then bind his arms close to his body," Truman ordered.

Though the vines were not by themselves very strong, the sheer number of vines wrapping his legs and arms formed an unbreakable casing. Truman and three other Maraia men dragged the beast to the wall at the back of the cave and propped him up in a sitting position.

"Have some of the men break branches from that dead tree over there." Truman indicated a tree that had tried to grow at the front edge of the cave and failed. The dry wood was brought to him.

Truman piled small splinters together then layered them with larger pieces. He removed the case containing the flint and steel from his pocket. Taking a small bit of kindling, he struck steel to flint. A spark leapt from the flint and caught in the kindling. Truman cupped his hands and blew. The spark glowed, casting an orange light out of his hands. Another soft breath and a flame caught. Truman transferred the flame to the stacked wood. In a moment, he had a fire going.

The flame rose higher and threw its light over the cave.

All the other Maraia except Juvenal issued sighs of awe.

The man-beast stared at the flames passively. "Fire," he said in English, his voice deep and guttural.

Juvenal put a hand on Truman's shoulder and leaned forward. "What does he say?"

"He is speaking a different language than yours, *English*."

"Do you understand him?

"Yes. Let me talk to him."

Truman stepped close to the beast and squatted in front of him. The Maraia stood in a line behind Truman, looking on.

"Who are you?" Truman asked.

"Cathcar." The sound rumbled from deep within the man-beast's chest. The trace of a smile twitched on the beast's lips. His teeth were large and blocky, discolored yellow.

"My god." Truman stepped back, as though pushed by an invisible hand. "You're...you're a--"

"Player." Cathcar did not smile this time. "I kill."

"Yes you do. Are you Hopkins?"

"No answer." Cathcar closed his eyes and leaned back.

"We should kill him now." Juvenal stared at Cathcar and drew his hand across his throat.

"How about it Cathcar. Either you decide to be more forthcoming or I leave you to these men."

"What want?"

"What are you doing here?"

"Guardian."

"Why is the guardian so important?"

"Make strong. Show past. Show future."

243

Truman thought about the guardian resting in his pocket. The cloth of his shorts seemed too thin a barrier to hide it from Cathcar. *Can he sense somehow I have it?*

But Cathcar's eyes left Truman and ranged over the Maraia behind him. "Who they?"

"They're the Maraia," Truman said.

"What do here?"

Truman didn't like the turn of interrogation. "I'll ask the questions."

Cathcar closed his eyes.

Truman decided he would get no further questioning the brute that night. "We'll leave him here," he said to Juvenal. "There's not much more we can do with him tonight, anyway."

"Why wait. Kill him."

"No. Not yet. We might kill him later but first I need to know more about what is going on. Put a guard on him. I think we all need some sleep." Truman yawned. "We'll deal with this in the morning."

Juvenal stared past Truman, causing him to turn.

Cathcar had opened his eyes again and glared in their direction. "You dead man, Truman Justis."

***

A nightmare chased away Truman's sleep. He jolted awake.

In the weak dawn light, the man-beast sat, as he had before, propped against the wall of the cave. His eyes were closed. A couple of meters away, the guard also leaned against the cave wall, sound asleep. So much for security.

244

Truman stepped to the edge of the cave and relieved himself over the slope. Heavy, gray clouds stretched as far as he could see, blocking any sunshine.

Despite the dreariness, Truman was in good spirits. If he could make it through the next few hours, then he'd be able to hitch a ride back to 2005 with the Shepherd. With Cathcar incapacitated, Truman could think of no impediment to staying alive until then.

Of course, the needs of the Maraia remained. Perhaps he could take Juvenal to collect Cathcar's tools. These would get the Maraia going in the right direction and save him a lot of time instructing them on tool-making. Then he'd retrieve his supply pod and move into the cave. With all the Maraia around, he'd be safe from wild animals and could also keep an eye on Cathcar.

Truman buttoned his fly and returned to the cave. The fire he had lit the night before still burned at the back of the cave. Its warm glow gave some cheer against the morning damp.

Juvenal squatted next to a rough pile of fruit someone had collected and placed on the cave floor. Bananas and papayas mixed with mangos and what appeared to be pomegranates.

"Who picked the fruit?" Truman asked.

"Owyn." Juvenal offered Truman a papaya. "This is a good place. We have water from the spring, and the jungle below contains much fruit. Jonah also saw game in the bush."

Truman took the papaya. As far as he knew, papayas hadn't been indigenous to this part of the world in thousands of years, yet now they seemed to grow in abundance. Perhaps global warming had benefits after all. He dug his fingers through the soft skin and broke the papaya in half. After scraping the slippery black seeds onto the ground, he chewed the meat of the fruit from the peel.

"We have kept the heat flower alive," Juvenal said proudly.

"I noticed. That's good. I'll show you how to rekindle it if it dies but for now it is well you feed it." Truman looked at Cathcar. "Our prisoner sleeps."

"The guard says Cathcar has not moved for a long time. I hoped he might be dead but when I examined him, his nostrils flared."

Truman threw the peel over the edge and wiped his hands on his shorts. "I want to investigate Cathcar's lean-to and collect his tools. I also want to get my...*supply pod* and bring it over here. No sense staying up in the ruins alone."

"What is *supply pod*?"

"The Shepherd gave it to me."

Juvenal stared at him without comprehension.

"God gave it to me. It contains items that help me live here, like the tools to make the heat flower."

Juvenal nodded.

After making sure the surveillance of Cathcar would be maintained, Truman headed for Cathcar's lean-to with Juvenal close behind.

Truman glanced at the sky. "We'd better hurry. It's going to rain."

"Does it always rain?"

"So I've been told."

Some minutes later, they came to the lean-to. Layers of palm fronds enclosed its three sides and

246

the roof, leaving one side open. The workmanship was very good, each frond tied with vine lanyards at regular intervals to a stick frame. Inside, the tools were stacked neatly.

Truman ducked under the open side and stepped over to the tools. "He's been busy."

"What are these?" Juvenal picked up a short stick with a shaped stone bound to its end.

"An *adze*. You can use it to kill an animal, or another human being, for that matter. I hate to think what Cathcar would do with it." Truman picked up another implement. "This is a spear. See how the point has been sharpened by burning it in... *fire*, the heat flower. The fire also makes the wood harder."

"The point would make it easier to penetrate flesh."

"You learn fast." Truman indicated the other tools. "These are scrapers for digging. These sharp stones are for working skins."

A stretched animal hide on a rack leaned against one wall. Next to it were the animal's meaty remains. The fat had been rendered and collected in crude earthenware containers.

"This is a... *lamp*." Truman picked up one of the containers. "Fire can be transferred to it to make light." He wrinkled his nose at the stench of rancid fat. "We can pile Cathcar's tools on this framed skin and carry them back to the cave."

After loading the tools, Truman hefted the front of the frame and led the way back to the plateau. They had reached its top when a crack of thunder preceded a morning rain.

"We better find some shelter and wait this out," Truman said. "The...*research ruins* are over there."

With large raindrops splattering around them, Truman hurried toward the ruins.

He ducked under the concrete slab of the vestibule and motioned for Juvenal to follow.

"What is this place?" He stepped into the vestibule, slicking water from his body.

Truman led the way into the main first floor space. Rainwater dribbled through the stairway opening from the second floor. Outside, water from the roof cascaded over the sides, obscuring some of the open windows in sheets of water.

"A long time ago, men much like you and me built this structure to study a mystery."

"A mystery?"

"The Shepherd, the object you refer to as God, appeared here many years ago. After he left, men built this place to study his departure."

"I don't understand. God is our creator. For that I am grateful, nothing else matters."

"He might be your creator but not mine. I'll be grateful when he comes back. Then I can return to my own time."

Juvenal eyed him. "You would leave us, Sedroth?"

"I can't stay here. It isn't my place, my time. I wouldn't know how to live."

"Then who is to help us against the beast Cathcar?"

"The Shepherd has thought this through. He wouldn't deposit you here to have you starve to death or be killed." Though Truman said this, he knew it was a lie. The Shepherd had brought him here to help the Maraia, to keep them from perishing. If he left, their chances of survival against Cathcar appeared slim. But why should he stay? What could make him want to give up his life of thousands of years ago to struggle here against the elements and alien beings that popped out of nowhere.

Juvenal stared at him.

Truman could almost imagine the poor guy thinking through what he had said.

Juvenal seemed to reach some conclusion. His gaze swept across the floor. He stepped over the tangle of roots and approached the door opening that led to the passageway. He stepped onto the landing and oriented himself. "This path goes down into the rock."

"It does," Truman said. "It also intersects with a... *tunnel* through the rock down below."

"*Tunnel?*"

"Come, I'll show you." Truman picked up one of the animal-fat lamps. With his flint and steel, he ignited dry kindling and transferred the flame to the lamp. It flared.

"What a stench." He held the lamp at arm's length.

"Cathcar is very clever," Juvenal said.

"I'm sure he's even cleverer than you or I imagine." Truman led the way down the stairs to the connecting hallway. He, too, was curious to see what was left of the tunnel.

At the end of the hallway, he thrust the lamp into the void and waited for his eyes to adjust to the dark. Slowly, he discerned the general outline of the tunnel and shadowy shapes on the floor below. The vault he had used to make his escape sat below him where he had pushed it against the tunnel wall. The rope was gone, rotted away.

"This is a strange place." Juvenal peered over Truman's shoulder.

"Stranger than you'll ever know." Truman shivered.

The reverberating roar of the rain lessened, then came to a muted end.

"I think the rain has stopped," Truman said. "If we hurry, we might make it to the cave before it starts again."

They retraced their steps, crossed the floor and exited the vestibule. On the way out, Truman added the supply pod to the pile of tools on the stretched skin. When they emerged from the ruins, the sun shone through a break in the clouds.

"It's nice to see the sun again." Truman took a deep breath of air saturated with the smell of rain warmed by the sun.

They marched along the path leading to the cave. By the time they reached the entrance, the sun had disappeared and it threatened to rain again. Truman scrambled through the slotted entrance on his knees. On the far side, he stopped and reached back while Juvenal passed the tools to him one by one.

Truman was stacking the tools next to his supply pod when a distinctive pop sounded, like a shorted electrical circuit. The sound, though not loud, seemed ominous, out of place.

Truman straightened and stared.

The scattered Maraia turned to gawk at a central figure in their midst.

Truman felt queasy. In his mind he knew what had happened but he didn't want to believe it. He slumped against the entrance rock.

"What is it?" Juvenal's head appeared on the cave side of the opening.

"We have a visitor."

***

Juvenal crawled through and stood next to Truman. He regarded the crowded Maraia. "I see a woman. She is not one of us."

"No, she isn't. She is from my time. Her name is Azizah."

"Did the Shepherd bring her here, too?"

"I wish he had." Truman took a step closer to the gathering.

Some of the assembled Maraia uttered expressions of awe. Others reached out and touched Azizah, as though confirming she was real.

She stood erect, looking bewildered, her hands at her sides, fists clenched. Her gaze swept the array of faces in front of her. Her only clothing was a skin wrapped around her waist. Otherwise, she was as naked as the day she was born, which Truman thought could be today, given her confusion.

She blinked at Truman and smiled. "*Jimmp.*"

He ignored what must have been a greeting in a language he could not comprehend. Feeling unsure of himself, he stepped up to her. "What are you doing here?"

"You *know* me?" Her speech came in English, as if nothing more than a lever had been thrown and now the current means of communication was English. She put the fingers of both hands to her temples and pressed. A frown creased her forehead,

251

the dawning of comprehension. "I understand. You and I... have met before...Truman Justis."

"You better believe it." Truman pointed at her, a motion that distanced himself from her but at the same time accused. "The last time I saw you, you had a gun. This time you don't have much of anything."

Azizah peered at her wrap and shrugged. "So? Are you going to kill me?"

Puzzled, Truman took a step back. "No. On the contrary, I was thinking you might know more about what is going on here. Maybe help me figure out how I can get back to 2005." The Shepherd had indicated there was a way back through him but what would it hurt to develop another option? Azizah seemed to come and go as she pleased.

She seemed surprised. "I misjudged you back in 2005, thinking you were only human when in fact you appear to be a very clever player. You have done well to get here so soon."

Back to square one. "I've told you before and I'll tell you again, I'm not a player. I don't want to be a player. I don't know what players are."

Azizah laughed. "That's funny, Truman. If you aren't a player then how did you get here?"

"The Shepherd brought me."

Azizah turned serious. "The Shepherd? The Shepherd is here?"

"He was here. He dropped me off and said he'd be back. If he keeps his word then I'm golden."

"I've never known the Shepherd to transport a player across time. Generally, we try to avoid any contact with the Shepherd."

252

"Well, he transported me…I mean he did bring me here but not because I'm a player."

She eyed him suspiciously. "Something doesn't compute. When last I saw you in Kanapoi, the Shepherd had sucked you up. At that time, you also had the guardian. Does he now have the guardian?"

"What's it to you?"

"Stop playing with me," she said with some anger. "You know I seek the guardian. If the Shepherd has it, I will never be able to get it. What I don't understand is why he would bring you here. You are not allied with the Shepherd...or are you?"

Truman tired of her grilling. Fortunately, he felt he held an advantage here that he didn't have in Kanapoi. "I'll let you figure that out."

Azizah frowned in frustration and let her gaze drift to Cathcar, who leaned against the back wall of the cave, quietly observing the whole scene.

"Who's he?"

To Truman's relief, she really couldn't tell who was and who wasn't a player. "His name is Cathcar. He admits to being a player." Truman didn't see any reason to withhold what he knew.

"Unlike you?" Azizah snapped. She approached the bound Cathcar. The crowd of Maraia parted and let her through. She peered at him. "Well, big man, are you a player?"

Cathcar glared at her.

"To my knowledge, there are no Neanderthals in this time. So my guess is that he's a player, who has taken on the physiognomy of a Neanderthal is this manifestation.

Cathcar's bloodshot eyes followed her.

"Why is he tied up?"

253

"He likes to kill people," Truman said.

Juvenal stepped up beside Truman. "We will kill *him*."

Azizah patted Cathcar on the head and straightened. "Who's this?" She indicated Juvenal.

"This is Juvenal," Truman said. "These are his people, the Maraia."

Azizah let her gaze pass over them with a renewed interest. "An odd name. Where did they come from?"

"The Shepherd made them after I arrived."

Azizah closed to within a decimeter of Juvenal and, standing nose to nose, peered at him. "So, you like to kill people, too."

To Truman's amazement, she spoke to Juvenal in his language.

Unfazed, he stared back at her.

"Interesting," she said in English. She stepped back and surveyed the people standing around her. "We have Homo sapiens. We have the Maraia, who appear to be almost Homo sapiens. And we have a Neanderthal." She ended with a wave of her hand in Cathcar's direction.

"We also have proto-humans," Truman said. "Although I've seen no evidence of them."

"Ah, yes. I forgot the protos. They tend to hang out in what is left of Nairobi. Five thousand years and humans have come to this? What's going on?"

"It has something to do with the degradation of the human genome. Mankind has devolved."

"I know nothing of this devolving genome." Azizah stepped close to Cathcar. When he didn't move or speak, she leaned forward and put her hands around his throat and squeezed.

254

Truman started forward. "What are you doing?"

"Testing. He seems content to remain where he is until you make a mistake. Players can be very patient."

Truman was about to remark on her statement of player patience when a scream pierced the air. He started, surprised at how tense he had become.

A Maraia woman clutched her abdomen and sagged against the man beside her.

Juvenal looked past Azizah to the woman. "Another is about to give birth."

Despite the distraction, Azizah's gaze on Juvenal never wavered. "I can help," she said.

A rivulet of sweat trickled down his temple. "If you can, then do."

Before anyone could react, Azizah was at the woman's side. She supported her arm and guided her to an area at the back of the cave where the floor was flat. She eased the woman onto the surface and knelt next to her. "I'll need some water and a strip of leather."

Juvenal hesitated, a questioning look on his face.

"Take one of the gourds from Cathcar's tools," Truman said. "There are also some leather ties."

Juvenal hurried back to the pile of tools. He returned with a gourd of water and a leather tie.

"We did not know how to help the others." Juvenal handed the leather strip and water to Azizah.

The head of the infant appeared. A moment later the infant slid from the birth canal along with the issue of afterbirth. A male child. His mouth quivered open and issued a ragged cry.

255

Azizah laid him, squirming, on the woman's stomach, then tied the leather strip around the umbilical cord, close to the baby's body and bit through the cord on the other side of the tie to separate baby from placenta.

She handed the gourd with water to one of the other women. "Clean up this mess."

Juvenal leaned close to Truman. "This Azizah knows about these things. I will be glad if she is here when my Lela gives birth."

Truman felt a vague premonition plan A was coming apart. Azizah had introduced a wild factor, creating in him a fear of the unknown. He knew little to nothing about her, and what he did know seemed contradictory. The Azizah of Kanapoi had been ruthless and driven. This Azizah seemed more compassionate and willing to help.

"I know little about childbirth," Truman said. "I also know little about this woman."

"But she helps us."

"Yes, she does." With everyone intent on Azizah and the infant, Truman returned to the entrance slit and grabbed his supply pod. If he stayed in the cave he would find it difficult to defend himself with Azizah so close. He would be better off returning to the research ruins. At least there he could control access to a more defensible space, or at least he hoped he could.

"I'm going to stay in the research ruins for a while longer. I think it would be better for you not to get too involved with this Azizah just yet," he said.

Juvenal seemed surprised. "But why? Does this woman have something to do with your decision?"

"Yes. I'm not sure I trust her."

"Then neither should we."

"Perhaps not. But she's already won over the women. You should keep an eye on her until we understand her motives."

Truman turned to leave, hefting his supply pod toward the entrance. "Can you have someone bring me food from time to time?"

"Of course," Juvenal said. "I will do it myself."

Truman glanced back at the crowd.

All attention was on the birth, everyone's except Cathcar. Truman locked eyes with the beast who glared. There seemed to be no end to the depth of his gaze. It was a blank, inky stare, the kind one saw in predatory animals.

It said, "I will kill you and feel nothing doing it."

Chapter Thirteen

After reaching the ruins, Truman scooted the pod up against the back wall of the main floor and sat down. He glanced at the square opening in the ceiling that led to the floor above. It would offer a better defensive position. He'd need it now that two players were here.

His annoyance with the Shepherd increased. Why had the Shepherd placed him in this situation without giving him the slightest idea of what he was up against?

First Cathcar and now Azizah. These players were insidious, showing up in one place, killing each other, shriveling up, reappearing in another.

He supposed they thought of him in the same way. They both knew who he was. Neither of them seemed to like him. Both probably regarded him as an agent of the other.

He lit one of Cathcar's animal fat lamps that he had retained, then removed the guardian from his pocket. He closed his hand around the cool metal and relaxed. The vision of a menu opened in his mind.

A heavy blow knocked him sideways.

An animal attack? No claws or teeth, only a frantic struggling.

He was forced onto his stomach and one arm twisted behind his back, his neck squeezed in a chokehold.

"Give me the guardian, Truman." A harsh whisper in his ear.

Azizah. Damn she's driven. She must have gotten here ahead of him and hid on the stair landing to the passageway. He was furious with himself. He had let his guard down. After her show in Kanapoi, he should have known better. He had seen what she was capable of doing.

He gripped the guardian in his free hand.

"Okay," he wheezed. "Take it."

She shifted her weight on top of him but maintained the pressure on his twisted arm and neck.

The room spun. He had only moments before passing out. He freed his hand from under his body. When Azizah loosened her grip on his twisted arm, he threw the guardian across the room.

"Get it yourself."

Azizah jerked his arm up behind his back.

Something crunched in his shoulder. Tears stung his eyes.

She tightened her hold around his neck, cutting off the air trickling into his lungs.

I'm passing out. That would be her intention. Render him unconscious, then grab the guardian and run off. He went limp, feigning unconsciousness.

She held her grip for a moment, then eased off him.

Truman brought his free arm across and slammed her body in a sweeping motion. He rolled on top of her.

Her arms flailed at his head. She pumped her knees, searching for his groin.

He ground his forearm into her throat. With his full weight, he bore down.

259

She gasped, choked. Her blue-green eyes bulged in their sockets.

Truman felt a rush of triumph, his head hot with the surge of effort. "If you don't stay still, I'll break your neck."

She convulsed and went limp.

Is she faking? He wasn't about to take any chances. Maintaining his pressure, he peered into her eyes. She stared unfocused. Her pupils dilated. She was either out cold, or a good actor. He released his forearm, sat back, and pinned her arms beneath his knees. He waited.

A moment later, she twitched. Her eyelids fluttered. She opened her mouth and sucked in a deep breath, coughed, then glared at him. "You play rough."

"Why the attack?" he asked.

"The guardian." She cleared her throat.

"You'll do anything to get it, won't you?" he said.

"Now that's an odd question coming from a player."

A wave of dismay swept over him. Was there no way he could divest her of thinking he was a player? She remained tense. There was a hunger in her eyes. To be so close, yet unable to obtain the guardian must be driving her crazy. Truman figured she wasn't done, just reevaluating her strategy.

She relaxed and smiled wryly. "I've got a proposition. I'll forget for the moment that I suspect you of being a player. So. If you let me have the guardian, I'll help you return to your own time."

Does she think I'm stupid? "You don't have the capability to do that."

260

She frowned, disappointed, then she threw back her shoulders, preening, pushing her bare breasts up on her chest. "I could make you very happy."

She's certainly working through her options. He had to admit she was beguiling. He shook his head, more to clear his thoughts than a negative response. Their struggle had brought them close to the guardian. He leaned and grabbed it.

Her gaze never left him.

He held the guardian between his thumb and forefinger in front of her face. "Do you know what it can do?"

"Of course. If I didn't, I wouldn't be trying so hard to get it."

She struggled to rise.

He clutched her throat and shoved her down, fearing a repeat of her assault.

Her head thrashed back and forth. "I'm not going to hurt you," she cried. "Release me. I want to leave now. I've lost the element of surprise."

He didn't know if he could trust her. Perhaps they had come to some sort of truce. He rolled off her, feeling confident that though he couldn't trust her, he could at least best her in a physical exchange.

She stood and brushed the dirt from her legs and arms.

Truman couldn't keep his eyes off of her. How could someone beholden to evil be so beguiling. He felt his own loneliness, a longing for companionship. "You don't have to leave." He felt awkward.

She glanced at him with a trace of a smile on her lips. "It won't work Truman Justis, or whoever you are. You've got the guardian, and I want it. Nothing else matters." She ducked out of the ruins and disappeared into the night.

Truman sat for a long time, wondering about his attraction to Azizah. A strange mix of emotions swept over him. The thought of her was comforting. It would be nice to have someone like her with him, even for a brief time. He couldn't talk to Juvenal about what was going on. Juvenal didn't have the experience to evaluate anything he said.

And Cathcar was out. Cathcar would kill him as soon as look at him, though he probably knew more than he indicated. In fact Cathcar probably knew as much as Azizah did.

Truman smiled to himself. Azizah had cleverly planted the beginnings of need in him. Very subtle. There was no telling what advantage she might gain with that.

Cunning bitch. She had taken him by surprise. He'd have to be more careful. The entrance to the ruin would have to be secured. Could he barricade it? Should he move? She posed no physical threat unless he let his guard down.

He grabbed the supply pod and dragged it over to the entrance, then rigged the pod to a string and ran the string across the entrance opening. Anything that tried to enter would trip the string and pull the pod crashing to the floor. Hopefully, the warning would give him time to protect himself before an attack was launched.

I need a weapon. The best he could find was a length of stiff root. It was better than nothing.

262

He stood under the opening in the ceiling that led to the second floor, preparing to climb up, when the supply pod clattered.

Truman whipped around, raising the root and realizing how ill-prepared he was.

Juvenal sprawled into the chamber.

"Sedroth!" He pushed the supply pod off his leg.

Relief. "What is it?"

"Azizah set Cathcar free."

***

The reality of Azizah's betrayal hit Truman in the gut like a heavy medicine ball. She'd attacked him, neutralized him and preened before him until he thought he could trust her. Then she'd sauntered out of the ruin and released the beast. Truman shivered. He'd come very close to succumbing to her charms.

"When?"

"While the guard slept," Juvenal said. "Others awoke and raised an alarm but it was too late. Cathcar ran out the entrance with her close behind. Why would she do this?"

"Maybe she thinks Cathcar can help her."

"Help her do what?"

"She and Cathcar are here in search of the guardian." Truman removed the sphere from his pocket and showed it to Juvenal.

"Then give it to them. They will leave us alone."

A simple solution to a complex problem. "I can't. It...it belongs to the Shepherd. I must return it to him."

Juvenal nodded sagely. "Then is must be done."

Good. Now we are back on track. "Did you see where they went."

Juvenal dragged his gaze from the guardian, seemingly still in awe of its omnipotent association. "I only followed them for a short ways. After they climbed to the top of the plateau, I feared they were coming here but they headed south instead."

"We'll have to see what they're up to."

Truman exited the ruin and ran south along a vague trail with Juvenal loping after him. A dense tangle of brush rose on either side and arched overhead, forming a patchy canopy. The moon, which had come free of a low-lying cloud, flashed through branches as they closed the distance.

Every few meters Truman stopped to study the ground. Two sets of footprints pressed into the rain-soaked sand, one set larger and deeper than the other. Judging from the length between the prints, Azizah and Cathcar had slowed to a walk.

Truman heard them up ahead and closed slowly. He stopped and, half turning to Juvenal, put his finger to his lips.

Juvenal opened his mouth to say something, forcing Truman to clap his hand over it.

Juvenal nodded he understood.

Truman crept forward.

Azizah and Cathcar had entered a small clearing, where Cathcar, who was in the lead, stopped and faced Azizah.

"What you want?" he grunted.

Azizah stopped so abruptly she almost stumbled. She seemed surprised but recovered, keeping her distance. "You, of course."

264

Cathcar surveyed the bush from which he had emerged. "Where others?"

Truman hunkered down, feeling as if he was at sea and a search light was scanning the water looking for him.

"There are no others."

He took a step toward her.

She retreated as though pushed by Cathcar's sheer animalistic presence. "Why didn't you try to escape earlier?" She quickened her awkward back-stepping.

"Not stupid." He reached out and grabbed her hair.

She flinched, recovered and cocked her head at an angle.

He drew her close.

"Let me go," she said matter-of-factly.

His other arm went around her waist.

She tried to pull her hair free, all the while being dragged closer to him. Her heels dug into the soft ground, slipped and left parallel groves.

He released her hair, then before she could flee, clamped his powerful hands on either side of her chest.

Her breath puffed from her lungs.

Lifting her, he buried his head between her breasts and waggled back and forth, making a blubbering sound. He came up for air and dragged his tongue in a long lick across one of her nipples.

"You are obscene." She seemed more bemused than afraid.

"No. Hominid." His erection stood out straight and stiff.

"All right," she said. "Let's get it over with."

Cathcar squinted at her. "No resist?"

"Nope."

"No fun."

"That's your problem."

Setting her down, he tore the animal skin cover from her hips. "Good." He stared lasciviously.

Azizah stood her ground, arms folded across her chest, waiting.

Juvenal eased forward but Truman pressed a restraining hand against his chest. "He'd kill you in a heartbeat," Truman whispered. "She's tough. She'll figure out a way to survive."

Cathcar clutched Azizah's hips. He pulled her in and tried to maneuver his erection between her legs.

"Trouble?" Her blue-green eyes flashed.

Cathcar pushed her away. "No resist. No good."

Azizah laughed with what seemed an air of false bravado.

Cathcar hit her hard across the mouth.

She put her hand to her bruised lips and pulled her fingers away bloodied. "That wasn't nice."

His hands flashed to her throat. He squeezed.

"This...will...not...go...unpunished," Azizah wheezed, her head jerking forward and back.

"She'll be dead soon," Juvenal whispered. "We must do something."

An air of foreboding came over Truman. His vision tunneled to a woman in the grip of a brute. Something inside him snapped. A rage against injustice, the injustice of Cathcar, all injustice, then an explosive desire to make things right. He lunged from his hiding place, screaming.

Cathcar cast Truman a baleful glance while still holding Azizah by the neck in a vice grip.

She hung limp.

I'm too late. Truman slammed into the beast. He might as well have run into a tree.

Cathcar grunted. He dropped Azizah.

She crumpled to the ground. Dark bruises mottled her neck.

He snatched Truman by the throat, one toy was as good as the other, and lifted him off the ground.

Truman kicked, then a heavy blow to his mid-section took all the fight out of him. He sagged like a sack of wet flour.

"God...damn...it." The words slurred from his lips, all that his remaining strength could muster. He clawed at the Neanderthal but Cathcar's reach was a good twenty centimeters longer than his.

Cathcar threw him to the ground and kicked him in the groin.

Juvenal charged, holding a basketball-sized stone over his head. Two meters from Cathcar, he hurled the stone.

Cathcar feinted to one side, an expression of mirth on his face.

He's enjoying this. Truman's throat felt crushed, his insides rearranged.

Cathcar stomped to a nearby shrub and pulled it whole from the ground. He twirled it, a baton, like some high school cheerleader, then swung the root end wide to catch Juvenal in the ribs.

Juvenal's mouth coughed open, expelling breath. His eyes bugged. He staggered sideways, stumbled and fell.

A gleam in his eye, Cathcar stepped over him. Grasping the shrub with both hands, he raised it, roots spreading out like twisted serpents, readying a killing stab at the prone Juvenal.

"Is this what you want?" Truman wheezed.

Cathcar stopped mid-thrust. He squinted, at first dismissively, then with dawning comprehension.

Truman rose to one knee, thrusting the guardian above his head.

Moonlight glinted off the guardian's faceted surface.

Cathcar's lips turned down with grim determination.

It was the first time Truman had seen him register any expression besides cynical rage, hate or lust. Maybe that covered the range of his emotions.

In a dreamlike state, Cathcar dropped the shrub. With an outstretched hand, he took one staggering step toward Truman, then another.

Truman waited. When Cathcar came within two meters, Truman drew back and heaved the guardian as far as he could off the plateau.

The guardian arced high and long, reducing to a pinhead sized dot before disappearing into the jungle below.

"Go fetch!" Truman shouted.

Cathcar's anguish constricted to a single stifled scream. He took a menacing step toward Truman, then stopped, his gaze drawn to the path the guardian had taken into the jungle. He scrambled across the plateau, holding to the line of the guardian's flight. At the plateau's edge, he plunged over with careless abandon.

***

The sound of Cathcar's tumbling descent rumbled up the slope to Truman as a muffled series of thuds. "That should keep him busy."

Juvenal helped him to his feet. "You have given him God's sphere."

"I think God is capable of looking after his own sphere."

"Sedroth, forgive me but I struggle to understand. You said it was important. How could you give it to him?"

"It was either that, or God was going to lose some of his worshipers. I couldn't think of any other way to distract him. Besides, I didn't make it easy. I don't think he'll be able to find it."

Azizah moaned.

Despite what she had done, Truman felt an odd compassion for her. She had stood toe to toe with the beast, though he was twice her weight and probably ten times her strength. She seemed like some sort of martyr, willing to risk everything to obtain the guardian.

He knelt and lifted her head. Then with a gentle finger, he massaged the bruises on her neck. Her throat was tight but soon relaxed at his touch. She began breathing normally.

Her blue-green eyes flicked open. A cloud of incomprehension passed over them, then wild fear glistening with tears. She swallowed. "I am..." she struggled to speak. "How did you get rid of Cathcar?"

Truman helped her to a sitting position. "Cathcar wanted the guardian more than he wanted to kill us."

"You gave it to him?"

"I threw it into the jungle. He'll never find it." *I hope*.

She appeared stricken, then a hunger came back into her eyes. She tried to stand but her legs wobbled. "The jungle? Where?"

Alarms rang in his mind. *She's still engaged after all this?* "Over that way." He waved his hand in the general direction of where he had thrown the guardian. *Would she never give up her quest for that lump of metal?* It didn't matter. If Cathcar couldn't find it, neither could she.

"We should go." Juvenal squatted a couple of meters away, scanning the bush.

"You're right. Cathcar might come back." Truman put one arm under Azizah's shoulders and the other below her knees. He was about to lift her when Juvenal put his hand on Truman's shoulder.

"I will carry her," he said. "You rest."

"Thanks. We'll take her to the ruins. I've got a *first aid kit* there." He knew Juvenal didn't have a clue what a first aid kit was but Juvenal complied, anyway.

Juvenal caught up Azizah in his arms.

Her head lolled back, raising her chest and bare breasts.

Truman draped the skin wrap over her. *She's a beautiful woman*.

Her eyes fluttered open. She caught him staring.

A hot flush rose to his cheeks. "Why...why did you untie Cathcar?"

270

Her eyes closed, then opened, a dreamy motion like a cat blinking. She smiled weakly. "I hoped for better results."

She seemed to see right through him to his loneliness and longing.

Struggling to recover, he hid his thoughts with incredulity. "With him?" *I almost had two players to contend with.* One had been bad enough, but if they had joined forces, he'd never get back to his own time. The Maraia would have been doomed.

"Player's motives are often complex and hidden."

Juvenal thrust his chin toward Truman. "You talk too much. Better we get to the ruins first and talk later."

"Lead the way." Truman had to appreciate the clarity with which Juvenal approached situations.

At the ruins, Juvenal stepped through the vestibule. He carried Azizah to the back of the ruin where Truman had built his makeshift bed and laid her down.

"I'll take it from here." Truman struck steel to flint and lit the animal fat lamp.

Juvenal regarded him.

"Go to your people," Truman urged. "You are needed by them."

"Yes, Sedroth, if you say so." He hesitated.

Truman clapped both hands on Juvenal's shoulders. "You saved my life. I want to thank you."

Juvenal nodded, then indicated the supine Azizah. "Is she dangerous?"

"Not without the element of surprise. I'll be all right."

271

Juvenal nodded and left the ruins.

Truman stepped to his supply pod, thumbed the hatches open and raised the lid. He pulled out the first aid kit.

Azizah stirred. She gazed at the pod. "You are well-stocked."

Kneeling beside her, he broke open the kit. "The Shepherd didn't leave me unprepared. I have a few things from the past. Like this pain medication." He held up a small bottle to the dim light of the lamp and shook out two capsules. With a gourd of water, he helped her swallow.

She leaned back. "I need rest."

Without thinking, he stroked her forehead.

"Thank you for helping me," she said, then winched as the effort to speak must have hurt.

"I... I couldn't have done less."

"I made a mistake. You saved me. If you are a player, then I don't understand why you would do that. If you are not, then I understand your helping me, but that still doesn't answer who you are."

"If I was a player and had the guardian, would I still be here?" Truman hoped to put his identity to rest once and for all.

She frowned. "No, I suppose not. But that only deepens my confusion."

"I've already told you who I am."

"I know. You're a human geneticist caught up in something you don't understand." She stared listlessly into the flame of the lamp. "I don't know why *Zug* leaves me like this."

Truman peered at her lying helpless on his bed. He, too, wondered why she was so weak but he

272

knew little about players. "The Shepherd mentioned *Zug*. How else would this *Zug* leave you?"

"I shouldn't have to suffer like this. If I die, that's simple but to get beat up and feel weak? I don't understand what's going on."

"You mean he could get you out of this jam?"

"Yes, and provide me with information so I don't try to make an alliance with a Neanderthal brute who has no intention of forming an alliance. Together, he and I could have had our way with you and these Maraia."

"Are you so ruthless?"

She gave him a tired smile. "I'll believe you for the moment and assume you are not a player. That doesn't help much, when even I am still much confused about what is going on."

"I'm confused, too," Truman said. "The Shepherd seems to have pegged me to help these Maraia. Why, I have no idea."

Azizah propped herself on one elbow and stared at him. "You seem to dismiss out of hand the task the Shepherd has placed before you. Instead, you focus your efforts entirely on being able to return to Kanapoi. Do you know what will happen to you if you return to Kanapoi?"

"No. I suppose I'll go back to work. I'll file a report on the Shepherd, and no one in our vast bureaucracy will pay the least bit of attention to it."

"You try to make light of a serious situation. It is not that simple." She put her hand on his. "I'm going to tell you something that may disturb you."

Truman felt a sudden chill. He could never anticipate what these players would do or say.

"What's that?" He knew full well he wouldn't like the answer.

Azizah closed her eyes for a moment, then she stared at him. "Before you and Hopkins arrived in the helicopter, before the tunnel entrances were dynamited shut, I shot a man who in retrospect resembled you in every way?"

"You what?"

"You heard me."

"But that's crazy. You said resembled. Maybe it wasn't me. Maybe this guy showed up out of nowhere. You don't know he came from the Shepherd."

"Fair enough. I'm only suggesting based on what I saw that I might end up killing you."

"Why are you telling me this?"

"You saved my life. I owe you. But if you don't want to believe me, then don't."

A knot formed in Truman's stomach. Had the Shepherd been forthright with him? Truman stood and paced the small chamber. "The Shepherd said nothing of this to me."

"Why should he?"

"For one, since he brought me here, you'd think he'd be more explicit if he wanted my cooperation."

"That's a big assumption." She shifted, turning her shoulders toward him in a provocative way. "Why don't you come and sit here beside me?"

Though tempted, Truman's longing came up against a wall of recent emotion, anger, resentment, at being attacked, kicked around by players and not wanting to be there in the first place. It was obvious she'd use her charms to ensnare him. Then where would he be? Even worse off. "What's this, more paying down of your debt?"

"You could look at it that way."

"It won't work." He saw the irony of him mouthing her earlier denials.

"No?" She seemed disappointed.

"I've got enough going on I don't understand, and you've admitted there are anomalies in your own world, crazy as it is. I don't think intimacy between us would help the situation." It wasn't what he felt but he knew it was the safest thing to do. Then feeling awkward with the moment he looked at his watch. "The Shepherd should arrive tonight."

"You said he was returning. I didn't expect it to be so soon."

"According to my watch and an estimated time of arrival provided by the guardian, he should be here in thirty seconds." He entered the vestibule and was surprised when she got up and followed him.

"Don't you need to rest?"

"I will in a moment."

He stepped outside and peered at the cloud-studded sky.

"What do you hope to see?"

"I thought something that would indicate his return. You know, a flash, a streak of light, a sonic boom. It's amazing how one misses such simple things as a cloudless sky. I haven't seen the stars since I got here." He frowned. "The constellations are different. Look at the Big Dipper. The stars are skewed."

"Stars move all the time. Some faster than others. Five thousand years is a long time."

"I had no idea they could change that much."

A bright light streaked across the sky, and for a brief moment turned night into day.

Azizah started at the sudden appearance. She gripped his arm. "Is that what I think it is?"

"Right on time. He seems to have landed on the other side of the river. "I've got to go meet him. Want to come?"

Shocked, she stared at him. "After Cathcar, I don't think I want to press my luck."

"He got to you, didn't he?"

Her gaze drifted away. "Yes, he did."

Truman checked his watch again. "I'd better go."

Her expression didn't change. Was she sad to see him leave? Happy? The moment became awkward. Truman stepped away from her. "I'll be back by morning...maybe."

276

Chapter Fourteen

Outside, the moon hung low, reflecting off the mirror black water of Lake Turkana.

Truman breathed in the night air. *This is a peaceful place.* It would be hard not to like it. He had friends here like Juvenal, who respected him, not like back in his own time. And there was his growing attraction to Azizah. Though he hadn't been able to bring her all the way onto his side, she was moving in the right direction. With more time, she could become an ally and maybe a companion.

He oriented himself, descended the plateau and struck out for the Kerio River. At the riverbank, he paused, hands on hips, surveying its languid flow.

God, do I have to swim this thing again?

He slipped into the warm water and let the current take him, stroking leisurely. No need to hurry tonight. There were no threats. He presumed Cathcar was still thrashing around in the jungle farther south, looking for the guardian.

Upon reaching the opposite shore, he heaved himself up, emptied water from his boots and wrung out his clothes. It appeared the Shepherd had landed in the same clearing where he had first landed and made the Maraia.

His rounded shape sat in high grass encircled by brush. The bright moonlight reflected diffusely off his exterior.

Truman strode up to the Shepherd and slapped the resilient side. "Shepherd, I am here."

"Who are you?" The Shepherd's voice was flat, without emotion.

What? "You can't be serious. You're the one who told me to meet you here."

"I am serious."

Truman was flabbergasted. "You don't know?"

There was a long pause.

"Did you hear me?" Truman asked.

"Patience. I am computing and will tell you what I decide in a moment."

"Great."

"I do not have any record of you, much less telling you to come here today."

"You...you don't?" *Damn, arrogant, useless machine.*

A seam, like someone had taken a razor and cut deep and clean into a ripe guava, formed on the side of the Shepherd.

Truman felt himself drawn toward it. The clean edges parted, exposing a chaotic mass of pink flesh. It too parted as he leaned into it. The feeling was not unpleasant, just close and confining. The seam must have closed and after some concerted rearranging, Truman found himself in the familiar womb.

The tissue was tense, almost as if the Shepherd was feeling some impatience. "Please tell me what is going on here."

The Shepherd was groping for understanding. This wasn't the reception he had anticipated. He adjusted his position, trying to calm down. "Aren't you the Shepherd that left me here two days ago?"

"I see." There was another pause. "My world line is the source of this confusion. In answer to your question, yes and no. The Shepherd you speak of must have been me but farther along my world line. After the Kanapoi Incident in 1985, the guardian instructed me to return to Earth on or about eight-twenty in the evening of Thursday, April 3, 7005. I have dithered near the Cygnus black hole for the intervening five thousand years and have now arrived. I thought I hit it quite accurately give or take a few minutes."

"I'll be damned. You don't have a clue what's going on, do you?"

"Clue?"

"Let me explain." Truman took an exaggerated breath. "I'm a geneticist who, in the year 2005, was sent to investigate a UFO sighting at the Kanapoi fossil fields. The UFO turned out to be you, and you brought me here. I arrived two days ago. You gave me the guardian and told me to meet you here and give it to you."

"You have the guardian?"

"It's here but I don't have it. I had to throw it into the jungle. I'm afraid we'll never find it. I was being threatened by a--"

Truman thought he heard a deep, throaty chuckle, a very strange sound to be coming from something as august as the Shepherd, then a zipping, like a bullet cutting through air.

"The guardian," the Shepherd said with a trace of triumph in his voice.

The guardian hovered before Truman. "How did you do that?"

"I called for it." The sphere rotated slowly as if it were preening. "So, you brought the guardian

279

from 2005. It has been prescient." The Shepherd was silent for a long while.

"What are you doing," Truman asked.

"I am confirming you are who you claim to be. I have used the guardian to examine your past. Indeed, I brought you here, though on another part of my world line as I have already surmised. What else were you instructed to tell me?"

"I was to tell you whether or not I wanted to return to my own time."

"I presume I am to take you back."

"Yes."

"And what is your decision?"

"I thought the guardian might have told you."

"It did but I detect reluctance on your part to state your decision."

"Hell yes, I'm reluctant. I've become uncertain." Truman hadn't expected to be grilled by the Shepherd. "When I first arrived, I wanted nothing better than to return. There was no way anyone could have convinced me to stay. But now I'm not so sure."

"Did I tell you, when last you saw me, it was necessary you go back?"

"You seemed sure it would happen."

"Has something changed your mind?"

"I..." *Could the Shepherd know about Azizah?* If Azizah was to be believed that he was to be killed upon returning that would have to affect his decision.

"Excuse me," the Shepherd said. "While you are pondering, I will consult the guardian." A moment passed. "I see."

"What do you see?"

"You go back. It poses an interesting problem."

"Does Azizah kill me?"

"Azizah?"

"Didn't the guardian tell you?"

"I only checked your return." Pause. "Ah, the players. They have been very busy looking for the guardian."

"What about my question. I die, right?"

"I do not know. The guardian does not seem to want to give me that information. Perhaps it does not want me to influence your decision."

That seems like dodging the question. Would the Shepherd lie to me? Truman decided the Shepherd would if it served his greater interest.

"I see that you have become quite intimate with the female player," the Shepherd said. "Usually players remain apart from the humanity that inhabits the time present they enter."

"I don't know anything about that. What's the problem you referred to?"

"The problem arises from your indecision about going back. The guardian shows you go back. If you decide not to return, then you will create the problem. Someone has to go back. The past is fixed."

Truman felt a tingling in his head. "What are you doing?"

"Scanning."

"Is that necessary?"

"Yes."

More tingling.

"You have a lot of psychological aberrations."

Truman felt the Shepherd rummage through his mind as someone would in a drawer full of socks.

Truman shook his head but could not relieve himself of the sense of intrusion. "What if I said I wanted to go home now and take my chances about being killed in Kanapoi? Would you take me?"

"Yes, of course. But I suggest you delay your decision."

"I don't know why this is beginning to sound complicated."

"As far as I can see, you still have a purpose to fulfill here. You are beginning to exhibit some attachment to these Maraia."

"How do you know about them?"

"Please, Truman. I do have the guardian."

"Oh."

"Given your indecision and the prerequisite that someone must return to Kanapoi, I am going to clone you...to give you more time to make up your mind and to cover the possibility you will decide to stay."

"You're going to what?"

"Clone. I do believe you are familiar with the term. Our problem is resolved if there is a clone. If you decide to stay, then the clone will go instead."

"He will return to be killed."

"We only know that from Azizah. But if it is true, then why not?"

"It doesn't seem right."

"Such sensitivities. Your clone is only a clone."

"But wouldn't he be me?"

"He could be but under the circumstances that would not serve my purpose. I need someone whose psychological makeup is such he will always be biased toward returning to Kanapoi. It would not do for him to also become attached to Azizah and the

282

Maraia. Then I would have another problem on my hands. Ah...I am using the latter expression figuratively."

"I understood as much." Truman wondered at the programming that had gone into the Shepherd. An odd mix of exotic technology and folksy personality.

"So he has to be different," the Shepherd said. "No spiritual stuff, *satori*, you know enlightenment. I could restore his self-esteem, make him more self-centered."

"I'm not comfortable being a part of this."

"You need not be."

The Shepherd seemed to withdraw, leaving Truman to wonder what was going on. When there was no further communication, he couldn't contain his curiosity. "What's happening?"

"I have made the clone. Now, I will fortify his self-esteem. So far, your search for *satori* has proved to be elusive, except perhaps your brief embrace of *Gilomir*. The clone, of course, will have no memory of that experience. I will have to suppress other key events in your life, like the sarin incident, the friendly fire. Your self-esteem took a... hit, is that a correct usage, after those incidents."

The Shepherd fell silent again.

"Yes, I think that will work well," the Shepherd said when Truman failed to answer. "We need someone so focused on getting back to the past he will never consider changing his mind. Someone who believes he can save humanity. A Captain Marvel."

Is he serious? "Captain Marvel has been out of the comics for decades, millennia if you count from the present. I'm more interested in how many of my memories you will give him."

"Up to your fall in the tunnel will suffice. There is a convenient moment when you fall and are knocked unconscious. I can have him pick up his reality from the blackout. He will not know anything about your being brought here, or what you have learned since about Cathcar, Azizah and the Maraia."

"I want to see him."

"I will deposit him outside. You can look him over before relocating him to his start point."

"I have to...there's a start point?"

"I suggest the clearing not far from the painting cave."

"You know about that?"

"Juvenal is there now. Start point or not, the clone is going to need a lot of help if he is going to survive even a day."

"You're being manipulative. I said I didn't want to be a part of this, and now you expect me to help him?"

"Not at all. You can sit back and watch him being eaten by some passing carnivore."

Truman didn't see he had much choice. The Shepherd knew all the buttons to push to make him agree, anyway. Plus, there was the subtle inference if he didn't cooperate, it would compromise his option of being able to stay. The Shepherd might kidnap him and force him home. "Okay, okay. I'll help. What's one more body in addition to the Maraia."

"I knew you we could come to an understanding."

"Yeah. The guardian again."

"Actually, no. I figured this out for myself."

Truman shook his head, wondering how a machine so advanced could also appear so dense. Maybe it was a cultural thing. "I assume I can't help him directly?"

"Of course not. If he sees you, it would be traumatic for him. I thought that would be obvious."

"Just checking." *Problems*? Helping the clone survive without any direct contact was going to be a huge problem. One that Truman would have to overcome. First one thing, then another. "Look, there's this beast Cathcar harassing us. He's a self-confessed player. I presume you know what that means. Can't you snuff him out? It would make our lives a lot easier."

"Snuff. Is that not some sort of addictive tobacco?"

"Could you kill him?"

"No. I cannot...snuff him out." The Shepherd seemed pleased with his expanded vocabulary.

This guy's way over the top. Don't start with the cynicism. "Forget snuff. What about neutralize?"

"You have learned much."

"For fuck's sake, you're the one who told me."

"Such language."

"If you want my help--" Truman's voice rose. "--if you want me to survive here, you've got to at least neutralize Cathcar."

The Shepherd consulted the guardian again. "You need not worry about Cathcar. But you do need to calm down."

"Great. Are you going to neutralize Cathcar or not?"

285

"I said not to worry about him. I am not at liberty to elaborate."

"You better elaborate or I'm...I'm going to sit down and do nothing."

"You are being childish. Juvenal can help you with the clone but you are going to need more than him. It would not be wise to involve any more of the Maraia. There are precious few of them as it is. That leaves Azizah as the only other resourceful person available."

"Azizah?" Truman was flabbergasted. "She can't be trusted. We had Cathcar at our mercy, and she let him go."

"You do not understand. She has an important long-term role to be played. The first stage is to bring her to your side. You are already well along that path. The second stage is to involve her more directly, and the clone is a way to do that. Here's the guardian. Entice her."

Truman felt the guardian being returned to his pocket. "Don't you--"

"No. Take it," the Shepherd said. "Offer to give it to her if she agrees to help you."

"She's going to trust me to do that?"

"What do you think? She is a player. If you betray her, she will wait for another opportunity. But I think she is at a point where she will trust you."

Before Truman could protest he was expelled from the womb and deposited outside.

"Hey!"

"What is it, now?"

"If you deposit the clone here and expect me to get him to the clearing in front of the painting cave, then I'll need some help getting him across the river."

The Shepherd shifted before him, then rose and headed for the river.

"Wait!" Truman shouted.

The Shepherd stopped. "I am moving across the river to deposit the clone on the other side...as you requested."

Truman looked skyward. "Hello? I was hoping you'd take me with you."

"Quite right."

Truman felt a compelling force yank him like a magnet acting on a nail. He was drawn to the Shepherd's side and stuck there.

The Shepherd rose and drifted across the river.

This is demeaning, being carried like a ship's barnacle by an arrogant superior being.

The Shepherd came to rest. "We are now on the other side."

"So I see. This will make my life a lot--"

Why would the Shepherd land in Cathcar's clearing?

A moment later, the clone tumbled down the side of the Shepherd. He dropped the last meter to the ground and lay pink and unmoving in his glistening mucus afterbirth.

"Take him," the Shepherd said. "His consciousness will light up in half an hour."

***

Thick, dark clouds drifted across the sky, obscuring the moon.

Truman leaned over the clone trying to get a look at his face.

Does he look like me or not?

287

It started to rain. Lightning flashed. The whole landscape lit up with a sizzling crack, turning rain to wisps of steam, followed by bone-crunching thunder.

Truman caught a glimpse of a bearded man with a head of hair. Otherwise it was impossible to see if there was any similarity. He grabbed the clone under the shoulders and began dragging him through the heavy downpour toward Juvenal's painting cave. He struggled, head down to protect his eyes from the stinging drops.

He came to the escarpment and followed the wall south, ducking rainwater that cascaded off the top of the plateau.

At the cave, a soft glow of light spilled into the chaos outside.

Truman released the unconscious clone inside the entrance and peered down at the silent figure. *It is me. He has hair and a beard but that's me.* The thought unnerved him. It was like looking at himself in the mirror and finding the reflection was real.

Maybe I'm *not real.*

Juvenal sat at the deep end of the cave hunched over his gourds with their assortment of colored clays.

"Juvenal," Truman whispered.

Startled, Juvenal glanced over his shoulder, then his expression changed to one of delight. "Sedroth. I have been painting." His gaze shifted to the clone lying in the mud outside the cave. "Who is he?"

"He's me. Sort of...." Truman glanced back at the clone, wondering if he was okay where he lay.

The poor sap gaped, unseeing, mouth open to the rain.

Juvenal walked over to the clone, wiped some of the mud from his face and clamped his mouth closed. "You are right. He looks like you, except for his hair and beard."

"The Shepherd has returned...is here. He produced this man to look and act like me. A being like this is called a *clone*."

Juvenal gave Truman a skeptical look. "The Shepherd is here?"

"Yes. He...ah...came back for the guardian and to resolve a problem."

Juvenal seemed confused. "If the Shepherd has made this man, this clone, then it must be right. But the guardian. You no longer have it."

"Like I said before, the Shepherd can look after the guardian by himself. In fact, he has already retrieved it."

Juvenal seemed relieved. Then he frowned. "What problem needs to be resolved?"

The light from Juvenal's lamp danced on the wall of the cave.

Truman considered the flickering shadows. "I have to decide whether or not I want to return to my time."

Juvenal regarded Truman sadly. "You must stay to help us. We will be lost without you."

"I feel that in my heart. That's what makes my decision so difficult."

The clone groaned.

"This man will soon wake up," Truman said. "When he does, he will think he is me. He will think

289

his name is Truman. I know you call me Sedroth but I want you to call this man Truman."

Juvenal started to protest.

Truman held up his hand. "I need another favor."

Juvenal nodded.

"I want you to take Truman back to your people. Care for him. Show him around. Let him get a feel of the place. He is going to be disoriented. Above all protect him. Will you do that for me?"

"Giving him shelter will not be a problem. But we are all newcomers here. I can only show him what I know."

"That's okay. He has to stay alive until I make up my mind."

"I understand. If you decide to stay, Truman the clone will go back. If you go back, then Truman the clone will stay. But we know nothing of this man. We want you to stay, Sedroth."

"I don't have time to argue the point, now. Truman will wake up soon. It would be best if he were placed somewhere outside and found his way here. It might be too much of a shock for him to awaken and have you be the first thing he sees."

"I will carry him back into the bush. Not far enough he will become lost. Near enough that I can help him if he gets in trouble."

"I better go. I can't let him see me."

Juvenal nodded. "I'll take care of him if it helps you decide to stay."

"Thanks."

Truman backed out of the cave and splashed through the mud and rain toward Cathcar's clearing thinking he would confront the Shepherd again about his situation. When he arrived, a blurred shape slipped out of the bush and headed for the Shepherd.

Cathcar? What's he got to do with the Shepherd?

Truman detoured and trudged back to the ruins more depressed than ever. He found them empty.

Where's Azizah?

***

Hours later the supply pod clattered to the floor.

Truman, who had taken refuge on the second floor, started awake and reached for the stick he and chosen as a weapon. Already, the dim light of dawn filtered through the open windows. He crept to the old stairway opening and took a look over its edge to the floor below.

"What's this doing here?" Azizah demanded. She kicked the supply pod out of the way, glanced around and spotted him on the second floor.. "What are you doing up there?"

"It's safer."

"And your supply pod?"

"I rigged it to alert me to an intruder. Where have you been?" Her skin was scratched and muddy. "You've been looking for the guardian, haven't you?"

She held her arms out and examined her scratches.

"So what if I have?" She picked at some caked mud. "It's too valuable to leave in the jungle or risk having Cathcar find it."

Truman swung his legs over the side, gripped the edge with his hands and lowered himself down.

291

"Do you realize the risk you took? What if he had seen you?"

"He didn't. I was careful. And if he discovered me, I can still run, can't I?"

Her flippant response annoyed Truman. "We're in a war here, not some treasure hunt."

"You might be at war." She glanced up from her idle grooming. "I prefer the hunt. Since you gave up the guardian of your own free will, you should have no objection I look for it."

"You are being very foolish."

"Why?"

"Don't you wonder about the Shepherd? Now that he is here, do you think he will let you and Cathcar do as you please?"

She hesitated. "What does he say about all this?"

"Something is afoot larger than you, or me, or Cathcar, or your players." *Do I tell her all this? Hell, she probably knows anyway.* "The Shepherd wants to make sure humans exist in the future so they can build the machine that ends up constructing him. If they don't, he can't exist. Since he exists, they do build the machine but there seems to be a number of different ways of getting them to do it. I represent one of the ways, the one he is currently working on. You and Cathcar are involved but I'm not sure how."

"And?" Azizah waited.

"I have to decide whether or not I want to return to Kanapoi."

She laughed, and covered her mouth with her hand, stifling another outburst. Then she turned

292

serious. "That's a tough one. I've told you, you will die if you return."

"I asked the Shepherd about that, and he didn't give me a direct answer."

"You can be sure he knows. He wouldn't be here if he didn't know what was going on."

"To cover the possibility I don't return, he has constructed another me, a clone. I left him with Juvenal."

"I know. I saw a being that resembled you in the Maraia cave. He seemed ill."

"You've seen the clone?"

"Truman, I live there. Juvenal carried this guy as a sack of potatoes and dumped him. I was curious and investigated. He does look like you, except for the hair."

"Did he recognize you?"

"No, he was delirious. Cathcar also came to the cave. I suppose he was looking for me but I hid. He got distracted when he saw the clone."

"What did he do?"

"Some threats. I heard something about the clone being a dead man."

"Then I'm screwed."

"That's the funny thing. Cathcar threatened him but took no further action. I suppose he didn't recognize the clone as you with his beard and hair."

"Okay. Maybe there's still time to set this up."

"Set what up?"

"I'm going to need your help with the clone."

She laughed cynically. "You are something. First you foil my attempt to obtain the guardian and now you have the nerve to ask me--"

"Recognize this?" Truman held up the guardian.

She tensed.

The same vacant look he had seen in Cathcar came into her eyes.

"I thought you threw it into the jungle."

"I did but the Shepherd retrieved it and gave it to me."

She relaxed, knees bent, as though going into a crouch ready to spring forward.

Truman took a step back. "Don't even think about it."

She straightened and circled to his left.

"I thought we had come to some kind of accommodation." He put the guardian in his pocket and braced himself for what he was sure would be an attack.

"You saved my life and I told you about Kanapoi. I consider us even." She lunged.

Truman sidestepped, slapped aside her outstretched arms to spin her around. He grabbed her from the back in a bear hug. "God damn it, I'm getting tired of this."

She heaved up and down but couldn't break free.

Truman leaned his weight on her until she stilled.

"Okay," she said, breathing hard, "this isn't going to work."

"I'm glad you can still be reasonable."

"Was that a clone I killed in Kanapoi?"

Truman shrugged. "Since I haven't made up my mind that remains to be seen."

He let her go and gave her a shove.

She spun to glare at him.

Truman tossed the guardian from hand-to-hand, taunting. "Have you ever used it?"

She pursed her lips. "No. I would have to possess it first, wouldn't I?"

Truman stepped up to her and, before she could resist, grabbed her hand. He forced her fingers around the small sphere, then placed both of his hands over hers and squeezed.

She stared at him with wild eyes and struggled to free her hand. Then she slumped forward onto him.

He staggered under her weight and counted the seconds. *Okay that's enough.* He opened her hand and removed the guardian.

"No. Don't." Her protest was immediate and desperate.

"Feels good doesn't it?"

"I've never felt anything like it. Please. Longer."

"I'll make a deal with you. You help me with the clone and I'll give you the guardian."

"You'd do that?"

"It's of no use to me, and the Shepherd doesn't seem interested in it. If he was he wouldn't have given it to me."

She eyed him. "You wouldn't lie to me would you?"

Truman smiled. "I'm not a player."

"Very funny. What do you want from me?"

"I want you to take the clone under your wing...you know the phrase?"

"Yes, Truman, I know the phrase."

"Juvenal said he would help but he can't be with the clone all the time. With two of you, you should manage to keep him out of trouble. He's disoriented."

"I know." She eyed the guardian. "Okay, I'll do it."

***

Truman heard them coming.

Voices drifted into the ruin from outside.

I must have dozed.

The sun shone in through the western facing windows.

Is it that late? After being up most of the night, he and Azizah had lain down exhausted and fallen asleep. The remnants of that much needed rest quickly dissipated to be replaced by sudden tension.

Truman rushed to one of the windows and peered out.

Coming out of the bush on the other side of the clearing to one side of the ruin was Juvenal followed by the clone. Juvenal seemed to be doing most of the talking, in his language, with the clone talking back to him in English.

"What is this place?" The clone's voice carried in the still air. He stopped and, hands on hips, surveyed the ruin in front of him.

Truman ducked back inside.

"You should not go there." Juvenal back-stepped and motioned for the clone to follow him but the clone couldn't have understood.

Instead, he limped across the clearing and climbed onto a concrete abutment that thrust up against the vestibule.

296

Cautiously, Truman returned to where Azizah still slept. "Azizah" he whispered, shaking her shoulder. "We've got company."

She stirred, then started awake. "What is it?"

Truman put his finger to his lips. "It's Juvenal. I told him to take the clone on an orientation tour but I didn't expect they would come here. We've got to hide."

Azizah motioned in the direction of the vestibule. "What about the pod?"

It lay where it had fallen.

"I'll stash it in the passageway. Wait for me." He lifted the pod carefully to avoid any scraping sound and carried it down the steps where he laid it against the wall in the dark passageway.

She stood waiting for him. "I think he climbed from the top of the vestibule to the second floor roof. We can't go out. He'll see us."

Truman paused, straining to pinpoint the clone's location. "Juvenal won't let him come in here. But just in case, we better get up to the second floor. There are more places to hide up there."

He grabbed her hand and hurried to the stairway opening, then helped her up first. He leapt and pulled himself up after her.

"What's he doing?" Azizah whispered.

Truman crossed to one of the windows and listened. "I think he's scanning his surroundings. I can hear him muttering to himself as he recognizes landmarks. His situation is beginning to sink in."

"You can't keep avoiding him," Azizah said.

"I have to. If I show myself, it would end my options with the Shepherd." Truman pointed. "They're leaving."

297

The clone eased himself down from the ruin the way he had gone up, then limped, his feet obviously tender, to catch up to Juvenal. They disappeared down a trail that led to the eastern edge.

"It's time for you to make contact," Truman said to Azizah. "You've got to meet him soon, or he's going to end up dead. Cathcar will only stay occupied with the search for so long, then he's going to come looking for me. If he figures out who the clone is, we'll have a dead clone."

"What do you want me to do? Just walk up to him?"

"I don't see how else to do it. I told Juvenal to take him to a cave we found south of here at the bottom of the escarpment. They'll be safe there for a while."

"Then what?"

"Then I'm not sure. They might go hunting. You'll have to shadow them and pick your opportunity. You can give him some information about what is going on but don't overdo it. I don't want him freaking out."

"You'd better not be toying with me."

Truman gave a short laugh. "Believe me, I'm not toying with you."

She peered at him as though hoping to find out if he was putting her on. "I hope not. Should I stay with him after first contact?"

"For a while. This shouldn't take more than a couple of days to sort out."

"Do you want me to stay here tonight?" Azizah gave Truman a questioning glance.

He felt awkward. Of course he wanted her to stay. And of course he couldn't let her. He had taken a chance falling asleep with her the night before. Fortunately, she had been as tired as he was. But he couldn't take that chance again.

Reluctantly, he pushed her away. "No. Get going."

Chapter Fifteen

The next day, Truman awoke with a start. From the slant of the sun it was late morning.

He quickly pulled himself together and left the ruin thinking he would try to take up a position overlooking the exit from the Maraia cave to see when Azizah made contact with the clone.

The sun was well off the horizon-line of the lake. The jungle brush still dripped with the night's rain. Prismatic colors sparkled in the slanting light, illuminating birds as they flitted through the air, chirping their morning calls.

No sooner had he gained the edge of the western escarpment that overlooked the Maraia cave exit, than Juvenal came out followed closely by the clone. They descended a trail that would take them to the jungle below on the western side.

Shortly thereafter, Azizah exited cautiously.

Truman ducked back when she looked around and up.

After presumably assuring herself that she had not been observed, she descended the same trail, then circled around to get ahead of Juvenal and the clone.

Truman followed her at a distance, unobserved, as she sauntered to take up a waiting position.

She is definitely different than the Azizah I encountered in Kanapoi. She seemed to have changed even more since using the guardian.

A few minutes later he heard Juvenal and the clone pushing through the bush.

Juvenal spoke to the clone the whole time, pointing at things and naming them but it was obvious the clone was much troubled and not listening.

The clone glanced with fear-filled eyes at the thick brush, then to the sky and clouds.

Truman felt a stab of guilt for what the clone must be going through. *If he is like me, then I can imagine what he's thinking and feeling.* He'd be taking in as much data as he could, all the while forming one hypothesis after another to explain his situation. Then he'd be pushing back an incessant assault by his emotions that threatened to overcome the only thing he could hold onto, his rationality.

Juvenal stopped and speared a pig.

Go on Azizah. Time to make contact, Truman thought.

She stepped into view, seemingly enjoying her role of informed protector. She feigned the right amount of surprise. Her brazen attitude impressed the clone. His face flushed dark at the sight of her nakedness.

Truman saw glimpses of himself as he was before the sarin incident destroyed his self-confidence. He saw a headstrong young man. Would the clone be enough on his guard to avoid Azizah's charms or survive Cathcar's assault should he be uncovered?

It started to rain, and the three of them headed back to the Maraia cave. Truman supposed Azizah would spend the night, as he had told her to do. Anyway, Juvenal had invited her.

Truman felt oddly jealous. *Strange emotion*, he thought. After all the man was only a clone. That's what the Shepherd had said, anyway. Truman sloshed his way in the deepening gloom back to the ruin

He retrieved the supply pod from the passageway, then climbed to the second floor where he would not be disturbed. He leaned back against a wall and took the guardian from his pocket. His fingers curled around the cool surface. The now familiar menus displayed in his mind.

He formed a thought question. *What happens here if I return to Kanapoi?*

The guardian presented a single choice.

Having no other option, Truman picked it.

The presentation began.

***

I see the Truman clone, Azizah and the Maraia are dead. The world is a dark place, and Cathcar holds the guardian.

***

The presentation stopped.

"That wasn't good." Truman muttered. If he went back to 2005 it seemed everything here in the future fell apart. He tried to bring up another world line but the vision remained dark. He refreshed the menu in his mind and posed a second question. *What if I stay?*

The guardian presented a single world line.

***

I see the clone coughs and lets a drool of blood escape his lips. He watches it drop. It splashes on the radiating wrinkles of the entrance to the Shepherd and oozes toward the center.

"Open," the clone says. "Please open."

The pucker relaxes and dials open.

The sky, dark with clouds, releases a torrent of rain.

The clone's head lolls over the opening. He feels a certain comfort staring down at the pink walls.

"Not going," Cathcar says as he pushes on the clone. His mouth curls into a snarl. The whites of his small eyes discolor red and test the confines of their sockets.

In a rage, he takes his anger out on Juvenal. He grabs Juvenal's chert knife, bends back his head and presses the knife up under Juvenal's chin.

"He player!" Cathcar shouts.

"No," Azizah protests. "He's not a player."

"Test if die." Cathcar starts the blade across Juvenal's throat.

Juvenal struggles but is no match for Cathcar's strength.

"Wait!" Azizah screams. "If you're looking for another player, try Sedroth."

Cathcar squints in the direction of the ruins. Then with a sudden movement, he draws the blade across Juvenal's neck, slicing deep.

The clone slides headfirst into the pucker that now is dialed open to its full extent. Once in, the opening closes behind him.

***

The guardian vision ended. Truman frowned and turned the sphere over in his hand, wondering if it had malfunctioned.

He tried to reactivate it but the guardian remained unresponsive. Confused, he returned the guardian to his pocket. He had learned nothing to confirm Azizah's prediction he would die if he returned to Kanapoi.

Perhaps even more troubling was seeing Juvenal's throat slit, then Azizah betraying Sedroth to Cathcar. If he did stay behind and the clone was sent back, then he would have to deal with Azizah and Cathcar alone. If he stayed, did everyone die, anyway? Why only the two scenarios?

Come morning he'd ask the Shepherd.

***

The next day, Truman beat his way through wet bush to the perimeter of Cathcar's clearing--deserted except for the Shepherd resting at the center.

Hopefully, the beast continued his search for the guardian. For Truman to wait around didn't make much sense. Either Cathcar was engaged, or just as likely, nearby and about to return.

Crossing in the open might be risky but I can get into the Shepherd quickly enough if Cathcar shows. The Shepherd's going to protect me, isn't he?

Truman hurried across the clearing. When he reached the Shepherd, he felt a moment of panic as he assessed the Shepherd's smooth sides without the faintest idea how to gain access.

He slapped the Shepherd's side. "Let me in," he said in an urgent whisper, looking over his shoulder.

The Shepherd's surface deformed, enough so Truman could get a foothold and haul himself to the top. He sponge-walked to the puckered entrance and waited.

A moment later, the sphincter dialed open and he tumbled inside.

"Why can't I get a straight answer out of the guardian about my future?" Truman complained as

304

he adjusted to the close confines of the Shepherd's womb.

"I have no control over the guardian."

"But I thought you said--"

"You did not come unobserved." The Shepherd directed Truman's attention to the edge of the clearing.

Cathcar stepped from the bush and strode up to the Shepherd. He thumped his fist on the resilient hide. Not receiving a response, he circled. "Want Truman!" he bellowed.

"Oh God, I'm trapped."

"You are not trapped. He cannot hurt you."

Cathcar leapt onto the top of the Shepherd and stomped his foot on the womb's opening.

Even Truman could feel the radiating ripples from the blows through the Shepherd's flesh.

"He will not go away. There may be advantages to letting him in," the Shepherd said.

"Are you insane?" Before Truman could react, the pucker opened and Cathcar dropped inside with only a thin membrane separating him from Truman. He held his breath, aghast.

"Breathe," the Shepherd said. "You have nothing to fear. Cathcar cannot see you. Nor can he hear or feel you."

"Who you!" Cathcar demanded, craning to get a look at his surroundings.

"I am the Shepherd."

Cathcar wriggled. "What do?"

"I make people."

"Make Truman?"

"No. I brought him here from 2005."

Cathcar seemed to digest the Shepherd's answer. "Why bring?"

"That information is privileged."

Cathcar grunted. "Can take back?"

"Yes. You are one of *Zug's* players, are you not?"

"*Zug* good."

"No, *Zug* bad." The Shepherd's womb constricted.

Cathcar screamed, then raged at the Shepherd's cloying tissue. "You no kill. You no kill."

"I am not going to kill you. I was only seeing if you could be killed."

Cathcar seemed distracted by something. "Who that?"

"Truman."

"Why hair?"

"To confuse you."

"I go now."

Truman felt a slight ripple, the Shepherd expelling Cathcar.

He rose and scrambled off the Shepherd.

"Why'd he want out?"

"I showed him a false vision of you, hair and all, going to join Azizah and Juvenal. He will think the clone is you when he sees them…"

"But you had him. You could have killed him!"

"Remember, I am not at liberty to kill players indiscriminately."

The scene in Truman's mind shifted.

Cathcar lurked at the western edge of the escarpment peering down at the Maraia men who had left the cave on a hunt in the jungle below.

Juvenal could be seen trudging up the trail to the top of the escarpment carrying a packet of food destined for Truman.

"What's Cathcar's doing?"

"Waiting. Things are about to get interesting."

***

Once Juvenal was well on his way to the ruin, Cathcar clutched a club sized length of branch and leapt over the edge of the escarpment. He clambered down the trail to the slit entrance that led to the Maraia cave where he peered through as though verifying all the men were gone.

Up on one of the terraces, the clone sat lacing on his sandals. Azizah was lower down with the other Maraia women.

Cathcar entered and sent the women into a frenzy. He stomped up to Azizah, who stood her ground.

Truman couldn't hear what was said between them, either because the vision's point of view was too far away, or the Shepherd chose not to transmit all the sounds.

In shock, he watched as Cathcar battered Azizah with the club, then took on a desperate attack from the clone. The assault didn't last long and the clone was dragged out of the cave, through the slit and over the plateau.

"Where is Cathcar taking him," Truman asked, alarmed.

"I do believe, his destination is here."

"Oh, God. Do I have to look at this?"

"If you want out, I will place you, now, beside me and you can deal with this situation firsthand.

As it is, this is a necessary step in the progression of this reality to its conclusion."

Whatever that means, Truman thought. "I'll stay put for the time being."

Cathcar entered the clearing, dragging the clone behind him.

The vision shifted again, back to the top of the plateau and the ruins.

Juvenal entered the ruins and exited a moment later. He looked around, obviously confused Truman was not there. After leaving the package of food inside the vestibule, he returned to the trail that led to the painting cave.

Azizah struggled up the far side of the trail and met Juvenal before he descended.

"Cathcar has kidnapped the clone," she cried.

Truman welcomed the return of sound.

"Where did he take him?" Juvenal asked.

"I don't know."

Together they followed the path down the eastern side of the escarpment in the direction of Cathcar's clearing.

The Shepherd's vision expanded to encompass everyone.

Azizah and Juvenal crouched at the edge of the clearing. Cathcar, having lashed the clone to a tree, started beating him.

"Aren't you going to help him?" Truman asked the Shepherd.

"Of course not. It would not be right for me to interfere. Most of this is preordained."

"I feel like he's beating me."

"In a way he is."

Frustrated, Cathcar brought both his fist down on the clone's shoulders. "Guardian!" he bellowed.

"It must still be in the tunnel," the clone cried.

Disgusted, Cathcar gave the clone a parting slap and headed for the Shepherd.

"He's coming here!" Truman cried.

Cathcar stood on top of the Shepherd peering at the puckered entrance. "Open!"

The Shepherd obliged.

Cathcar slid down into the slippery womb. His body pressed against Truman's, separated by the thin membrane.

Truman held his breath.

"You are going to suffocate if you do not breathe," the Shepherd said.

"But--"

"Relax. This will only take a moment."

Cathcar struggled.

It seemed the membrane would tear.

"Where guardian? Speak!" Cathcar yelled. "Pile of excrement." He pushed at the wall only to have his arms absorbed as though he had pressed them into pink bubble gum.

"Be still," the Shepherd said. "Truman tells the truth. The answer lies in the tunnel."

"What did you mean by that?" Truman demanded.

Cathcar grunted. "Out me." He struggled to extract his arms.

"Though the guardian no longer lies in the tunnel, I thought I might use a...sleight of hand and make a reference to the real answer. You. Sedroth."

"Me? And don't call me Sedroth."

"Your question will be answered in due course. Look." The Shepherd directed Truman's attention to the edge of the clearing. Azizah stepped forward and ran to the clone. She fumbled with the lanyards.

"What's she doing?" Truman asked.

"Out me!" Cathcar roared.

"Excuse me," the Shepherd said. "I almost forgot our guest wants to leave." The Shepherd expelled him.

He hit the ground and sprang to his feet.

Azizah looked up, horrified.

"He'll kill her," Truman cried.

Cathcar ran full tilt at Azizah. With one arm outstretched, he caught her under the chin.

Her head snapped up. Her feet left the ground, and she fell flat on her back.

He stepped over her.

"Bitch." He grabbed her hair and dragged her to the tree where he bound her next to the slumped clone. After checking they were both securely tied, he grabbed a handful of digging tools and headed for the tunnel.

Once Cathcar was gone, Juvenal emerged from hiding and untied them both.

"See, no problem," the Shepherd said. "Cathcar is engaged in a futile search. Azizah has insinuated herself with the clone, and Juvenal is a hero."

"You planned this from the start?"

"I...no, to be honest I had no idea how this would turn out."

"But he might have killed her."

"I calculated Cathcar was more interested in the guardian. He will not kill anyone until he gets it. He has to keep his options open."

"Who's in charge here? I thought the guardian was."

The Shepherd vibrated. Truman supposed it was his equivalent of a laugh.

"The guardian has given me a certain amount of leeway," the Shepherd said, after becoming still. "Leeway is necessary as the guardian does not always tell me everything it sees. I suppose, since it already knows what is going to happen, then whatever happens will happen anyway whether I know ahead of time or not or indulge the leeway it has provided me. I find this lack of information very frustrating at times."

"I'm confused. You with your leeway. The guardian seeing the big picture. All the while there's *Gilomir*. Where does he come in?"

"You have asked a good question. He is in charge of the guardian, I think. I am a mere servant of my masters, though as I said I still have to figure out a lot of things for myself."

"Can you do that?"

The Shepherd seemed to inflate, then deflate, perhaps his way of showing he had been insulted. "Of course."

"That leaves me to wonder how this is all going to play out. I thought my going back to Kanapoi was up to me. All I had to do was show up here and let you know my decision."

"That is still the case. The only one holding everything back is you, Truman. You are the one who cannot make up his mind."

"How much time do I have?"

"I am leaving the day after tomorrow to ferry you or the clone back to Kanapoi."

311

A great depression pressed on Truman. "I quit," he said, frustrated. "I want to go back."

"Are you sure?" The Shepherd seemed concerned.

"Yes, I'm sure. Or isn't that permitted?"

"Of course it is. But there is nothing for you back in Kanapoi. You…you will be killed."

"How come you know this, now?"

"I knew before. I did not think it appropriate to tell you."

"So who told you?"

"The guardian."

"The guardian? It refused to tell me anything about Kanapoi, only that there would be death and destruction here."

"Up until now, we have been contending with two options. The first is that you return to Kanapoi and are killed at the tunnel. Your aggregate world line loops and disintegrates into multiple world lines in 2005. The second option is that the clone returns to Kanapoi and is killed at the tunnel. You remain here to aid Juvenal and the Maraia. You bring Azizah over to our side, Cathcar is defeated, and mankind's advance to the future is assured. Perhaps you should talk to the guardian again. It may now show you other options."

"Other options? Yeah, like how about the clone and I both go back? Let the clone die, and let me go back to being myself."

"That is an option but one that is not possible in the current context. Within the current context, there is only one person returned to 2005, and he dies at the tunnel."

"This all sounds suspicious. Azizah has her reasons for telling me I will die, and you have yours to keep me here. I'll take my chances in the past. Let the clone become your messiah."

"The guardian has put a lot of thought into instructing me to bring you here. You are special. As you know, the clone is flawed, not as it pertains to him going back but as it pertains to his potential as a leader of the Maraia if he stays. He is not you. Only you are capable of swaying Azizah. Only you are capable dealing with Cathcar. Only you are capable of giving the Maraia the direction they need."

"But you could change the clone. Why couldn't he do it?"

"I could. But that would not conform to the--"

"--context we are dealing with. It seems to me, I never had a choice in the first place."

"Of course you have a choice. But so far you have made the wrong one. There is still time to change your mind."

Chapter Sixteen

Truman felt a mounting frustration. No matter which way he turned, no matter what solution he thought up, he was outmaneuvered, nudged, prodded, and pushed in a single direction against his will. "I want to think about this some more," he said, not at all sure more thought would help.

The Shepherd opened a vision that showed Truman the outside.

"It's night already?"

"Indeed. Before you go, there is something I want to show you."

Truman sensed movement. The vision showed the Shepherd lifting off from the clearing and sailing high above the jungle. The steep slopes of Mount Kenya rose in the distance, lit by the light of an almost full moon.

"Where are we going?"

"To the ruins of what was once Nairobi."

The vision gave way to a flat, grass covered plain, then an unruly lumpiness. The outlines of crumbling structures loomed on the horizon.

"What are those?" Truman asked.

"Skyscrapers. They have rotted through and toppled over. Poor construction. Not the government sponsored excess of the research ruins. Long ago whatever reinforced this concrete dissolved. Without the reinforcing, the concrete crumbled."

The Shepherd swooped in and landed in a clear area surrounded by ugly monoliths of fractured concrete.

"Okay. Nairobi is a ruin. So what?"

"Be patient. You will see."

Truman waited. His eyes adjusted to the low light level. Then something scurried in the dark. Out of the shadows scampered first one, then another human form. They coalesced. The group shifted. Their numbers increased. When Truman estimated they had reached about a hundred, they swept toward the Shepherd.

Truman screamed. He struggled to bring his arms up to cover his face.

"Do not worry," the Shepherd said. "You are safe."

The hoard clambered over the Shepherd. Like rats, they swarmed. Sharp sticks rose and fell on the Shepherd's exterior. Stone clubs thumped and scraped. A deafening, animal cry rose from a hundred open mouths.

"I've had enough!" Truman shouted.

The Shepherd rose, tipped one way, then back the other, shrugging the vermin off his hide. When they were all on the ground, he rose straight up until they lost individual definition and merged into a carpet-like, squirming mass.

"What was that all about?" Truman tried to sound calm.

"They are the remains of humanity. Proto-humans. They come out at night to forage. The daylight bothers them and makes them vulnerable.

"But they're not human."

315

"True. Protos reached this stage of de-evolution a few hundred years ago, then seemed to stabilize. Eventually, all of the *Gilomir* genome in their DNA will be gone, and they will resume their downward descent into barbarity."

"They already look barbaric. Why did you show this to me?"

"I am still trying to convince you to stay. If you return, you die, your life is wasted and mankind continues to devolve into these pitiful beings. If you stay, you have a future insuring that the Maraia have a future. Would you like to meet a few protos?"

Truman peered at the shadowy figures. "Of course not. What would be accomplished by meeting them?"

"Certainty."

"You could have shown me anything. For all I know, what I saw was a vision you conjured."

"I could have done that, but I did not."

"I don't believe you. Mankind couldn't have degraded that fast. Return me to the plateau. I've had enough."

"Of course."

He felt a slight prick, low on his thigh.

"What the hell was--"

The last thing he felt was the Shepherd descending.

***

He opened his eyes to a dim light. He was outside the Shepherd but not back at the plateau. The floor beneath him was smooth, perhaps concrete. Dark monoliths rose in a threatening circle. A cold fear caught in his throat.

Nairobi?

He jumped to his feet and spun around, searching in vain.

"Shepherd!"

The sound of his voice rose and bounced from the still walls. Something in the darkness shifted. *Oh God, this can't be happening.*

Hunched shapes slipped from the black recesses of the ruins, merged with one another, and drifted toward him.

The whites of eyes in misshapen faces gleamed. Open mouths showed discolored teeth. A murmur rose.

"Take it easy now." Truman backed up a step, both hands extended. He glanced over his shoulder. He was surrounded.

The multitude didn't sweep over him like it had the Shepherd but skittered up to him in an agitated suffocating press. Hands touched his face, his chest and stomach, his groin. He squirmed to be free but had nowhere to go. The intensity of the touching increased. The murmur rose to a keening cry. Wave after wave of sound washed over him. The touching transformed to distinct pinching and squeezing.

Terror rose in Truman's throat. "Help! Help!" But the sound of his voice was lost in the greater tumult.

He felt a sharp pain in his leg, then another on his forearm. He jerked it free and brought it to his face. A half-moon of teeth marks dripped black in blood, then more pain, everywhere. He slipped, and the hoard closed over him.

All right, Truman thought. *Times up, Shepherd. I believe you. Get me the hell out of here.*

But the Shepherd was nowhere in sight.

The feverish touching stopped. One diminutive proto, who still had his teeth sunk into Truman's arm, was ripped free and flung to one side where he landed with a yelp.

In his place, a proto twice his size and every bit as ugly grasped Truman's leg and began dragging him toward the dark recesses of a crumbled building.

The other protos fell back, forming a corridor of snarling faces, glittering eyes and sharp pointed teeth.

A constant howling jeer rang in Truman's ears. He kicked with his other foot to no avail. The brute who was dragging him was twenty kilograms heavier than Truman and well-muscled. A leader, given the distance and respect he commanded.

At a pile of collapsed concrete slabs, the massive proto located a dark entrance that led in under them. He ducked his head and dragged Truman after him..

The smell of human feces and urine assaulted Truman's nostrils. Now in total darkness, he bumped along, hitting his head on unseen obstructions.

The darkness began to lighten, shadows flickered.

They entered a cramped smoke-filled room. What used to be a large steel garbage container sat on a fire, the water it contained already boiling. The bones and half carcasses of large and small animals lay strewn about.

Other protos crowded in, pressing close to the open flames. Their howls now coalesced into a mind piercing chant.

With sudden horror, Truman realized they were about to cook him. He kicked. This time the big proto lost his grip. Truman lunged at the wall of degraded humanity, who continued chanting, slipping into a near trancelike state of rapture. They pushed him back toward the fire, and pressed forward.

No way out.

Truman grabbed one of the burning logs, ignoring the pain of the hot embers, and the stench of his scorched flesh. He swung the log, knocking heads and shoulders.

The protos fell back in confusion. The chant lost its cadence and degenerated into the former howling and jeering.

Truman ran through the breech, and hit the opposite wall hard. The burning limb skittered from his grasp.

The protos closed.

Truman punched and kicked the nearer ones who fell back giving him a brief respite. He located the entrance farther along the wall and slewed in that direction.

The clawing and pinching resumed as he tumbled into the narrow passage, slipping on soft solids and splashing through puddles of what must be human waste by its smell.

The protos pursued.

The passage narrowed.

Truman paused to kick a proto that had caught up to him.

319

He burst free into the clearing outside. *Shepherd where are you*? He ran, stumbling, not knowing a direction, except away. His foot caught on the uneven surface and he fell. The skin on his burnt hands peeled away as he broke his fall.

The protos swarmed over him again, holding him down.

The big proto approached but this time he raised a club and brought it down hard on Truman's head.

Everything went dark.

***

Truman opened his eyes. The Shepherd's slick, pink walls pressed against him. He flinched, reflexively kicking, punching.

"God damn you. What did you do that for?" Angry red wounds on his arms closed, turned pink and disappeared.

"You did not seem convinced they were real," the Shepherd said. "Now do you believe me?"

"Yes, get me out of here."

The Shepherd rose, leaving the squirming mass of humanity behind. The monoliths diminished in size and disappeared into the gloom. The Shepherd leveled out and skimmed the tops of dark trees. Mount Kenya loomed on Truman's right, its snow-capped peak lit by the morning sun not yet above the horizon.

Truman relaxed, feeling at peace as the familiar scene slid by below him.

When the outlines of Cathcar's clearing came into view, Truman gave a sigh of relief. He never thought he would consider the clearing, the plateau, and the ruins as coming home.

They landed. "Can't the de-evolution be reversed?"

"Yes, and it has been." A flickering of images raced through Truman's mind. Swirls of helical molecules. Alternating strings of acids and alkalis. "You see the problem?"

"Yes, it's amazing." Truman marveled at the clarity of the vision, the complexity of the problem, the simplicity of its solution. "But how has it been reversed?"

"The Maraia. When I created them, I did so with the only genome I had at my disposal, the last best combination of *Gilomir* and hominid DNA."

"John Lohner's DNA."

"Yes. Interesting how he keeps reappearing in the conversation. We can thank A4-Ni again or condemn her for creating the whole problem in the first place by her theft."

"I read Lohner's diary."

"Except for A4-Ni's nurturing, the hominid part of the entwined *Gilomir*-hominid genome would aggressively attack the *Gilomir* half to re-establish itself. Hence, after A4-Ni perished, the genome degraded as you have already discovered. Since she was the only one who knew how to separate the two genomes, I had no choice but to find the solution I just showed you in an attempt to prevent the genome from further degradation."

"But the guardian must have seen all of these complications."

"It is my understanding, and I daresay hope, the guardian did. Be that as it may, mankind reaches a point where they can care for their genes by themselves."

321

"You will get your A4-Ni built."

"We know she is built but consider this."

The vision shifted to show grotesque human forms. Truman grimaced. "When is this"

"The future."

"Who are these people?"

"The descendents of the Maraia."

"But they look horrible. What happened?"

"Designer genes."

The vision swirled to a close-up of a misshapen man hunched over a short baton-like cylinder. He took something that resembled a pellet from the end of the cylinder. He placed the pellet in his mouth, and swallowed. Almost immediately, his body began to transform. It then stabilized into another form, equally grotesque.

"He recreated himself," Truman said, astonished.

"Yes. These humans use nano-assemblers to alter their genes. They ingest homemade DNA and hope for felicitous changes. There is very little of hominid purity left, let alone traces of *Gilomir*."

"Does no one survive?"

The vision shifted again, this time to beings who appeared very human. "Regard," the Shepherd said. "Pure Maraia."

"Incredible. They must not have experimented with the…designer genes." Truman wondered at his excitement.

"Yes. Early on, they foreswore use of the nano-assembler and managed to preserve their original genome, the *Gilomir*-hominid mix I first gave them, and evolve naturally from that base."

"But how?"

"With the help of a quasi-religious belief. They belong to a cult, the Cult of TrueMen. Their creed prohibits altering their genes. It is they who build A4-Ni."

Having failed to make the right decision on his own, Truman now felt he was being subjected to almost unimaginable pressure to change his mind. So much for free will. "I need some time alone," he said.

"You can have some time but not a lot."

"And if I can't make up my mind in time?"

"You will."

"You can let me out, now." Truman relaxed, preparing for the exit. "No, wait," he said, troubled. "This Cult of TrueMen, does it have anything to do with me?"

"What do you think?"

"I think it's obvious they do. It's also beginning to appear obvious you know I will change my mind and decide to stay."

"The guardian knows."

"Then all this show-and-tell is for nothing. I have no choice."

"You always have a choice," the Shepherd said. "Though some events are foretold, shown as strong probabilities, they can be arrived at by many different paths. Take the case in point. The Maraia survive. They build A4-Ni. I exist. Everything that goes into making that a reality is happening now, including this little speech I am making. It all gets wound together and put in front of you to guide your decision."

"But you are manipulating me to change my mind and, to make me conform to what you keep telling me is preordained," Truman said.

"You can die here or die there."

The Shepherd placed the guardian into Truman's pocket.

"I suppose you expect me to ask the guardian for advice?" Truman asked.

"That might be a good idea."

Truman fingered the guardian, reassuring himself it was still there. "I'll see you in the morning." He again readied himself to be exited but nothing happened.

"Azizah and the clone approach." The Shepherd seemed apologetic. "We will wait until they pass."

***

Azizah and the clone descended the escarpment and struck out toward Cathcar's clearing.

The clone emerged first from the jungle into the clearing. He crossed without hesitation to the Shepherd. After circling the Shepherd once, he tried to climb on top of it but kept slipping.

Apprehension paralyzed Truman. "I suppose you are going to let them in."

"Why not? They are curious and will not know you are here. I can repair the damage Cathcar has inflicted on the clone. I can scan Azizah. Who knows when such information might be useful against a player?"

Azizah helped the clone onto the Shepherd. After he pulled her to the top, they approached the puckered entrance and were admitted.

Separated by the membrane, Azizah pressed up against Truman, her brow creased with worry, almost as if she knew he was there.

"Hurry," Truman said to the Shepherd. "I think she suspects my presence."

"Why yes, I believe you are right. She is very perceptive."

Azizah wriggled in the close confines.

In an effort to see more, the clone turned until his face came within a millimeter of Truman's. Truman stared into the clone's eyes, thankful the membrane was only transmitting images in one direction.

The clone blinked, then glanced sideways, a look of fear mixed with wonder. How easy to read the clone's emotions, Truman thought. *Do I wear my feelings so obviously?*

The clone faced Azizah again, their heads close. He ducked, his lips brushing against hers.

"He kissed her!" Truman shouted.

"Yes, he did," the Shepherd said. "Are you...jealous?"

"No..." Truman stammered, "...just surprised."

"They seem to be getting along quite well. Is that not what we had hoped for?"

Truman shook his head. "This is something you had hoped for. I have always been a reluctant part of this whole thing."

The clone began quizzing the Shepherd.

"While I am answering his questions," the Shepherd said to Truman, "I will examine Azizah."

How the Shepherd performed the examination was a mystery to Truman. Azizah didn't appear to be aware she was being studied, either.

325

"Amazing," the Shepherd said.

Truman had trouble concentrating on the two conversations, his with the Shepherd as well as the clone's with the Shepherd.

"What's amazing?"

The Shepherd's dense flesh rippled, a sign Truman interpreted to mean he was agitated. "Though she is a *Zug* player, her genome is no less pure than the *Gilomir*-hominid combination of the Maraia, or for that matter of yourself."

"I guess you don't remember you neutralized her. Didn't the guardian bring you up to speed on what you had…are supposed to do?"

"The guardian made no mention of that. It probably did not see it as temporally relevant to what was going to happen."

"Great. Azizah will cease being a player but we'll both be slaughtered by Cathcar, who still is a player, since you failed to neutralize him when he was last here."

"But I did neutralize him. I have not had the opportunity to inform you."

Truman was stunned. This whole episode seemed to lurch by fits and starts. "So that's why you said I didn't have to worry about Cathcar."

"As you seem to know, the conversion is not instantaneous and is also affected by the strength of the player. But the guardian has assured me Cathcar will cease to be a problem."

Why the convoluted answer? Was Cathcar going to be a problem or wasn't he?

"…I don't want to exit," the clone shouted.

Truman redirected his attention to what was happening on the other side of the membrane. It

326

seemed the Shepherd was about to expel the clone and Azizah.

"One moment," the Shepherd said to Truman. The walls of the womb flexed and deposited the clone and Azizah on the outside.

"It is starting to rain," the Shepherd said. "They will seek shelter in the painting cave."

"You didn't want to take him back to Kanapoi? You could have dumped me out instead and taken off. You could have pre-empted my choice."

"Sometimes I despair at your ignorance, Truman. There is a world line to which I have no choice but to adhere. I cannot jump off to Kanapoi simply because the clone sees it to be in his best interest. There are events that have to happen. Besides, you have grown attached to Juvenal as he has to you. He saved your life once. You are indebted to him. This indebtedness will take some time to bear fruit."

"You're putting Juvenal and a handful of Maraia up against my returning to Kanapoi and saving the whole human race?"

"You seem to have difficulty accepting the fact that you will die."

"As far as I'm concerned the jury is still out on all this world line, preordained stuff. I might just take my chances as far as being killed is concerned. I also know I can exercise my free will. I do still have that, don't I?"

"That is a vacuous assumption."

Chapter Seventeen

Truman stood outside the Shepherd in the rain. Water cascaded off the Shepherd's smooth dark sides and flashed a glistening white with each lightning strike.

Truman had always thought the Shepherd was the dominant force in this whole episode. Now, according to his own admission, he was nothing but a servant to one or more masters. And if the guardian and *Gilomir* were the masters, which one was the master's master?

In the dim moonlight diffusing through dense clouds, Truman climbed to the top of the plateau and arrived smeared in mud and soaked through. He stood at the entrance of the ruins, letting the run-off that cascaded from the roof scuppers wash down upon him. He rubbed his arms and chest, tipped back his head and drew both hands over his face until he felt cleansed.

Inside the ruin, the roar of the incessant rain receded to a background rumble. The walls felt comforting, like he was home.

Juvenal burst through the sheet of water falling across the vestibule door opening and stood dripping before him, breathing hard from his run. "Cathcar is looking for you."

"I know. I was in the Shepherd and saw Cathcar exit the tunnel."

"He must have gone directly to the Maraia cave. We fought him at the entrance but I fear he will keep returning and wear us down. He dragged a stone box with him."

"It's a vault, constructed long ago to contain the guardian. The clone told him the guardian was still in the tunnel. Cathcar dug his way in and not finding the guardian thought it might be in the vault. Since it isn't, Cathcar is enraged. Did you see which way he went?"

Juvenal pointed south, away from the ruins. "Toward the big mountain."

"I hope he doesn't find the painting cave. That's where Azizah and the clone have holed up." Truman thought for a moment. "I am going to consult the guardian. I'll be okay here. There are plenty of places to hide. If Cathcar comes for me, it will take him a while to find me if he ever does."

"Are you sure? I could stay to help you."

"No, your people need you more than I do. I've got some thinking to do. The Shepherd leaves tomorrow, and I must make my decision."

"You must stay," Juvenal insisted. "What match are we against Cathcar? If you are not here to guide us, he will destroy us."

"There are worst things than Cathcar in your future. The Shepherd took me to the ruin of an ancient city called Nairobi. I saw what becomes of the human race. They have devolved into animals. You must promise me if something happens to me, you will guide your people and tell them to keep their lineage pure. Promise."

"I would promise you anything, Sedroth, but I do not understand why this is a problem. Why are you so concerned?"

"First, I am concerned for you and your people. Some will stray. There is nothing you can do to prevent that. But others must hold true. Second, you consider the Shepherd a god because he created you. But the Shepherd was created by something known as A4-Ni. She in turn was created by the descendants of the Maraia here today.

"If the Maraia do not remain pure, they will not be intelligent enough to build A4-Ni. With no A4-Ni the Shepherd cannot be built. Your god, will cease to exist."

"But, Sedroth, the Shepherd exists."

Even Juvenal sees the obvious contradiction. "I could sit here and speak to you of many strange things. But I won't since even I am not sure about them. Take me at my word when I tell you there are realities that exist beyond my capacity and yours to understand."

"You are wiser than all of us, Sedroth. Another reason you cannot leave. I will go to my people as you ask but I do so reluctantly. I will also think about what you have said."

Juvenal exited the ruin.

The rain tapered off. The moon shone and sent ghostly gray sparkles dancing on the walls of the ruin near the windows. Truman stepped under the stairway opening and leapt to catch the lip of the floor above. With an effort he dragged his legs over the edge and heaved himself up. If Cathcar did try to climb onto the second level, it would be defensible. Not that Truman thought he had some superior weapon but the high ground would provide an advantage.

330

Truman looked for a secluded place where he could use the guardian without being disturbed. An abandoned closet served his purpose. He stepped into the tight space, kicked aside some broken concrete and hunkered down.

He removed the guardian from his pocket and curled his fingers around the sphere's faceted surface.

Truman formed his thought question.

What happens to me when I return to Kanapoi? Azizah says I will die. So does the Shepherd. I want to know it from you.

"*You do not return to Kanapoi. The clone returns to Kanapoi in your stead and is killed at the tunnel.*"

But I can't stay here. I'd have to contend with Cathcar. I'm only human.

"*Cathcar will cease to be a problem.*"

That's what the Shepherd said. Why am I not convinced?

"*You may choose to believe or to disbelieve. Everything that can happen in your reality has happened. The totality of your existence is preordained. The only variable in the entire mix is your consciousness and its ability to observe.*"

I'm sorry, guardian. You lost me.

"*By making an observation, you make a choice. You realize reality for your point of view.*"

Sounds like quantum mechanics, Schrodinger's wave function.

"*Occasionally, there are theories you and your scientific peers conjure that turn out to be rather accurate descriptions of what is real.*"

Every time I ask a simple question, you, or the Shepherd, or Azizah end up giving me a mind bending explanation that is difficult to accept, or you don't give me a direct answer.

"*Perhaps giving you a direct answer would...bend your mind even farther. Do you have a specific instance when one of your questions was avoided?*"

Truman thought for a moment. *Yeah, I do. After the Shepherd picked me up, I asked him where Zug and Gilomir came from and he evaded the question.*

"*He should have. At that time, given your existing state of anxiety, lecturing you on their origins could have been traumatic.*"

How about now?

"*All right. But promise me you will indicate when you mind starts to bend.*"

Agreed.

"*What you call your universe is better described as an anomalous part of the universe that Gilomir and Zug inhabit.*"

A universe within a universe? I kind of got the impression Gilomir and Zug weren't from around here.

"*You're a scientist. You've heard of closed-timelike-curves.*"

Truman drew back. Yeah, he'd heard of CTCs. Somewhere back in an undergraduate physics class. *Given a Lorentzian manifold, a closed-timelike-curve is the world line of a material particle in a space-time that is closed. Kurt Godel found them in 1949 as a special solution to Einstein's General Theory of Reali--*

"Good. You know what it is. What you don't know is you exist in one."

What I learned referred to a single particle. Are you saying our entire universe is closed?

"That's the essence of it. It is a bubble embedded in a larger universe. What is in the bubble stays in the bubble and cycles around endlessly. Hence it's designation as an anomalous zone. Although the bubble is closed, it contains an almost infinite number of realities."

Infinite?

"Essentially. Some infinities are larger than others but that's another matter. Since the bubble is closed and contained, and there are a limited number of world lines, there are also a limited, though large, number of possible combinations of those world lines. But there are perhaps even a smaller number of realities than all the permutations would allow."

How so?

"A reality exists only when a conscious observer is present. The only conscious observers in the bubble are those who carry Gilomir's DNA. The finite number of conscious observers is quite small by comparison to the number of realities."

What about the universe in which our bubble is imbedded. Is it one of an infinite number of universes? Truman sought to make a glib remark.

"Indeed. It is one of an infinite number of universes."

Truman was startled, then realized he shouldn't be surprised anymore by anything the guardian had to say. *I know it's been theorized. It's remarkable to hear it talked about as though it were true.*

"Given that space and time exist in many more dimensions than the three physical ones plus time you consider the norm, other universes are quite possible and do indeed exist quite close to this one. Fractions of a millimeter, like pages in an infinitely long book. You can't sense them. But there are those, including Gilomir and Zug, who are extended entities that can move back and forth amongst the pages and do so frequently."

I don't understand. The Shepherd, the players, they travel through time almost at will. And they don't muck things up?

"All the almost infinite number of world lines that make up your closed reality are like long strands of hair. An outside force can intervene and finger through the hair, or twist it into knots but the individual strands remain the same and circle back on themselves. The outside interference can be seen as changing reality but it only does so from your point of view. Since the strands are forcefully self-consistent, they return to their path as soon as the perturbing influence is removed."

This all seems very complicated.

"I don't doubt it. Since CTCs are pathological, there is usually nothing in a CTC that has the capacity to worry about whether there is determinism or not, much less 'why am I here' or 'what is the meaning of life'. It is only by a fortuitous circumstance you are conscious enough to even pose these questions.

"The light of your consciousness turned on when A4-Ni inserted the Gilomir genome into an ancient hominid. That light will go out when the last of your kind dies. As a race, your awareness has a

beginning - approximately four million years ago and an end a few thousand years in the future."

Only a few thousand years?

"I am sorry. None of this was meant to be."

You're saying we humans are a mistake, an accident.

"You are a tragedy in a way. Humans look out at a universe they were never meant to see or wonder about, much less have the capacity to understand."

Next you'll tell me I have no free will.

"On a sub-atomic scale, free will does not exist. At the scale you operate, the macroscopic, you think you are exercising free will, when in fact you are merely serving as the conscious observer that makes explicit a specific reality. You observe with your senses, which do not transmit stimuli instantaneously to your brain. Consequently, you have adapted to this time delay by thinking you are exercising free will, when in fact all you are doing is observing the macroscopic manifestation of one of an almost limitless number of random combinations of sub-atomic events.

"You are nothing more than the combined world lines of every sub-atomic particle that makes up your body. While you are alive those particles are constantly changing. When you die, those particles go their separate ways. Eventually, all world lines circle the closed-timelike-curve and begin over again."

The guardian fell silent.

Truman expelled a long whistling breath. *This all sounds like a lot of mumbo jumbo.*

"It is expected that you have doubts. Consider this…"

"Truman!"

The sound drifted to Truman as though from far away.

"Where the hell are you?" This time an annoyed demand.

"Azizah?" Truman struggled to regain his focus, to reprise the moment. "I'm up here." He scrambled to the stairwell opening.

Azizah stood on the floor below, impatient, her arms extended. "Help me up."

"Why aren't you with the clone?"

"He's sleeping. Are you going to help me up or not?"

Truman dropped to his knees, grabbed her hands and hauled her to the second floor.

She brushed dust from the loose-fitting skin that clothed her, then peered at him. "You were there today, weren't you?"

Truman was taken aback by her brusque manner. He had thought he was getting somewhere with a gentler, more accommodating Azizah, and now this. What had happened? "Yes, I was there. I'm surprised you noticed. I'm surprised you even care."

She eyed him. "What's that supposed to mean?"

If she's prepared to be direct, I can be, too. "You kissed the clone."

Her lips slid into a teasing smile. "Let's get the facts straight. He kissed me."

"Anything else going on?"

336

"Truman." Her gaze slid away, and she resumed her idle brushing. "Are you getting jealous?"

"Jealous? Why should I be jealous?" *Damn it. Am I jealous? What's going on?*

"You shouldn't be. Jealousy can be a corrosive emotion. The clone and I are getting along just fine. Tell me, why did the Shepherd scan me?"

"How fine?" Truman couldn't leave the subject of her relationship with the clone alone. "I didn't expect you'd be spending all your time with him."

"So you are jealous. At least the clone pays me some attention. I've grown quite fond of him."

"That's a change. A matter of hours ago you seemed quite fond of me."

Azizah thrust her head back and glared at him. "You'll recall you showed little interest. I have my needs."

"So you take what you can get?"

"Let's not be petty. I've been keeping up my end of the bargain. I've shown my commitment. Now I want to see some goodwill on your side." She stuck out her hand. "I have come for the guardian. Either you give it to me now, or you can have the clone back."

"I thought you cared about him?"

"I said I was fond of him. He's the one who cares about me." Azizah waved her hand impatiently. "Guardian or the clone."

"That's easy." Truman reached into his pocket and removed the guardian. He tossed it to her. "You don't know what you're getting into. It's almost more trouble than it's worth."

"I'll make that determination. You never answered my question."

"Which was?"

"Why did the Shepherd scan me?"

"I wondered if you felt what he was doing."

"Of course I knew what he was doing. I felt naked. Out of control. It was like Cathcar groping me. Did the Shepherd find what he was looking for?"

"I don't think he was looking for anything in particular. But he did seem surprised."

"About what?"

"Though you are a *Zug* player, you possess a complete *Gilomir*-hominid genome, like mine, like the Maraia."

She stared, astonished. "How is that possible?"

"He thought he might have given it to you."

Azizah paced. "He must have inserted it when I was chasing you in Kanapoi. I'm told it takes some time for the *Gilomir* genome to convert a player."

"I don't know."

"I knew there was something going on inside me." She stopped and faced him. "It's not often the Shepherd neutralizes a player. Why me?"

Truman struggled to step back but she would not let him go. "You're asking the wrong person. But the guardian probably knows. Since you now have it, why don't you use it."

She eyed the small sphere. Apprehension played across her brow. "It can wait."

A loud crash reverberated from the floor below.

Truman ran to the stairwell and eased a look over the edge.

Cathcar ranged across the floor of the ruin looking first down the abandoned elevator shaft, then crossing over to the stairs leading to the passageway.

"It's Cathcar," Truman whispered. Without waiting for Azizah's reaction, he grabbed her hand and dragged her to the far side of the floor.

Below, the supply pod banged against a wall. Its contents clattered across the floor.

In desperation, Truman grabbed a fist-sized chunk of concrete and ran to an open window on the north side. He threw the stone out the window. It plowed through branches with a crash and rolled with a thump into the bush.

Cathcar's thrashing stopped. His ponderous footfalls clomped to the north side of the ruin.

Truman picked up another chunk and threw it out the window, farther east of the first.

Cathcar exploded in furious pursuit.

"Good thing Neanderthals are so stupid," Azizah said over Truman's shoulder.

"You know he's not stupid." Truman eased himself up to the window and peered out. Cathcar was visible in the moonlight. He punched his way through the scrub, stopped to get his bearing, then resumed his pursuit. His path took him toward the north end of the plateau.

When Truman turned from the window, Azizah stepped up close to him. Heat rose from her body. She played her tongue across her upper lip.

"Give it up, Azizah. I know where your sympathies lie."

Her face hardened. She hefted the guardian. "I guess I better get back to the clone."

339

"I guess you better. What happens now that you have the guardian?"

"I don't know. I suppose the game, my searching, is over."

"All that effort for nothing."

"I never thought of it that way," Azizah said. "What is the point of a game, anyway? Each side works so hard to win, then one does. After that, what happens?"

"They play another game?"

She snorted a laugh. "Tomorrow is your big day. Have you made up your mind?"

"Yes."

"Then you will...stay?"

"I'll let you know tomorrow."

Azizah patted him on the cheek. "Have a nice life." She placed the guardian in a small pouch that was slung from her hips. She smiled wanly in the dim light, then heaved herself over the edge of the stairwell, grasped it with outstretched arms, and dropped to the floor below. She glanced back with a grim expression and was gone.

I should have known from the beginning. Truman felt like an idiot. But he supposed in all of eternity he wasn't the first man who had been played for a fool by a beautiful woman. The upside was that her attitude and attraction to the clone only made his decision easier.

***

Truman opened his eyes an hour later, wishing he could remain curled up in the cozy confines of the closet. The morning was clear for a change. Sunlight streamed from the east across the distant

340

lake above the top of the jungle and surrounding bush and into the second level of the ruins.

He'd have to hurry if he was to notify the Shepherd of his decision before Cathcar and the clone showed up. That was assuming the guardian had forecast the future accurately.

In the back of his mind, Truman felt a great unease, as though the guardian might be capable of skewing the visions it created to its own purposes. In that regard, the future could be self-fulfilling, closed world lines aside.

Truman dropped to the floor below. The supply pod lay at an odd angle against one wall. The contoured lid leaned askew and cracked, its contents strewn across the floor. No time to gather them together now. Would he even need them?

He exited the ruins and after splashing water onto his face and rubbing his smooth scalp, headed for the Shepherd.

The sun pushed a heavy humidity into the air. By the time Truman arrived at the clearing his skin was slick with sweat mingled with moisture poured from a thousand leaves.

He hurried to the Shepherd and slapped its side. But the Shepherd was expecting him. He lifted Truman off the ground, dragged him up the curved side, and drew him into the womb.

"Well?" The Shepherd didn't wait for the puckered entrance to close over Truman's head.

"How much time do I have?"

"Cathcar and the clone have left the Maraia cave." The Shepherd opened his vision for Truman to see. "They will be here soon."

"I gave the guardian to Azizah."

"I see. I think I know your answer as to whether you will go or remain."

"How so?"

"You know when I return to Kanapoi, with or without you, I will subsequently return here with the guardian. The same guardian you have given to Azizah. I could not very well transport you back to Kanapoi, you having the guardian I am to recover."

"I see. Actually, I hadn't thought of that. I gave Azizah the guardian because she demanded it and wouldn't have agreed to see the clone to whatever end awaits him unless I gave it to her. You'll have to excuse me. These time loops are confusing."

Truman saw movement in the vision.

"Here they come," the Shepherd confirmed. "This is your last chance. You or the clone."

Truman's shoulders slumped. He felt an overwhelming depression. This was all too much, too surreal. He had the solution to fix the degrading genome. It was beholden on him to try to use it to save mankind. Any relationship with Azizah was a fantasy. The Maraia were going to have to look after themselves. "I want to go back."

"I understand your motivations. I do not understand your logic."

"I don't give a damn. Can we go before they get here?"

"We could but I think it is important for you to see what happens."

"I suppose I have no choice."

"In this case, no."

Cathcar burst through the thick bush, dragging the clone by the hair. He pulled him over to the base of the Shepherd and dumped him.

342

Azizah and Juvenal stumbled out of the bush soon afterward, but kept their distance.

The clone cast about dazed, as though thinking he would crawl away and make a break for it, then he glanced at the Shepherd and seemed to remember he was about to be sent home. The clone staggered to his feet and made a feeble attempt to climb onto the Shepherd.

Cathcar grabbed the back of the clone's thighs and shoved him high up onto the Shepherd.

Inside the Shepherd, Truman felt a faint reverberation from the clone landing on the spongy surface.

Cathcar leapt onto the Shepherd and stomped across to the clone. He dragged the clone's head and positioned it over the puckered entrance. "Open!" He stomped on the entrance, sending shockwaves throughout the Shepherd.

"Are you going to let him in?" Truman asked.

"No. He is to remain here."

"But Cathcar will kill him."

"Perhaps. It is one of the consequences of your decision. There are others."

Azizah came to the side of the Shepherd and strained to see what was going on up top.

"No enter," Cathcar growled, staring at the closed opening.

"Didn't he let you in before?" Azizah asked.

"Always open. I go. I come."

"When we were last here it opened automatically."

Truman felt a tinge of alarm. He knew the Shepherd could protect him but in light of what he

343

perceived was an unpopular decision, would the Shepherd do so. "Can we go, now?"

"In due course," the Shepherd answered.

Cathcar dropped to both knees and tried forcing his fingers into the center of the pucker. "No open. Like clay!"

"It seemed willing to respond to Truman." Azizah gave the clone a quick glance.

But he only stared past them both at the tangle of jungle beyond, probably wondering when his ordeal was going to end.

Cathcar shoved the clone's face close to the pucker. "Ask open."

The clone coughed. A drool of blood escaped from his lips, splashed on the radiating wrinkles, then oozed toward the center.

Cathcar kicked him.

"Open," the clone said. "Please open."

Cathcar stared myopically at the closed womb. He leapt off the Shepherd.

As soon as Cathcar hit the ground, he bounded up, fists clenched and glared at Juvenal. "No open!" Cathcar's rage rose to his face. His mouth curled into a snarl. The whites of his small eyes discolored red and swelled, seeming to test the confines of their sockets. He grabbed Juvenal's head in two massive hands, bending it back.

Juvenal strained. His jugular pulsed on the side of his throat.

"Shepherd open!" Cathcar bellowed.

"You have to do something," Truman cried. "He's going to kill Juvenal."

The Shepherd remained silent.

344

Juvenal struggled but was no match for Cathcar's strength.

"Don't kill him!" Azizah screamed. "This is all for nothing. I have the guardian!" She held it high.

Cathcar's nose twitched, his lips fluttered. He seemed insane. His eyes rolled in their sockets, giving him the look of an enraged simpleton. Then with a sudden movement, he wrenched Juvenal's head.

The crack of Juvenal's neck snapping seemed to echo across the clearing.

Juvenal twitched, his head screwed at an impossible turn. He pitched forward onto the grass and lay still.

Azizah stared. "Why?" she cried in anguish.

Cathcar stepped over to her and wrenched the guardian from her hand. He shoved her to the ground and eyed the small sphere while fingering it with both hands.

Truman struggled to close off the vision the Shepherd was projecting into his mind. "Why are you showing me this?"

"You must be aware of the consequences your actions precipitate. You may, in your arrogance, decide to return to Kanapoi despite warnings you will die, all the while leaving the Maraia behind to the mercy of a deranged player, who now has the guardian."

Truman felt a needle prick in his lower thigh. "What are you doing?"

"Sedating you for the trip."

The Shepherd rose a meter off the ground and tipped sideways.

The clone began to slip off the Shepherd's hide. He clawed, digging fingernails into the surface. "Don't leave! Take me with you!" he screamed in desperation.

The Shepherd tipped farther and the clone rolled off and landed in a heap on the ground.

"What's to become of him?" Truman asked. "Why did Juvenal have to die?"

"Sleep well Truman Justis. Your next stop will be the tunnel at Kanapoi."

"But I want an explana--"

346

Chapter Eighteen

Truman awoke. The horror of Cathcar breaking Juvenal's neck came fresh to mind, then his impulsive decision to return to Kanapoi instead of sending the clone back. He was still in the Shepherd. But where? When?

"I'm awake," Truman announced.

"Yes, I've been monitoring your signs and have brought you back. We are minutes from landing in Kanapoi, 2005."

"I want you to know I don't feel good about this. Bottom line, I felt I didn't have a choice but to try to take my chances being killed. If I survive, I can do a lot to help humanity survive."

"We are almost there. I will supply you with a rifle. Once you are outside, I will give it to you."

Truman couldn't be certain but it sounded like the Shepherd was miffed with him. "Do you really think I'm going to go down to the tunnel knowing Azizah will shoot me?"

"Back in the future you so abhor, there's the small matter of Juvenal's death. If the guardian is not placed in the vault in 2005, Cathcar will do what he did. By placing the guardian in the vault, the contextual reality surrounding events in the future will change. Cathcar will obtain the guardian when he first searches the vault. Azizah will then never come into possession of the guardian. And you can hope Cathcar's course of action will change, perhaps enough that Juvenal and by extension the rest of the Maraia, men, women and children are not slaughtered. I say hope, since I cannot foresee the future. But the alternative is not something I would want on my conscience if I were you."

"What do you know about conscience?"

"You are being very cynical in an attempt to avoid facing the issue. Be that as it may, I have stated my position and will now expel you to your own devices."

Truman wasn't amused. As far as he was concerned he'd paid his dues, suffered enough, been hauled to and fro and called upon to do things he would never have otherwise contemplated doing. Who was the Shepherd to exert this kind of pressure? If he was so interested in seeing that the guardian was placed in the vault why didn't he do it himself? Yeah, why not? "Why the hell don't you place the guardian in the vault yourself?"

"My placing the guardian in the vault is not a part of this reality. So, I can't do it."

Before Truman could respond he felt the constriction of the Shepherd's womb about him preparatory to expelling him.

With a strong upward thrust, Truman was deposited on the Shepherd's rounded exterior. A moment later a rifle oozed through a small opening.

Truman pulled the rifle to him and examined it. A 450 Marlin big game rifle by all appearances. What was he supposed to be hunting, rhino?

The sound of two gunshots rang in Truman's ears.

Clutching the heavy rifle, he slid off the Shepherd's rounded exterior and trudged toward the western edge of the escarpment.

He squinted and pushed on. His decision to abandon the Maraia and the Shepherd's admonition zigzagged in his mind. It probably wouldn't hurt to try to put the guardian in the vault. If it changed everything, then so much the better. If he did nothing, there would be a massacre. *God, I hate guilt trips*.

At the plateau's edge, Truman flopped onto his stomach, then inched his way forward to peer over. Down and to his right, the western entrance to the tunnel gaped open. The Shepherd must have deposited him minutes before it was dynamited. Were the shots he had heard fired at Moye and Azizah? Her Land Cruiser stood undamaged on the road below. No sign of the helicopter. Still too early for that. What would happen, if he met himself? *Whatever I do, I don't want to meet the helicopter*.

He pushed the thought to the back of his mind. Presumably, the Shepherd had also foreseen there was a potential space time contradiction looming if Truman was to meet Truman. *Even if none of it makes much sense to me right now*.

Okay, procrastination over. Go down and put the guardian in the vault. Be a good guy. He knew what he'd have to look out for. Azizah. Turn his back on her and *blam*. Moye would be good as dead but who pulled the trigger? Azziah didn't say anything about shooting Moye. Probably this guy Jomo.

As Truman eased over the edge, a large man, carrying a rifle, exited the tunnel and headed for a canvas satchel that rested fifteen meters from the opening. He picked up the bag and returned to the entrance.

That must be Jomo.

A moment later, the man hurried to the edge of the tunnel entrance and taped what Truman assumed was an explosive charge to the rusted, iron gate. After checking the charge was secure, the man thumbed a switch which set an LED blinking. He stood and returned inside.

Guessing the man would cross to the opposite entrance to mine it, Truman scrambled down the escarpment. When he got to the bottom, he ran to the entrance and peered into the tunnel.

Constable Moye slouched against the wall of the tunnel, holding his gut with both hands in a failed attempt to stop the hemorrhaging of blood from his mid-section.

"Truman?" Moye's face contorted with pain.

Truman stepped to Moye's side. "Yeah, it's me. Who did this to you?" He kept his voice low, glancing all the while into the dark eastern depth of the tunnel. *Where the hell is Azizah?*

Moye took two quick breaths, his face slick with sweat, his eyes wide with fear. "What are you doing here?"

"Later. Where's Jomo?"

"You know Jomo? That's the fucker who shot me. He's at the other end of the tunnel."

Truman scanned the floor of the tunnel looking for Azizah but couldn't locate her. An unfamiliar opening gaped at ground level. *Haven't seen that before. It was dark last time I was here.* "What's that over there?"

Moye groaned. "You want a tour?" He tried to stifle a chuckle that started pumping blood out of his wound.

"Please, tell me."

"It's the entrance to an abandoned elevator shaft. Happy?"

"Yeah, thanks. Where's Azizah?"

"Jesus Christ, Truman, you know all these people?"

"It's a long story, Constable. Right now I've got to get the guardian back into the vault."

A moan, far to Truman's left, carried across the rocky floor.

Azizah.

Truman located her lying in a dark shadow. "Jomo shot her, too?"

"AK-47. Appeared out of nowhere and opened fire."

The sound of footsteps echoed off the rocky floor from the east. Truman stared, a sudden fear seared his mind. He was glad he hadn't refused the rifle.

Jomo appeared from the shadows, looking ominously strong and muscled, his black skin shiny from his exertions, his red hair plastered across his forehead.

"What the--" He raised his AK-47 like a toy and fired a continuous burst moving from Truman's left to right.

Bullets whined overhead.

Sweat stung Truman's his eyes, blurring his vision. He brought the heavy hunting rifle up to his shoulder and fired.

The 450 caliber, belted magnum cartridge thwacked into Jomo's chest and blew through like it was piercing a thick melon.

351

The force of the blow lifted Jomo off his feet and slammed him onto what was left of his back.

Twitching in agony, the man rolled over and crawled deeper into the tunnel, dragging his legs after him.

"Strong motherfucker but I think I got him," Truman said. He laid down the rifle and ran over to Azizah.

She opened her blue-green eyes and gazed at him. There was a flicker of recognition, then she fainted.

Truman undid the laces to one of her boots and tied her hands behind her back, then returned to Moye. "Where's the guardian?"

Moye shook his head. "God-damned guardian. I should have given it away."

"Where's the guardian? We don't have a lot of time."

"Fuck you, Truman, I'm the one who's dying."

"I'm sorry. Please. It's important you tell me where the guardian is. It has to be put back in the vault."

Moye's eyes went to where Jomo had disappeared. "He has it."

The last thing Truman wanted was to revisit a dead Jomo. *I should have finished him and frisked him before.* Truman stepped into the tunnel.

He came upon Jomo and was surprised the man was still alive.

With what seemed a supreme effort, Jomo turned his head around and stared. "You are not part of this," he said through clenched teeth.

"But I am." Truman trained his rifle at Jomo's head.

Jomo lunged for something near his thigh.

Truman fired.

The top of Jomo's head snapped back and splattered the area with shards of brain and cranium.

Truman stepped forward and, with distaste, pushed up Jomo's shorts. A gun rested in a holster strapped to his thigh. The iron smell of blood thickened the air.

He patted down the dead man's pockets, trying to ignore the gore above Jomo's neck. In his left front pants pocket, Truman closed his fingers around the guardian. He returned to where Moye lay bleeding.

He sat ashen-faced, his breath sucking into his lungs as if passing through dry reeds, then rattling out with a long hiss through his teeth. "God I hurt."

Truman grabbed him under the shoulders to pull him out of the tunnel.

Moye screamed in agony. "Forget me. I'm done. Get the girl."

Truman hesitated but Moye was right. Better to pull Azizah out before the tunnel blew. She wasn't a threat trussed up the way she was. But the guardian had to go in the vault. Was there time? Girl first. He could always re-enter from the ruin. The key to the vault.

"Do you still have the key to the vault," Truman asked Moye but the constable had lost consciousness. A quick frisk of his pockets yielded a large key. Truman shoved it in another of his pockets and headed for Azizah.

He dragged her toward the Land Cruiser, passing the LED on the way out of the tunnel. Five minutes left. He gave a silent thanks to the erstwhile

Jomo for setting such a long time on the timers. *Plenty of time*.

Truman released Azizah and jogged back to the vault. He dropped the guardian in, slammed the lid shut and locked it. He returned to Azizah.

At the Land Cruiser, he opened the rear hatch door and shoved her inside. If she died from his mishandling he wasn't going to lose any sleep over it.

The distant clop-clop of a helicopter reverberated through the superheated air.

Already?

If he hung around, the helicopter would land and he'd end up meeting himself. Better to get the hell out of there while he could. He'd done what he had to do. Time to get on with his life. He could drive north under cover of the deepening darkness. The entrances would blow soon. That should give him a head start, while his doppelganger and Hopkins tried to sort things out.

He jumped into the Land Cruiser, thankful the keys were still in the ignition and started the engine. He raked the vehicle in reverse, then accelerated forward with the lights off toward the north end of the plateau.

In the dark, he failed to see a large rock. The front left tire hit the rock. The Land Cruiser pitched onto its side.

"God damn it!" Truman screamed, slamming his hand on the steering wheel in frustration.

The helicopter loomed up behind him, went into a hover and settled to the ground. Its landing lights flicked on, banishing the gloom that had begun to settle on the area.

Flashlight in hand, Hopkins jumped out the raced toward him.

Truman twisted around looking for a weapon of any kind, regretting leaving his rifle on the tunnel floor next to Moye.

Hopkins rushed up to the driver side window and shone his light into Truman's eyes. "For fuck sakes! What's going on here? Truman?" He peered at Truman as though he were the last person in the world he expected to see.

Truman wasn't sure how to react. This was a player. He looked exactly like the Hopkins who had picked him up at the hotel and ferried him up here, how long ago, he could only guess. "Yeah, I'm Truman." He looked apprehensively over Hopkin's shoulder for himself. But saw no one else. With a small sense of relief, he looked at the man in front of him. "You must be Hopkins."

"Yeah, hey, I'm Hopkins, Brad but how'd you know?"

Truman was speechless.

"Never mind," the exuberant Hopkins said. "Ditch that question. Sorry I missed you at the airport. Some fuck up in schedules. Boy, I took a chance figuring you might have tried to make it up here on your own. Hot damn, I scored. You okay? That was a hard hit you took."

"I'm okay. We're in the middle of an incident here."

"I like incidents." Hopkin's smiled. "Involve that UFO we were supposed to check out?" His head whipped back and forth as he searched for the UFO.

"Negative. I've got a passenger in the back that's wounded. Some crazy shit is happening here."

Hopkins angled his light and craned to see into the rear compartment. "Jesus. She looks like someone shot her."

"Someone did. We've got to get her to a hospital."

"You administer any first aid?"

"I've got nothing here. Help me get her to the helicopter."

"We've got to stop that bleeding first. I have some EMT training. Let me have a look. There's a first aid kit back of the pilot's seat in the copter. You get it and I'll get started."

Truman wondered for a moment about the arrangement, then Hopkins became his 'take-command' self, and there was no arguing. Truman ran back to the helicopter and located the first aid kit.

A shot rang out.

Truman had another déjà vu. But how could Azizah get free to shoot Hopkins. Truman hoped she had. He returned to the Land Cruiser to find Hopkins standing with a .45 caliber service revolver in his hand.

Azizah had a neat hole in her forehead.

"She bit me," Hopkins said with a smirk on his lips.

"So what now, Brad, she going to shrivel up and disappear?"

He cocked his head. "You're maybe not who I think you are. Move over there, cowboy." He waved his gun for Truman to step beside the vehicle.

"Hands on the hood. Legs spread. Just going to pat you down."

From the back of the Land Cruiser a shoe clumped to the ground.

Hopkins glanced over. "Guess your lady friend went bye-bye."

Truman hung his head and shook it. The situation was quickly exceeding the surreal.

With the gun in one hand, Hopkins stood back of Truman and frisked him with the other hand. He slid his hand down up and down Truman's legs, then to his sides and out his arms. He returned to clutch at Truman's pockets. When Hopkins came to the vault key, his hand froze, then he felt earnestly with his fingers. "What's this?"

"It's a key."

"Geez, Truman." Hopkins looked at him as though he was stupid. "Yah went and locked the guardian in the vault."

"I…how do you know about the vault?"

Hopkins raked his hand through his red hair. "Look familiar?"

"Why should it?"

"Jomo, Hopkins. Hopkins, Jomo. I know," Hopkins grinned. "The skin color threw you off."

Surreal just got more surreal.

Hopkins hefted the key, then looked down to put it in one of his pockets.

Truman whirled and caught Hopkins with a chop at his neck, feeling the hard cartilage of his larynx give but not break.

Hopkins dropped the key and clutched his throat. He fell to the ground in an agonized faint.

Truman grabbed the key and zigzagged for the tunnel.

Shots popped in the dry air. Bullets whined overhead.

Truman ran into the tunnel, glancing at the LED. Ten seconds.

He lunged into the dark as a bullet caught him in the thigh. He clutched his thigh and hobbled. *Shit, another thigh wound.*

A blast of air from the explosion at the eastern entrance staggered him and almost blew him back out. Then the western entrance blew and he was propelled forward onto his face as total darkness descended around him in a choking cloud of dust.

***

I'm drowning.

Truman gagged on water sliding down his throat into his lungs, then started drowning some more. He fought to open his eyes, which felt like they were glued shut. Their lids came apart and he stared wide-eyed.

Rain fell in a torrent. He spit and snapped his mouth closed. No wonder he was drowning. *What am I doing outside? Torrential rain in the desert?* He groaned. *Oh, no. I'm back.*

He rolled onto his knees and shook his head to clear it. No pain. He reached to his leg, brushing a pocket. The key. Still there. Hopkins hadn't gotten it. He felt his thigh where Hopkins had shot him. Healed. *If I didn't know better, I'd think I was the clone.*

He felt for the watch on his wrist. Still there. Still a Casio. It gave him a thin thread of security knowing at least that was real. He pressed the light button on the side of the watch and peered at the display. 9:25 P.M., Sunday, April 7. Still '05. He tried to think where everyone was supposed to be at the current time. Juvenal had barged in and warned him. Then Azizah had confronted him and demanded the guardian. She'd been holed up in the painting cave with the clone, and returned there for the rest of the night. The Shepherd had left for Kanapoi the next day on the April 8, shortly after noon. Would they all be where he expected them to be now?

A flash of lightning silhouetted the outlines of the escarpment through a tangle of jungle.

He didn't care if Azizah and the clone were in the painting cave or not, he needed shelter, fast. He slogged his way in the direction of the escarpment, and upon reaching it, took a chance and turned to his left, hoping to come to the painting cave. After feeling his way along the wall he felt the opening.

A rustling noise indicated someone was inside. He hoped it was Juvenal. Truman stepped into the cave and stood, letting his eyes adjust to the flickering light from a single animal fat lamp that sat off to one side on a ledge.

In the middle of the floor, the clone lay on his back, his feet angled away from Truman. On top of him sat a naked, thrusting Azizah.

She looked up from her exertions. Her gaze fixed on Truman. No hint of surprise or embarrassment. No glitch in her steady motion.

Truman wheeled back outside. If she hadn't been shocked, he was. Then something else hit him. The clone's head was shaved. His beard was gone. *What the hell*? He staggered north along the wall

359

seeking out the path that would take him up to the ruin. Finding it, he slipped and clawed his way with abandon to the top, not caring about the bruising his body was taking, hating himself he knew not why.

At the top, he almost ran into Juvenal.

"Where have you been, Sedroth? You are in great danger. Cathcar is looking for you."

"I know. I don't think the son of a bitch has ever stopped looking for me."

"He came to the Maraia cave. We fought him at the entrance but I fear he will keep returning and wear us down. He carried a stone box with him and kept demanding to know the whereabouts of the guardian."

Truman felt a moment of despair. He'd put the guardian in the box and locked the lid. Yet here was Cathcar assaulting the Maraia and looking for Truman as he had before. The future was supposed to change. Had it? It didn't seem so. Maybe Hopkins survived and returned with the key and got the guardian.

"It's my fault," Truman said. "The guardian was supposed to be in the box. The clone told Cathcar the guardian was still in the tunnel."

"*Clone?*"

Is that different, too? But I saw him. "You don't know anything about a clone?"

"I'm sorry Sedroth. I do not even know what the word means."

"Who is it that Azizah is with?"

Juvenal peered at Truman. "She is usually with you, Sedroth."

"No clone."

360

"If there is this clone among us, I would know and tell you."

At least something has changed. Truman would need time to sort that out. In the meantime, there was the issue of Cathcar. "Did you see which way Cathcar went?"

Juvenal pointed south, away from the ruins. "Toward the big mountain."

"I hope he doesn't find the painting cave. That's where Azizah and...that's where Azizah is."

"Sedroth, there is something else I must tell you. Lela has given birth to a male child."

Something else new. "That's wonderful." Truman shook Juvenal's hand with Juvenal staring at the formality not knowing what to make of it.

"Thank you, Sedroth."

A fleeting anguish passed over Juvenal's face. As a father, his responsibilities had increased tenfold. "Is Lela all right?"

"She is well but tired. She is also very worried about the future. I have told her you are thinking about returning to your own time."

"I'm sorry if my indecision has caused apprehension. You can tell her everything will work out in the end. She has nothing to worry about."

Juvenal looked skeptical. "If you say it will be so Sedroth, then it must be."

"You better return to the Maraia and your Lela." Truman thought for a moment. "I'll go to the ruin. There are plenty of places on the second floor where I can hide. If Cathcar comes there, it will take him a while to find me if he ever does."

"Are you sure? I could stay to help you."

"No, your people and Lela need you more now than I do. I've got some thinking to do."

"I beg you to stay."

"Go to your people."

***

Truman had just finished transferring all his gear and the supply pod along with his bed to the second floor when someone entered the first floor of the ruin. He grabbed the stick he had picked out for a club and prepared for the worst.

"Hello!" Azizah called. "Is anybody up there?" This time an urgent whisper.

Truman scrambled to the stairwell opening. "I'm up here."

She stood on the floor below, her face showing a mix of anguish and fear, or was it anxiety?

He leaned over and offered her a hand up.

She hesitated, then clasped his hand as he pulled her to the second floor. She stood before him, looking a bit embarrassed, almost shy. "Juvenal said he met you on the trail. I couldn't believe it was you since you were asleep deeper in the painting cave."

"The clone is asleep in the painting cave." Truman corrected.

"Clone?" She looked him over. "You and Truman are identical. But obviously, you and he cannot be the same person. But a clone? Why? How? Maybe twins?"

"I have no twin. The man you were within the cave is a clone. I know. I was present when the Shepherd created him."

Azizah looked skeptical. "Truman has never given any indication that he is a clone. He was present at Juvenal's creation. Juvenal has said so

362

himself. Truman has told me he is from 2005 and that the Shepherd transported him here. He has been helping the Maraia ever since he arrived."

Truman felt the ground he stood on was shifting. What had the guardian done. Where was he on his world line? Was it the same world line? Everything was changed, yet oddly the same. "That's quite an endorsement. But what does he know of this past he claims. Has he mentioned sarin, friendly fire?"

"I don't know of these things. Should I expect that he would tell me every detail of his past in the short time I have known him? Anyway, I was not of a mind to determine who or what he was or to doubt how he got here. He's not a player, so the only way he could have gotten here was if the Shepherd brought him. He was helping the Maraia when I arrived. And I have joined him in that effort. Given your confusion, I should be the one quizzing you about the details of your past."

Truman could only stare at her. Questions crowded his mind without any answers being offered. If he was honest with himself, and now seemed to be a time for honesty, then he was at a loss to explain what had just happened to him. It was not only the big gaps in memory, but the massive shifts in the direction of what he could recall of his life these past days that gave him pause.

His shoulders slumped. He felt beaten down. "I don't know what is real and what isn't anymore, if I ever did."

Azizah reached a hand to his arm, an effort to comfort. "There is only one entity in existence that could possibly cause your disorientation. The guardian."

Truman nodded. "I have a clear memory of events that seem to have never happened. Earlier today, in what had to be the same day, the Shepherd said I should consult the guardian about a decision I had to make--whether I returned to Kanapoi or stayed here to help the Maraia. I retired to the ruins and asked the guardian for guidance. It gave me a bunch of cosmological stuff that I questioned, then it shut down, almost petulantly with a parting, "Consider this..."

"Soon afterward, you came to visit me. You were brusque, unlike the Azizah I thought I was beginning to know and like. You demanded the guardian in return for your efforts of protecting the clone. I gave it to you. You also said you preferred the clone to me. Bottom line, I was disappointed the way things were turning out. I slept. The next day when I saw the Shepherd I told him I wanted to go back to Kanapoi. There was a horrific scene with Cathcar, you, the clone and Juvenal. Cathcar killed Juvenal. The clone was dumped and I went back to Kanapoi. I survived the events back there. You didn't kill me as everyone seemed to be telling me you would. And now I'm back here. I remember it all."

"You must have been dreaming."

"But it's true." Truman grabbed at his pockets. "Look. I still have the key to the vault."

Azizah shook her head. "That means nothing to me. From my point of view, this is the first contact I have ever had with you. I could never have said that I preferred Truman to you. There has only been

Truman here…at least until tonight when you showed up. And to my knowledge, Juvenal is alive and well in the Maraia cave with his mate and newborn. As for killing you in Kanapoi, I don't know what you are talking about or why I would. The last thing I remember from Kanapoi was being shot by a brute named Jomo."

Truman felt like a drowning man. Desperately, he grabbed for a life raft. "Are you sure you haven't seen me before this? Maybe…maybe as Sedroth?"

"Juvenal is the only one who calls you Sedroth. He has from the beginning."

Nothing made sense. Had they lived separate realities and were only now trying to make them congruent. There must be a coincident experience they could agree upon. "I was in the Shepherd when you and the clone were there. I saw him kiss you."

Azizah looked surprised. "Truman has kissed me but Truman and I have never been in the Shepherd."

Truman felt dazed. "The Shepherd scanned you. When I last talked to you, you said you felt violated, like Cathcar was groping you."

Azizah eyed him sympathetically. "It didn't happen."

She blushed and stared down at her clasped hands. "I'm sorry you had to see me and Truman as you did. It was the first time. But we have felt strongly about one another for a long time before that."

Her tryst was the least of his concerns. "I admit, I feel some small jealousy. I thought you and I were developing a relationship, one that I valued. One that I thought you valued. But things have changed.

365

At least you, Juvenal, everything here has changed." Truman shook his head in despair. "Unfortunately, I have not. I am still me. I have lived every moment of this experience and more."

"I thought the guardian only showed visions. Maybe it has powers even I don't know about."

"The ability to commandeer alternate realities at will?"

"Somehow I'm not surprised." She reached for his hands, and when he didn't pull back she grasped them. "I too feel change. You say the Shepherd scanned me, did he tell you what he found?"

"But it seems he did that in a different reality. What bearing does it have on what is happening now?"

Her anxiety had returned. "Let me deal with that. What did he find out?"

"I don't think he was looking for anything in particular but he did seem surprised. Though you are a *Zug* player, you possess a complete *Gilomir*-hominid genome, like mine, like the Maraia."

She looked at him with astonishment. "How?"

"He thought he might have given it to you."

Azizah let go his hands and paced. "He could have inserted it at any time he had contact with me. But I don't remember such a time. Inserting the *Gilomir*-hominid genome is a way to neutralize players."

"I know."

She stopped and stared at him, probably wondering where the knowledge had come from. "It's one reason we shy away from the Shepherd," she continued. "If indeed he has inserted the genome in me, then I have little time left as a player. In fact, I may already have crossed over."

"Is that so bad. Even I can tell you are different than the woman I met in Kanapoi."

"I am more different than you can imagine." She reached into a leather pouch strapped across her waist and retrieved the guardian. "Truman asked me to give this to you."

Truman was stunned. So that was why everything was changed. "I placed the guardian in the vault like I was supposed to. How did you get it?"

"Truman and I went looking for it. We feared Cathcar would find it first, if indeed it still existed. Prying the lid off the vault wasn't easy but our efforts were rewarded. I have no recollection from 2005 as to how it got back in the vault.

"When I caught up to Truman here, all he ever talked about was getting the guardian back and giving it to you...when you came. He always said that you would come. That he had to return to his time. That I should not despair because he would still be here with me...as you. From what I have seen, it is true. You are both one and the same."

"He knew I was...coming?"

"He seemed to know everything that was going on, even ahead of when it happened."

"He knows I'm here, now?"

"I can't be sure but I think so."

What does that make this man? Had the Shepherd or the guardian primed him with foreknowledge? If so, then he must know his destiny. *He's been here, biding his time, waiting for me to show up, so he can go home*. Was he a clone?

367

If not, was there a clone? And if so, who was the clone?

Truman took the guardian from Azizah. "You don't want it?"

She looked thoughtful. "I recall a time when I wanted it very much. But, now, no, I don't want it. I used to think it was important to be able to possess it and be able to see the past and the future. Truman has told me it has greater power than that."

"You've never used it?"

"I've only had it recently. Though, I've held it, nothing has ever happened. I guess I don't know how to use it. I assume you do. Could you show me how?" She extended her hand.

"I have no control over the guardian. If it responds to you, it will be because it wants to. And I must warn you, I know from experience that what it projects, or chooses to project is not always pleasant."

He gave her the guardian.

As soon as her fingers closed around the sphere, her knees buckled, and she fell forward.

He caught her in an awkward embrace before she hit the floor and eased her down onto her back. Her eyes rolled up into her head, showing white where emerald-blue had been moments before. He straightened her legs and positioned her arms at her side, then waited. She seemed serene, as though lying in state.

After a couple of minutes, she twitched. She blinked and smiled.

"I..." She cast about confused. "I'm sorry." She burst into tears. "I have never felt anything like that before." She sucked in air as if she were drowning and put her hand to her forehead. Then her shoulders rolled forward and she was wracked with heaving sobs.

"What did you see?" Truman asked.

"Everything. *Gilomir* is with me." Tears streamed down her cheeks. She brushed them away unabashedly. "It's incredible. I'm so happy, I cry."

"I used it once and felt the same way."

"We prevail." She still seemed in awe of the guardian's power.

"Now it's we?" Truman asked but she didn't answer. She seemed so far out of focus he became concerned. "Are you going to be all right?"

"Yes, I think so." She gazed around with a renewed vision, as though seeing the walls of the ruin for the first time. "Where am I?"

Truman put his arm around her shoulder. "Take a deep breath. You know this place."

"Who am I?"

"You're Azizah. You know that, too."

"Azizah?"

"Who do you think you are?" Truman asked.

"I don't know." She dabbed at the tears on her cheeks. I feel like I have a new purpose in life."

"Did the guardian tell you what it was?"

"No. It's just an impression it left me with." She struggled to stand. "Thank you for helping me. I better get back to Truman before he wakes up. He said he has a big day tomorrow. Do you know what he means?"

Truman walked her to the open stairwell. "A while ago, I might have said that I knew. But after all that has happened I can only speculate. He will be offered a return to Kanapoi."

369

"If he refuses, will you go back to Kanapoi in his stead?"

Truman shook his head. "I don't think I have that option any longer."

"Realistically, he can't stay. Then there would be two of you."

"And that would be difficult."

"Then he has already made up his mind to return."

"I think so."

She grasped his hand in both of hers, pulled him close and kissed him on the cheek. "My feelings are terribly mixed. You are Truman, but you aren't Truman. How am I to feel?"

"I'm sure everything will work out."

"Perhaps. Hold me."

He gave her a hug, feeling her tension.

She smiled in the dim light, then separated herself from him. She sat with her legs over the stairwell, grasped its edge, and dropped to the floor below. She glanced up with a brief smile and was gone.

Fate works in strange ways. He found himself rethinking all he had ever thought about the nature of fate. After what the guardian said, fate was real, something almost physical that could not be changed. Not unless, of course, one was the guardian.

Chapter Nineteen

Truman walked over to his makeshift bed and sat down. He removed the guardian from his pocket. His fingers trembled uncharacteristically as he curled them around the sphere's smooth surface.

He formed his thought question.

I don't know what is real anymore.

"*It is all real.*"

I blacked out. When I came to I was back here. How'd that happen?

"*I will show you.*"

***

I see Truman lying unconscious on the floor of the tunnel. The entrances are closed. It is pitch black. The smell of dynamite lingers in the dust filled air.

Truman stirs. He awakes and is disoriented. He clutches his thigh. Pain shoots up to his groin. He curses Hopkins. Then panic washes over him. He grips his pocket and feels the vault key. Hopkins wants the guardian and knows there is another way into the tunnel, through the ruin, down the passageway.

Hopkins will be here in a heartbeat. I've got to get out. But how? The door opening at the end of the passageway is too high to reach. What else? The elevator shaft. Maybe the vertical guide rails are still intact.

Truman stands, suppressing the pain in his thigh that threatens to render him unconscious. He staggers forward, trying to orient himself. *I'll keep walking until I run into something.*

He trips. A body. Suppressing his revulsion he reaches out and pats down the body. It's Moye. Thank God. Moye, even dead, helping him get the hell out of here.

Now the elevator shaft.

Turning toward what he hopes is the opposite wall of the tunnel, he walks carefully, hands stretched out in front of him. After thirty steps he bangs into the wall. He scrabbles to his right and comes to the recess leading back to the elevator shaft.

He enters and feels his way around. His panic rises as he touches nothing but rock. The rails must have been stripped away. *I'm finished.* A moment of despair, then his hands land on the rung of a ladder embedded into the concrete. *They couldn't scavenge that.* What luck.

Footsteps echo down the passageway above. They pause where the passageway runs adjacent to the elevator shaft. A beam of light from Hopkins flashlight plays over the shaft.

"Truman?" Hopkins calls.

Truman presses up against the wall, praying the light misses him. It does.

The light shifts back to the passageway and shines out the end into the vastness of the tunnel.

Truman begins a slow careful climb of the elevator guide rail.

A rope thumps onto the tunnel floor from the direction of the end of the passageway.

Truman comes level with the passageway. Hopkins has tied a rope to one of the wall anchors and climbed down into the tunnel. A glance into the tunnel shows Hopkins standing over Moye's corpse. The beam from Hopkin's flashlight moves to the vault.

Truman continues his climb. He gains the passageway when Hopkins slams his hand onto the metal lid of the vault having been unable to open it.

As Truman transfers his weight from the rail to the passageway, he bumps his thigh and grunts in pain.

Hopkin's shines the light into the recess, then runs across the tunnel, his gun in his hand. The light falls on Truman as he lunges into the passageway.

Hopkins fires.

Bullets splatter the rock over Truman's head.

Staying low, Truman limps up the passageway to the stairs and climbs.

Hopkin clumps up the rung ladder breathing heavily.

Truman tumbles into the ruin. The gloom lessens from dim light coming through the vacant windows. He orients himself and heads for the vestibule that leads to the outside. Once clear of the ruin, he looks for the Shepherd. *He saved me once. Is he going to save me again*? Truman hobbles south. No Shepherd is in sight.

"Hold it right there, buddy!" Hopkins shouts.

He has cleared the vestibule and stands gun pointed at Truman who is forty meters away.

Truman runs as best he can.

Hopkins fires again but misses. The next shots are snaps of the hammer on an empty chamber.

Truman stumbles and falls flat. He rises and pushes on desperately.

"You stupid son of a bitch." Hopkins lunges in pursuit.

Truman struggles to rise.

Hopkins flops on top of him, his weigh shoving the breath out of Truman's lungs. "Where the hell is it?" Hopkins drags at Truman's pockets, searching for the key.

"I left it in the tunnel," Truman lies.

"I don't believe you." Hopkins pistol whips Truman on the side of his head.

Truman stares upward. A black shape moves across the field of stars. *The Shepherd.* Truman never thought he would be so glad to see him.

The Shepherd descends. The dark shape parts to reveal a lighted pink interior.

A force tugs at Truman's shoulders.

Hopkins thrashes desperately, closing on the key, trying to dislodge it. He screams. His clutching hands fall away.

***

Truman wiped sweat from his forehead and cheeks. So that's what happened. *Then the Shepherd brought me back here to start all over again.*

"*It is true you are here again. But to say you will start all over is to ignore the experience you have just had.*"

Truman re-traveled his timeline in his mind. He had left the Shepherd after he, Azizah and the clone had been inside. It had started to rain. Azizah and the clone went to the painting cave to find shelter. He went to the ruin to consult the guardian about his decision to stay or return. The next day he was returned to Kanapoi, then he awoke in a downpour back here, staggered to the painting cave and discovered the clone and Azizah having sex. Later Azizah denied ever being in the Shepherd.

There's something I don't understand.

"What might that be?"

You said that my recent experience was relevant. If that is so, then please explain how I can have one memory of me being in the Shepherd with the clone and Azizah, and a second later memory of Azizah denying that she and the clone were ever in the Shepherd at any time. I woke up here almost coincident with when I remember being in the Shepherd with the two of them.

"Did you have a question?"

How is it possible that both of these memories can co-exist? It seems to me they are mutually exclusive since the Shepherd cannot be here entertaining a visit from the three of us at the same time that he is in transit from 2005 A.D. with me on board.

"I see no contradiction. If you consider the events from your point of view the timeline of your memories is self-consistent. One moment please."

What are you--

Truman gasped. Stark terror washed through his psyche. Underlying horrors welled to an all-encompassing despair.

Stop! He jerked violently. His chest convulsed in sobs. Tears streamed down his cheeks.

"Just some mumbo jumbo," the guardian said.

The walls of the room darkened, then came into view through tear blurred vision. Truman had no way of knowing how long he had been in the guardian's grip. He trembled. Crossing his arms and

375

clasping his shoulders, he tried to calm his shaking. He formed his thought question.

I don't know what is real anymore.

"*It is all real.*"

When I was taken back to Kanapoi, Cathcar broke Juvenal's neck. Did he survive?

"*Juvenal survives. I will show you.*"

***

I see Juvenal an old man. He lies on lies on his deathbed. The Maraia elders gather around him to pay their last respects.

He lies on a bed of fine linen, white sheets with a black trim around the base of the bed. Lights glow from glistening walls of a room buried deep in the rock of the plateau. A side table of shiny steel holds medications. A solitary candle dances with every movement of air.

He rises onto an elbow and with his other hand outstretched, offers the guardian to his son Osa. "Take this and return it to Sedroth and his mistress."

Osa nods. "It shall be so, father. But is there nothing more that it can teach us?"

"It has told me that we have everything we need to progress. The nano-assemblers will do our bidding. They must be used wisely. I have given the guardian to you because only you know where Sedroth and his mistress are buried. Their location must remain secret. Promise me that."

"Of course, Father. I promise."

"We have come to a crossroads," Juvenal says, giving last instructions in a weak voice. "One that I cannot help you navigate. The Maraia have come far in a short time. They still have far to go, and that path will be difficult. Soon, a great evil will visit us.

376

Some Maraia will take the easy way and embrace the evil. Others will turn away and resist. Those that resist will know no peace for the evil will pursue them all their days."

"What is this evil?" Osa asks.

"I am not meant to tell you. Each of you will recognize it in your own way, in your own time, and make your own decision not based on what I might say. Hold true to the words of our messiah, Sedroth. His teachings alone can guide us through the troubled times to come. It is now time for me to go." Juvenal clutches his chest and winces with pain. "Carry my body out on the plain so the night animals might feast. I shall always remain a part of this place."

Juvenal dies.

***

That was moving but how do I know it was true. You could have shown me anything.

"It is a pity you have become so attached to your cynicism. You ask to see. And I comply. If you choose to disbelieve what you see, that is your choice, not mine."

So I'm stuck here.

"Indeed."

Then if you want me to help the Maraia, I demand two things.

"Only two? What are they?"

First off, I want to make sure Juvenal does not die tomorrow as a result of Cathcar's brutality. Second, I want Cathcar taken out of the equation.

"I see no problem meeting your request. When you next see the Shepherd, communicate your demands to him. He will see that they are fulfilled."

It's going to be that easy?

"What you request is the easy part. What happens after that remains to be seen. I know this must be trying for you," the guardian said, *"but you will, you will find the right path."*

***

Truman opened his eyes an hour later, wishing he could remain sprawled on his bed. The morning was clear for a change. Sunlight streamed from the east across the distant lake above the top of the jungle and surrounding bush and into the second level of the ruins.

He'd have to hurry if he was to notify the Shepherd of his decision before Cathcar and the clone showed up. He dropped to the floor below and exited the ruins. After splashing water onto his face and rubbing his smooth scalp, he headed for the Shepherd.

The sun pushed a heavy humidity into the air. By the time Truman arrived at the clearing his skin was slick with sweat mingled with moisture poured from a thousand leaves.

He hurried to the Shepherd and slapped his side.

But the Shepherd was expecting him. He lifted Truman off the ground, dragged him up the curved side, and drew him into the womb.

"I have two conditions that have to be met if I am to help the Maraia," Truman said without preamble. "The guardian said I could communicate them to you, and you'd take care of them."

"What are your conditions?"

Amazing. Not the slightest hint of surprise. The guardian probably knew long beforehand what his

378

request would be and had already primed the Shepherd with responses.

"First, you take care of Cathcar. If I'm to remain here, I don't want to have to deal with him anymore."

"It will be some time before the genome takes effect, assuming it does. I suppose something can be arranged during the interim."

Truman shook his head. "I need more assurance than that. Why don't you take him back to 2005 with the clone? Let Azizah kill him. She's got a gun and doesn't seem coy about using it."

"Yes, I suppose I could do that." The Shepherd adjusted Truman's position. "You said two conditions."

"I won't stay if Juvenal has to die. He's a father now. I don't want that on my conscience."

"Juvenal does not have to die." The Shepherd convulsed and pressed something into Truman's hand.

Truman tried to look down but couldn't see below his chest. "What's this?"

"It is a packet that contains a nano-healant. Apply the salve to Juvenal's neck. It will stimulate and guide his healing. A few seconds are all that is needed but I have included a sterile dressing to cover his neck. Though healed, the area will remain tender for an hour."

"A salve is going to fix a broken neck?"

"Cathcar slits Juvenal's throat. The salve will heal a slit throat."

"Something else that is different than what happened before."

"Did this happen before?"

"I can't tell what is real and what is simply…stuff…that you and the guardian are throwing up to make sure I adhere to a certain path."

"What you should realize is that the guardian is something we all look to. It is not mired down in your self-centered debates about whether you will or will not help the Maraia. It has a higher calling, a higher purpose. You have to trust that even if it does deceive you sometimes, it only does so for your own good."

Truman thought the Shepherd was in the process of admitting his own impotence and throwing everything that happened and was to happen onto the guardian. No one yet had stepped forward and told him what the guardian was or represented. Ostensibly, the guardian represented *Gilomir* but who was in charge?

"How much time do I have?"

"Cathcar and the clone have left the top of the plateau." The Shepherd opened his vision for Truman to see. "They will be here soon."

Truman dug into his pocket and produced the guardian

"I guess you'll want to take this."

The Shepherd vibrated. "Is it still so hard for you to understand what is happening?"

"You don't need it?"

"It must remain here for the time being. In a moment, I will return to Kanapoi, 2005. I cannot very well be carrying it at the same time I pick it up, can I?"

"You'll have to excuse me. These time loops are confusing." Truman put the guardian back into his pocket. "What am I going to do with it here?"

"Nothing, other than what you will do. The guardian has already seen to that."

Truman saw movement in the vision.

"Here they come," the Shepherd confirmed. "One last chance to stay or go."

"I stay. Let me out," Truman said.

***

It was raining, when Truman fell the last meter onto wet grass, hit hard on his shoulder, and rolled to his knees. The bush beyond the edge of the clearing thrashed violently. Cathcar and the clone were coming straight for him. He leapt to his feet and dove behind a dense thicket on the side of the clearing away from the noise.

Truman's initial anger at the Shepherd for misjudging the distance to the ground was replaced by anxious concern. He patted his pockets. The guardian rested in one pocket and the first aid packet in the other.

A moment later, Cathcar shoved what had to be a clone through the brush.

With an agonized cry, the clone sprawled on all fours and gazed directly to where Truman was hiding without seeing him.

Good God, he has hair and a beard. Has my reality changed again? Try as he might, Truman could not identify any other physical characteristic that differed from himself.

Cathcar stepped free of the jungle, put his foot to the clone's backside and gave him a shove, which propelled him closer to the Shepherd.

Dazed, the clone scrambled to his feet and stumbled forward. He clasped his hands in front of him, bowed his head and let the rain wash over him.

Seeing the clone degraded, seeing him struggle to regain a semblance of dignity, Truman fought back a desire to help the poor man.

Azizah rushed to Cathcar, stumbled and fell at his feet. Her arms wrapped his legs. "Don't hurt him. Please, don't hurt him," she begged.

Cathcar kicked her away, then knocked the clone sideways. He reached down and grabbed the clone by his ankle and one arm, took a practiced swing and heaved him high up onto the surface of the Shepherd.

"Oh, Truman, what is he doing to you," Azizah wailed in anguish, unable to mask her feelings for the man.

The Neanderthal leapt up after him. There followed a muffled challenge by Cathcar to the Shepherd, which Truman could not make out, then the Shepherd began to draw the clone inside.

"Goodbye," Azizah cried

With the clone half swallowed by the Shepherd, Juvenal lunged from the jungle. "Don't leave us, Sedroth!" He slipped and sprawled onto the wet grass. "Don't leave us," he sobbed, pounding his fist on the ground in despair.

The last of the clone slid into the Shepherd.

"Please, forgive me," Azizah begged to the emptiness left behind.

Truman pitied the poor woman. She was losing a lover to a probable death in Kanapoi at the hands of another Azizah, presumably not the reformed Azizah Truman saw before him. Truman pressed his hand against his forehead and squinted through the rain.

Cathcar whirled and glared at Juvenal. With one great stride, he jumped from the Shepherd to the ground.

Before Juvenal could react, Cathcar straddled him, grabbed his hair and yanked his head back to expose his throat.

Azizah screamed and ran at Cathcar.

While Azizah battered Cathcar with ineffectual blows, he bent over and grabbed the chert knife at Juvenal's waist, then casually slit his throat. He stood straight, brushing Azizah aside with a massive arm.

Juvenal lay twitching, the red blood from his neck spraying patterns across the green grass.

Truman struggled to contain his anger and fear. If he revealed himself now, he was a dead man. But could Juvenal last long enough for the first aid packet to still be of use?

Chest heaving, Azizah clasped her hands to her cheeks in horror. "What have you done?" she shouted above the roar of the falling rain.

"Shepherd fault."

"You idiot." She knelt next to Juvenal, her hands pressing to staunch the blood pouring from his neck.

Cathcar went for her. The back of his hand came hard across her cheek.

She recoiled, lost her balance and fell onto the grass.

He lunged on top of her. "Choose. Me or them."

She batted at his groping hands. "You don't understand," she cried with effort. "I have no choice. I am no longer a player. I am who I am, a lost soul, adrift."

Cathcar slapped her. "No believe...stupid bitch...no lost." He clutched her neck and slammed her head on the ground. The blows hit with a steady cadence. He stopped to catch his breath.

She looked about, dazed. "Let me go. Juvenal needs help."

Truman felt a pang of sympathy for these creatures, thrust into the universe with a mission, then abandoned to their own devices.

"Guardian!" Cathcar bellowed.

Words slurred from her mouth, unintelligible gasps. She stopped struggling.

Cathcar released her and bent forward, resting on his hands, breathing heavily. Then he clasped the fingers of both hands together in a massive fist and raised it for a killing blow.

"You fool," she managed to say. "You are sending...a clone back to Kanapoi. The real Truman Justis is still here, alive."

"You lie!"

"In the ruins," Azizah whispered.

Cathcar stayed his blow. He blinked. His eyes rolled in his head as if comprehension was something impossible to achieve. He sat back and wiped sweat and rain from his face with both his hands, drawing them across his eyes and pulling down on his cheeks, leaving angry red streaks where his nails dug in.

"You know. All time, you know."

"Yes."

"How you know!" A large vein across Cathcar's forehead swelled near bursting.

She coughed and rubbed her throat with her hand. "He arrived last night. The clone told me to give him the guardian."

Cathcar grabbed her hair and twisted.

Truman cringed. His heart went out to Azizah. Though she had betrayed him, he understood she was using the only thing she had left to survive. Cathcar swayed.

Azizah's hands grappled with his wrists. "*Gilomir*, the Shepherd, Truman, they are all in this together for the guardian."

"No!" Cathcar shook his head, a madman. "No!" He spun off Azizah, raised the chert knife, and lunged at the Shepherd. The knife sunk deep. Cathcar pulled it out, watched the wound close, then stabbed again. Heavy blow after blow thumped into the mottled, green exterior.

His rage dissipated. The blows slowed, then stopped. Spent, he leaned against the Shepherd and turned his bloodshot eyes toward Azizah.

She tried to stand but couldn't. Instead, she dragged herself to Juvenal.

Cathcar stumbled forward. But it wasn't Azizah he wanted. With the chert knife in hand, he veered away from her and staggered into the jungle toward the ruins.

Truman burst from his hiding place.

Startled, Azizah gazed at him, her hands soaked, her face flecked with Juvenal's blood. "Thank God, you're still here." She pressed at Juvenal's neck, trying to stop the hemorrhaging.

385

Truman stumbled over to them. "Where are the Maraia?"

"After the attack--" Azizah leaned over Juvenal, frozen with anguish and apprehension. "--After the attack, Juvenal told them to wait. He wanted to stop the clone from leaving. It was too late."

Truman snatched at his pockets. He pulled out the first aid packet along with the guardian, which fell into the grass. He ignored the guardian as he tore at the packet. Its contents spilled out.

"What's that?" Azizah asked.

"The Shepherd gave it to me. It will save Juvenal's life." Truman picked up a small tube, unscrewed the cap, and squirted a gooey, gray substance onto his palm. He hesitated, looking at his hand and the spattering raindrops. Then, with a single motion, he smeared the salve in a swath under Juvenal's chin, following the path of the blade.

Truman's hand came away covered in blood. He wiped it clean on the wet grass.

Almost immediately, the blood on Juvenal's neck caked and dried. Falling raindrops dislodged flakes from around the wound, leaving two clean edges of skin, which exposed the interior of his neck as a meat-red gap. Then the two edges inched toward each other, met, and sealed to an angry red line. It too disappeared, leaving a pink expression of new skin.

Juvenal groaned.

"Is he going to be okay?" Azizah asked.

"I think so."

Juvenal blinked. His initial disorientation gave way to a slow smile. "Sedroth, you are still here." His hand went to his throat. "I am not dead."

"No, you're not dead," Truman said.

Juvenal struggled to his knees, then tried to stand. He wobbled forward.

Truman caught him before he fell. "You'd better sit for a while."

Juvenal sat down and pressed his hand to his neck. "It feels tender."

"It will take some time before you feel one hundred percent."

Azizah surveyed the scene around them. "Why is the Shepherd still here?"

"He's going to take Cathcar with him," Truman said. "That was a condition of my agreeing to help the Maraia."

"The Shepherd agreed to that?"

"Yes. Is that so strange? I didn't want to be left here and have to deal with Cathcar on my own."

The ground trembled.

The Shepherd rose a meter above the ground and hovered.

"What?" Truman screamed. "You can't leave!" He slapped both hands onto the Shepherd's rubbery side. Rainwater cascaded from the smooth surface and washed over his fingers.

The tough hide twitched, the skin of an animal chasing away a fly.

Truman jumped back.

The Shepherd shifted in the downpour, one way, then the other and shot straight up, punching a hole in the dense clouds. A mist of vaporized rain curled through the clearing, followed by a thunderclap. The sad gray of the soaking jungle returned. The rain resumed its chaotic splatter of water falling onto leaf.

"Why have you betrayed me?" Truman shouted, arms raised skyward.

Azizah looked around nervously. "What do we do when Cathcar returns?"

Thoughts cascaded through Truman's mind. Sarin. Death. Betrayal. "We have to get Juvenal out of here."

A tree branch cracked, followed by a bellowed cry of rage.

Chapter Twenty

Cathcar lunged into the clearing. The hair on his body clung in a sweat-smeared, rain-soaked sheath. He gasped for breath. The run to and from the ruins must have been exhausting, even for a Neanderthal. He took a staggering step forward and squinted.

Truman felt a deep resignation. Nothing was going according to plan.

Juvenal jumped to his feet. "Sedroth. I will--" He took one unsteady step forward, and buckled into a slumping swoon onto his knees. His head pitched forward in a faint and struck the grass, where he lay still.

"Tru...man," Cathcar wheezed looking at the stricken Juvenal. His gaze lifted. A smile creased his lips, then disappeared as he jerked his head back to Juvenal. "Not dead?" He tilted his head to get a better view in apparent disbelief.

"No, he's not dead!" Azizah raised her voice above the pounding rain.

Cathcar grunted. He surveyed the area, then stopped when he saw the guardian lying in the grass surrounded by pearls of splattering raindrops.

Truman lunged.

Cathcar, a second late, crashed onto the slick grass.

Truman grabbed the guardian and scrambled back as Cathcar slid a couple of meters with hands outstretched to where the guardian had been.

Truman gave Azizah a fleeting look, then sprinted toward the plateau. A glance back over his shoulder showed Cathcar struggling to his feet.

I can outrun this guy. Though strong, the Neanderthal weighed twice as much and ran with an awkward gait, something between that of an ape and man. Truman scrambled up the escarpment.

At the ruins he paused at the vestibule doorway, leaned against its frame and tried to catch his breath. The room gave off a damp musty smell born on the spray of rain blown in through the open windows.

He crossed the inner room to the spot below the open stairwell and jumped. Wind-driven rain washed across the floor above and poured down the opening, making the edge slippery. In a rising panic, he grabbed at the slab, struggling to get his legs up and over the lip.

Cathcar barged into the ruin. He hesitated a moment, then duck-walked over to Truman and grabbed his ankle before he could pull it away.

He kicked to no avail. His grip on the slab came loose, and he tumbled onto the seething hulk.

"Guardian," Cathcar spat. His eyes darted over Truman trying to ascertain where the guardian might be hidden.

"Let me go!" Truman screamed but wherever he engaged Cathcar, the beast countered by either gripping his fists or blocking his kicks.

The heel of Cathcar's open hand caught Truman in the nose with a force that traveled to the back of his skull. Blood gushed from his nostrils.

A closed fist landed like a sledge-hammer, on the top of Truman's head. Stars swam before his eyes. His knees buckled. "I--"

"Guardian!" Cathcar slammed him with the back of his forearm.

Truman hit the wall like a rag doll. The concrete rattled his brain. He slumped to his knees. A desperate plan took shape.

Cathcar lunged at him with both hands extended.

Truman lurched to one side.

Cathcar's empty hands smacked the wall. He wheeled around, bellowing with pain, blood dripping from bashed knuckles and a broken finger.

In a limping run, Truman staggered for the doorway leading to the passageway. He slipped on the top step and rumbled down the remaining steps to sprawl at the bottom. The light spilling down the stair dimmed as Cathcar's bulk filled the door opening above.

Patience.

Cathcar began a cautious descent of the steps.

Truman let him close the distance between them, then in a pain-filled stumble he ran.

Cathcar grunted and lunged in pursuit.

Truman lagged letting Cathcar catch up to him, then in a full sprint he ran toward the end of the passageway, hoping Cathcar didn't know the passageway ended four meters above the tunnel floor. Truman hurtled into the void. He twisted mid-air.

Cathcar skidded to a stop at the edge of the passageway.

Truman landed hard. His arm above his elbow gave way with a loud crack and dislocated his shoulder. Something buckled in his chest.

Cathcar's booming laugh exploded off the arched roof of the tunnel. "Not stupid! Not stupid!"

For a moment, Truman's world imploded, mingling with the darkness of the tunnel. Then pain brought him back to stark reality.

The rough walls arched overhead like exposed ribs, catching light from the open eastern entrance. Warm liquid slid beneath his body where the rain run-off from one end of the tunnel coursed its length and joined the lake at the other end.

When he focused on the passageway a nauseating panic rose in his throat. Cathcar was on his knees, extending a leg over the edge in an attempt to lower himself into the tunnel.

Cathcar raised his head. He stared back up the passageway toward the stairs.

A soft padding sound grew louder.

With a wild shriek, Azizah appeared at a full run.

Cathcar grunted and raised one arm to ward her off.

She never lost stride.

Smack.

They launched into air.

Truman gazed, mesmerized.

They twisted in what seemed a slow motion pirouette. With a muffled thud, Cathcar came down on his shoulders and lay flat out.

Azizah flopped stomach first on top of him, her hair drifting up around her head in a lazy spray, then settling into a disheveled mess. She loosed a sharp yelp of pain.

The two of them lay still on the tunnel floor.

Dragging his broken arm, Truman crawled over to her.

"Azizah," he wheezed. Pain stabbed his chest. He saw anguish and fear in her eyes, then the tip of the chert knife glinting in the light where it exited from her lower back. The blade thrust clean through her stomach.

She attempted a smile, then grimaced and tried to roll off of Cathcar. "I seem to be stuck," she said wondrously. The knife's tether still held the blade to Cathcar's waist.

"Don't talk," Truman said but the color drained from her face. Her breathing became ragged.

He pulled her.

She came free of the blade with a sucking sound to an open wound that soon filled with dark blood. She rolled onto her back, clutching her stomach.

With a struggle he eased her away from Cathcar, who lay still, seemingly dead.

"The salve," Azizah whispered.

"There is none." Truman pressed his hand over her wound. In his heart, he knew she was finished. The blade had done its work.

"I told him," she whispered.

"I know." Truman coughed and doubled up in his own pain. A cracked rib must have pierced his lung. A vice closed on his chest.

"I had to tell him, he would have killed me."

"He would have killed you, anyway."

She touched his forehead with a shaky hand. "I have come a long way haven't I, Truman Justis?"

"Yes you have."

"I've learned to love. It is a great gift."

"It is very human."

"I have broken through." She gasped in pain. "What is to become of me now?"

Truman reached into his pocket and took out the guardian.

"Once more." Her voice fluttered with effort as she extended her hand. "Please."

Tears stung Truman's eyes. He placed the guardian into her hand and helped her close her fingers.

She relaxed. "Peace," she murmured, eyes closed, lost in a world of her own. Her hand opened and the guardian rolled out.

Truman picked it up. "You have seen?"

She opened her eyes and turned her head to Truman. "I..." A shadow of concern passed across her face. She smiled as her gaze drifted from Truman to over his shoulder.

He turned.

A head-size stone whistled past his ear and hit with a sickening crack off Azizah's forehead.

She slumped back, eyes glazed, staring vacantly, her smile fixed in place.

"Now dead." Cathcar swayed above them.

***

"You son of a bitch!" Truman staggered to his feet, slewed drunkenly, and swung at Cathcar's chest with his one good arm.

Cathcar absorbed the blow and regarded him. Then his eyes locked onto the gleam of the guardian still clenched in Truman's fist. He grabbed Truman's hand and pried at his fingers.

Truman kneed him in the groin.

Cathcar grunted. His eyes bulged in their sockets. Blindly, he shoved Truman to the ground, then dropped spread-eagle on top of him to begin a methodical pounding of Truman's head against the stone floor.

Darkness closed around Truman's vision. Time seemed to slow into an eternity. Truman's fist relaxed, and the guardian spilled out.

Cathcar grabbed at it.

"Mine." A grin of demented satisfaction broke across his face. He rose to stand over the bloodied Truman, raising the guardian high until it caught the light. "Mine, all--"

The blow from Juvenal's stone adz slammed into the base of Cathcar's neck.

His head whipped-lashed with a reverberating crack, then flopped forward onto his chest. His knees buckled.

Juvenal stepped around and swung the club in an uppercut. It smashed Cathcar's forehead, lifted the giant up and sent him thumping to the floor on his back.

Juvenal raised the club for a killing blow.

"Wait," Truman whispered through bruised lips, his eyes puffed near shut.

Cathcar stared at the roof of the tunnel, an ugly welt swelling above the bridge of his nose, his massive arms at his sides, his legs twitching spasmodically.

"His neck is broken," Truman said.

Cathcar's breathing caught in his throat. His lungs labored to function.

Truman dragged himself over and leaned up against Cathcar's massive chest. "You're through," Truman said, his face millimeters from Cathcar's.

"No through." The words slurred from his mouth mixed with blood and saliva. He strained to move. A small artery running alongside his temple pulsed with the effort.

Juvenal hovered close, club at the ready.

"*Zug* is still strong in you," Truman said in a low voice close to Cathcar's ear.

"Strong."

"The game is played on many levels."

"No levels." He blinked and a tear formed at the corner of his eye. "You god?"

"No."

"Hurt."

"I know you hurt."

"Where *Zug*?"

"That's a good question." Truman reached for Cathcar's massive hand, which held the guardian in his palm. Truman curled the gnarled fingers closed. "You have the guardian. Ask it."

Cathcar's panic-filled eyes snapped back and forth in their sockets. He blinked, and blinked again, refusing to close his eyes.

Truman saw none of the bliss Azizah had registered. Instead the small capillaries around the beast's irises swelled, then burst, washing the whites of his eyes in red.

"What do you see, Cathcar?" Truman wheezed. "Tell me what you see."

396

"No," Cathcar panted. "No... no." His mouth gaped open and closed. Then the artery on his temple swelled one last time and went limp. He lay rigid, his eyes open, staring at the tunnel roof.

Truman sensed a change in the still form.

First Cathcar's toes disappeared, as though some invisible blade was working its way up his body. His feet and legs were next. In a quickening ripple, his torso deflated, rolled up and vanished.

His head went last.

Truman lost his balance and fell forward into the void left behind. He winced at the pain tearing his insides.

Juvenal knelt beside him. He stared to where Cathcar had been.

Truman could see Juvenal questioned what had happened but in the end Juvenal must have pushed it from his mind. Practical Juvenal.

"It is time to go." He lifted Truman's head above the dirt and water on the tunnel floor.

"Wait," Truman said. "The guardian."

Juvenal scanned the rocky floor and located the guardian. With distaste he picked it up and placed it in Truman's outstretched hand. "You must hold it. I cannot."

"Yes." Truman clutched the guardian, then stared at Azizah's bruised body. "It is time to go."

Epilogue

I'm floating.

Juvenal carried him effortlessly. Heavy rain lashed at them with a windblown fury but for once Truman thought it felt good.

Juvenal strode in silence, keeping close to the escarpment, ducking his head and turning Truman away when the wind bent a sapling over the path.

At the painting cave, he entered and made his way to the back. He laid Truman on the floor next to the painting wall.

Though it was warm, Truman shivered. The shock of events had caught up to him. Every breath he took clogged in his throat, making him think it would be his last.

Juvenal arranged Truman's legs so they were straight, his arms at his sides. Juvenal paused to wipe his eyes of the tears that fell unbidden down his cheeks.

"Azizah," Truman whispered.

Juvenal nodded. He turned to leave.

"Light," Truman said.

Juvenal felt around in the gloom and found his fire-making materials. A moment later a small flame flickered in an earthen lamp. Its warm glow filled the chamber and brought to life the dancing figures on the walls. He returned to the entrance and was gone.

Truman let his gaze drift over the painted figures. They flowed in and out of focus, his vision blurring from tears welling from his puffy eyes. The story of my life, he thought. Azizah, the Shepherd, Sedroth, the guardian, even Cathcar, they were all there on the wall, coming and going. He closed his eyes, welcoming the darkness, and slipped his hand into his pocket for the guardian. Without removing it, he closed his fingers around it.

Is this real? I can't tell anymore. Did I really go back to Kanapoi?

"*You should not trouble yourself with these questions. They have no meaning. You are here. You have found the right path.*"

Then give me peace. I have stayed and done your bidding, yet I feel empty.

"*I see an infinite two-dimensional plane and a line running across the plane, coming out of a dark abyss and plunging into a brightness with no end. Humans plod along the line, their steps marking time, always heading in the same direction.*"

What does it mean?

"*They know no beginning and see no end but they are also the center.*"

Their journey is futile.

"*I see two beings, good and evil, being and nothingness, yin and yang hovering in the plane to each side of the line. As the plane rotates about the axis of the line, the beings sweep out their destinies in a greater space and time.*"

Gilomir and Zug.

"*I see they toy with the humans who inhabit the line. For this reason, He bestows his attention upon them.*"

He?

"*He pities them.*"

There is a god?

"I see He is everywhere. You may embrace Him."

But who is He?

"I am here."

For an instant, Truman felt as though his soul lifted out of his body and spread into all space and time. He shook with awe. *You know everything.*

"No, I evolve."

Truman lay back exhausted but content. He had achieved what he had always wanted. For a brief moment he saw and knew a greater whole.

A scraping sound drew his attention. Juvenal had returned.

"Sedroth?"

"I'm here," Truman said.

"I thought you were dead." Juvenal stepped into the cave, Azizah draped in his arms. "You did not respond the first time I called."

"I was learning." Truman tried to smile and opened his hand to show Juvenal the guardian.

Juvenal glanced at it. "I have brought Azizah. The rain has cleaned her." He laid her in front of a small opening at the back of the cave that led to a chamber beyond.

At the sight of her, an ache came into Truman's heart. Her beauty radiated even in death.

"I will place her in the chamber and seal it closed," Juvenal said.

"Thank you. When I am dead, I want you to place me beside her."

Truman laid his hand across her stomach but she was already cold. "Take her."

Juvenal crawled through the opening on his hands and knees, then reached back and pulled

Azizah after him. After a few moments, he backed out of the chamber. "I have arranged her to be at peace."

"Take this," Truman said offering the guardian to Juvenal.

He hesitated. "It has brought only trouble to everyone who touches it."

"No. You must take it, and keep it with your people. If I survive, I will guide you, and if I don't then it will be with you."

Distastefully, Juvenal took the sphere from Truman, then sat down next to him. "In the tunnel, Cathcar disappeared. Azizah did not. You said before they were both players."

"Azizah became one of us. Cathcar did not."

"We are on a side?"

"Yes, at least here. You, me, Azizah. The guardian used us to forestall Cathcar and the evil he represents. The future is safe for the Maraia. They will prosper and build A4-Ni."

"A4-Ni?"

"You will learn soon enough."

Juvenal put his hand on Truman's. "I sense you are different. Have you found the answers you sought?"

"I have found them." Truman winced. "The guardian is the way to *Gilomir*."

"I do not understand what you say."

Truman must have blacked out momentarily. When he came to, Juvenal was at the wall painting.

Truman strained to raise his head. "What are you painting?"

Juvenal stepped back to reveal a caricature of Truman. The figure stood with arms outstretched in the direction of an object not unlike the Shepherd. Between Truman and the Shepherd stood an assembled group, the Maraia.

"Why have you painted me?" Truman asked.

"You are our savior." Juvenal pointed to the assembled Maraia. "And here you are instructing the Maraia to remain pure."

"I have only told you."

"But you can tell them all later."

Truman shook his head. "I think I am dying."

"You will not die, Sedroth. You have made too great a sacrifice for us to die now. The guardian and the Shepherd will see to it that you live."

"Somehow I think they have been trying very hard to kill me."

Juvenal smiled. "I see your pain. You have suffered more than any individual should. It is because of this you will live and guide us into the future. Let's leave this cave of death and emerge into the sunshine."

Truman couldn't answer because of the pain he was in, though he liked what he was hearing.

Juvenal rolled a heavy stone across the opening to the chamber. "In the end, she was a good woman. I am sad for you Sedroth that you did not have more time to spend with her."

Juvenal gripped Truman under the shoulders and legs and lifted him, then stepped out of the cave to bright sunlight. The rain had stopped and left the vegetation wet and sparkling with prismatic colors.

"It is going to be a good day, Sedroth."

Truman tried to open his eyes but the light was too bright. He'd have to wait and hope Juvenal was right. That he would survive.

402

In the distance, he heard his name called, a low chant from the voices of the remaining Maraia.

"Sedroth, Sedroth."

The Maraia broke from the jungle, some carrying their children, and hurried toward him.

He raised his hand in weak greeting.

The future beckoned.